The Greeks have a ⟨...⟩ from Greece. The ⟨...⟩ with it all the yearning ⟨...⟩ the isolation of living among strang⟨...⟩ *xenitia* is hard, and it is where I've lived for twenty-five years.

I'm not like other Greek immigrants. I didn't leave Greece to make money. I left Greece to keep my heart from breaking. Unlike other immigrants, I have never gone back, not even to visit, not even after I made money. My need to forget was so great that I never even talked about Greece. Other Greeks talk incessantly of their country, their family there, their desire to return, but I never said a word. Never, until my Katie stumbled upon the two pictures of my father and my family and started asking questions.

Irene Livadopoulos was born in Thessaloniki, Greece, and emigrated to the United States at age thirteen. She currently lives in Los Angeles where she works as a lawyer. *The Consolation Prize* is her first novel.

The Consolation Prize

Irene Livadopoulos

CORONET BOOKS
Hodder and Stoughton

First published in 1994 by Hodder and Stoughton
A division of Hodder Headline PLC
A Coronet paperback

British Library Cataloguing in Publication Data
Livadopoulos, Irene
Consolation Prize
I. Title
813.54 [F]
ISBN 0 340 60961 3

Typeset by Phoenix Typesetting, Ilkley, West Yorkshire.

Printed and bound in Great Britain by
Cox and Wyman Ltd, Reading.

Hodder and Stoughton Ltd
A Division of Hodder Headline PLC
338 Euston Road
London NW13BH

This book is dedicated
with all my love
to Apostolos and Eleni Livadopoulos

CONTENTS

Part One

The Foreign Land

1

My Daughter Katerina

Sunday afternoon is my time to relax. After church and lunch by the pool, I take a beer and whatever part of the Sunday paper has survived the morning, and I sit in my favourite armchair in the small family room. It's usually the classifieds that are left these days, and not by accident. My daughter Niki thinks I should buy her a car now that she's turned sixteen, so she circles all the used convertible BMWs for sale and then she leaves the classified section in the small family room for me to find. She knows I won't relent and buy her one; she's just trying to annoy me. It's one of her less successful tricks, but by no means her only one.

The classifieds are fine with me because I only need the paper as a prop. Before I've spent five minutes reading, Diane, my wife, peeps into the room and spies the beer next to me. She disappears silently only to appear without a word once more, and replace my beer with a glass of iced tea. She thinks I should drop a few pounds. In vain I tell her that there is no Greek in existence who doesn't sport a bit of a belly at the age of forty-two. It's genetic, I tell her, but she insists that if I only exercise and give up beer I will again become the skinny, sinewy immigrant kid I was when we met. I don't want to be skinny and I don't want to be a kid. It's taken me more than twenty-five years to become what I am and as far as I'm concerned it's an improvement. Besides, I'm short, and short men should never be skinny if they want to be taken seriously. A grown man needs to have the look of substance. I never do business with skinny men. I don't trust them. They might disappear.

Anyway, the beer switch is not what I'm waiting for in the small family room on Sundays. What I'm waiting for is my little pixie, Katie. She tries to sneak up on me and stick her little face under the paper on my lap to surprise me, but I hear her. I always snatch the paper up just as she thinks she's made it, and this delights her. She laughs and pulls my moustache, and then she settles on my lap and we leaf through the paper together until she gets around to the real reason for her visit.

'Tell me about the family in Greece, Daddy,' she commands, pointing to the two yellowed pictures on the wall. The light of my life, the joy of my heart, wants to hear every Sunday what I most want to tell her.

'Well, now, let me see. You see that man in the portrait, the one with the hat and the handlebar moustache? That was your *papou*, my father, *papou* Yiannis. He was a baker. He would wake up in the middle of the night every day, at four, to go make bread for the whole village. All morning he baked and sold bread, and on Sundays the housewives would arrive with their roasting tins filled with whatever they wanted roasted, and he would put it in the big oven with his long wooden paddle to cook.'

'Why didn't the housewives cook at home like Rosa does here?'

Rosa is our cook.

'Because they don't have ovens at home in Greece. At least not back then, not in Panorama in the fifties.'

'And did they come back to get their food, Daddy?'

'Yes they did. And a hard thing it was, my baby, because those who were better off would be picking up roast lamb or pork, and those who didn't have much would pick up roast beans or maybe a scrawny chicken, and have to smell the lamb as they waited for their own roasting tin.'

Katie ponders this. She is very interested in lying, because she's learning not to make up stories. That explains the next question.

'But didn't they lie and take someone else's?'

'No they didn't. People in Greece don't lie and they don't cheat or steal.'

Oh but they do, they did. They don't steal roast meat, but they steal other things, vital things.

I had been made a father twice before Katie arrived more than ten years after John, my son, but for my heart Katie was the first. We almost lost Katie. We were living in Brentwood at the time, and Diane was having the second bathroom upstairs remodelled. Christos, the handyman doing the tile work, had left some tools on the top of the staircase, and the door bell was ringing. In her rush to get downstairs, Diane tumbled halfway down the staircase before she could grab hold of the banister and stop herself. She was barely in her seventh month.

I hope the Catholics are right about there being a place in the hereafter where you can spend some time being punished before you move on to heaven, because otherwise I cannot wish justice on Christos. May he rot in purgatory for the first half of eternity for almost killing my Katerina before she was ever born, but let him go to heaven for the other half, because he rushed Diane to the hospital. This was a miracle because it was probably the only thing he ever did right. I only hired him because he is a *patriotis*, and we Greeks have to support one another in a foreign land, but the man is a complete imbecile. Back then he had been in America for three years and still could not speak a word of English. To this day he cannot speak English. But then why should he speak English? He barely speaks Greek. The only people who will hire him are other Greeks, and only to help out a fellow Greek, because nine times out of ten whatever Christos does must be taken apart and done again. Even the tile he botched.

So Katie was born prematurely. Christos thought to take Diane to the hospital, but didn't think to call me. I came home a few minutes before the dinner rush at my two restaurants, and found a locked house and two panicked children in the yard, who had returned home from school to find their mother gone. I knew immediately something must have gone wrong, because Diane is the perfect mother and would never leave the kids waiting like that. I started knocking on the neighbours' doors and finally someone said they saw some guy in a battered Toyota drive off with her. I knew it had to be Christos. The Toyota is his prized possession. Anyway, I drove to the nearest hospital with the kids in tow, but of course Christos wouldn't take Diane anywhere that logical. He had no phone, so I couldn't call him. So I called every hospital in town from a phone booth, instead, and finally learned my wife was downtown. To this day I don't know why Christos drove miles to get downtown, passing at least two major hospitals on his way.

When I arrived, Katie had already been born. Later that night, when I had taken John and Niki home and put them to bed, returned to the hospital and looked in on Diane who was fine, I went to look at the baby. She was the most pitiful thing I ever saw. She was in an incubator, no more than a handful of baby, skinny and pale, very still. There were tubes running through her and she was hanging to life by a thread. But her eyes were big and brown and alive, and even though I already had two children, as I stood behind the glass looking at this unlikely human being, I felt for the first time that this was flesh of my flesh and blood of my blood and I felt a love as strong as, no, stronger than any I ever felt in all my life.

For six weeks Katie stayed in the incubator. For six weeks I let my business run itself and spent hours pacing in front of the glass wall separating me from her and muttering to her to get strong, to not let go, to hang on, to gain weight, to breathe, to live. And Katie did.

The first time I held her is as alive to me as my own sainted mother's last goodbye before she died. I remember it that vividly. Both John and Niki were full-term healthy babies, who smiled early and talked early and did as early as they could everything babies do that gets them everybody's love and affection. But I never held them or wished to hold them while they were newborns. They looked like they could break, and I didn't comprehend that they were mine. They were Diane's project, her accomplishment, her wish fulfilled. I loved them because that's what a father does, but I was busy building my business and making my fortune.

Katie came at a different time, and came in need. When the nurse put her in my arms, I had already spent countless hours boosting her in her effort to live. She was tiny and fragile and pitiful-looking, but she was mine. It was in the afternoon, in the hospital. The sickly, hazy Los Angeles sunlight was streaming through the window, the PA system was urgently looking for a Dr Hajani, and I had just talked to Leandros, my manager, who had told me that the Health Department had just reported twenty code violations at Artemis Garden and was threatening to shut us down. But there was my littlest daughter, very serious and quiet in my arms, looking up at me, or at the blur that my face must have been to her, with her huge, liquid brown eyes. This was one newborn who didn't start life blue-eyed.

'What will we call her?' asked Diane, who was standing next to me. She had named the other two children herself, choosing my father's and my mother's names to please me. Having run out of sure bets, she thought she would ask.

The name, the right name for my love, rushed to my throat. I swallowed it down. The moments ticked by.

'Melina, maybe?' asked Diane, thinking of the famous Greek actress whose picture graces one wall of Artemis Garden.

The name rushed up again. Again I swallowed, but it wouldn't go down. Why not, I thought, why not. And I did it then, I gave my tiny daughter, the person I love most in the world, the name I've whispered to myself more times than any other.

'Katerina,' I said. 'Katherine,' I corrected. 'She'll have no trouble with that one in school.' But to myself I whispered again 'Katerina,' and if I weren't a grown man I would have cried.

Only to me is Katie 'Katerina' and only sometimes. Only when we are alone and always when she pops up in my thoughts when I'm away from her, and then I whisper 'Katerina' and the sound caresses my face. I lived without love for twenty years before I found it again in my little girl's eyes, and even though it's not the love of a man for a woman but of a father for his child, I've known both and I can tell you the one is just as sweet as the other, and that they both start from the same place, and bare your soul the same way. Both make you feel like you could faint from happiness or die of sadness. I pity the man my Katie chooses for her husband, because if he causes her so much as a moment of grief, I will hound him to the ends of the earth and with my bare hands rip out his heart to bring to her.

So Katerina nestles in my lap every Sunday and points to the next picture. She's heard this a million times, I have no new stories to tell, but she likes the repetition. Sometimes I swear that somewhere in her pure child's heart she's doing this for me.

This picture is smaller than my father's portrait. It was taken in the yard of our house, built in the thirties in what then was considered a prime spot, next to the church of Saint George, patron saint of Panorama. The picture shows my father, my mother Niki, my brother Andreas, my uncle Demetres, and me at the age of twelve. We didn't know it then, but my mother was already sick with the cancer that killed her. She is sitting by the acacia tree where every summer she set up a small iron table and some chairs for her friends to sit and work on their embroidery while sipping thick Greek coffee from tiny cups. My father is behind her, his hand resting on her shoulder. Next to him is my uncle Demetres, a malevolent smirk on his face. Andreas, already seventeen, is sprawled on the ground in front of the group, propped on his elbow, one leg bent and one extended, a blade of grass between his teeth, a nonchalant expression on his face. I am off to the side, skinny and short, wearing short pants and holding the ball that I had hoped would make me king of the soccer games in the neighbourhood.

The photographer was not careful enough when he framed his shot in the viewfinder. Off to the side, if you look up close, you will notice a foot. It is a slim and dainty foot, swimming in a worn plastic sandal. The sandal is much too large, and the foot is much

17

too small. You can't see the heel, but the arch is half visible and it is a great arch, full of grace and charm. Its owner is outside the picture.

I tell Katie about the ball, I tell her about my uncle, I tell her about the coffee ladies, and how they turn their coffee cups upside down on a napkin when they are finished. The thick coffee sediments that settle in the bottom while you sip, trickle down to the paper napkin when the cup is upended, and leave traces inside the cup where those with talent can read the future. I've said all this perhaps a hundred times, but every time I tell it it's like the first. My words transport me to the stairs of our house in Panorama where I sit as a child in the mild breeze of springtime, listening to the women of the neighbourhood chuckle and sigh over the fortune that Kyra Maria, the village sediment reader, is intoning to Antigone, the old maid.

Diane comes in to take Katie to her swimming lesson, and her appearance at the door always ends my stories abruptly. Never have I told Diane, or anyone, these stories. Never have I spoken to anyone other than Katerina. She alone knows, and even though I never said it was a secret, she never repeats a word to anyone, and she knows that if anyone enters the room the stories stop. I've never told her, but she knows.

2

The Call From Manos

There is no country in the world more beloved to its people than Greece is to Greeks. There's something about its pure, distilled light, its clear, weightless air, the peerless azure blue of its sea and sky. Whatever this something is, it pierces the soul and declares it its own, enters the bloodstream and floods every corner of a Greek's being, gathers and pools in muscle and sinew and grows into a love that knows no bounds. The love of Greece to a Greek is an addiction, almost a vice. Maybe some day scientists will isolate and identify some element in the Greek air that works this magic. Until then, every Greek knows what I'm talking about. We're only half alive away from our country. The love of Greece is our first love and our last. You've heard stories about dogs who die when they are separated from their owner? Well, there are stories of Greeks who die because they find themselves in foreign parts and they cannot return to Greece.

Loving Greece is a lot easier than living in it. For all its heart-rending beauty, Greece is a poor, harsh country with very little in the way of raw material that a man can turn to food and clothing for his family. Its turbulent history makes even what there is harder to get at than it has to be. In this last century alone, Greece was invaded by the Germans, torn asunder by a bitter civil war and flooded with millions of poor, homeless Greeks chased out of their Asia Minor birthplace by the Turks.

For centuries, to escape grinding poverty and have some hope for tomorrow, Greeks have reluctantly left their homeland to strike out for places with jobs, money and stability. Thousands upon thousands of Greeks over the years have emigrated to rich countries like Germany, Australia, South Africa, America. They take few things when they leave – a mother's blessing, a few names of people to contact, and the burning desire to come back. They get to these places and they work like men possessed from sunup to sundown and beyond, saving every penny they make except what they send back to their family. In all their struggles, they have one dream that sustains them. It is the dream of the day they will return, finally with the wherewithal to live in comfort, to give their sisters a dowry, to build a house for their aging parents, to dedicate a school in their poor village.

Some of them never make it back. They never manage to hit the big one, and they are too ashamed to return as paupers. Some others make it, but find that the foreign land has taken too big a hold on them. They get married in the foreign country, they have children who grow up there. The children don't want to go to Greece. The soil and the sea and the light of Greece have not had a chance to drip the love into the soul of these foreign-born children. They lack the hard little knot of yearning that presses on the heart of every Greek immigrant. So the parents stay with their children, because family is everything, but staying is never less than a huge sacrifice. The Greeks have a word for the state of living away from Greece. The word is *xenitia* and it carries with it all the yearning to go back, all the isolation of living among strangers. *Xenitia* is hard, and it is where I've lived for twenty-five years.

I'm not like other Greek immigrants. I didn't leave Greece to make money. I left Greece to keep my heart from breaking. Unlike other immigrants, I have never gone back, not even to visit, not even after I made money. My need to forget was so great that I never even talked about Greece. Other Greeks talk incessantly of their country, their family there, their desire to return, but I never said a word. Never, until my Katie stumbled upon the two pictures of my father and my family and started asking questions.

She was not the first person to see the pictures. Diane had found them, too, many years before Katie, but I never answered her questions, and she stopped asking. But by the time Katie asked she had already cured my heart and saved my soul, and I could once again reclaim my past and let myself relive my childhood.

Katie discovered the pictures in the attic, in my old duffel bag. Diane had decided to clean the place and had taken Katie up there with her. When Katie asked about the pictures Diane told her to take her questions to me, and Katie did that night when I got home.

'Who is that?' she asked, waving my father's face at me as soon as I got home.

I stared at his stern face. It was the fashion among men of his generation never to smile when photographed. For most Greek patriarchs this pose was natural, but my father was a laughing, lighthearted man, and the picture makes him look like a stranger. He never looked like that when the picture was taken. He only took this look on when my mother died, and then he took it permanently and never laughed again. His face became a rock and stayed that way until he died, too.

I didn't answer Katie that day.

'Why don't you wait until tomorrow,' I told her, 'and after church, when I sit down with my paper, you can come to me and I will tell you.'

That was the first Sunday of our ritual. Her interest never waned. On my next birthday, she presented me with her gift, the two pictures framed. It must have been Diane who guided her choice and took her to pick the frames and have the pictures mounted, but it was Katie herself who picked the spot on the wall and directed me to hammer the nails and hang the pictures. From that first Sunday on, the people in the pictures became real to her, more real than her own brother and sister who never have a kind word for her. They shove her out of their way no matter how hard she tries to beguile them, and it is my big failure in life that no matter how much I love her I can't give her the attention she craves from her brother and sister. They are my own children, and I cannot wish harm on them, but time and again it's on the tip of my tongue to wish them misery for making my Katerina sad.

It was just a few hours ago on such a day, a day when I had to remind myself that Niki is my child and I cannot bring upon her, through a parent's curse, the punishment she deserves, that the phone rang and set me on my way back from the *xenitia*. But no, I take that back. What set me on the road back to Greece was the same thing that sent me away to begin with: two large and liquid brown eyes. And my trip didn't start a few hours ago but almost six years before, when my daughter first melted my frozen heart through the glass of her incubator.

So, six years after I had, unbeknownst to me, already started my trip back, I was sitting at the kitchen table going over the books to make sure my accountants were not robbing me blind. My house is big and has a room that Diane set aside to be my 'office', but I could never get any work done in there. When I was a boy I used to do my school work at the big kitchen table in our house, with my mother washing dishes in the sink and my father dozing next to the fire, and ever since when I have to do paperwork I have to do it where I can smell food. My 'office' has become the small family room. I was checking the take from Poseidon when I heard a door slam upstairs and my Katie's voice, hysterical and thick with tears wailing: 'I didn't mean to do it. Really I didn't.'

I got up, raced up the stairs and found Katie knocking on the door of Niki's room, her face bathed in tears, her small hands clenched into tiny fists. I kneeled down, put my arms around her, kissed her wet cheek.

'What is it, my love, what did she do to you? Tell your *paterouli* what it is you want. Come on, my love, what is it?'

Diane appeared on the top of the stairs, but saw I was already there and stayed put.

'Stop these tears, my darling girl. Stop and I'll take you with me to work tomorrow. You can play with Christos, and cook your own hamburger,' I said, and turned Katie's face to me. Her left cheek was flaming red and Niki's fingermarks were still visible on it. I felt an overpowering rage. I got up, grabbed the door handle and found it locked.

'Niki,' I said, 'open this door this instant or I will bust it down and you will be in more trouble than you already are.'

The door swung open and Niki glared at me.

23

'This little monster comes into my room, takes my things and ruins them and I'm the one in trouble?' she yelled.

I grabbed her by the shoulders, brought her within an inch of my face and asked: 'Did you hit Katie?'

'She took my lipgloss and smeared a whole page of my notebook with it and now it's all gone and I've told her not to take my things!' she said all in one breath.

She was afraid, I could tell. She had hit Katie once before that I knew of, and I had grounded her for a week. I know from bitter experience the tyranny an older sibling can exercise over the young, and I meant to stop it dead in its tracks before it could poison my Katie's life.

'Did you hit your sister?' I asked her again.

Niki is a witch, but she is no coward.

'Yes, I did,' she answered me.

I let a split second pass to get my rage under control, and then I slapped Niki, hard enough to teach her a lesson, but not hard enough to hurt for longer than a minute. Then I picked Katie up and started carrying her down the stairs, past Diane who was standing there like a pillar of salt. She never interferes when I discipline the children. By the time I was halfway down, Niki was at the head of the stairs yelling down at me.

'That's right, hit me when she is in the wrong. But she is never in the wrong as far as you can see. Oh no! Not Papa's little darling, not his little baby. Tell me, am I your daughter, too?'

I turned to her then, this viper in my house.

'Jealousy does not become you, Niki,' I said, and moved on to the phone which had started to ring in the middle of Niki's tirade.

'Vasilikos residence,' I said.

'George, it's Manos, how are you?'

24

Manos is the man who brought me to America. He comes from Panorama, too. He left Greece when I was just a kid and went to New York where, after washing dishes and saving every dollar he made, he bought his own hot dog stand. He worked sixteen hours a day come rain or come shine and finally put together enough money to open his own restaurant. It took him a while to make money, too long. By the time he came back to Panorama in his expensive car, loaded down with gifts for every man, woman and child in the village, his mother was on her deathbed. He sat by her bed, married a village woman to please her, buried her two days after his wedding, and a few weeks later left again, taking me with him. He is the only person who knows both my family and my whereabouts. Nobody else has heard from me since I left, but Manos knows where to find me. He knows my story first hand, and he understands.

Manos and I talk regularly twice a year. On Christmas he calls me. Easter Sunday I call him. This was neither Christmas nor Easter. I knew something was wrong.

'What is it, Manos?' I asked, my thoughts racing to the worst news I could think of.

'It's Andreas, George. His heart. He's had a heart attack, he's in the hospital. It's really bad, they don't know if he'll pull through. He asked for you. Petros called me and said if I know where you are to tell you to come home.'

It's hard to describe my feelings. Relief was first, that it was Andreas and not someone else. What followed the relief was a flood of memories. Andreas as the older brother I idolised, Andreas as the other brother who sometimes paid attention to me and sometimes ignored me. Andreas who tormented me with his insults and protected me from the bullies. Andreas who taught me soccer and bought me my ball. Andreas who saved my life from my uncle's drunken rage, and Andreas who took my life from me as surely as the good Lord will take it some day. He might be dead already, I thought.

'George, are you there?'

'I'm here.'

'I think you should go back, George. It's been twenty-five years for Christ's sake. It's time to let bygones be bygones.'

'I don't know, Manos. I don't know.'

'Listen to me, you stubborn mule. He may be dying, he may be dead already. Get on a plane this instant. You'll never forgive yourself if you don't go. Family is the most important thing. That's all I can tell you.'

'I have to think, Manos.'

'Think later. There may not be time to think. Think about your mother. What would she have told you to do?'

When I hung up the phone I realised that Katie had been standing next to me the whole time, holding on to my trouser leg and looking up at me.

'What is it, Daddy?' she asked.

She had forgotten her tears, even though her cheek was still red and swollen.

'That was Uncle Manos, my love. He called to say Uncle Andreas is sick. He had a heart attack.'

'Will he die?' Our last cook, Cora, died of a heart attack, and Katie remembers.

'We don't know, Katie. Honey, I've got to go upstairs. Why don't you go into the kitchen and get yourself a cookie? You and I will talk later.'

She wore a worried expression, but she went. My Katie always does what I ask her. I stood in the half-light of the hallway, dazed. Think! I commanded myself. I went back up the stairs slowly, my mind in turmoil. I headed straight for the bedroom, and opened the drawer where Diane keeps our important papers. I located my passport. If I want to go, I can, I thought to myself. I shut the drawer again, and walked into the bathroom. I poured some water on my face. Then I stared in the mirror. Andreas had a heart attack, I thought. He might die. Death is final.

Back in the hallway, I heard Niki's voice through her closed door.

'I can't stand it any more! I hate him!'

'You don't hate him,' I heard Diane reply. 'He is your father and he loves you and you love him, too.'

'Oh Mom! This is pathetic. You know he doesn't care about me or John. The only person he's ever loved is Katie.'

Oh no, I thought. Not just Katie. There is at least one other person I have loved and even as you speak these awful words she is standing at my brother's deathbed.

'You're wrong, Niki,' came Diane's soothing voice again. 'Your father is not a demonstrative man, but he loves all of us. He loves us very much.'

Niki's voice interrupted with harshness.

'A Greek who's not demonstrative! Wake up, Mother. He doesn't love me, and he doesn't love John. And he doesn't love you.'

Diane never raises her voice, but she raised it now.

'Don't you ever say that to me,' she said. 'Your father loves me. I know he does!'

I didn't stay to hear more. I continued down the hallway, past John's door. It was open and when I glanced in I saw him sitting on his bed with a book on his knees, looking at me. He didn't say anything, he hardly ever does, but his eyes were the eyes of a stranger. Niki hates me, I thought, and my son is a stranger. I turned and stumbled down to the kitchen.

3

A Sleepless Night

I found Katie sitting at the kitchen table. I sat down across from her.

'Will Uncle Andreas die?' she said.

'I don't know, my heart, I don't know.'

'I don't want him to die.'

I knew I had to talk to her and reassure her, but my mind had no peace to impart to her. I motioned for her to come over, and when she did I put her on my knee and rested my chin lightly on her dark head. Of my three children she is the only one who looks Greek. She has dark brown hair and eyes, an olive complexion, and she is short. My other children also have brown eyes, but their mother's blonde hair has made theirs light brown. My son John at seventeen is two heads taller than I am, and shows no signs of having reached his final height.

Katie has an instinct for silence. Sometimes during our Sunday talks my stories take me to events I do not want to describe, and then I stop. Katie never pushes me to continue. She lets me stay silent, even if I have stopped mid-sentence, and never resists my changing the subject once I have reclaimed my voice. She let me stay silent this time, too. I knew she wanted to talk, but I selfishly took her gift.

We sat like this for a few minutes, and then Diane came in.

'It's your bedtime, sweetie,' she told Katie.

Without a word Katie got up, kissed us both and took herself off.

'Why don't you go in the small family room and I will make us some tea,' Diane said to me.

I shuffled off and waited for her. It seems a talk was in the works after all.

After Diane brought in the tea and squeezed half a lemon in my cup the way I like it, she settled herself on the sofa tucking her feet under her. Diane is a tall woman, but when she sits like this she becomes a tiny bundle. We sat sipping in silence.

'George, do you love me?' she asked suddenly.

Diane is not like other women. She never asks for demonstrations of affection or verbal reassurance. It is enough for her that I am a good husband and father, that I take care of my household, come home every night, and don't look at other women. In nineteen years of marriage I have never told her I love her and she has never asked. But there's a limit to everything. Having heard Niki's words to her earlier, I wasn't surprised at her question. No, what rendered me speechless was that I couldn't answer her truthfully without wounding her badly. I care for my wife, I respect her and want her to be happy, but I have had love, and what I feel for her bears no resemblance to that other feeling. I looked at her, this handsome but not pretty woman with the blonde hair and the calm clear blue eyes. For more than twenty years, ever since she met me, this woman has stood by me and cared for me, has given me every comfort and attention, has never had a harsh word for me, has never made a demand. In every way she has been a perfect wife and mother, putting her needs second to mine and those of the children. If there is anything she lacks I do not know it, for she never complains. When I worked round the clock for years, she smoothed my life at home into a seamless cocoon to help me rest. And when, after Katie was born, I cut down on my workload and started spending more time at home, she welcomed my presence. So now I looked her straight in the eye and I said: 'That was Manos on the phone. My brother Andreas has had a heart attack. They think he may die. He asked for me.'

Some expression passed over her face too quickly for me to catch it. Then she got up and came over to my armchair, put her arms around me and kissed me lightly on the forehead.

'Oh George, I'm so sorry. Of course you must go. When do you have to leave? Can I come with you? George, are you going?' Here was another question I couldn't answer and I had run out of ways to change the subject. I remained silent.

'You never talk about your family, so I know something went wrong and that's why you left Greece. Can't you tell me now, dear, won't it help you?'

'I have to think, Diane,' I told her. 'I have to be alone to think.'

She let go then and she went out of the room. Her shoulders had a weary look as she walked away. They stated clearly that she had interpreted my avoidance of her last question as my answer to her first.

I had a glancing moment of guilt. I've always put Diane last on my list of priorities, and this night was no exception. Listen, I told myself, I cannot help the way I feel. I give her everything I can. And even as I thought this thought, my mind was jumping away from the subject, my heart was humming, and my thoughts were

31

racing to Greece. I put the tea away and poured myself some Scotch, because Scotch is a drink for thinking. I had a lot of thinking to do, and if my wife was feeling sad, well there was not much I could do about it, because she has never been a part of my other, earlier life in Greece, and it was that life which had my full attention at the moment.

I wandered over to the pictures on the wall, and lingered on the group shot. Diane receded and other faces flooded my mind. Should I obey my brother's dying wish? The five years that separated us had always seemed to me like a lifetime. My childhood seemed unbearably long when I was living it, because I always wanted to catch up to him and never could. I always wanted the things he had, from the peach fuzz that started to grow on his face when I was nine to his easy way with women. He always seemed to know what everything was about, and he was a man when I was a boy. A man can have things a boy can only dream of. And I had only one dream in those days, a dream I cherished and nurtured, a dream that used to nurture me back. But now we are both men, I thought, and he is dying.

So this is where I am right now, in the small living-room, halfway to dawn. Tomorrow I am leaving for Greece. I am no longer the skinny child I was when Andreas snatched from me the only thing that mattered and chased me out of my home. Back then I had nothing to fight back with. But now I am a grown man, a man of means and substance. And it is time to face him once again. It was a hard decision to make, a jump over a bottomless chasm, but now that I've made it, it seems inevitable. I told myself earlier that I would make my decision and then I would think about Diane and how to make her feel better, but I was wrong. All I can think about is halfway across the world, to the east. I've had no sleep, but I feel awake, alive, alert. I'm going back to the scene of my defeat, and to the people who hurt me the most in forty-two years of living, but there is a voice inside me that keeps repeating, 'I'm going home, I'm going home,' and I am bowled over by the strength of my happiness. Until I told myself a bit ago that I am going back, I never knew how much I wanted to go. That hard little knot of my yearning had been buried under scar tissue, but now it has started to melt and it's running down my face. The last twenty-five years seem like they never happened. I don't know how I'll feel when I get there, I don't know what I'll find, but tomorrow, tomorrow, in a few hours, if I can sit still that long, I come in from the *xenitia*. My heart is glad and my pulse races. I'll think about Diane some other time, I'll think about Niki, I'll think about John some other time. And if there is any whispering guilt at some corner of my soul for neglecting my American home, I cannot hear it, because the bells of Saint George are ringing for my return.

Part Two

The Beloved Land

4

My Brother Andreas

Few Americans know of it, but the prettiest city in
Greece is Thessaloniki. While tourists flock to the
commercialised antiquity of Athens and the overpriced
picturesqueness of the Aegean islands, Thessaloniki lies
precious, gorgeous and unknown to tourist agents, nestled
around Thermaikos Bay, six hours by car from Athens.
Like every treasure of true worth, it's hidden, tucked away
up north, out of the beaten path, subtle and authentic.

Her low profile belies her importance. Thessaloniki
is actually the second largest city in Greece, and the
second most important port after Pereas. She is an
ancient city, named after the sister of Alexander the
Great, and known as the bride of Thermaikos. Pretty
as a bride she is, bathed in golden light and the blue
reflection of the water, smaller than Athens and that
much easier to love; intimate, unassuming, comforting
as the girl next door, a real sweetheart of a city.

If you find yourself in Thessaloniki, turn your back to
the bay before the colours of the setting sun steal your
heart, and face the Hortiatis mountain range to the north-
east. If you have the eyes of a poet, the mountain peaks
will arrange themselves in the shape of a woman lying on
her back, the observatory on top of Hortiatis Mountain
forming the nipple of a firm, conical breast. Mark the spot

and follow the twisting road that ascends Hortiatis. Push your car over the steepening upgrade, be careful on the turns, and in about a half-hour, you'll come to Panorama. It's perched halfway up the range and boasts a regular bus service to the city. Most of the village is built in a shallow dip of the mountain, but a part of it, the best part, circles a small peak, and offers a sweeping view of Thermaikos Bay and Thessaloniki. It is that view that gives the village its name, which means view from above.

I was born in Panorama just as the fifties were getting started, to the village baker and his pretty wife Niki. I was the second of two sons. The story of my birth was one of my mother's favourites. My father was a firm believer in progress, and wanted my mother to give birth in a modern hospital in Thessaloniki. From the very beginning of the pregnancy, he took my mother to Dr Mavros downtown, shunning the services of Kyra Marika, the village midwife. He had arranged for everything, including the availability of the only privately-owned car in Panorama to drive my mother into the city once her pains started. The car belonged to his friend Stamos, the local pastry-shop owner, who had been making money hand over fist ever since the smart set from Thessaloniki had discovered his custard-filled filo pastry. In preparation, as my mother's time neared, Kyr Stamos changed the oil, checked the spare and polished the chrome. Then he waited for the signal.

At four a.m. on the morning of my birthday, my father got up as usual to go to the bakery, accompanied by his partner, his brother Demetres. My mother fed them breakfast and went back to bed. At seven she got up again, to start her day. She went out to feed the cats living in our yard and on her way back inside she saw Kyra Marika hurrying past. She invited her in for a cup of coffee, mindful to be extra nice to her to erase the insult of my father's choice of a doctor for her pregnancy. Inside the house, Kyra Marika took one look at her and said: 'It looks to me like you're ready to drop that child any minute.'

My mother explained that she was three weeks away from her official due date.

'Your fancy doctor may say what he wants, but I think you're having that child today,' Kyra Marika answered.

She left our house and went straight to the bakery, where she informed my father of her opinion. My father shook his head to indicate 'she never gives up' and went on selling bread.

Around nine the snow started falling. It snows at least once a year in Panorama, but November snow is a rare event. By one o'clock an unprecedented blizzard was under way. And by two my mother was in labour. Making it to Thessaloniki was out of question in the storm. My father, who had closed the store and returned home in the blinding snow, had to go out again together with my uncle and knock on Kyra Marika's door to ask for her help. The wind was howling and driving the snow hard enough to bruise. My father and uncle carried Kyra Marika to our house in their arms, stumbling and falling all the way. The round trip to her house and back to ours took them over an hour, even though she lived only a few blocks away. My father said she gloated all the way, but he never replied except to thank her. He knew when to put pride aside. 'And that's how,' my mother would conclude, 'you set the course of modern medicine back by about ten years in Panorama.'

My parents named me Giorgos, but Kyra Marika, still teasing my father for his faith in progress, translated it to George. 'The child of progress should have an American name. I think he even cried in American,' she laughed at my baptism, and so I remained George.

My father's favourite story was how he met and married my mom. He loved to tell how he saw her for the first time the year the baker of Hortiatis, the village on top of the mountain range, fell sick and couldn't work. To help the neighbouring village, my grandfather baked extra bread every day for the two months the baker was laid up, and he would send my father up every day with a donkey and all the bread it could carry. My mother was one of the Hortiatis women who would come out to buy the bread. Day after day my father would see her, and day after day he loved her more. But there was never an opportunity to talk to her. Despairing of ever seeing her alone, he tried to communicate his feelings by keeping back for her the best loaves, the ones with the crispiest crust and the best colour, but she didn't seem to notice.

After a month of this subtle courting, he finally talked to Stamos, whose mother had relatives in Hortiatis, and asked him to find out what he could about a girl named Niki. It took Stamos two days to report back, and the news wasn't good. Niki by all reports was a fine girl, but her parents had targeted the Hortiatis tavern keeper for her groom, and Niki was almost engaged. To make things worse, the tavern keeper was in his late thirties, and had a gimp leg. My father almost lost his mind. The next day, when he went to deliver the bread, he couldn't stop himself: 'I hear you're getting married,' he told her.

My mother was astonished that this stranger would have heard, and she made no reply. The match was not finalised yet, and it embarrassed her to have a stranger refer to it openly, so she blushed and stammered. Through the eyes of love, my father interpreted her reaction as a sure sign that she was not anxious to marry the tavern keeper. Back in Panorama he consulted with Stamos. Stamos thought my father should kidnap Niki.

'But I don't know if she wants me, Stamos,' my father said.

'So ask her,' Stamos replied.

The next day my father screwed up his courage and when my mother showed up to pick up her order he made sure to serve her last. This did not mean they were alone, because the women always hung around to chat and wait for each other, but luck was with my father that day, and he and my mother were almost out of earshot.

'A tavern keeper keeps late hours,' he whispered, looking away from her, 'and he's always drinking to keep his customers company. Wouldn't you rather marry a baker and have your husband home at night?'

'No baker has asked me,' my mother replied.

That's all my father needed to hear. The next afternoon, when everybody was asleep, Stamos and my father sat in the yard drinking coffee and planning the kidnapping. Thank God my grandfather overheard them from the house, where he was supposed to be taking his afternoon nap. Bride kidnappings were not unknown, but they often ended in trouble and sometimes even in bloodshed, when the groom didn't manage to make his getaway, and the bride's relatives saw the botched bridenapping as a blot on their honour. Once a kidnapping had ended in the wrong marriage, because in the darkness the groom had stolen the wrong girl. He ran off with her in the middle of the night and didn't discover his mistake until he took her to a deserted church in the woods where he had planned to hide out until his friends could bring the priest to perform the ceremony. By the time he peeled back the blankets covering his precious burden, the girl, who was his beloved's cousin come to visit, had been irredeemably compromised. Even though he returned her untouched that same night, he had to marry her anyway. By all accounts they lived happily together for many years, but this is the kind of thing that can easily lead to misery. Grandfather dashed out in the yard, grabbed my father by the scruff and told him that if he wanted to marry he had to do it right.

This set things in motion. Grandpa made inquiries as to Niki's character and having satisfied himself as to her good reputation he saddled the donkey, put Stamos's mother on it, and set off for Hortiatis accompanied by my father. The party made it to Niki's house where Stamos's mother vouched for the character of the Vasilikos family, and my grandfather explained that my dad had fallen in love with their daughter.

'I don't know how you feel about all this,' he told them, 'but it's good for a man and wife to love each other. I know my son loves your daughter, and if your daughter is the girl I saw looking out the window when we were arriving, I think she loves him, too. My son is a good boy and he will take care of her. He is a hard worker, and he will inherit half my bakery and half my house when I die. The other half goes to his brother. We ask for no dowry. You think about it, talk to your daughter, and let me know.'

They left shortly after my grandfather's pithy speech. My father didn't know it then, but the tavern keeper had asked that he be given the house my mother's parents lived in in exchange for marrying the daughter. The parents had balked at that, because they had another daughter, too, and if their Niki got the house, what would be left for her? In his ignorance, my dad worried all the way down the mountain that his father had spoken too plainly. But shortly after that the word arrived that Niki's parents agreed to the match. And so it was that every Sunday for six months my father went up to Hortiatis to visit my mother and his in-laws, eating lunch with them and never seeing my mother alone, until the wedding was held and my mother moved to Panorama.

'The only thing he didn't tell me was that if tavern keepers keep late hours, bakers keep very early ones,' my mother used to say every time my father would tell the story. But this was no rebuke, because as she said it she would gaze at him fondly and he would wink at her.

After the wedding, my mother moved into a house full of men. My grandmother had died giving birth to my uncle, and since then my grandfather had lived alone with his two sons. When my mother moved in, she had to take care of all of them. Now I think that her life was far from ideal. My grandfather was no trouble at all, he was a good man who asked for very little, but my Uncle Demetres was not so easy. He was a hard worker, like my father, but he was also a drinker. Every night he headed out to the village tavern under the huge century-old buttonwood tree in the village square and drank ouzo with his buddies. Sometimes he came home singing in the night, but other times he came home in a rage, cursing one buddy for having cheated at cards, and another for having cheated at backgammon. My earliest memory is of just such a night. I remember seeing my uncle propping himself up on the door separating the dining-room from the family room, and speaking in a loud voice. I remember my mother in a long white nightgown telling me to go back to bed, and I remember ignoring her command. But most of all I remember my grandfather getting up from his bed in the room I shared with him and Andreas, gently pushing me out of the way, and then striding up to my uncle and slapping him hard on the face.

*   *   *

The house we lived in was my father's ancestral home. It had two storeys. At ground level was a cellar, filled with provisions, tools and odds and ends. Above the cellar was the house itself. It had a formal dining-room with two bedrooms on each side, one for my parents and one for my brother, me and my grandpa. Past the dining-room, there was a small sitting-room where the family gathered on winter evenings, with the bedroom where my uncle slept on one side, and a large kitchen on the other. The house had high ceilings which kept it cool in summer but made it hard to heat in winter. We had a wood-burning stove in the sitting-room, and another in the kitchen on top of which my mother did her cooking, but there was no heat in the bedrooms. Each night after escorting me to the bathroom, my grandpa would rub my hands and feet real hard before I went to bed, to keep them warm until my body had a chance to heat up the space under my blankets.

The bathroom was outside, a tiny outhouse containing only a hole, over which you had to squat. To help centre you over the target, my grandfather had placed two cement blocks shaped like a giant's footprints on each side of the hole. There was a cloth strip tied to the door and you were supposed to hold on to that when you were inside. It kept the door securely closed, and it gave my grandpa some leverage, so he could straighten up when he was done. Most households, including our own, never bought toilet paper. Instead, the housewives cut the daily newspaper into squares, and skewered them on a wire nailed to an inside wall of the outhouse. I was eight years old before my uncle bought toilet paper for us to use, but my father continued to use the newspaper. He said it gave him an opportunity to comment on national politics.

During the day the bathroom was just a fact of life. At night, however, it became a thing of terror. It had no electricity, so I would take a flashlight with me. The flashlight cast shadows and the hole seemed menacing. Anything could leap out of that darkness and grab me. My grandpa was my sentinel outside, ready to come to my rescue. My brother Andreas also offered to be my guard, but I knew from bitter experience that once I was in there he would disappear, and soon I would be hearing strange whoops and whistles which I now know he was making to scare me. It is a miracle to me that my toilet training was successful.

Our house had a large yard where I did most of my growing up. The yard was filled with acacias, but there were also pomegranate bushes, two almond trees and two fig trees. Fig trees grow branches straight out of the ground, and very early in life I discovered that I could hide in the heart of a fig tree and watch the yard from there unobserved. My mother never knew my hiding place, but my brother did, so it wasn't much of an asylum.

There was plenty for me to do to keep myself amused. I could spend my time exploring the yard in summer, or breaking into the cellar in winter to dig through the boxes and tools stored in there. I could go to the bakery and ask my father to let me handle the long wooden paddle to check on the baking, or let me hand the scalding hot bread to the women and jiggle their drachmas in the till. I could join the other village children in a game of hide and seek or an exploration of the village environs. I could run with a gang bent on stealing watermelons from the orchards, or I could join the game of war staged almost every night on the steps and open porch of the church of Saint George. I could wait for evening and count the cows coming back from pasture, and marvel over the cow patties they would drop on their way. I could make fun of the girls and old ladies who walked behind them scooping up the dung to dry and use as tinder for the fire. I could even hang around within earshot of my mother and neighbours as they settled down to their daily coffee ritual, pretending I was paying no attention to them, but all the time straining with all my might to hear adult secrets. Any of these things I could do, and each was amusing in its way, but what I wanted more than anything was to hang out with my brother Andreas.

To other people Andreas went through childhood, just like everyone else. But to me Andreas was never a child. He already was five years old by the time I was born. He was a boy when I was a baby, an adolescent when I was a boy, and a man when I was not yet a teenager. My first memory of him is of the two of us sitting under one of the almond trees. He was picking up almonds from the ground, peeling their fuzzy green covering, placing each carefully on a stone slab, and then, while holding the almond in place with one hand, cracking it open with a rock to eat. I picked one up, too, and put it in my mouth.

'Not like that, you little fool! You have to strip it bare, and then you have to crack it,' he said. 'Spit that out.'

I did as he told me and then he handed me an almond ready for cracking.

'Here, you can use my rock,' he said.

I must have tried to imitate him, but I was a baby. I hit my hand and howled in pain.

'You're such an idiot, George,' he said.

But after examining my hand for damage and finding none, he placed the rock back in my palm, covered my fist with his own, and guided my first successful attempt to crack an almond open.

I was drawn to him like a moth to a flame, and remember having no other hero. You see, Andreas was not just my older brother. Andreas was a leader of boys and inventor of games, a tireless adventurer, and a fearless warrior. He won every fight, came first in every race, rode his bike with his hands off the handlebars and usually scored the winning point in soccer. He was a master at sneaking into the movies without paying and had discovered that by climbing a particular tree he could watch the butcher's wife undressing for bed. He charged other boys money to share his secret. Everything every little boy dreams of becoming, Andreas was without even thinking about it. He was not afraid of anything, not the dark, not dogs, not even disobedience. He knew full well every time he violated my father's rules that he risked a sound beating, and yet he did what he wanted. When he was found out he faced the consequences without complaint. I remember the time, for example, that Andreas announced he planned to lead a bike expedition to Sedes, the next village down the mountain. My father told him to put such plans out of his mind immediately.

'I mean it, Andreas,' he told him. 'That road is dangerous, and I will not have you getting run over or getting one of your friends run over. If I hear you've been on that road I will beat you so hard you won't be able to sit down for days.'

My father was right. The forbidden road was frequented by speeding trucks loaded with stone, barrelling down the mountain from the quarry near Hortiatis to Thessaloniki. But sense and threats meant nothing to Andreas. He had already talked to his gang about the great bike trip. He had already made plans, shamed the boys who were afraid to follow him into promising to do so. He couldn't back out now. Only a few days after my father issued his edict, Andreas mounted his bike, motioned his buddies to follow, and set out for the big adventure, leaving me to wring my hands in worry and anxiety. The boys were gone all morning, and I, who was in the know, worried all morning. Strangely enough I did not worry about the murderous trucks. I worried about my father's rage once he found out, as he would, that he had been disobeyed.

The morning passed without incident, but when time for lunch came and there was no sign of Andreas or his gang, parents began to worry. One by one they showed up in our yard, having learned from other boys that in all probability their sons were in Sedes. My father got the story out of me. Yes, Andreas had disobeyed. Yes, he had gone to Sedes. By the time Andreas and his band of merry mischief-makers rode back, tired and triumphant, I was crying in the corner and blaming myself for cracking under my father's questioning. My father grabbed Andreas by the scruff of the neck in full view of the other miscreants and their outraged parents, and beat him long and hard. Then he grounded him.

Andreas took his punishment like a man; silently, stoically, without complaint. Later I slunk into the bedroom, where Andreas was lying on the bed, staring at the ceiling.

'I'm sorry I squealed on you,' I said, crushed with shame, filled with self-loathing, ready for the scathing words of blame that I deserved.

'It doesn't matter,' Andreas shrugged. 'It was no secret, everybody knew except the grown-ups.' And then he told me of the hair-raising trip down the steep mountain, the bikes' brakes overheating and losing their hold, the trucks whizzing by and the truck drivers shouting out curses, the watermelon field baking in the sunshine that the boys stole into to quench their thirst, the dozens of watermelons they stole and crushed open by dropping them on the hard pavement, the triumph of finally pulling into Sedes, then the horrible return in the heat. The plan was to make it back before they were missed, but they had not realised how hard the return trip would be. The mountain that had speeded their descent now worked against them. The afternoon sun was hot, and the boys could not pedal up the steep incline. For half an hour they strained their muscles and let the sweat pour, unwilling to admit defeat. But it was too hard. Finally they had to give in, Andreas last, of course, and walk, pulling their bikes beside them.

'But you know what? It was worth it!'

If it were possible to admire my brother more than I already did, the trip to Sedes and his casual forgiveness of my cowardly betrayal would have done it. But it was not possible.

Even apart from special events, Andreas was a king. When the neighbourhood kids played hide and seek, nobody ever found him. I was afraid of the dark and always hid in the obvious places, behind a ledge, in a nearby shack. Even there my heart would beat in fear, and I almost wished I would be found, so I could have company. Once in a while I would try to follow Andreas to his ingenious hide-outs, but I was too slow. In the space of a second Andreas would melt into the night, and I would be left straining behind him, guessing this or that disappearing shadow to be his, but unable to follow. When the seeker would move away from the designated spot to find the other kids, and Andreas got tired of hiding, he would stealthily move through the shadows to reach the spot and spit at it to mark his victory. He always let out a huge glob of spit that made a splat and was the envy not only of my bedazzled baby eyes, but of the whole neighbourhood.

The boy who was discovered first, and didn't manage to outrun the seeker to the spitting post, had to be the next seeker. I was not only afraid of the dark, but also a bad runner. Since I knew the chances of me outrunning the seeker were slim to none, I always played defensively, making no effort to sneak to victory, but rather just cowering behind something, taking defeat for granted, and hoping another boy would lose first so I would not have to be the seeker. The thought of having to keep my eyes covered in the darkness and count slowly while everybody else hid filled me with terror. So I would wait till it was safe, and then let myself be found, getting no pleasure from the game, just hanging in there.

Despite my defensive strategy, the night came when I was discovered first, and had to look for everyone in the darkness. When the counting was over and I opened my eyes, the silence around me was terrifying. There was light from the lamp-post where I was standing, but everything else was pitch black. I took some tentative steps around, looked behind some bushes, made a pretence of moving away from the post, but stayed well within the nimbus of light. It was a long time before I could gather enough courage to look anywhere where a boy might be hiding, but I found no one that night, and no matter how far away I eventually walked from the post, no boy came running out of the darkness to spit. Tired of my cautious ways, and despairing of ever seeing me move far enough from the post to allow anyone a fighting chance to win, Andreas had gathered up the boys one by one, and they had all taken off for a stroll down the village main street, leaving me alone to search in vain, as punishment for not playing fair. When I finally caught up with them, Andreas wouldn't let me join the crowd.

'You are a cheat!' he yelled in front of everybody. 'Nobody talk to George for the rest of the week!' And the boys obeyed him.

They always obeyed him. No vote was ever taken, but Andreas was the acknowledged leader of the neighbourhood. All his other talents aside, his prowess at soccer was enough to secure him the position. Soccer was the big game. Every boy played, and every boy followed the professional games. Most kids were good enough to hold their own, but Andreas was gifted. There was magic in his legs. When he had the ball nobody could trick it away from him. When he saw his way clear to the goal, he kicked with everything he had, strong straight kicks that either won the point by sailing through the stones that stood for goalposts, or bruised the goalie who used his body to deflect the shot. Andreas's team was usually the winner.

My father thought Andreas should take care of me, and he was always telling him to take me with him when he wanted to go off with his friends. Andreas would obey my father, but sometimes, as soon as we were out of sight, he would quicken his steps and urge his friends along, until I could no longer keep up. I would try to run and the tears would start rolling down my cheeks.

'George is such a baby,' he would yell, looking over his shoulder. 'George is a little girl. Stay there if you're not a little girl. Stay there and wait for me.'

And I would wait, sometimes for hours. Never, not even once, did I tell my father.

But there were other times, too, when he would take me with him. His friend Pavlos complained once that I was slowing them down, but Andreas said, 'I say he goes with us,' and then he picked me up and put me on his shoulders and carried me around. I felt as though I'd never have a prouder moment.

What he did usually when he left me behind was climb the tree to watch the butcher's wife, or hide with his friends to smoke and talk dirty. In the afternoon, when everybody would be sleeping, I would hear him get up and walk out of the bedroom we shared. He would tiptoe to the family room where Uncle Demetres usually left his cigarettes and, if the pack was fairly full, he would steal a couple. Later, in the evening, he would sit behind the church with his buddies and they would smoke. Our neighbour, Antigone, saw them once, and went to tell my father.

'Right next to the church they were, Kyr Yiannis, they have no respect.'

Antigone's words were spoken with malice, but then she had plenty of reason to hate Andreas. Antigone was in her thirties and unmarried. She was an old maid, forever on the fringe, forever hoping that someone would marry her. Day after day she drank her coffee and turned her cup over carefully for Kyra Maria to read her fortune. But the entwined rings that meant marriage never showed up in her cup, and she remained unclaimed. She did have a fiancé once. His name was Petros, and he had asked her to marry him when she was in her twenties. Then he left for Germany where he would work in a brewery and save the money necessary to set up house. The years passed and Antigone waited. At first there were letters. Then the letters grew scarce, until they finally stopped altogether. Still Antigone waited. She had already been waiting for a decade when Andreas learned the story and came up with a cruel game for the neighbourhood kids to play. Whenever things got boring, he would get everybody running from the square to Antigone's house, yelling at the top of their lungs, 'Petros is here! He's arrived! Come out, Antigone, he's here.' Antigone knew who invented the game, and missed no chance to turn in Andreas to my father.

Andreas received a sound beating that night, both for smoking and for stealing the cigarettes, but he never cried. Instead, he gave me his 'it was worth it' look, and went right on smoking and announcing the arrival of the faithless Petros.

You'd think a boy who had so many talents, including a talent for mischief, would have a few enemies, a few detractors. At the very least, the adults or some of the older boys should be set hard against him, and set him down a peg. Not so. Andreas did get in trouble a lot, but not near as much as he deserved. He had a way of cajoling the people around him into forgiving him, taking his part, seeing his side. If he was too high-handed around the neighbourhood and some of the boys began to resent it, he would soon realise it and bestow some favour or compliment on the disaffected to soon have them in his camp again. If the favour or compliment didn't work, he would pull the other boys so far over to his side, that whoever questioned his authority soon found himself alone, and had to submit or have no one to play with.

Adults were easy for him to handle, too. He could be the nicest, politest boy to his friends' parents, so that they often ended up blaming their own kids for the trouble Andreas led them into. Andreas was successful because he didn't wait until he needed someone before he would turn on the charm. Oh, no! He cultivated everybody in case the need should arise, so that when it did, the groundwork was already laid. My uncle, for example, was a taciturn man who had a habit of talking only to complain, threaten or curse. I thought it best to keep out of his way. Andreas, however, befriended him, and was always whispering and laughing with him. The result was that if he needed money, he could always talk my Uncle Demetres into giving it to him. And if my father didn't find out on his own Andreas's newest misdeed, Andreas could always get my mother to cover for him. Even though to me and his friends he always made light of my father's beatings, he made sure our mother knew the extent of his injuries each time, and he was not above practising a pained limping walk in her presence after a well-deserved caning. When news of his latest exploit would reach my mother, he would let her rant and rave and threaten to let my father know at the earliest opportunity, and then he would allude to the punishment that he would get amid subtle, indirect assurances that he would never do again whatever it was that had upset my mother. Soon my mother would be thinking that my father was really too harsh with his son, and she would keep the infraction to herself.

My father was the only person Andreas never managed to con. He punished Andreas without mercy, in keeping with the theory, popular in Greece at the time, that to spare the rod was to spoil the child. The rod fell on my brother often, but its effect missed him entirely, and fell on me, instead. Andreas was not afraid of punishment. He would try to escape it if he could by hiding his feats, but he never to my knowledge refrained from doing something because he might be slapped around for it. It was I who lived in fear of my father's discipline, even though it never had to be directed at me. There was an air of oppression in the house when my father paced around waiting for Andreas so he could unleash his wrath on him. I would watch him gnash his teeth, look angrily at his watch and slap his belt against his hand, and I would cringe in fearful anticipation. One of what I suppose must be my earliest memories was of just such a beating, administered by my father while I lay in my bed and Andreas in his across from mine. I have no idea what the provocation was, but I remember my father lifting Andreas bodily and slamming him down on his bed again with an angry thud. Andreas was not saying anything, but I was crying. This became the pattern. Andreas would do whatever he wanted, and as soon as I knew it I would be driven mad with worry and fear that my father would find out. When he did, and began his beating of Andreas, it was me who cried and hurt.

My dad never had to discipline me. I grew up dutiful, respectful and obedient. Dad used to say I was his 'good' boy, never suspecting that it was Andreas's punishment that kept me on the straight and narrow.

You'd think that given these circumstances, I must have been the favourite son. Not so. My father took great pains never to favour one above the other, and always to treat us equally, but there was a hint of pride when he complained to his friends about Andreas that was never there when he talked about me. And it was obvious to me that he admired Andreas for taking his punishment like a man.

Almost every night of my childhood I prayed that I would wake up the next day fearless, courageous, admired and respected just like my brother Andreas. My prayers were never answered. It was as though God had exhausted his bounty on my brother, and had no good qualities left by the time I was born. Where Andreas was fearless, friendly, commanding and confident, I was shy, withdrawn, cowering and uncertain. It wouldn't have been easy on any boy to follow in the footsteps of Andreas, but it was even harder on me. I was not only younger, but also small for my age. I had no natural ability in games, and my shyness hindered me further. I felt everyone measuring me against my brother, and I knew I came up short in the comparison. If we were closer in age I might have ended up hating him, but five years was a big enough difference to allow me the illusion for several years that it was just a matter of time before I would catch up with him. I kept waiting to grow up into another Andreas, and by the time I realised it would never happen, I was already his adoring slave. He was my hero. I swear I learned to walk just so I could run after him. When I heard other boys speak of him with wonder or admiration, my chest puffed out with pride. When he won the soccer game, I felt as though the glory was mine. When he wrestled an opponent to the ground and confirmed his supremacy once again, I was the boy cheering the loudest.

He was the centre of my universe, but it was clear to me from the start that I would never be much to him. This was as it should be, and I understood it. I had no accomplishments to stack up against his own. If he treated me with contempt, or did things to hurt me, it was no more than I deserved. And there were times when he was nice to me. It was times like that I lived for. When Andreas would confide in me, throw his careless smile my way, or decide to pay attention to me, I was the happiest boy on earth. I basked in the sun of his approval, and noted the circumstances so I could duplicate them in the future to get him to pay attention to me again. Alas, there was no way to manage this. How Andreas would treat me at any given moment had nothing to do with anything I could control or even predict. If I happened to be around when we had visitors, and hid a piece of his favourite kind of cake to give to him, he might take it from me with a smile and a nod of thanks, or he might toss it away and tell me to get lost. If I hovered around the sidelines when he played soccer to hand him a towel to wipe his sweat, he might ask my opinion of his playing as though it mattered to him, or he might tell me to get the hell away from him. More than anything I wanted Andreas to love me, but there was nothing I could do to make it so. Like a puppy with a cruel master, I spent my childhood coming up to Andreas time and again with eyes bright and my tongue hanging out, to receive sometimes a pat, sometimes a kick.

5

Artemis

Unlike other boys who have no interest in girls, and who hide even when they do have it, even before he hit puberty Andreas made no secret of what would become his life-long pursuit. For a while he called himself the kissing bandit. He would tie a kerchief around his head so that one eye was covered, and he would hide with his buddies. As soon as a likely prospect would walk by alone, his friends would pounce on her and hold her still, while Andreas kissed her on the cheek. Many of the girls would fight and try to twist away, but there were those who would deliberately walk that stretch of street alone, hoping to become the newest victim. Finally one of the ones who really minded got over her embarrassment enough to tell her mother, and a severe beating put a stop to the kissing bandit.

Soon after, Andreas picked Fani, the girl living around the corner, as his special lady love, and courted her roughly. He teased her without mercy, and one day took a long stick and used it to raise her skirt from behind while she was standing talking to her girlfriends. He did this in full view of his buddies who laughed uncontrollably and caused Fani to run home in tears. Her mother complained bitterly to my father, who slapped Andreas and made him apologise to Fani. Andreas apologised, but never again spoke to her. When he later became the heart-throb of Panorama, Fani regretted having discouraged him so.

The spring he was sixteen, his interest focused on Artemis, the seamstress's daughter. Artemis was a pretty girl, some said the prettiest in the village. She was short and well developed, with bright brown eyes and dimples. At fifteen she looked as juicy and delicious as a plum fresh from the tree.

Artemis lived with her mother in a small cottage three doors down from ours and our mothers were friends. The cottage had two rooms. One was a bedroom, and the other was everything else, including Kyra Toula's work room. My mother visited often, and I accompanied her because I loved being in that room where I could examine the battered sewing machine, an American Singer with a faded rose on the side, pick up the rags that littered the floor, or play with the scattered pins and the horseshoe-shaped magnet. When I got too old for rags and pins, I kept going to Kyra Toula's cottage for her collection of ancient fashion magazines in full colour, showing pretty young women in a dazzling display of dresses for all occasions. Well, most occasions. There were no dresses for milking cows or for boiling water in a huge cauldron to do the family's wash, and I guess that's why nobody from the village ever asked Kyra Toula to make them one of those dresses.

I got to be friends with Artemis because she was always around, helping her mother. She was a good-natured girl and liked me, so although she was four years older she paid attention to me and always had a kind word. Then one day she took me aside and handed me a note.

'Give this to Andreas for me, will you, Georgie?' she asked me.

I was stunned and curious. Teenagers didn't date in Panorama. Boys and girls talked to each other only in groups, after they reached puberty. Romance was hidden and furtive and usually by the time anyone found out about it, the couple were announcing their engagement. I had never seen Artemis and Andreas glance at each other, let alone talk. Why was Artemis giving me a note for him? I had no time to ask. My mother was already saying goodbye and explaining that she had to get back to her cleaning.

Andreas was still at school when we came home. Younger children like me only had to attend for half a day, but Andreas had to go back after a two-hour lunch break and stay till six. Artemis was not attending school because her mother thought it was more important for a girl to learn to sew so she could some day earn a living. It took me all of ten minutes to decide to open the note, reasoning it was allowed, since Artemis didn't say not to.

'Can't make it tomorrow,' I read. 'Day after at three, usual place.'

This mystified me. Unless Artemis meant that she would meet Andreas in the dead of night, she had named an hour when he would be in school. And where could they possibly go where the whole village wouldn't see them?

I gave the note to Andreas when he got home, after having rehearsed how to say 'of course not' when he would ask me if I had read it. He never asked. He just took the note, glanced at it and stuck it in one of his school books. That night in bed, I decided to follow Andreas and solve the mystery.

Two days later, when Andreas set off for his afternoon session at school, I followed him at a distance. He walked the road to school for a while, but then I saw him veering away. He was heading up the hill, towards the slope of the western outskirts of Panorama where rich men from Thessaloniki had built their summer villas to enjoy the view of the bay below. Andreas was walking purposefully. A couple of times he looked around, but I was being careful and managed to stay concealed behind trees and bushes, only breaking cover to dash to my next post. Soon he was striding past the high fences and gates of the villas, nearing the most envied one of all, Villa Karras, the one that had a pool. The only other place the kids in Panorama had ever seen a pool was in the movies. When he reached the wooden plaque identifying Villa Karras, he left the road and started circling the tall wooden fence. Soon he was nowhere to be seen. I stayed put, wondering what to do. Then I saw Artemis. She also left the road, circled the fence and disappeared.

I waited a few minutes and decided to explore the fence. Sure enough, I found a spot behind a bush where somebody had pulled aside a couple of pikes, leaving a margin wide enough for a body to squeeze through. With my heart beating a mile a minute, I wiggled to the other side. There was no one in sight. I stood looking at the house. It was big and white with the doors and windows made of dark wood. Decorative wrought-iron lamps hung on each side of the arched door. Everything looked new. The ground was covered by smooth grass that looked as soft as silk. In the back of the house the pool was visible. It was empty. Beyond it, you could see Thessaloniki and the bay, bathed in sunlight. I couldn't figure where Andreas and Artemis had gone. And then I heard Artemis laugh inside the house. Inside the house! I was shocked and frightened. It was one thing to crawl through the fence and maybe roll on the grass. It was one thing to stick your face to a window and see the beautiful furniture, the cavernous fireplace, the pictures hanging on the walls inside. Many children did this when the owners were not in residence. But to my knowledge nobody ever went inside the homes. And to laugh out loud! These visits to the summer villas were always carried out in either complete silence or conspiratorial whispers. We knew that if we were discovered the police could haul us away. To go inside and then to laugh was to invite disaster.

I considered running away, but I wanted to see how far my brother could possibly go in this madness. With a quick prayer to Saint George I approached the house and peeped in one of the windows. I had a full view of the living-room. It had a recessed marble floor and was furnished sparsely. There were some armchairs and a sofa covered with sheets and arranged around a square coffee table, a bookcase taking up an entire wall, a piano off to the side, and the view from the picture window. Andreas was sitting on the sofa with Artemis on his lap. Her blouse was open and his face was pushed into her chest. As I watched in fascination, Andreas tipped Artemis over till she fell on the couch. I heard her protest, but her words were muffled when Andreas moved his face to hers. My brother was kissing her and at the same time was manoeuvring his body and hers so that they lay on the couch, with her underneath and his body half to her side and half on top of her. His one arm was beneath her shoulders. His other arm, after having positioned her to his liking, was gripping her thigh.

I couldn't have moved away even if I had heard police sirens. Three years before, when I was pretending to play during one of my mother's coffee klatches, I had heard Kyra Maria, in her best sediment-reader voice, whisper to the women who sat in rapt attention around her: 'Thirty-five years of marriage, I tell you, and he never jumped her. She stayed with him and said nothing, and when people asked what about children she looked sad and everyone assumed she was barren. And maybe she is, who's to know. But one thing's for sure, so help me God. She's still a girl just like she was and thirty-five years of marriage didn't change that. She'll die a girl. I asked her, I said, "Hariklia, how come you didn't leave him, why didn't you do something?" and she said to me, "I was ashamed."'

I knew what I had heard was good. I could tell by the look on everyone's face and the blush on Antigone's cheeks. If Antigone blushed, then the topic under discussion was sure to be related to sex. I had seen the animals around me of course, and I knew more than city kids knew, but the subject of sex between people was still a mystery, and I could not connect what I had seen animals doing with the people around me. What did Kyra Maria mean that Kyra Hariklia was a girl? I knew Kyra Hariklia, I had seen her recently at her husband's funeral. Our house's proximity to the church meant that we shared in all weddings, baptisms and funerals even more than the rest of the village, because, after all, it all happened in our back yard, and we had a ring-side seat. I remembered Kyra Hariklia crying and standing on the church steps receiving condolences. She was no girl, she was an old woman. And why was it bad to be a girl, and what did it all have to do with jumping?

I went to Andreas with my questions. I knew from experience that he loved to hear whatever gossip I could gather from the women who drank coffee in our yard, and he often laughed at my words and ruffled my hair. Sometimes he would get mad or impatient, however, and tell me that I was talking nonsense and was too stupid to remember what I heard. This time my news made no sense, and so I approached him warily, but he seemed to understand in an instant and he laughed long and hard.

'And to think he used to sit around in the tavern and sigh and roll his eyes whenever a summer girl would go by and wish out loud he had his youth back!' he managed to say when he was done laughing. And then he explained to me that Kyr Agisilaos couldn't do the deed that separates the men from the boys.

'If she wasn't such a fat cow,' he boasted, 'I would go to Kyra Hariklia and throw her down and I bet she'd be so grateful she'd leave me the house when she dies.'

As I watched through the villa's window I reasoned that my brother was doing now what Kyr Agisilaos couldn't do to Kyra Hariklia. His hand was moving steadily up Artemis's thigh and her skirt was being dragged along with it. I could see her white cotton panties. Andreas was moving urgently against her, rubbing his body on hers. Then he let his hand move on her bare leg and for a moment his fingers disappeared under the white cotton. Artemis started to struggle hard and threw him off. She sat up, red all over and breathing hard, and she smoothed her skirt and then her hair. She said something but I couldn't hear, because her voice was soft. I did hear my brother, who was now pacing up and down the room.

'Why do you come here if you don't want me?' he asked her. 'Why, eh? Why?'

She whispered something again that I couldn't hear, and then she started to cry. My brother looked annoyed for a few seconds, and then he sat back on the couch and held Artemis in his arms. He rocked her back and forth and soon they were kissing again, but this time my brother did not reach under her skirt. Instead, he opened her shirt all the way and when he leaned back to look at her I could see too, see Artemis's smooth breasts with their brown nipples. To this day this first glimpse of a woman's breasts is one of my most sensual memories. Artemis was only fifteen, but I can see now that she had remarkably mature breasts, not only big but fully formed. My brother groaned and fell on her again, and after furiously rubbing against her for a few minutes finally let her go and got up. I knew it was time for me to get out before they left the house and saw me. As I raced down the hill I marvelled at my brother's daring.

It was several hours later when I saw Andreas again. I was in the yard, sprawled on my belly watching an army of ants haul food to their home. Most ants were dragging small seeds and tiny bits of food, but one was trying to haul an impossibly large piece of bread, not realising that even if he brought it to the hole, it would never fit. I took the bread away from him as gently as I could and with my nail broke it up into tiny pieces, but I must have scared the little fella, because he gave the crumbs a wide berth and returned to the hole empty-handed. By the time the other ants had discovered the new crumbs, I was feeling guilty of having deprived the ambitious ant of its glory. Then Andreas's shoes entered my field of vision.

'Where were you this afternoon, George?' he asked me, his voice dangerous.

I felt the world stand still.

'Around here,' I replied, not looking up at him. A furious, uncontrolled blush was painting my face red.

'That's funny. Then it must have been your twin I saw up in the Villa Karras.'

I decided it was best to say nothing.

'Listen, you little piece of snot,' he said bending over me and grabbing me by the shirt. 'If so much as a word escapes you, you are dead. And learn to hide behind things that are bigger than you next time. Hiding your eyes doesn't mean I can't see your big butt.'

I had expected a big scene, maybe a kick or two, but

nothing else happened. As a matter of fact, Andreas softened towards me. That evening I joined my friends for a game of soccer. My brother, who was too good by now for the neighbourhood games, had left a legacy of excellence for me to follow. Unfortunately, I was no good. At the age of eleven I played worse than the nine-year-olds on the team, and I was always one of the last boys to be picked on a team. That year, Andreas had begun to play with the young men's teams in the league that competed against other villages. Still, he often watched the neighbourhood games and sometimes gave advice or criticism. That evening, the other team scored because I mistakenly passed the ball to one of my team's opponents. Thanases, my team captain, was furious with me.

'You're hopeless, George. You are an idiot. I don't ever want you on my team again. What do they do? Pay you to give away the game?' he yelled at me in front of everyone.

Shamed and depressed I slunk back into our yard and hid inside the fig tree. There I let my tears roll down my face. After a while I heard someone approaching.

'Come out of there, George,' I heard my brother tell me. 'Stop being a baby and let's do something about your problem.' His arm reached through the fuzzy fig leaves and dragged me out of my hiding place.

'You and I have a lot of work to do,' he told me, 'and we start right now.'

And with a ball borrowed from Kyr Stamos's boy my brother started coaching me.

Spring brought warm weather and with it the start of the evening promenade on the village main street, a thoroughfare that never received a proper name and was christened 'Main Street' through usage alone. Every night after dusk, the whole village would gather there and walk leisurely up and down the few blocks where Panorama's restaurants and shops were ranged in a row. Those who could afford it would sit at the little tables in the gravel-strewn yard of Kyr Stamos's shop and order coffee or 'triangles', the filo pastry that was fast becoming the signature speciality of the village. Teenagers and young men and women saw the promenade as their chance to see and be seen. They generally wore their best, and prepared for the evening's exercise with as much care as possible. Girls never walked with boys except in the company of their peers. Still, many a romance was born, lived and died on Main Street.

The route of the evening promenade was determined by the boundaries of the village. It was okay to walk up to Stamos's shop, because the street was lit and crowded up to there. After that, it was dark and no girl could hope to go beyond and escape censure. No one ever broke the rule in this direction, because Stamos's shop was always full and his clientele always eager to observe the passers-by. In the other direction, the boundary was more fluid. The lights did not stop abruptly like they did with Stamos's shop, but petered out slowly until they reached the sloping turn that led up the hill and to the villas. Boys were always signalling girls to take that turn and follow the dark road around the hill, but few dared to do so. The hapless girl who was persuaded to such folly might find the news spread far and wide the next day. Koula, the tavern keeper's daughter, walked the hill with two boys one night and the next day, so the story goes, her father beat her soundly and took her to a doctor downtown to find out if she was still a virgin.

I would stroll around with boys my age, but that spring I was still too young to want to circle the hill with anyone. I had developed a mild and secret interest in girls that was probably fuelled by the sight of Artemis's bare breasts, but darkness still meant fear to me, instead of the opportunity to be alone and unobserved. Now that I knew Andreas's secret, however, the stroll took on a whole new meaning. I'd seen him with his buddy Pavlos, the general-store-owners' son, stake out a spot by the open-air cinema, which operated only in the summer, and watch the girls go by. The girls would pretend to be interested only in each other, but I would catch them slide their eyes under demurely lowered lids towards my brother, and I would see the coy smiles that lit their faces. I noticed that they always stood taller and thrust their breasts forward when they neared the cinema. Little by little it dawned on me that my brother was much sought after, and that the girls were vying for his attention.

I started watching him with a fresh eye. I knew that he was good at games, that he was fearless, that he smoked and cursed and had the love of Artemis. What I hadn't known was that he was also good looking. He had always seemed tall to me but now I noticed that he was taller than all his contemporaries except for Pavlos. Pavlos was skinny, however, whereas my brother had wide shoulders and a narrow waist. His hair was dark and curly and his jaw was square. His smile was wide and teasing but when he saw a girl he liked he would lower his eyelids and tilt his head back as though he both appraised what he saw and was a little bored by it. At sixteen, he had the look of a man.

Most of all I watched Artemis. She tried the hardest not to look at Andreas, but I was sensitive to the subtlest nuance. Every time I saw her I remembered her breasts and her tears and the thought was like an electrical current running through me. It was a habit of mine by now to follow Andreas to the villa when he met

Artemis once a week. I'd set my face to the window and watch my brother kiss and hold Artemis, bare her breasts and nuzzle them urgently, and I wished with all my might to exchange places with him and be the one who won at soccer, and won at soccer cards, and had Artemis in the palm of his hand.

Every couple of weeks he would try to worm his way under her panties, but she always stopped him and started to cry. Andreas would first be angry, then comfort her, and then take her down on the couch again to rub himself furiously against her thigh. One day he wrapped her legs around his waist but she cried out in pain. My brother rose in disgust and quit the sofa, and I could see that his trousers bulged between his legs and his hands were shaking. Artemis cried twice that day.

I suspected that my brother knew I watched him. There were times when the way he undressed Artemis, and the way he pulled away from her bareness seemed directed to an audience. But I didn't know for sure, until I found a whistle in the Greek equivalent of a box of Cracker Jack.

'That's good,' my brother said when I showed it to him. 'You should take it with you when you go up to the villa, just in case you need to warn anybody that there are people approaching.'

After that I knew I could watch without reprisals and that Andreas liked it. My pride at being his acknowledged accomplice at this, his most delicious escapade, knew no bounds. My friend Nikos noticed that I would disappear to parts unknown once a week, and finally asked me what I was doing. With the smug air of someone much wiser, I condescended to let him come with me one day. I had made it a habit to arrive early at the villa, use the kitchen window that Andreas had jimmied open to break into the house, and crack my window open a bit so I could hear what Andreas and Artemis said. Nikos and I hid behind the house and waited. Andreas arrived first and then Artemis, and soon Artemis's blouse was up to her throat, she was on her back, and Andreas was assaulting her panties. So far Artemis was true to the script.

'No!' she yelled and threw Andreas off.

Andreas got up in a fury and threw her discarded cardigan at her.

'Leave,' he barked at her. 'You say you love me but you won't let me do anything. I'm tired of your games. I can have anybody I want, and I don't need this nonsense.'

Artemis started to cry.

'Leave, I tell you. I don't ever want to see you again.'

Artemis continued with her tears.

'Okay,' he said. 'If you won't leave then I will.' And he turned to go.

Artemis rushed up from the sofa and ran after him. She threw herself on him and started kissing him and begging him not to leave her. Little by little he let himself move to the sofa, and when he got there he made Artemis sit down and he stood in front of her. Then he took her hand with his, and he put it on his crotch. As Artemis cried and hid her eyes, he pressed her hand over his trousers for a few minutes, and soon he was lying on top of her moving fast against her, still with his trousers fully buttoned, but with his hand inside the white cotton panties.

Nikos beside me was breathing hard and his eyes seemed to have grown to twice their normal size. But when Andreas and Artemis finally stopped their game and left, he turned to me and said something I had never thought before.

'He's hurting her.'

The words shocked me. Week after week I had watched

with mounting fascination the sexual play between my brother and Artemis, but it was only after Nikos's simple statement that Artemis became a flesh and blood participant in what I had been watching. For the first time it occurred to me that Artemis's tears were tears of pain, and that maybe my brother was not a hero for throwing her down on the couch and forcing his fingers in her panties, but a bully. I walked down the hill with Nikos in shame instead of triumph at having introduced Nikos to a delightful secret, and I knew that my plan to impress my friend with my brother's accomplishments and my own participation in them had backfired. Every night on Main Street, while I watched Artemis trying not to look at Andreas, I thought only of her tears, and I vowed never again to be a witness to her humiliation.

6

The Summer People

Summer arrived and I was free from school and ready to play full–time. At the end of the term the teacher informed my father that Andreas had failed maths and history and would have to sit a retake exam in September which he had to pass or repeat the whole grade.

'But why?' my father asked. 'Andreas is a smart boy. How can he fail?'

'Andreas is very smart, Kyr Vasilikos, but school requires studying. You can't expect the boy to help out at the bakery and also keep up with his studies. I realise that times are hard and you have financial problems, but if Andreas helps out less often, I'm sure he can find the time to study.'

My father was speechless. Help out at the bakery? Financial problems? He had never asked Andreas for help, and as for financial problems, he was quite able to provide for his family single-handed, thank you.

When he came back from the school my father was more furious at Andreas than ever before. Andreas wasn't home, but Dad sat down in our bedroom to wait for him. My mother fluttered around him, anxious to defuse the situation, but she could do little more than wring her hands. I had done nothing wrong, but I hid myself in the corner with my heart beating wildly, and waited for the storm to break.

After a couple of hours Andreas came home. By the time he was halfway into the living-room he knew he was in trouble, and made as if to back out again. My father's voice froze him on the spot.

'Andreas, come here,'

Andreas walked inside the bedroom and my father closed the door. At first I could only hear my father's raging voice. In a few minutes, however, I heard a sickening thud, and then another, and it was plain that my father was beating my brother and knocking him against the wall. My mother rushed to the door begging and pleading with my father not to hurt her son.

'You stay out of this, Niki,' he yelled out. 'This useless carcass will learn that he can't lie to his teachers and that by God, if he does lie, he cannot shame me by pretending I cannot support my family and need his help to make ends meet.'

And with that my father continued to pummel my brother until he ran out of strength and rage and walked out to find my mother awash in tears on the floor in front of the door. She wanted to rush in and see Andreas, but with infinite care and tenderness my father picked her up and carried her in to their bed. Behind their closed door, I could hear him murmuring soothing words to her.

I peered into our bedroom. My brother was lying on his back on the floor. His lip was cut and bleeding and his shirt was torn. I knelt down and touched him, but he winced.

'Bring me some water,' he groaned, and I ran to the kitchen. I got some water from the icebox and rushed right back to my wounded brother. I helped hold him up to drink and then he said he felt nauseous. I brought the pail in and he threw up in it, grimacing with each spasm because my father had punched him in the stomach and he was in pain. After a while I helped move him to the bed, where he stayed all night.

Our evening meal was silent, except for my father who was pretending that nothing had happened. My father didn't know about Artemis, but to my mind the beating was not about skipping school and shaming my father. It was divine justice for Artemis's tears, and now that it had been meted out I felt my brother was cleansed and I could worship him again.

I went to bed relieved, but woke up in the middle of the night from some slight noise. In the moonlight coming in from the window, I saw my mother bending down over Andreas and caressing his forehead.

The next day my brother got up with many bruises and a split lip, but I could feel he was excited and even happy. School was out, my father's inevitable discovery of the winter's misdeeds was over, and it was time for the summer people to arrive.

Panorama, with its fresh air, its stunning views, and its proximity to the city, was a prime location for rich city dwellers to build summer houses. The village was familiar to them, because it was close to Anatolia, the American Academy where, for an astronomical fee, rich kids could be enrolled for grades one to twelve and take most of their courses in English, thus learning a second language to perfection. In the summer, the men could commute to the city every day to tend to business, while their wives and children stayed in the villas, away from the heat of the city and close to the amusement offered by tennis and swimming lessons at Anatolia. The summer people arrived every year in June and stayed till August, and for three months the village took on a different character.

The summer people dressed differently and behaved differently. The women of Panorama dressed in housecoats that they bought from Kyr Mitsos, the travelling salesman. Once a week he would appear with his donkey in tow, laden with two big green cupboards. He would stop in the middle of the dirt road and he would cry out in his sing-song way, 'Housecoats, skirts, nightgowns,' to bring the housewives out to buy. Kyr Mitsos would open the cupboards and there would be riches inside. Needles and thread, pillowcases and sheets, towels and washcloths, slips and even housecoats, skirts and nightgowns. Kyr Mitsos's fashions were accessorised with thick stockings and sturdy shoes made for dirt roads, with stretched-out hand-made wool sweaters, and faded cotton underwear.

The summer women, though, wore high heels, had their hair done, used perfume and sported manicured red nails. We saw them mostly at night in the restaurants set in a row all along Main Street when we strolled to pass the time.

The summer men and women wouldn't join the promenade until after a late dinner at one of the restaurants, and then only briefly. Their sons and daughters, however, walked up and down Main Street as determinedly as the villagers, and they were beings from another planet. The summer girls wore tight skirts and make-up. They gazed at men and boys frankly and they spoke to them without fear of being seen. They and their brothers had money and they sat at Stamos's every night in noisy groups that ordered the most expensive ice cream, with chopped nuts, sour-cherry syrup and whipped cream, costing thirty drachmas including tip. They went to the cinema as often as the features changed, and if they didn't like what they saw they would just walk out, without minding the

waste of money. They were exotic birds, and every lad in
Panorama lived with the dream of capturing one.

Among the summer girls Anna Karras ruled. Her father
was the richest in her set and she probably got her confident air from him. She was not the prettiest girl, but at
sixteen she had clear skin, good teeth, long hair in a rich
shade of blonde that some whispered came out of a bottle,
and long slim legs that she exposed without concern in one
pair of shorts after another. She was the centre of every
group she joined, and she was always laughing. If her nose
was a little too large, her eyes nondescript, and her hips
a little too heavy, these were minor details, and not to be
counted against her. Every local boy pined for her. In the
back of every young man's heart was the hope that Anna
might fall in love with him and marry him, and then he
would have solved his problems for good.

My brother was among Anna's admirers, but he was
much too smart to join them as they obsequiously vied for
her attention. He kept his distance wearing his lowered-lid
look and waited for his opportunity. And as luck would
have it, when she hit a tree with her bike to avoid running
over a dog, he was there not only to help her get up from
the street, but to straighten her bent wheel with his bare
hands and allow her to go on her way.

I wasn't there when he rescued Anna, but the village
was filled with the news. That night, when Andreas was
walking past Stamos's, Anna, who was sitting there with
her friends, invited him over. I was on the street when that
happened, and heard her call out to him: 'Andreas, come
and meet everyone. And please allow me to treat you to
thank you for helping me today.'

Andreas gave a smile, and then casually walked up to
her, inquiring about her bike. Soon he was sitting with the
summer group, and bending over to see the bandage that

covered the scratches on Anna's tanned leg. Ever since that night, Anna always stopped by to chat when she saw Andreas standing in his usual place by the cinema, and it was clear that she liked him.

It was my uncle's custom in the summer to give Andreas and me money so we could go to the cinema once a week. The cinema was just a wall housing the ticket booth and two bathrooms, and a screen. It had no roof and its floor was dirt, covered with the gravel that formed the floor of every open-air establishment in Greece. Canvas chairs were arranged in rows on the gravel.

It was in the cinema that I realised the relationship between Andreas and Anna was more than gratitude for a straightened bicycle wheel. I was never allowed to sit near him, of course, or even approach him in the cinema. But one night, as I was searching for my seat next to Nikos in the dark, I saw Andreas sitting next to Anna two seats in on one of the back rows, holding her long slim hand in his.

By the time I found my seat my mind was full of my brother. Whatever Andreas might be, however he might bully me or enrage my father, I had to hand it to him. He had a knack for managing the impossible, and he knew how to get things in life. He was as dashing as the men on film.

After the film I hung back and watched Andreas and Anna, no longer holding hands, walk to the end of Main Street and start to climb the road up the hill. That's where she lived, of course, but I knew that going up that hill was more, much more than it appeared. And it was only when they disappeared around the bend and I returned home and to bed that I thought of Artemis and what this new development might mean to her.

*   *   *

It became my mission in life to find out where things stood between my brother and Artemis. With the Karras family installed in the villa, they were barred from their meeting place. Now that Andreas was walking up the hill with Anna, had he broken off with Artemis? The only way to find out was to become Andreas's shadow. So I watched him. Andreas spent most of the morning and a good part of the afternoon at a small table underneath one of the acacias in the yard. My father had decreed that he spend eight hours a day studying, and Andreas did just that. Every morning he would gather his books, a pitcher of water and a bowl with ice chips from the big block of ice delivered to our door every morning for the icebox, and sit in the shade to expiate the sin of failing two courses. After lunch and a short nap, he and my uncle would sit under the tree sipping coffee and whispering to each other, every so often laughing at some private joke I would have killed to share in. Then Andreas would study some more. When he had completed eight hours exactly, he would saunter out to the open field where the village soccer team practised and he would play ball for a few hours. Later, he would join Pavlos for their usual evening activities, which more and more often included Anna and her friends. I marvelled at his discipline until one day I snuck up on him under the acacia tree and saw that inside the open maths book in his hands he had a comic book. Andreas may have been beaten, but he was not defeated.

I was sure now that he was not seeing Artemis. In the evenings I would watch her walk by him with her friends, and I sensed her despair. She who had taken such precautions not to be seen looking at him, would now stare at him openly. He avoided her eyes, never meeting her gaze. The pain she felt was plain on her face.

For weeks her silent plea continued until she passed me a second note. Once again I opened it.

'I'm sorry,' I read. 'Walk up the hill at ten.'

I delivered the note to Andreas under the acacia tree. He read it quickly, smiled to himself and put it in his pocket.

That night on Main Street I watched him from a distance anxiously. Would he climb the hill? Ten came and went and he was still standing outside the cinema with Pavlos. Around ten-thirty Anna came by, and he followed her to Stamos's. That's where he was when Artemis walked by shortly before eleven, and even though he could plainly see her on the street, he never once let his attention waver from Anna.

I showed up at Kyra Toula's cottage the next day to see what Artemis would do. She gave me another note.

'Give me another chance,' it said, 'and I will prove I love you.'

This time, when I took it to him, I stood by.

'What do you want?' he asked me after he read it.

'Are you going?' I dared to ask him.

'Why don't you follow me and see? You always do anyway,' he replied, and turned back to his comic book.

And that's how come that very night, in the full illumination of bright moonlight, I watched my brother flip Artemis's skirt over her waist, drop his pants to just below his knees, and take her on the hill while her hands gripped the summer's brown pine needles on the ground. Afterwards he sat holding her, and when she asked him if he loved her he said of course. Artemis's face shone, and it was plain that what she had hoped to gain by her sacrifice was hers for the moment.

At least once a week that summer Andreas met Artemis on the hill among the trees and there were no more tears.

Sometimes Andreas would lay her on her back and push himself inside her. Other times he would lie down and pull her on top, holding his engorged penis up for her to lower herself on. Afterwards he would sit a while with her, stroking her hair or nuzzling her breasts. Andreas still kept company with Anna, but when Artemis complained he told her it was just a front, and she was his true love. Didn't he prove it to her on the pine needles?

7

Measuring Up

I was still a boy, far from adolescence, but watching my brother's sport was stirring things in me that should have remained dormant for years. Time after time on the hill I watched Artemis's gleaming thighs open to receive my brother. And time after time I wished that it was me who moved against her in the dark, that it was my penis looking dark and huge with menace. Sated with sex, my brother spent that summer in a great mood. He was nicer to me than ever before, letting me watch soccer practice, kicking a few balls my way, and even calling me over to his post outside the cinema one night, to have me testify to a magnificent shot he had executed that day on the soccer field. Standing in the glow of his magnificence, I decided to get for myself some of the things he had, and see if I could be his equal.

Being Andreas's brother had many advantages, not the least of which was the notion some girls had that making friends with me might gain them his attention. If they went past our yard and saw me there they would stop to talk, the whole time casting glances at Andreas under the acacia, lazily leafing through his books. Nor was the worship of Andreas a cult only among those girls of an age that may reasonably interest him. Many of his admirers,

83

and the most persistent ones, were young girls, barely out of childhood. Among them was Lila, who was only ten. She was a summer girl and neighbour to Anna, so in my eyes she belonged to the fast set. And she was so besotted with my brother that she made sure to come round every day and talk to me. I picked her out to be my Artemis.

Lila may have loved my brother, but she got to like me, too. I encouraged her insatiable curiosity about him, and tirelessly gave her as much information as I could, identifying for her Andreas's favourite colour, his favourite singers, his favourite actors. She wanted to know what he ate, what he wore when he slept and who his friends were. Some of the information I made up, but most was true. She was also aware of Andreas's relationship with Anna, and very curious to know what they might be doing together.

'I bet he kisses her,' I said one night, as Lila and I walked up and down Main Street, where our young age granted us immunity from the custom that kept boys and girls from walking together in pairs.

'Have you ever kissed anyone?' I added.

'No,' she said. 'Have you?'

'Yeah, many times,' I lied.

'How is it?' she asked.

'It's great,' I replied, 'but you have to learn how. For example, if someone wanted to kiss you, would you know what to do?'

I could feel her thinking now that if Andreas ever tried to kiss her, she may not know how and then what would she do?

'I could teach you,' I stammered.

Our plan was simple. First, I would head up the hill alone and unobserved. Then she would follow. I rounded the bend on wings, but immediately was seized with fear.

I was alone in the dark. I hugged a tree and began to recite a prayer to Saint George.

I waited in the darkness forever before I heard Lila's footsteps crunching on the gravel road.

'Here,' I whispered.

She joined me under the tree. Now that she was with me I was no longer afraid of the dark. The only thing I feared was kissing her.

'So what now?' she asked me.

'You have to close your eyes,' I said.

She obeyed me and stood expectantly. I couldn't do it.

'Come on!' she said impatiently.

'I can't, like this,' I said.

'Why not?' Her eyes were open now. I cast about for an excuse.

'You have no breasts, you're not a woman.'

She was no woman, but she was also no Artemis to be so easily intimidated.

'And you're just a boy. It's just for practice,' she retorted. I took her by the shoulders, then, and quick as lightning, I stuck my lips on hers and took my first kiss, half lip, half tooth. It was a miserable first kiss, passionless, loveless, forced. I kissed her again, this time staying on her lips a long time like Andreas and running my hands down her back. The kisses I had observed my brother exchange with Artemis had sliced through my guts with heat. But my own kisses were a hollow disappointment.

'This is dumb,' she said when I let go, echoing my own thought. We separated after a few minutes, she heading back to Main Street to join her friends, and I walking home. I felt a failure. The next evening I followed Andreas again and once more stumbled down the hill after he had made love to Artemis, feeling crazy with a desire that had neither shape nor outlet. There had to be a way, I just hadn't tried hard enough to duplicate the feeling.

In the village square, near the tavern, there was a free-standing board, protected by mesh wire, where the cinema proprietor pinned pictures from scenes of current attractions to advertise. A few nights after my inept romancing, Lila got the idea to steal a picture of Sophia Loren that was displayed there, to give to my brother as a gift. She asked for my help. The theft had to be accomplished in the dead of night, when nobody would be around. I had to sneak out and meet her, then help her cut the wire and take the picture. She was afraid to do it on her own.

'Well, you'll have to give me something for my trouble,' I told her.

'What?' she asked.

'You'll have to let me do some stuff that Andreas does with his girlfriends,' I said. I felt pushy and slimy saying it, but my need was great.

It took some persuading. First she wanted to know what it was I wanted to do, but I couldn't get past my shame to describe what I wanted. Then she wanted my promise that I would never tell anyone, and to this I readily agreed. And I could only have ten minutes with her. Breathless with excitement I got her to agree that we would meet at two a.m. and she would let me do what I wanted behind the buttonwood tree. Then we would steal the picture.

It was no trouble sneaking out of the house. If my grandfather or Andreas heard me, they would think I was going to the outhouse. And they were unlikely to stay awake to time my absence. Still, my heart was thudding violently when I walked out of the room and into the night. I had never been out that late. The moon was bright, and everything looked unfamiliar. I got down to the square and waited. As expected, nobody was around, the whole village having long ago settled into sleep. Lila arrived panting from running. It was even easier for her than it was for me to sneak out, because she had her own bedroom, but she had to make her way down the hill alone in the dark, and she was still trembling like a leaf by the time I led her behind the buttonwood tree.

I got her to lie down on the ground with her shoulders resting against the ancient trunk and, feeling awkward and afraid, ran my hands over her body. She was a little girl. She had none of the lushness of Artemis. I felt nothing as I touched her hard body, but I persisted. I thought of my brother's laboured breathing, and the bulge in his trousers. She giggled when my hands passed over her chest.

'If you do that then it doesn't count,' I whispered fiercely.

'Okay. It's just that it tickles,' she whispered back.

I felt angry, at her I thought. Artemis had cried when Andreas had tried to touch under her panties. With grim determination I put my hands between Lila's legs and felt for the cleft between them. She didn't expect that. Her legs snapped together, hurting me. I pulled away from her.

'Forget it!' I snapped in a venomous hiss. 'You are just a little girl. You know nothing. Get the picture by yourself.' But I made no move to get up.

'I'm sorry. I'll be still. Just get it over with,' she said. I bent over her again. I opened her shirt and looked for her tiny nipples with my mouth, rubbed my hand over and under her panties, cupped her hard bottom in my palms and nuzzled her stomach. I did all these things that I had seen Andreas do, but nothing was the same. Lila just lay there, with none of Artemis's surrendering passion. No matter how I rubbed and kneaded the body offered to me, the terrible dark desire never caught me in

87

its grip. The hot alien wave that rose up inside of me every time my brother's erection slid into the secret depths of Artemis, never claimed me. My small and insubstantial penis stayed curled up in my shorts. I wanted to cry out my frustration, but bit my lip and concentrated. My touch grew rougher with the despair of feeling nothing, until Lila couldn't stifle a cry of pain.

'You're hurting me,' she complained, and her voice was not the pleading croon of Artemis, but rather the petulant cry of a spoiled child. I let her go.

My blush of anger and shame was invisible in the night under the buttonwood tree as I laboured with the pliers I had brought with me to cut the wire and hand Lila the picture of a lush and moist-lipped Sophia Loren. She took it with her face shining with joy and raced back home.

It was a relief to watch her disappear in the darkness because I could finally let my face reflect the pain and humiliation I was feeling. I wearily took the way home, struggling to contain my unmanly tears. And then I heard footsteps behind me. I turned in panic and saw my uncle weaving his unsteady way behind me. I had lived with him all my life, but I hardly knew him, except as a mean-spirited man with a sly air who paid me only nominal attention. Tonight, however, he was hurrying to catch up with me, and I was caught redhanded.

'Wait up,' he commanded, and I waited.

He put his arm around me to steady himself. He smelled of ouzo.

'No need to hurry now,' he told me. 'I've caught you. Your father would use you to wipe the room with if he knew you were out here at this hour. But, hey, you have nothing to fear.'

He winked at me and pulled my ear. Where had he been, I was thinking. What had he seen?

'Yes, you can slow down now and help your uncle. You and I, we will both sneak inside today. Don't worry, I'll never tell.' He leaned his face down to mine. His breath reeked of drink and cigarettes. His skin was pitted and slack in the moonlight and I didn't want to have secrets with him.

'I was there, you know. The tavern closes too early, but I was sitting in the dark. I saw you take that picture. And you know what else I saw, don't you. So tell me, little Georgie. Are you fucking her? Are you fucking her little cunt? Do you like it?'

His breath on my face made me want to retch. Suddenly his hand flashed out and squeezed my crotch.

'Didn't know you had it in you already. Thought it was just your brother fucking the little girls and now here I find you doing it right under my nose.'

His hand was hurting me, but I didn't dare speak.

'So come on. Tell me. Are you fucking her?' His voice was growing louder and in the perfect stillness of the night I was sure it would wake up the neighbours. I put my finger to my lips to motion him to silence, but he knocked my hand down.

'Tell me, damn it! Are you fucking her?'

'No,' I whispered.

'You're lying. I saw you. You are fucking her. Tell me. Tell me you're fucking her,' he said louder than ever.

'Yes, yes,' I hissed to silence him.

'Yes what?'

'Yes, I am.'

'Yes you are what?'

'Yes, I'm fucking her.'

'And do you like it?'

'Yes, I do.'

'Yes you do what?'

'Yes, I like fucking her.'

This satisfied him. With his arm draped around my shoulder and most of his weight on me, we walked back to the house.

'Help me to the outhouse,' he said when we got inside the yard.

I walked him over to the small structure. He let go of me to go inside, stumbled and grabbed my hand. I made to leave him alone, but his grip tightened.

'Wait,' he said, and pulled me in with him. He leaned against me and with his other hand took his penis out of his pants and peed with a sigh. Then he stood there, one hand holding my hand, the other shaking his shrivelled genitals.

'You and Andreas fuck the girlies and I just pee,' he murmured. 'Might as well cut if off. Might as well cut it off.'

I half carried him, half dragged him into the house and finally snuck to my bed, heartsick and heartsore. The last thing I saw before I fell asleep was my brother Andreas, reaching to scratch his balls in his sleep. 'He doesn't have to cut his off,' I thought, and fell asleep to dreams of Artemis straddling my brother and taking in her belly his impossibly thick, impossibly strong erection.

The next afternoon Lila stopped by. My brother and my uncle were in the yard drinking coffee. I saw her standing by the gate, and I hurried inside the house, consumed with shame. Hidden behind the curtain that covered the doorway to keep the flies out, I saw her motioning to Andreas to go with her. With a wink and a smile to my uncle, Andreas got up and approached her. They talked for a while, she handed him the picture.

'Thanks,' he told her, 'but you're prettier than she is,' and he leaned down to kiss her on the cheek. My brother, the smooth talker. At the last possible moment she turned her face, so his lips landed on her mouth. Lila, the little bitch. She turned bright red and ran off. Andreas sauntered back to where he had been sitting. My uncle said something I couldn't hear, Andreas laughed shaking his head.

It was late August by this time. The summer people had begun to leave. I saw Lila several times before her parents took her back to Thessaloniki, but I never again spoke to her or even acknowledged her. She was my Waterloo, she was my Hariklia. She never seemed to mind. She tried to speak to me a couple of times, but when she realised I was avoiding her she just shrugged her shoulders and went right on chasing Andreas, who seemed amused at her slavish devotion. For the rest of the summer I never once followed Andreas to his rendezvous with Artemis. I needed no reminders of his mastery. I wasn't a man. I was like Kyr Agisilaos, and if I ever got married Andreas would know and he would take my wife and throw her down and claim her.

8

The Daughter of the Soul

Two days after my birthday in November that year, we got the news that Olga, my mother's best childhood friend, had died in a fire. Olga and my mother had grown up together side by side, neighbours, friends and closest confidantes. It was to Olga that my mother had confessed her dislike of the tavern keeper for a husband, and her resignation to her fate since she could hope for nothing else. And it was to Olga that my mother had whispered her liking for the baker's son who brought the bread. Together they had tried to interpret his subtle courting behaviour and figure out whether he gave her the best loaves by accident, or whether he was singling her out. Together they had waited in agony for him to make a move, and it was together that they danced around the room after my dad, my grandfather and Stamos's wife had visited Hortiatis to ask for my mother's hand in marriage.

Olga got married too, to a Hortiatis goat shepherd, and moved to his cottage at the top of the mountain. By all accounts he was a mean and hard man, who married because he needed an extra pair of hands. Olga married him because poor and a drunk though he was, he was the best a girl without a dowry getting on in years could hope for. She lived in his bare and isolated cottage for years, enduring his rough treatment, tending the goats, making cheese from their milk and scratching out an existence as best she could.

Over the years Olga and my mother saw each other no more than a handful of times, when my mother ascended the mountain to attend a wedding or funeral that Olga was also able to attend. My mother came back from each such meeting sad at her friend's fate, and full of rage at the shepherd's brutal treatment of Olga and her daughter, Katerina. By my mother's account, the shepherd beat them both regularly and often let them go hungry, to spend their meagre income on the cheap resinated wine called *retsina* that he drank almost every night. Then, two days after my birthday, the cottage burned down in the night. Neither Olga nor her husband survived the fire. The cause was never clear. It could have been started by a spark that jumped out of the fireplace and on to the wooden planks that made up the floor. Or it could have been started by the shepherd's cigarette, left burning in his hand while he was sleeping off his regular drinking binge. Olga's husband died in his chair. Olga stumbled out of the house, but died later of smoke inhalation. Katerina survived by jumping from the window to escape the flames that were already engulfing the cottage almost completely. She found her mother who, barely alive, told her to run to Hortiatis. Katerina ran, and got the priest to ring the church bells to summon the villagers to the rescue, but by the time they arrived there was very little left.

The news was delivered by Kyr Mitsos who said the funeral would be held the next day in Hortiatis. My mother started crying when she heard the news and she still hadn't stopped by the time my father came home from the bakery. Her grief moved me immensely, and I had trouble controlling my own tears, even though I barely knew Kyra Olga. The next day, when my father gently led my grieving mother to Kyr Stamos's car, which he had borrowed for the trip up the mountain, I got in, too, determined to provide whatever support I could.

The sun was bright, but it had 'teeth', which means it was cold. In the car, however, once the heater got going, it felt cosy. We made it up the mountain in half an hour, and stopped outside the church. There were two coffins inside, and pretty much the entire population of Hortiatis in attendance. Olga had lived there all her life, and so had the shepherd. Hortiatis was burying two of its own. I stood at one of the pews with my parents, and held my mother's hand throughout the interminable ceremony. Priests chant in the ancient Greek of the Bible in church, so most of the congregation does not understand even a fifth of what is being said.

After what seemed to me like hours, we followed the hearse to the cemetery, where two graves had been dug. That's where I saw her for the first time. She was a tiny girl, barely over five feet tall, dressed in a black dress and an ancient bottle-green coat. She stood by the graves with her hands clutching a handkerchief. I knew right away that this must be Katerina, Olga's only daughter, now an orphan. The sight of her made me feel very vulnerable, and I clutched at my mother's hand. My uncle smoked and drank. That could be me standing by the two graves, I thought. Suddenly the whole scene of the funeral and the internment became real to me. That was a real woman in the plain wooden coffin, a mother who had loved her girl and provided for her and was no longer alive to do so. I stared at the girl in horrified fascination, thinking how alone she must feel. There were people around her, and one of them, a big dark woman, put her arm around the girl's thin shoulders in a gesture of support. It was clear to me, however, that the woman's well-intentioned arm was the arm of a stranger. Katerina did not lean into the embrace, nor did her face lose its stony look.

After the coffins were lowered into the ground, the crowd started heading back to the village. Coffee and the traditional boiled, sugared wheat would be served. As we headed down the hill my mother stopped and looked behind her, searching for Katerina. When she saw her making her way down next to the big dark woman, she walked over to her, with my dad and me right behind her. Katerina and the woman stopped when they saw my mother.

'Hello, Niki,' said the woman.

'Hello, Polyxeni,' replied my mother and then turned to greet Katerina.

'My dear,' she said, and her voice broke and she couldn't continue. Instead, she hugged the girl and stood there with her arms around Katerina's slender frame. Katerina hugged her back. After a while my mother let go.

'Your mother was my best friend,' she said.

'I remember you,' I heard Katerina say, and for the first time I saw a tear make its way down Katerina's face.

The wake was at Kyra Polyxeni's house. She was the shepherd's second cousin and, as it turns out, the closest remaining relative. While my mother stayed close to Katerina, hugging her for comfort, my father and I walked around Kyra Polyxeni's overcrowded house, where people were milling about and speaking in hushed tones.

'So what happens to the girl now?' my father asked a stooped wrinkled man who was shovelling one spoonful of wheat after another into his mouth.

'Someone will take her in, I suppose,' the man replied.

'Yes, but who?' my father insisted. 'Who is the closest relative?'

'Well, that's a tough question. She has no relatives of the first degree. Just second and third cousins. She's been staying with Polyxeni. I guess Polyxeni will keep her.'

Now my father searched for and located Polyxeni. She was in the kitchen, making coffee to take to the mourners.

'Tell me, Polyxeni, will Katerina live with you now?'

'For another week, she will. But then my son Odysseas comes back from the army, and I can't have a girl of fifteen in the house with him around.'

Fifteen, I thought! But she's so small!

'He has an eye for the girls, that son of mine, and I have no room to give her,' Kyra Polyxeni continued. She was lining up the small cups, and carefully measuring coffee into each.

'She's sleeping in his room right now, but after he comes back I'll have nowhere to put her except the living-room, and that's no good with Odysseas coming in and out at all hours of the night. It isn't seemly.'

'But then where will she go in a week?' my father persisted.

'She could go stay with Pantelis. He's Olga's third cousin,' said Kyra Polyxeni, and turned away to make more coffee.

Pantelis was a fat man with a moustache, sitting in the corner with his coffee cup delicately balanced on his puffy hands.

'I have five children, and nowhere to put her, but if she has no place to go she can sleep in the wood shed,' he said.

'Is there heat in the wood shed?' my father asked.

'Of course there's no heat in the wood shed,' Pantelis replied, looking at my father like he was crazy to suggest such a thing.

'Then how can the girl sleep there in the winter?' my father retorted.

'It's the best I can do.' And with that, Pantelis turned his eyes to his coffee, as though he could already read the future in his cup even though it was still full.

Our next prospect was Olga's second cousin, Telis. He was smoking a cigarette near the door and arguing politics with a short wheezy man who kept waving away the smoke Telis was blowing in his direction.

'I don't know where she'll go,' he said, a little annoyed, when my father finally managed to get his attention. 'I don't know if she can stay with us, I'll have to ask my wife. She's away right now, at her parents' village, but she'll come back in a couple of weeks.'

Theodoros, a tall gaunt man with yellow teeth and a strong smell of sweat, seemed willing to take Katerina in.

'I suppose she could sleep in the kitchen,' he said, but then his wife, enormous belly balanced on two stick legs, stuck her elbow in his ribs.

'But then that could only be for a few days,' he corrected himself quickly. 'We cannot take on another mouth to feed.' Again the elbow.

'That is, there must be someone who is a closer relation. This is a family responsibility.'

'We hardly knew them,' the wife chimed in. 'And I think it's too much for us to take on Katerina, when Olga never bought anything from our store. After all, if she had supported us when we opened the grocery store, we would now support her child. But never once did she darken the doorstep, and never once did she spend a single drachma. They had their own milk and cheese, I grant you, but where did she buy soap, where did she buy matches? Maybe Harilaos can take Katerina in,' she finished with a flourish, naming her chief competitor in the grocery business.

'This is beginning to look really bad,' my father whispered to me. We spent the next half-hour moving around the smoke-filled room from person to person, determining the degree of blood tie, and asking if they had room for Katerina. Nobody did.

'I'll have to ask my husband.'

'Only if the other relatives can contribute to her keep.'

'It is too much responsibility, and I'm too old.'

'The girl grew wild in the mountain, who knows what her habits are.'

'We have no room.'

Little by little I could see my father losing his patience. First his voice got louder. Then he began to answer the excuses with sarcasm. 'Of course you have no room, after all she'd take up so much room.' 'Yes, I can see that she must have grown wild, and would be a bad influence on your children. I guess your children are growing up in the convent, and can't be contaminated by the girl.' Finally, he had all he could take.

'We'll take her,' he announced in a loud voice from the middle of Kyra Polyxeni's living-room. 'She'll come with us. And she can stay all her life, just like it was her home. And I don't have to ask my father, or my wife, or anyone in my family, because they are all human beings and they wouldn't leave an orphan on the streets,' he said, and with that he gathered up my mother, me and Katerina and asked Kyra Polyxeni to give us Katerina's things.

Katerina had been sitting with my mother all this time. She didn't say a word when my father made his announcement. Obviously she knew her predicament well, and knew that this was the only solution that was likely to present itself. Silently she gathered her few things in a sheet, tied the ends into a bundle and followed my father out to the car. The mourners did nothing to stop us, and I believe they were relieved to have such a simple solution to the problem of the orphaned Katerina.

It wasn't unprecedented for a family to take in a stranger in need in Greece. People were poor and didn't have much, but nobody lived on the streets. Orphaned children would often be taken in by strangers, so often that there was even a word for them. They were called *psychopedi* and *psychokori*, meaning 'son of the soul' and 'daughter of the soul', because the good deed of providing for the destitute was insurance that the benefactor's soul would be admitted to heaven. Sometimes the *psychopedi* would be treated like a servant by these benefactors, expected to show his gratitude through hard labour. Many a *psychopedi* has harrowing stories to tell of brutality and work without cease, and if Katerina's relatives had had to take her in, she probably would have joined their ranks. There were also examples, however, of 'children of the soul' who came into families that took them in with love and never treated them any differently from the real family members.

My parents were going to be good to their *psychokori*. On our way down they discussed where Katerina would sleep. They decided to make room for her in the cellar. They would stack everything to one side and hang a curtain for now, and they would put a cot in there and a wash basin, a chair and a cupboard, and that could be Katerina's room.

'It's warmer than the house upstairs,' my mother told her, 'and of course you only have to be there when you sleep. You are my daughter now and you'll be the same as my two boys. I always wanted a daughter, Katerina, and I am glad I finally have one.'

For the last half of our trip we were silent. Katerina was sitting next to me in the back seat, her head turned out the window. I sat on my own side behind my father and wondered what she must be thinking. In a few days her whole life had been turned upside down, and here she was among virtual strangers, leaving her birthplace, unwanted by her relatives. My heart went out to her, and I turned to my own window to control my urge to cry.

And that's how Katerina entered my life. That first night at dinner she sat on the edge of her seat and kept her eyes down as she took a few bites of the food on the table. This made it easy for me to examine her finally, and I drank in her appearance. Her hair was darkest brown. It was gathered in a long braid, but little tendrils had escaped the confinement and were curling around her face. Her wide forehead was adorned by a widow's peak. Beneath it, long lashes cast shadows on her cheeks. Her nose was short and straight, and her lips pink and delicately curved. Her dress was too big for her. The shoulder seams hung halfway down her arms, and the sleeves were rolled up several times to let her small hands peek through. Despite her fifteen years, she looked like a little child, but a sad one. I watched her trying to take up as little room as possible, scrunching her narrow shoulders and never once relaxing her posture, as if she feared that any moment now my parents might decide she was too much trouble and ask her to leave. She must have felt the weight of my stare, because all of a sudden she lifted her eyes to mine. I turned away embarrassed, but not before I caught the full impact of velvety round black eyes wetted by barely-contained tears and framed by the shadow of pain. I didn't know it then, but I was already hooked.

My dad set up his old army cot for her in the dining-room when it came time for bed. I saw her small form curled up in a ball under the blankets when I passed through to go to my bedroom. She wasn't sleeping yet, maybe she never did fall asleep that first night, but I tiptoed to my bedroom nonetheless. I went to my own bed and prayed for morning to come soon, so I could once again look at her.

It started that first night and that's how it continued. Day after day my eyes strayed to Katerina. I watched her at every opportunity and never watched my fill. At first I thought I stared at her because I felt sorry for her. Then I realised that most of the time when I looked at her I wasn't thinking of her sad life. Instead, my eyes were simply drawn to her, like pins to a magnet. I stared at Katerina because she attracted me, and she attracted me because she was beautiful. I would have noticed sooner if Katerina looked like the women I had considered beauti-ful until I met her. Artemis was beautiful. Fani was beauti-ful. Rounded young girls with full breasts, bright colours, ripe lips. Katerina was subtle and delicate instead. She was a slim reed, an insubstantial waif with a pale face and a quiet manner. Her beauty was all in her eyes, her bottom-less eyes, so black you could not separate the pupil from the iris. They were enormous eyes that swallowed the rest of her face. They were eyes as round and guileless as those of an infant, but filled with sadness and mute feeling.

At the first opportunity my father set to clearing the space in the cellar for her and painting the walls and an old chest of drawers for her to use. Meanwhile, my mother began to stitch some curtains to hang in Katerina's cellar, to soften the harshness of the room. Katerina remained silent and sad throughout these preparations. Each morning she woke up to help my mother with her chores. First she would tuck away her temporary bed. Then she would set breakfast for me and Andreas in the kitchen. I started getting up earlier so I could sit in my chair and watch Katerina heat the water for tea, get the butter and jam and measure two spoonfuls of sugar in my glass of milk. Andreas often tried to talk to her in the morning, asking her if she slept okay and if it was too cold for her in the dining-room, but it was obvious that his friendly attention made her uncomfortable. He would shrug his shoulders and leave her alone.

In a few days the cellar was ready, and Katerina moved in with her few possessions. Winter was upon us now. The winds howled and the rain pelted our house. If she was alone and afraid down there, I never knew. Her face, already taken over by grief at losing her parents and her house, had no room to register other emotions.

My parents had given me a bike on my birthday, second-hand but in good condition. My days were filled with that bike, and school, and watching Katerina. Little by little her grief lessened. She remained quiet and withdrawn, but she was warming up to my mother who did everything she could to make her feel at home. When the neighbourhood women came by for coffee, she introduced Katerina as her new daughter and invited her to sit down and keep them company. When Kyr Mitsos went by with his donkey and cupboards, she bought coloured threads and some fabric from him and set to teaching Katerina embroidery. Many an evening the two would sit companionably by the fire in the family room stitching in silence while my father dozed near by and Andreas and I did our homework in the kitchen. I got into the habit of sitting in the chair that afforded me a view of Katerina in the other room, and knew that sometimes Katerina would stop her embroidery and stare into empty space. I thought she must be remembering her family, and my mother must have had the same thought, because at such times she would get up, go over to her and put a hand on her hair, or kiss her forehead.

My mother's love was a boon to Katerina. As we moved deeper into winter it was obvious that Katerina loved my mother back. The two would make short work of the chores every day. When my mother got a lingering cold in January, Katerina took on all the heavier tasks and wouldn't relinquish them even after my mother protested that she was feeling better.

'Better, but not a hundred per cent yet, Aunt Niki,' Katerina told her, and went right on mopping the floors.

Katerina was right. My mother never got a hundred per cent better, but Katerina was the only one who noticed at first.

By February Katerina was coming out of her shell. She was still quiet, but she smiled often now and seemed to be over the worst of her grief. I still saw sadness in those eyes, but I also heard her crystalline laughter when Andreas would deliver with aplomb the jokes he had heard in school. Since the day's shopping had become her responsibility, it was she who would forget occasionally to buy tea or bleach, and she would send me to bring the forgotten item home when I was back from school. I had always done this for my mother, but it was different when Katerina did the asking. Then the chore became a mission, a knight's errand for a beautiful lady, and I would race to the store on my bike to get Katerina whatever she wanted. 'Back already,' she would marvel, and I would swell with pride.

It was while I was out on such an errand that I miscalculated in my efforts to ride like the wind and I fell off my bike. She cried out when she saw the blood on my forehead, but she didn't berate me for my carelessness. She simply got hold of the medicine kit and dressed my wound with tenderness. I remember the moment as though it were yesterday. The iodine smarted, but the only thing that registered with me was the feel of her hands on my face. I suddenly felt hot as she bent over me, and curiously sensitive to her hand on my cheek, holding my face steady.

'Good as new,' she said when she was done, and her lips parted in a smile to reveal her white, pointed teeth. Confused and embarrassed, I bounded out of the chair and stumbled outside for some cool air.

Almond trees are too impatient in Greece. In February, when the worst of the winter seems to be over but all other trees are still in their winter slumber, they alone burst into flower. Their blossoms, white with a delicate hint of rose, seem to mock the other trees, still bare and brown. Too often the almond tress are punished for their *hubris*. March unleashes a storm and many flowers are torn from the branches and fall to the ground. It was to the blossoming almond trees that I stumbled after Katerina stuck a Band-aid on the worst of my scratches. I felt anxious and unsettled, and I had a hard time quieting my racing heart. I couldn't fathom why I felt so strange. I stared at the new blossoms until I felt peace return to me, and sat there wondering what it was that had happened.

I was still sitting under the almond trees when I saw Andreas coming into the yard, his face looking dark and brooding. This was unusual. Even when he was at his meanest, Andreas never looked anything but lighthearted. There was a time when I would have pondered on this and tried to find out what was up, but I was too busy with my own feelings and shrugged the matter out of my mind.

'Katerina,' I whispered to myself for the first time, and marvelled at the warmth that gathered in my belly at the sound of her name.

9

Artemis in Trouble

A few days later my mother decided that Katerina needed some lighter dresses for the coming warm weather. Nothing special, mind you; Katerina would have to wear black for a year in accordance with mourning custom, and that only because she was a young girl. Grown women stayed in mourning for three years, and middle-aged and older women who had lost a husband would never wear again anything but black. Katerina and my mom ordered some black cotton fabric from Kyr Mitsos, and when it arrived they set off for Kyra Toula's cottage. I followed them.

I had to stay outside while Kyra Toula was measuring Katerina's slight frame, but I was admitted inside for the ritual of coffee and gossip. I sat in my usual corner leafing through the fashion magazines, but I was really watching Artemis. She seemed uneasy and distracted. She let the coffee, which was prepared in a small copper coffee pot, boil over. And when she set the tiny cups and saucers on the small table, she sat down herself, forgetting to bring the sugar cookies until her mother reminded her. Most unusual of all, she hardly had a word to say, to me or to the women. My brother's bad mood came back to me then, and I wondered what might be happening between them. I had not followed them all winter, and now I was curious once again. Could it be that Andreas had stopped seeing Artemis? This would explain Artemis's state, but not my brother's.

The next day I decided to follow Andreas and find out what was happening. Soon he was climbing the road to the villas. There was no reason for me to stay behind him. I knew where he was going. Fast as the wind I rode my bike through the side streets in a big circle, bypassing my brother and getting to the Villa Karras before him. I left my bike on the far side of the fence and climbed through the familiar opening. Fast as I was, I barely had time to crack the window open and hide under it before my brother came in. In days past he had spent his time waiting for Artemis by fixing his hair, smoothing his clothes and whistling to himself. This time he paced nervously up and down. Soon Artemis arrived.

'Well?' he asked her.

'Nothing,' she replied.

They stood silent.

'What are we going to do?' Artemis broke the silence.

'We don't have to do anything. This doesn't mean anything. You're just late, that's all.'

'Andreas, it's been a month!' she said, and started to cry.

My brother walked over to her, raised his arm to touch her, but changed his mind.

'You're over-reacting,' he told her. 'I told you I took care of things. You can't be pregnant. I pulled out every time. There's not a chance in a million.'

'Stop doing this,' she yelled at him through her tears. 'I'm not over-reacting. I've known pregnant women and I know! I feel like throwing up in the morning, my waist is getting bigger. Andreas, I'm pregnant!'

'You're not, I'm telling you. There's not a chance

in hell. Who do you think you are, the Virgin Mary, to get pregnant when you know I never came inside you?' he yelled back at her. His face was red and he seemed to be sweating. 'But maybe that's just it,' he continued. 'It's not mine, is it?'

She was stunned. And I was stunned along with her.

'Andreas, what are you saying?'

'Well, if I know it couldn't be me, and if you are pregnant like you're telling me, how else could it have happened?'

'Andreas, you know there has never been anyone but you,' Artemis cried.

'Well, then you are not pregnant,' Andreas insisted.

Artemis looked at him through her tears, pleaded with her eyes.

'I've got to get out of here,' Andreas said, and with that he turned and left.

Artemis threw herself down on the sofa, crying with gut-wrenching sobs. She must have wanted to do that for a long time, and finally she was alone and away from everyone so she could give vent to her grief. I considered leaving then, so Artemis could be by herself, but I stayed. My brother had wronged her, had made the worst nightmare of a village girl come true for her, and I felt that someone from my family should stand by her, even in complete silence and in hiding, even without her knowing. I sank to the ground and listened to Artemis and I think she and I kept coming back to the same thought: 'How could he do this?' And for the first time in my life I felt ashamed of my brother.

Andreas continued in a black mood. He picked fights at the slightest opportunity, cut classes to play pool and smoked incessantly whenever he could hide from my father. Now I know he must have been scared, but back then it looked to me like he was just mean. All his life everything he wanted had come easy for him. He was fearless, undefeated, a leader, a protagonist. At sixteen he had managed the unthinkable given that he was growing up in a small Greek village in the sixties: he had a girlfriend who was giving him everything. He never had a real problem in his life or a real difficulty until Artemis told him her news. Here for once was a problem he could neither brave his way nor charm his way out of. And even if he didn't try to escape his fate and faced it, a beating from our father would not be the end of the matter, but barely the beginning. It was unreasonable and unfair of him to accuse Artemis of sleeping with someone else, but in the end it was the only possible escape route for him. During the next week I could see him try to talk himself into believing his senseless accusation.

I was squarely on Artemis's side on the issue, and so I missed no opportunity to mention her name when Andreas was around. I appointed myself his conscience. But still it wasn't enough. I kept wondering what she must be feeling, and found a thousand excuses to go by the cottage and look in on her. Day by day she grew more desperate, and I thought that at any moment she would burst into tears and never stop. The ruddy colour left her cheeks and black circles appeared under her eyes. What will she do? I kept wondering.

I considered talking to her, offering my help, but I decided against it. First, there was nothing I could do. Second, she looked so remote and unapproachable that I was afraid to let her know I knew the secret. I was afraid she might do something desperate. I had heard stories of girls in trouble who had swallowed rat poison or slit their wrists to escape the shame. I was scared of what might happen, and so I started following Artemis whenever she left the cottage, uncertain what I could do, but determined nonetheless to be there. As it turns out, I was there when Artemis tried to end her troubles, but I could do nothing to prevent it. It was a Sunday. At church, I had seen Artemis, dressed in her best dress, her hair neatly combed and tied in a ponytail, praying fervently with her eyes closed. She looked innocent and blameless. I wondered if it was possible to ask God for help when she was in trouble, since her trouble was the consequence of her sin in the first place. After the service, I stayed behind her as she climbed the incline to Main Street. She started walking along it towards Stamos's. When she passed the sweet shop it became harder for me to follow her without seeming obvious, and so I fell back. She stopped every so often, as if to consider something. Then I saw a car coming down the mountain. She saw it too, and turned to face the road as if waiting for the car to go by so she could cross. I remember wondering why she would want to cross to the other side when there was nothing there except empty fields when, at the last possible minute, Artemis seemed to stumble, flail and fall in front of the rushing vehicle. There was a sickening screech of brakes, a mad veering to the side, a body on the road, screams and a soft thump as the car drove over Artemis's leg. My heart stopped. I started running to Artemis. The car's occupants were already out, bending over her. The driver was a young man.

'She jumped in front of me,' he kept saying. 'You saw her, Poly, she saw me coming and she jumped in front of me.'

'She stumbled and fell,' I butted in, wanting to protect Artemis and her secret.

The young man was upset. Artemis seemed unconscious on the ground and her ankle was a bloody pulp. I felt my stomach give a lurch.

'Run and get an ambulance,' the woman called Poly told me, and I backed away gratefully. I had to get away from the sight of my brother's victim. I ran to Stamos's, told him there was an accident and to call the ambulance from Thessaloniki. As he rushed to his phone, I set off running to find Kyra Marika, who as a midwife was also the person to provide first aid.

I found her in the yard of my own house, where she was drinking coffee with my mother, Katerina and the rest of their friends. My news, delivered between gasps for air, was greeted with a show of horror. Then the whole party rushed out to the site of the accident. I wanted to follow them, but my legs were trembling from my headlong run. I sat down to rest a few seconds, and then I saw Andreas.

He was sitting away from where the women had been. There was a stick of wood and a knife in his hands. He was nervously scraping the knife against the stick, his face turned a deathly pale.

'You know what she did, don't you?' I said to him.

'I don't know what you're talking about,' he replied, and now his hands began to tremble.

'Yes, you do,' I told him. 'She threw herself in front of the car to lose the child.'

My words hit him full in the face. He was speechless for a moment. He had thought nobody knew. Then I saw his face crumple. And then he surprised the hell out of me, my proud, arrogant brother, because he said: 'It's not mine, don't you understand? I was careful. Please understand. Uncle Demetres says if you're careful it can't happen.'

And he turned his face away from me. I had never seen him in despair. I had never heard the word 'please' from his lips. It was a strange moment. Just as my brother humbled himself for the first time, I felt nothing but contempt for him.

'You are the lowest of the low, Andreas,' I told him, and I meant it. 'And I'm ashamed to be your brother.'

I sounded sanctimonious and self-righteous. At any other time Andreas would have called me a little prig and would have pushed me out of the way. But this time he just looked at me with his face naked of mockery.

'Even if it were mine, what could I do?' he said bitterly. 'I have no money for an abortion. So what do I do? Marry her when I'm only seventeen and bring my wife and baby home while I finish high school?'

'You should at least run and see how she is,' I told him, and took off for Main Street, determined that my family would not let down Artemis any more than was already inevitable.

During the next few days we learned the consequences of Artemis's desperate act. Artemis was out of danger, but her ankle had been shattered. The doctors could patch it up so she could walk, but it would always be with a limp. In a week or so she was released from hospital, her leg in a cast. And perhaps worst of all, she was still pregnant. I carried a note to her from Andreas, which had only two words on it: 'Not yet?' I gave it to her while she sat on the sofa in her mother's work room with her leg up and her crutches by her side, her face a mask of despair. She didn't brighten up when I passed the note to her. She read it quickly and returned it to me and then she said bitterly, in a whisper I could barely hear: 'Tell him not yet. Not even now.'

I came back with the message. Andreas had been hoping, I could tell. He knew the minute he saw me, but he asked anyway: 'What did she say, did she give you a note?'

'She didn't give me a note. She just said, "Not yet, not even now."'

Andreas threw himself on a chair. His last hope had just disappeared.

'What happens now?' he murmured.

'I have some money,' I said. 'You can have it.'

'Yeah! Big help! Fifty-six drachmas! I'd need two or three thousand, or more, for an abortion. And where would I find a doctor to do such a thing?'

He knew the exact amount I had in the tin under my bed. He must have been going through my things. I didn't let that thought distract me. Instead, I concentrated on a flash of inspiration. There was one person who had money.

'What about Uncle Demetres? He could give you the money.'

'Yeah, and then tell Dad the next time he gets drunk. Talk sense, George.'

I was mad now. He was telling me to talk sense when he was the one who had accused Artemis of being the village slut.

'Well, there's no other way,' I told him. 'What do you think Artemis will try next? Isn't it enough that she's a cripple now? Do you want her to die?'

He hung his head in misery.

That night he took a walk with my uncle. They were gone a long time and when they came back he gave me a wink and a nod, to indicate that they had spoken and that a plan was under way.

I don't know exactly how the arrangements were made. Abortions were illegal in Greece, but many doctors performed them, nonetheless. My uncle must have put up the money and found the doctor. Then, on the pretext of having to go to Thessaloniki for business, he borrowed Stamos's car and, as an afterthought, offered to take

Artemis to her doctor, because she had been complaining of pain. They were gone all day. I don't know if Kyra Toula suspected anything. I don't know how Artemis concealed from her what had happened, or if she did.

Andreas must have been immensely relieved when Artemis came back from Thessaloniki without her burden. He actually smiled when my uncle returned and said, his voice filled with double meaning, that everything had gone fine, and Artemis was back in her cottage.

During the next few weeks Andreas tried to revert to the way things were before. Once again he hung around the streets of Panorama with Pavlos, joking with the girls, sneaking cigarettes, combing his hair into a flirty sidesweep, playing ball effortlessly. But things were not the same. Artemis hardly ever left her cottage any more, but he saw her often enough walking to an errand or in her own yard two doors down from ours. He'd be standing in the village square laughing with Pavlos, or kicking a soccer ball to the small fry, when she would go by, carefully keeping away from him, her head bent to the road, dragging her left foot behind her. A shadow would flick across his face at such times. Guilt at what he had done to this poor girl who loved him and gave him everything he asked for would darken the moment and destroy his pretence that nothing was different from the way it had been. So Andreas's eyes still twinkled with mischief, but their sparkle was never so bright. He still flirted with all the girls, but he never went to the Villa Karras with any of them. He had once more managed to get what he wanted and keep going, but this time there was a victim to his misdeeds, and her self-effacing manner made her all the harder to ignore. Artemis never blamed Andreas to his face, never told anyone, but it was obvious to me that her existence was a torment to my brother.

His guilt softened him. He was less demanding with the people around him, less caustic towards those who were not as able or as brave as he was. He was trying to recapture his earlier state of grace, but it was lost forever. He had to pay for what he did, and part of the price was the loss of my worship. My brother no longer seemed to me the shining being he used to be. My hero had feet of clay. When he paid attention to me, I didn't beam with satisfaction. When he cast a careless insult my way, I was not plunged headlong into misery. He sensed the difference, and he knew what made my feelings for him change. He had never seemed to value my adoration before, but now he missed it. My changed manner towards him underscored the unwelcome change in his life, and he tried to turn the tide. He showed up one day with a brand new football for me.

'This will do it, George,' he said with a bluff smile as he handed me the precious gift. 'If they want to use your ball, then they'll have to let you play. Talent is nothing. Having the ball will do the trick.'

There was a time when a gift such as this from my brother would have made my heart sing. It was an expensive gift, and one that had both thought and caring behind it. Now it was too late. I accepted the ball and thanked him, but he knew he had failed with me. He went away without another word.

The ball didn't restore my feelings for my brother, and it didn't cure my deficiencies, either. It did make me one of the first to be picked on a team, because the boys wanted to use my brand new ball, but they rarely passed the ball to me, and then only when my team had a comfortable winning margin. I knew it was the ball the boys valued. The ball seemed as tainted as Andreas.

10

The Summer of Loss

I was finally free of my brother. He was still taller and
better at everything, but I knew now that he could be
scared, uncertain, guilty, just like me. I felt a little ashamed
at having idolised him all my life. And I felt no small
measure of satisfaction at rebuffing his veiled attempts
to win me over once again. Finally, in a small way, I
had the upper hand. Every time I turned away from his
pathetic attempts to reclaim me, I felt contempt at what I
considered lack of pride on his part. Because I had loved
him so well and admired him so blindly, because he had
been my symbol of perfection and the standard against
which I had always measured myself and found myself
lacking, that one flaw, that one mistake, made me reject
him completely, and break free from him. In a thousand
little ways he asked to have my love back. The ball was only
the beginning. Andreas who had never been influenced by
my presence began to show off when I showed up to watch
the village team practise soccer.

'Did you see that shot, George?' he would ask, waiting
for me to chime in as I once would have.

'Yeah, that was great. They never knew what hit them,'
I would have said and I would have continued in my
praise, my face flushed with excitement, until he found

something else of interest and interrupted me in mid-admiration to go off on a different subject, or worse yet to talk to someone else, or walk away altogether, as though I had not been speaking.

But no more. Now I would greet his invitation to comment on his game with silence, or with a few words to the effect that he had played well. The more I resisted him, the more he tried. He offered me cigarettes. I declined. He explained to me the trick of riding a bike without holding the handlebars. I didn't take his advice. Nothing worked. Each new sign of favour was to me a sign of weakness. If he was begging for my attention, then he must not be worth it.

I felt mean and small every time I turned Andreas away. But that was only deep down, where I was barely aware of it. My over-riding sense was a righteous satisfaction, a sense of come-uppance, a sweet revenge for every humiliation of the past, whether he had inflicted it on me or I had inflicted it on myself. I, who had been a graceful loser, became a bad winner. But I couldn't see it. I was mean to my brother and the meanness became a hard shell that covered my heart, but I mistook it for the strength of the righteous. Andreas had done wrong and he must suffer. Eagerly I became his tormentor. Pointedly I referred to Artemis in his presence, bemoaning her handicap, parading my pity for her only so he could hear it and be reminded. He winced every time, and put up with my assault on his psyche, but even the meek way he accepted my punishment was not enough to satisfy my fervour. I was like one of those religious fanatics who preach the Bible to everyone, but neglect to practise the love it preaches.

My mother noticed my new attitude. She didn't know what had happened and so my hardness towards my brother, and his own answering meekness, were unexplained mysteries to her. She chose to bring it up one day in May. I was sitting in the yard studying for my finals. It was three in the afternoon, and the whole village was asleep. The heat had come early this year, and I had trouble staying awake in the sweltering atmosphere to pay attention to my history book. Instead, it was easier to let my eyes rest on the yard around me, painted a wild and vibrant red by the poppies that spring unbidden everywhere in Maytime Greece.

My mother came and sat down next to me.

'Aren't you sleeping?' I asked her.

'I couldn't keep my eyes closed and I thought it might be better to leave your father alone instead of driving him crazy with my restlessness,' she said.

She seemed tired and worn out.

'You need to sleep,' I told her. 'You look tired.'

'It's restful just sitting here,' she smiled at me. 'I've been meaning to talk to you anyway, and this is as good a time as any, with everyone else asleep. George, has something happened with you and Andreas?'

Her question took me aback. Except for occasionally asking Andreas to be nice to me, she had never interfered between us.

'No, nothing, why do you say that?'

'It just seems to me that you are rough to him these days. Things are not the same.'

She was searching for words.

'Maybe it's nothing,' she continued, giving up. 'He's always been too big an influence on you, and maybe now you're growing up and coming into your own.'

'I am growing up. And Andreas has to learn that he doesn't rule me.'

'He can be overbearing sometimes,' she agreed. 'And it's good for you to not look up to him too much. But you're brothers, George. Be careful not to forget that while you're busy growing up. Okay?'

If you only knew, I thought, but didn't say. And I continued meting punishment to my brother.

This is the last conversation I remember having with my mother before I learned that she was dying. I got through my finals and summer came, the summer people arrived, the days were given over to play. My only worry was avoiding Lila, who didn't seem to take any notice of me anyway. Apart from this small concern, I could devote the whole day to my bike and watching Katerina.

Oh how she blossomed! She was still dressed in black, of course, but her summer black had been made for her instead of being handed down. Her summer black had a cloth belt that cinched her tiny waist. It flared around her slender legs with grace. It fitted her delicate arms and hugged her small round breasts, perched high on her rib-cage. Katerina in her simple black dress was a vision of loveliness, the very picture of girlish beauty on the brink of full womanly allure.

I wasn't the only one who noticed. One morning she was doing the wash in the yard. She had lit a fire under the big black cauldron and after the water began to boil she put the clothes in. She was stirring the water with a long wooden paddle, every so often stopping to mop the sweat pouring down her face. The day was very hot and soon her dress was soaked and sticking to her form. Her breasts, impossibly high, perfectly round, were clearly marked against the fabric when she turned sideways. I watched for a while but soon turned away in shame, only to see Andreas staring, with a glint in his eyes that I knew so well. My anger scalded me! How dare he! I stood up quickly, went up to Katerina and took the paddle from her hand.

'It's too hot for you. Let me do it,' I told her.

'George, you are a sweetheart,' she smiled at me and ran off to her next chore.

I glanced over at Andreas, intending to give him a thunderous look, but he had already turned away.

In winter, we bathed in the family room. Every Saturday evening, my mother would stoke up the fire in the stove and bring in a large copper basin. She would boil water in large pots in the kitchen, and then mix it in a bucket with cold. With a bowl in hand, and the doors closed, each of us in turn would sit in the basin naked and pour water over ourselves while we soaped and scrubbed. Then my uncle and my father would lift the basin, pour the dirty water on the street, rinse the basin and set it down for the next person. A bath was so much trouble that once a week was all the household could handle.

In the warmer weather, washing was simpler. There was a small shed in one corner of the yard. It was just a square room with a door made of rough planks, a hole at the bottom of one wall for water to escape from, and a small plastic chair in the middle. To wash you had to do nothing more than carry a bucket of water in there with you and sit on the chair or use it as a support. No worrying about everything getting wet. No basin to empty. Just close the door and splash away.

The planks making up the door were not fitted very well. There were any number of holes through which it was possible to see inside. And that's where I saw Andreas the day after Katerina had done the wash, his body stuck to the side of the door, his head craning to the planks and his eye glued to an opening, oblivious to my approach, while Katerina was bathing inside.

I didn't scream my rage. I didn't make a sound. I didn't want to scare or embarrass her. But I hurled myself at my brother with all my might, in complete silence, targeting his waist with my head. He lost his balance in surprise, and I took him down, rolling with him on the ground and pummelling at him furiously. He was too good and he was too big. After a couple of moments he rolled me on top of him, seized my hands with his, locked my legs with his own and held me from where he was lying on his back, amused at my anger.

'Goddamn you, you stay away from her!' I spat at him.

'George, don't be such a sap. You can watch, too. No harm in watching.' He gave me a conspiratorial wink.

I redoubled my attempts to twist free of him. It was impossible.

'Goddamn you!' I said again, my face red with anger, the sweat streaming down my back. I felt as though I was about to burst a vessel.

'What is the matter with you? What are you so angry for?' he asked in puzzlement.

'If you don't let go of me this minute, I'll tell Dad about Artemis,' I threatened.

He let go. Immediately. Without a word. I picked myself up and watched him rise to his feet, the victor who had lost.

'And I'll tell him if I ever see you sneaking looks at Katerina, too. I'll tell him if you so much as think of her! I won't let you make another Artemis out of her. Not as long as I have breath left in me, you son of a bitch!'

Andreas just looked at me. He didn't call me a coward, he didn't make fun of me for having to resort to threats of involving our father to get my way. That's what the old Andreas would have done, and it would have stung me to the core, and I would have walked away feeling lower than a snake on the ground, or I would have asked for his forgiveness, or pretended in vain that I never meant to tell at all. That's what would have happened in the old days.

'I only looked, George. There won't be another Artemis.' Just like that. Not 'please don't tell,' not 'I won't do it again.' Just 'there won't be another Artemis.' Then he turned on his heel and left. I knew it wasn't the threat that beat him. I knew it was the reminder alone of Artemis that made him back down.

I watched him closely from that day on, and I watched Katerina. I was guarding her. Maybe that's why I didn't notice that the summer was taking its toll on my mother, that she was losing weight, that she was plagued by fatigue, tired by the slightest effort. When my father took her to Thessaloniki for tests, I was barely aware of it. It was only when the results were in in a few days, and my father set us all down to explain that my mother was going to the hospital for exploratory surgery, that I felt the world slide out from under me.

It was cancer. Inoperable cancer. Cancer of the pancreas. Fast-spreading cancer. For years it had lived in her body, eating her life, spreading its tentacles, taking my mother. They opened her up and then sewed her shut again. Nothing to do but wait for her to die. She went in weakened by the disease, and she came out even sicker, stooped over, shrivelled, gaunt.

I never left the yard for the remainder of that summer. None of us did. My father placed the bakery in his brother's hands and sat with my mother. He held her hand night and day. He fed her, fanned her, carried her up and down the steps from the yard to the house and back every day, crushed ice to put in her water glass, held a mirror for her to fix her hair. He took care of her every need with exquisite attention to every detail, but he forgot to eat his own food, to shave his beard, to change his clothes. He was always with her.

I sat near them at first, but I felt there was no room for me. My father's love for my mother was occupying all available space, was using all the oxygen. I moved farther away, where I could see the two of them together. They hardly ever spoke. In nineteen years of marriage they had said everything they had to say to each other in words. Now they spoke by just being next to each other.

Katerina was the only one who kept to her routine that summer, but that's because she hardly ever left the house even under normal circumstances. She applied herself to the housework. She scrubbed, cleaned and polished better than ever. She was determined that my mother would go to her grave with her house spotless. Only in the evenings would she let up. Only then she would sit down next to me in the yard, letting her eyes fall on the couple holding hands. She was a comfort to me when she sat like that. I remembered the sight of her standing by the grave of her mother. I knew that she knew the pain I was feeling first hand, had experienced it only a few months ago, and, indeed, was still in its grip. And because she also loved my mother, I knew there was new pain added to her old loss. Katerina became my solace that hot, heavy summer.

There are couples who fall in love and marry and stay that way, until they have children. Then they turn the love to their children, and they forget the love they had for one another. But there are couples who do not make their children the centre of their bond. They love their children, but their core relationship remains the relationship they have with each other. My parents were the second kind. Yiannis loved his Niki too well, and Niki loved her Yiannis. Many Greek mothers worship their sons and hold them first in their heart. But there was never any doubt that first place in my mother's heart belonged to her husband. She was tender and good to her children, but when her husband walked in the room his needs and desires came first. Maybe that's why I never envied Andreas our mother's love, even when I envied him everything else. In the mother-love sweepstakes we were both a distant second.

If they had not loved each other so much, perhaps my parents would have considered more the impact my mother's death sentence was having on me and Andreas, and even Katerina. But they did love each other enormously. At the prospect of this first and final parting, they had hardly a thought to spare for us. My mother would ask me to go to her every so often. She would caress my hair, kiss my forehead, hold my hand, but soon my father would reclaim her attention and I would wander off to leave them alone. I didn't resent them their time together. I just felt lonelier and more scared than I would have if my father had worried a bit over me and had made an effort to ease my burden. But all his love and support were channelled to my mother. She was saying goodbye to me, but my father was saying nothing. Everything he had, everything he was, he was giving to my mother.

That's how I got through the three months it took my mother to die. Abandoned by my father, estranged from my brother, never more than a stranger to my uncle, I turned all my fears and grief to Katerina who absorbed them as best she could and gave me the strength to cling on. In return, I suppose I did the same for her. Seated together on the steps we wordlessly counted the time. Once in the gathering gloom of the evening she took my hand in hers. It was such a comfort that from then on, as soon as dusk would fall, I would search for her hand and hold her slender fingers gently, tightening my grip momentarily when my mother would sigh or moan or speak.

In September my mother entered the hospital, never again to leave it. She was alone with my father when she died. She had earlier said goodbye to my uncle, my grandfather, Katerina, Andreas and me. She was very weak and in a lot of pain. I had to bend to her mouth to receive her kiss and her blessing. I didn't get a last glance at her, because my eyes were full of tears. I backed out of the room and the door closed behind me. It didn't open again until my father came out, his face a stony mask of pain. He ordered everybody home in a gruff voice and went back inside. She was dead already, but he wanted to sit with her.

He didn't leave her side again until the earth covered her. When they brought her home and the women came to wash and dress her, he sent them away. He would wash her himself, he said, and the women departed whispering in shock to themselves that this was too much, and whoever heard of a man washing the dead. My father didn't care. He took her in his arms and set her in the coffin in the living-room, washed and changed her himself, fixed her hair, and then sat next to her, reaching out every so often to touch her hair or her hands which he had folded together.

The mourners came in a steady stream all day. Then night-time arrived. Andreas and I went to bed. My uncle and grandpa tried to stay up with my dad, but he sent them away. He sat alone with her and I spent that sleepless night thinking of him sitting in the dark with his only love.

Is he crying? I wondered, but I was too scared to get up and look.

We held the funeral the next day. As the pall bearers carried the coffin down the steps my father broke tradition again. Instead of letting some woman do it, he personally took the clay water jug selected for the purpose and threw it to the ground, breaking it in a million shards as was customary, to break the bad luck and scare death away from the house.

Back at the house people milled about and hugged and kissed Andreas, me and Katerina. They nodded sadly and said my mother was too young to die, and made the traditional wish that we should live long. I got through the day by shutting down my feelings. I came close to losing my self-control only when Kyra Hariklia, crying freely, remarked that I was such a little man not to cry. Katerina was serving coffee and dabbing at her eyes every so often. I concentrated on her and bit my lip, and the moment passed.

My father just sat in a chair, said nothing and looked at no one. His father stood beside him, his hand on his son's shoulder. It was he who answered the villagers as they stopped one by one to offer condolences. After everyone left, we sat down to eat the food the neighbours had brought. All of us, except my father. He went in the bedroom, his bedroom now, and shut the door. A few minutes later we heard a sound. It was the most horrible sound on earth, a keening, wrenching moan of a dam breaking, the earth splitting open, the world coming to an end. My father was crying for my mother.

It was the only sound we heard out of him for days. The next morning he went to the bakery and resumed his routine. He ate, he read the paper, he worked, but it was as though nobody lived in his body. His face had only one expression, a stern, hard look. My father had stopped living.

I lost both my parents on the same day. For all practical purposes, my father was no longer with us. Little by little he started talking again, only the bare essentials. He didn't hear what we said to him. He didn't care.

My mother's death had devastated me, but it was something I could understand. It was natural. My father's behaviour, however, was beyond anything I had heard of or seen. As the days passed, instead of healing, my sense of loss and abandonment intensified. I sat on the steps one evening feeling lonely and sad when Katerina came over.

'It's hard to be in the house without her, isn't it?' she said as she lowered herself on the steps next to me. I said nothing.

'And it's even harder with the way your father is taking it,' she added.

I seized the opportunity.

'Why is he acting like we don't exist, Katerina? I think he hates me. I talk to him and he looks right through me like I'm not even there. What have I done?'

'You've done nothing. He loved your mother very much, that's all, and he finds it hard to go on without her. Remember how I was when I first came here? Well, he's like that. It will get better.'

I thought about that, but I didn't find it satisfactory.

'But you weren't like that, Katerina. You were sad and quiet, but you knew we were around. You talked to us and you heard us. My dad is like he's not even there.'

'Well, I guess it's harder when you lose your wife or your husband. It's quite a different kind of love. It's the biggest love there is. It's like they say in church. Two people become one. One flesh, one person. If one of them dies, the other is only half a person.'

This seemed a better explanation. If my mom and dad were one person, then no wonder my father couldn't go on without her.

'Then in a way, since they had to die, I guess it's a good thing that your parents died together,' I said, 'so they didn't have to be apart from each other.'

Katerina chuckled harshly.

'It would have been better for my father only to have died. I think my mother would have been happy to outlive him.'

Her bitterness startled me. I looked at her, amazed at what she had just said.

'And I would have been glad of it, too,' she added. 'I wish to God that he had died and my mother had lived.'

'Katerina, how can you say that about your father?' I cried, ever the little prig.

'He beat us, George. At night he would drink, and he would get mad at anything. Even nothing. If my mother spilled some soup, if she asked for money, if the crickets made too much noise, if the dog barked. His face would get red and he would beat her. And then he would beat me. She would try to save me and he would beat her some more. He broke her arm once and she had to say she broke it herself when she fell. Well, she did fall, but only because he pushed her. And she didn't break her arm in the fall. He broke it for her when he twisted it to get her off him because she was trying to get him to stop hitting me. So you see, Georgie, married people don't always love each other. But your parents did, and if it means that your dad can't stand the loss of your mother you should be glad, because he loved her that much, and he would never hurt her for the world.'

Tears had started falling in the middle of her speech. Her lashes were wet with them, made darker and thicker with the moisture. Her lovely eyes were large with grief. Instinctively I put my arm around her and I hugged her. She put her head on my shoulder and we sat like that for a while, me holding her and she softly crying. Out of that summer of loss there was this one shining moment when I sat with Katerina in the faint light of sundown feeling stronger than I had ever felt. I could take anything, I could take my mother's death, I could take my father's desperate behaviour. I could withstand it all. I could make it and not crumble because Katerina needed someone, needed me, to hold her in the dark while she cried.

I must have loved her before. I must have fallen in love with her some time in the preceding months. But it was that evening that I first realised it. She kept her head on my shoulder even after she stopped crying. I wished that she would stay like that all night, but my uncle's voice pierced the moment. He was calling her from inside the house to iron his shirt for him so he could go to the tavern. She sprang out of my embrace and hurried to do his bidding. I sat there drunk with my feelings. I touched my shoulder where her head had been. I breathed in deeply to catch the last lingering bit of her scent. I closed my eyes to preserve the sight of her wet lashes. And I whispered to myself, 'Katerina!'

11

The Wages of Grief

Only Katerina made life bearable that year. My thirteenth birthday came and went without anyone remembering it. My father continued to pay no attention to anything. Soon he started joining my uncle at the tavern. He would sit speechless in a corner and drink one ouzo after another while all around him the men of the village played backgammon on large wooden boards, slapping the dice and the game pieces loudly, cussing and arguing politics, playing cards, or just flinging their worry beads expertly in a hand dangling from the arm of a chair. Late at night my dad and my uncle would stumble home together, one supporting the other as they weaved around the dark rooms crashing into furniture.

My grandfather tried to intervene. He would wait up for his two sons and start a litany of advice and criticism as soon as they came in.

'What are you trying to do, Yiannis? This isn't like you. Drink if you want to, nobody says you don't have a right to, but drink in moderation. Drink a few. Drink and come home at a decent hour. How will you wake up in a few hours to go to the bakery? You're killing yourself, don't you see?'

All the advice was directed at my father. My grandpa

had long ago given up on his other son, the bad seed, who showed no signs of getting himself a wife or settling down to a normal life. My father never seemed to hear his father's words. He would move past him and crash on the big double bed without a word or a glance.

Until one night on the four-month anniversary of my mother's death. My grandpa started his litany as soon as his two sons walked in. When my father continued moving towards the bedroom, my grandpa followed him and grabbed his sleeve to turn him around.

'What are you doing to yourself, my son? You'll kill yourself if you keep on like this,' he was saying.

My father tried to yank his arm away, but when he failed he turned to the old man.

'I wish I could kill myself. I wish I were dead.'

'Yiannis, don't say that!' my grandpa cried.

My father crumbled now. He sat down on the floor and keened, rocking himself back and forth.

'I don't want to live without her, Pa. I don't want to live without my Niki. Nothing is good without her.'

Grandpa sat on the floor with him, took him in his arms, this grown-up boy of his who was in so much pain.

The noise had woken me up and I was standing scared and shaking at the door to my bedroom. Inside, Andreas was sitting up on his bed. Grandpa was talking to my dad nonstop, telling him he had to go on, that it was a sin to treat life this way, that it was the will of God that took my mother, that my dad had to accept the will of God, and finally that he had his sons to think of, his boys who needed him. Nothing seemed to console my father.

'I cannot do it, Dad,' he interrupted the old man's homilies. 'May God forgive me, but it's beyond me.'

'You have to think about your sons. Your boys. They need you,' my grandpa repeated. Then he motioned me over. I stepped over hesitantly. My father's tears were scaring me. His naked grief was more than I could bear, but I stood by as Grandpa instructed.

'Here is your son, Yiannis. You have to go on for him.'

But my father was not listening. His face was closed again. He let the last tears fall from his eyes, and then he turned and looked at me as if he didn't know me.

'I have nothing any more,' he muttered, and picking himself up unsteadily he went into his room and shut the door.

Grandpa turned to Uncle Demetres now.

'This is partly your fault,' he said sternly. 'You take him with you to the tavern and you teach him your ways. It's not enough for you to ruin your own life with your drinking, now you have to ruin his, too.'

My uncle shrugged and turned to his own room.

Things got worse after that. All winter long my father remained drunk and closed in on himself. Grandpa tried talking to him a few more times, but my dad ignored him as he ignored all of us. More and more I turned to Katerina.

Andreas had no one to turn to. He became angry and depressed once more. He started skipping school regularly and coming home late at night, never telling anyone where he'd been. He was in twelfth grade now, a few months away from graduation. His teacher sent a note home with me, asking Dad to come in for a consultation about Andreas's progress. The note warned sternly that unless Andreas turned the situation around immediately he might not graduate.

I put the note in my dad's hand, but he didn't read it. He just continued sitting in front of the fire, staring into the flames. The next day I found the note on the floor, still unfolded and unread. At school the teacher asked me when he could expect my father.

'I don't know,' I said. 'He's not himself just lately.'

I told Andreas about the note, but he just shrugged. Finally, I decided to give the note to Grandpa. He read it, and the next day visited the teacher. Then he sat to wait for the confrontation with Andreas.

'Andreas, I want to talk to you,' he said when my brother walked in.

'Not now,' Andreas replied as he pulled some bread out of the breadbox and sat down with a hunk of cheese and a tomato. 'I'm just here to eat something and then I have to go right out again.'

My grandpa got mad at this. He got up, went up to where Andreas was sitting at the kitchen table.

'You listen to me, you little punk. Your teacher says you're not going to school. You're going to stop that right now and start acting like a human being again. Just because your dad isn't paying attention doesn't mean you can run wild. You'll stop going out all the time, and you're going to start studying, and that's that.'

My grandad had been a fierce man when he was younger. He had ruled his household with an iron fist. Even grown up, his sons showed their respect for him and feared his wrath. Even my uncle was afraid of him, and kept drinking only because his need for alcohol had long ago become a compulsion stronger than any human fear. But grandpa was no longer the man he used to be. He was a stooped old man with a tremulous voice, bad eyesight and legs made unsteady by arthritis.

'Leave me alone,' Andreas said, not even looking up.

Grandpa raised his cane and brought it down on Andreas's shoulder.

'Damn!' Andreas yelled and jumped up. He towered

over the old man. 'What place is this where a man can't even eat in peace!'

'So you think you are a man now,' my grandpa mocked him. 'You who never worked in your life think you are a man. You're still a puppy, a child, and as long as you live on your father's sweat you will do what you are told.'

He raised his cane as he said the last few words, to hit Andreas again. Andreas did the unthinkable. He grabbed Grandpa's hand in mid-air and stopped the arc of the cane. Then he forced the gnarled, arthritic hand open, took the cane and threw it across the room.

'Leave me alone!' he yelled once more and, grabbing the bread and cheese, bounded out of the house. My grandpa sat in the chair that Andreas had occupied.

'Bring me my cane, George,' he said. His voice was breaking. By the time I retrieved the cane and brought it over he was wiping a tear from his face with the back of his hand.

'I'm sorry, Grandpa,' I whispered.

'Your father is right. Nothing is the same,' he told me.

With no one to discipline him, Andreas got worse. There were nights when he didn't come home at all. Nikos told me he heard my brother and Pavlos were gambling down in Thessaloniki and running with fast women.

'That's ridiculous,' I told him. 'Where would Andreas find the money?'

Where indeed. My father and uncle would bring the bakery's take home every night. Seated at the kitchen table they would sort the money in piles and make entries in the ledger they kept on top of the icebox. Then they would lock the money in a strong box, kept on a small table in my parents' room. At the end of each week, on

Sunday, they would total up profits and losses and they would divide the take between them, my uncle getting a much smaller portion because my father had to run the house and pay for everything out of his. Still, my father must have allotted my uncle more than his fair share considering the services that my mother and then Katerina performed for him, because my uncle, who was a complainer, never complained. We didn't have money for luxuries, the money was always tight, but my father was more than a fair man; he was generous.

My uncle kept his money in his mattress. I don't know why he took this elaborate safety precaution of cutting a hole and then taking pains to conceal it. Everyone in the house knew his hiding place and he certainly wasn't hiding it from us. As for burglars, there were no such things in Panorama. We never locked a door or latched a window unless somebody was taking a bath or changing clothes. We guarded our modesty, but there was no reason to hide our money.

As it turned out, Nikos was right. Andreas was spending money in Thessaloniki. And he was getting it from my uncle's mattress. Whenever he found himself alone in the house, he would go in Uncle Demetres's room and take a few bills, never too much, just enough. My uncle was unlikely to notice, since he was usually too drunk to know what he spent. Then Andreas's luck turned. He lost a good deal of money, and his creditors wanted to get paid soon. So he took more. My uncle might have been a drunk, but he was no fool. He noticed. And since he was no stranger to the ways of the world, he also had a good guess who the thief might be. He didn't say anything. He just watched and waited to catch the thief redhanded.

He started spending his nights in the tavern with his eye glued to the window, watching the road outside to see if Andreas might be heading home. When Andreas did one night, he followed him quietly, and managed to walk into the darkened family room just as my brother was trying to stuff the bundle back under the mattress, his pocket filled with his loot. The family room looked directly into the bedroom. When my uncle turned on the light, there was no way Andreas could hide.

'So you're a thief now, you piece of shit,' my uncle yelled and fell on my brother.

The scuffle brought me and Grandpa, who had been sleeping, out to the family room. Even though we didn't know at that moment what the fight was about, Grandpa was not about to interfere unless Andreas was getting the upper hand. As far as he was concerned, Andreas deserved a good beating, whatever the reason.

Uncle Demetres was kicking Andreas, who was trying to squirm away from him on the floor, when my father walked in, reeking of ouzo.

'Your punk son is a thief,' my uncle yelled without letting up. But the distraction was enough. Andreas grabbed his leg in mid-kick and brought him crashing to the ground. Then he got up and hurried out of the room. But my uncle was still not done.

'You give my money back,' he yelled as he scrambled to get up. Andreas stopped to toss the bills on the floor and Uncle Demetres was on him again.

'All of it, you son of a bitch! Everything you've been taking,' he screamed.

'If I had it I would, you dumb fuck,' Andreas screamed back.

'You're nothing but a thief,' my uncle continued, shaking him. 'A thief and a punk, getting girls pregnant and then begging for abortions, and now stealing from your own flesh and blood.'

My heart stopped. The secret was out. I braced for the storm. I cringed. And nothing happened. As though this was not his own family being torn apart, as though this wasn't his own son being exposed as a thief and a spoiler of women, my father just said, 'You'll wake the neighbourhood if you don't stop,' and walked into his bedroom. My uncle continued to rage at my brother until he grew hoarse and tired and Andreas managed to disentangle himself from him.

'You'll pay it all back,' my uncle said shaking his fist and went into his room. Grandpa just shook his head.

Somehow we made it through that winter. Grandpa's heart was torn to pieces watching his son deteriorate. He began to lose his grip. He started forgetting and losing things. He began to sleep at odd hours and spent most of his time dozing as though he didn't want to be around any more than my father did. In March a fierce storm ripped the blossoms off the almond trees. I cried when I saw the tender pink-white flowers on the ground, but my tears were common these days. It seemed to me that I had spent months with a lump in my throat. I would swallow it down all day, all week, all month, and then something would happen, something trite in comparison with the tragedy of my family, and I could not stop the tears any more. I could only hide them from the people around me.

May brought the poppies again. Every Sunday that month Katerina and I left the house and went to the meadows surrounding the village. She would walk deep into the sea of red and I would watch her from the edge, a slim black shape in the middle of the riot of spring colour. She would gather the flowers and bend them into wreaths for us to wear. Poppies are very delicate. Their petals pour all their strength in their colour and keep none back to bind them to their calyx. At slight pressure, a strong breeze, the petals fall to the ground. Our wreaths were plain bands of green after a few minutes.

These are the only happy moments I can recall of that season. These, and the presence of Katerina at home. She was the only reason I still called our house a home, and many times I thanked the Lord for having had the good will, since he had taken everything else from me, to at least give me Katerina.

In June my father got his wish. He died. They say that the first year of widowhood is hard to survive. Many widows, and more widowers, die within that year. Having known my father, I understand this statistic completely. I think it would have been unusual indeed if he had lived.

One morning he just didn't get up. My uncle, who had been waiting for him in the kitchen so they could start for the bakery, went to see what was keeping him. When he got no answer to his knock he went in. He found him dead on his bed. It looked as though he had been dead a few hours.

My father's death was not a shock to me. In most respects he had been dead already. I accepted the news sadly but with equanimity, and felt glad in a way, because his torment was over and he could finally be with my mother. We buried him next to her, side by side, and returned to the house to resume our lives.

12

The Tyrant

Andreas didn't graduate. He failed almost every course.
There was a time when this would have meant a row and a
beating. But there was nobody around to punish, nobody
around to pay attention. Grandpa had been hard-hit by
my father's death. He aged ten years in a matter of days.
His mind started to wander. Part of it was old age, part of
it was grief. Whatever the reason, he grew more stooped
and feeble, and he began to drift off into the past. He
called Andreas 'Yiannis' more often than not, and he
seemed not to recognise Katerina. Often, he would call
my mother and then complain when she wouldn't show
up to fetch his slippers or make him coffee. Katerina cared
for him with tenderness and compassion, but it was clear
that he would never recover.

My uncle was now the head of the household. All his
life he had to obey his father and take second place to
his brother, who was both older and more respected
since he had a family and family responsibilities. But
now there was nobody to check him. The first thing he
did was demand that Andreas help at the bakery.

'You're not going to school, you're not studying, you're
doing nothing. If you want to eat, you have to work,' he
announced.

Andreas made a show of protest.

'I'm only waiting till August,' he said, 'when I have to enlist. Let me have this summer.' Enlisting in the armed forces was compulsory, and service lasted for two and a half years. Every male had to serve unless he was attending college, in which case military service was postponed until college graduation.

Uncle Demetres didn't even listen to Andreas's protests.

'You'll rest in the army,' he told him. 'Until you leave, you will work fulltime and put bread on the table.'

There was nothing Andreas could do. He began getting up at dawn to knead dough and bake bread, and sell loaves all morning. For a full day's work, my uncle gave him a meagre allowance. When Andreas insisted that since he was working fulltime he must get a full day's wages, my uncle laughed.

'And your debt to me?' he asked him. 'What about the money you pissed away on cards and whores? I mean to get paid back, and this is the only way.'

After that Andreas worked without protest, but you could see he was counting the days. Finally, in August, he packed a small bag and showed up to enlist. The army shaved his head, issued him his boots and khakis and sent him to Kavalla for his basic training. Later he would be stationed elsewhere, maybe even Thessaloniki, if he could pull a few strings or get his commanding officer to like him. Since Pavlos was starting college in Thessaloniki that autumn, Andreas was going to move heaven and earth to charm anyone he had to into stationing him in Thessaloniki.

I hadn't expected to, but I missed my brother after he left. After the abortion, I had stopped spending time with him and thinking about him, but the year had had too many losses in it for me to accept his departure with equanimity. It bothered me that I missed him, and I caught myself thinking kinder thoughts about him and wishing he would be stationed in Thessaloniki soon so I could see him. Increasingly I felt like a stranger in my own house and clung to everything that reminded me of the old days.

But the old days were gone forever. Autumn found Katerina and me practically alone in the house with Uncle Demetres. To his credit, he worked even though neither my father nor grandpa were there to require it of him. He got up every morning just as early as he ever had, drank the coffee Katerina made and left for the bakery. He hired the cobbler's son to help him, and even though he cursed the young man nonstop for being an imbecile and lazy to boot, the bread was baked as always, and the villagers came and bought it. He'd come home after closing down the store, do the books by himself, eat and go to the tavern.

The way he chose to celebrate his new-found independence was to start drinking at home. Always before, when my father was alive and my grandpa had his faculties, Uncle Demetres did his drinking at the tavern. We would have wine with the midday meal on Sundays, but on those occasions my uncle drunk no more than anybody else. Now, however, he started bringing a bottle home, and he would start his drinking as soon as he sat down with the books. By the time he put the ledger and strong box aside, he was well on his way to tying one on, and he would weave his way both to and from the tavern.

While Andreas was still at home, they would do the books together, and Andreas would put aside money for the house that he would give to Katerina to do the shopping and pay the bills. Once Andreas left, however, my uncle seemed to forget that a household doesn't run for free. In a couple of days we ran out of everything. Katerina was too shy to ask for money. She approached me instead.

'Please ask your uncle for money to do the shopping,' she told me. 'And the electric bill needs to be paid.'

That evening I approached my uncle. He readily agreed to give Katerina the money, but then he questioned her about how much was needed, and made her explain the cost of everything before handing her a few bills. Just enough for a couple of days. After the money ran out I had to approach him again.

'Why doesn't Katerina ask me?' he said. 'Is she mute that she has to have you do the asking? Or is it you who does the shopping these days?' Katerina was there when he said this, and blushed deep scarlet at his words.

'I didn't want to disturb you, Kyr Demetres, and it's hardly my place. This is your house.'

'You don't need to stand so much on ceremony,' he told her with a smile. But he still made her give a full accounting of how much she needed.

'You pay the grocer too much, and that's a fact,' he told her. 'I'll give you thirty drachmas and you try to talk him down. If he doesn't go for it, you come back to me, and I will give you more.'

It became a ritual. Every night Katerina had to stand in front of him and explain what she needed and why. Every night he would chide her for being taken advantage of and paying too much. I found this incomprehensible. Katerina had been doing the shopping for a long time now, and nobody in the village would even think of cheating Yiannis's daughter of the soul. Overcharging was reserved for the summer people, and only because they could afford it and seemed to expect it.

I knew Katerina minded. Hell, I minded. But there was

no higher authority to appeal to. She began to get that scared look when Uncle Demetres was around, the one she had the first few days with us, when she would hunch her shoulders and keep her eyes fastened to the ground. One night when he insisted too long that Katerina was paying to much for cheese, and I could see that Katerina was barely restraining her tears, I intervened.

'Uncle, she's not paying too much. The price is marked on the tin, and Kyr Nestor charges everyone the same.'

'Then he's putting his finger on the scale when he weighs it, and she's not catching him,' he retorted.

'Kyr Nestor is an honest man, and he wouldn't cheat like that,' I replied. My uncle's hand rose, circled the air and landed squarely on my cheek before I knew it.

'Damn insolence!' he bellowed. 'I know what a kilo of feta looks like, and this is no kilo she's been bringing home. Now, either she's eating it on the way, or he's putting his thumb on the scales!'

I was scared. His face had grown red during his little speech, and his anger, fuelled by the ouzo he was drinking, seemed out of all proportion. My face was burning where he had hit me. But this was Katerina he was picking on. I squared my shoulders.

'She's not eating it, and he's not cheating her,' I yelled back. 'And if you didn't drink like a fish all day you'd have eyes to see that she runs this household as well as Mother ever did.'

I had more to say, but I didn't get a chance. My uncle rose from his chair, slapped me hard twice, shoved me to the ground and kicked me in the stomach.

'You talk to me like that one more time and you won't live to talk to me another day,' he roared at me. 'The times you knew are gone. I am the master in this house now, and if I say she's paying too much for cheese, then she's paying too much for cheese.' He sat back down and drained his glass of ouzo. Then he re-filled it, threw some water in it to make it milky white, and went on poring over the books. I slunk away, hurt and humiliated. I couldn't protect my love.

After my uncle left, Katerina came to me in the family room. She touched my shoulder as I sat curled up in a ball of hate and shame on the sofa.

'Thank you, George, for helping me.'

'Big help!'

'You're always a help to me. Just by being here you're helping me. If you weren't here I'd have to go, and I have no place to go.'

I hadn't thought of that. Katerina had had two adult allies in this house, two protectors who offered her this haven when she was destitute. But they were both gone now, and she was at the mercy of a man who had not chosen to make her his daughter of the soul. He was a complete stranger to her. And he held the purse strings. My mother had brought her in out of love. My father took her on out of Christian charity and because she was the daughter of his wife's best friend. But none of these reasons was likely to sway my uncle to gentleness.

What if Uncle Demetres decided that Katerina could not handle running the house? What if he decided to throw her out? What then? I turned to her and I could see she was thinking the same thing.

'I've got to try harder to cut the household expenses, George. Your uncle doesn't trust me. I've got to get him to trust me. You can help. He gets mad when people tell him what to do. So you have to not do that. I know you want to help, and you did help, but we have to avoid getting him angry.'

'But, Katerina, I had to do something. I can't let him

do this to you every night. I can tell it makes you sad. I don't want that. It makes *me* sad. And angry.'

'If he gets angry he might throw me out, George. And then what would I do? Where would I go? I have no other place to go.'

Tears were rolling down her cheeks now. I reached out for her and put my arm around her slender shoulders. I held her while she cried softly.

'How I wish your mother had lived!' she whispered.

I reached out with my other hand and caressed her hair as she rested her head on my shoulder. Together with Andreas I was my father's heir to half the bakery and half the house. If my uncle wanted to stop supporting me then he would have to give me my quarter of the house and the bakery. He was not supporting me. He was simply working part of my inheritance and letting me live in my house, as I had a right to. But Katerina was here on his sufferance. If he decided to throw her out, what could I do to stop him? Why, I could ask for my quarter and support her out of that. I brightened at the thought.

'Don't worry, Katerina. This is my house, too,' I told her, 'and so is the bakery. He can't throw you out. I won't let him.'

'You're sweet to say that, George. But he's your guardian, and what he says goes. Just, please, for my sake, don't upset him.'

I promised her I wouldn't. Then I sat quietly with her body pressed next to mine and I thought, I'll grow up and I'll marry you, Katerina, and you'll never have to fear anything ever again, because this house will be yours, and so will the bakery, and so will I. I will love you and provide for you, and I will make you happy, and even though your eyes are so beautiful when you're sad, you'll never be sad again.

It was hard to keep my promise. My uncle liked his new game of questioning Katerina and making her feel uncomfortable. Sometimes his questioning was perfunctory, but more often he drilled her thoroughly, getting impatient when she hesitated. On most such occasions he made a great show of holding his temper, and spoke slowly and distinctly to her, as though to an idiot. Several times, though, he raised his voice and once he got very angry and threw his chair to the floor. Then he swept his arm over the table, throwing the books down, and slammed out of the house in a fury.

I blamed the drinking for these displays. My uncle now kept a bottle at the bakery and he spent all day in a haze, sometimes burning the bread slightly. The things he had to do all day at the shop had been ingrained into his muscles over the years, however, and his mistakes were few and slight.

I reminded myself that if I tried to protect Katerina he was likely to get angrier and tell her to leave. I swallowed my pride and my instinct to stick up for her and made myself sit very still in the family room while his own voice rose steadily in volume while Katerina's replies grew softer and slower at each of his questions. Sometimes Grandpa would be sitting in his chair next to the fire, but he seemed not to hear what was happening.

It was a torture to me to witness these scenes, but I was unable to stay out of the house while they were going on. Afterwards I would try to console Katerina, telling her funny stories, complimenting the way she ran the house, and reading to her from my books.

Household expenses were not the only way my uncle harassed Katerina. After winter came, he began to grow petulant in his demands for food, coffee, the laundry.

'Katerina, this shirt is not clean!'

'Katerina, this coffee tastes like mud.'

'Katerina, where the devil are you? I've been waiting for ever to get some food in this house.'

Katerina would answer meekly, rush to make him another cup of coffee, give him another shirt, set the table, apologise. He would smile with pleasure when she did these things.

'You do a good job when you try,' he would tell her, 'but you're lazy. If I don't keep on at you, you'll never do anything right.'

One day Katerina lost the change she was bringing back from the grocer. In a panic when she realised it, she retraced her steps, turned her clothes inside out, went back to the grocer to ask if he found the money, looked everywhere, but to no avail. The fifty drachmas was lost. She told me when I got in from school, and the two of us searched everywhere again.

'He'll kill me when he finds out. He'll think I stole it,' she said. Fear was twisting her features and a thin film of sweat was breaking out on her forehead, even though the day was cool.

'I'll give you the money, Katerina. I have some saved.'

She was reluctant to accept my savings at first. As the time for my uncle's return home approached, however, her fear won over her reluctance. She took the money.

When she stood in front of my uncle to give her accounting, her voice was shakier than usual, but the change was correct.

'Very good,' he said, his voice already blurred from drinking. 'This is correct. Isn't it nice how you've learned to keep a correct account!'

From my post in the family room, I thought there was a funny tone to his voice. Something false and dangerous.

'Still, it's a little funny,' he continued. 'Kyr Nestor came round after he closed down the shop, and it seems to me he said you lost some money today, and came to his store asking him if he had found it. So how come the money is all here?'

The minute I heard the grocer's name I went to the kitchen doorway. Katerina was speechless. She opened her mouth a couple of times, but nothing came out.

'Did you happen to find the money?' my uncle asked, in a deceptively calm tone.

Yes, Katerina, I thought. Say you found it.

'Yes,' she said, as if she had read my thoughts. Unfortunately, she blushed as she said it and looked away from my uncle's eyes.

'And where did you find it, my dear?' Again the calm tone. Katerina hesitated only a second.

'In my pocket. It was crumpled up in my pocket and I didn't feel it.' The slap exploded in the stillness that followed Katerina's answer. The force of it whipped her head sideways.

'You're lying!' he bellowed. 'You little bitch, so you think I don't know when you're lying to me?'

'No,' I yelled and rushed at him. I grabbed his hand which was rising again and hung on to it.

'Run, Katerina,' I yelled again.

He threw me across the floor as if I were no more than a puppy dog tugging at his trouser leg. Then he grabbed Katerina who was standing rooted to the spot and shook her.

'Where did you find the money? Did some prick give it to you? Did you whore for it?'

I had a sudden vision of his bloated face under the moonlight, asking me if I had fucked Lila. Revulsion rose in my throat and it was the fuel that led me to rush at him again, grabbing him from behind. I pummelled my fist on his back, but he didn't seem to feel the force of my ineffectual blows.

'Tell me, you little whore, did you spread your legs for it? Did you? Do you have more? Have you made a brothel of this house?'

'I gave it to her!' I screamed. 'It was mine!'

The cry was wrenched out of me, and I didn't know what effect it might have. Would he accuse me of sleeping with Katerina?

He stopped shaking her. He stood motionless. She was crying now. Silent tears were running down her face, but she still faced him, defenceless and resigned.

'What is the matter with you? Why do you act this way? It's only fifty drachmas. We knew you'd be upset so I gave it to her.'

'You stay out of this,' he told me, but the fire had gone out of him. 'And the next time she loses money she can tell me. Do you hear me?' He turned to her. 'Don't lie to me. Just tell me.' Then he sat back down at the table and gathered the books in a pile.

'Now bring me some food.'

Silently, trembling and unsteady, Katerina got a plate and filled it with the cabbage and pork she had cooked that day. Her face had no expression in it. She's thinking of her father, I thought. This house has turned into the same miserable place that her own house was like. Once more a drunken brute is terrorising her, and I can't do anything about it.

Most days were not this bad. Often Katerina would simply have to go through the humiliating accounting and a few whiny complaints about the way she did her chores. There were even days where my uncle praised her for something, a cake that turned out good, a stain that she had removed by scrubbing. Then he would wink at her and reach to tweak her cheek, and he would boast that his control was making a difference.

'You need an iron fist, Katerina, to bring out the best in you,' he would say with a satisfied grin.

Katerina would flinch imperceptibly at his words. She would shrink from his hand. His face would cloud over but he didn't give up. When she turned away from his outstretched, beefy hand, he would simply reach out a little more and pinch her harder. She learned not to turn away.

Are there any conditions to which human beings cannot become accustomed? The home that used to be so happy and tranquil had turned into a minefield, with my uncle's steady drinking likely to push him over the brink at any moment. Still, Katerina and I got used to getting along as best we could. We tiptoed around him. We tried to anticipate his every need. We accommodated his moods and put ourselves at his service. Sometimes this was enough to keep him quiet. Other times nothing worked and the circle of screaming, cursing and slapping would play itself out. Katerina's cheeks reddened time and again with his hand print, but he did no worse harm to her. I got shoved around a few times, hit my knee hard against the wall, got a few bruises. We learned to live with it. We even had some good times. A lot of good times. At night, when he was down at the tavern, Katerina and I would sit together, she with her knitting and mending, me with my books, exchanging a word here and there. Sometimes a neighbour would drop by, Antigone or Kyra Marika, for coffee, a brief exchange of news. But much of the time we were alone for hours on end.

Half the time I spent bent over my homework was really

spent daydreaming. In the warmth of the kitchen, with the clickety clack of Katerina's knitting needles keeping time, it was easy to pretend that I was not fourteen but twenty, and that I was married to Katerina. That she was my beloved wife, and as soon as I was finished I would get up, kiss her on the forehead and say, like my father used to, 'It's time for us to go to sleep, my little wife.' Then I would lead her by the arm into the bedroom and I would close the door. I would put my arms around her, kiss the top of her head and coax her face up towards mine, and I would kiss her pink lips and encircle her fragile waist. Unbutton the front of her dress, bury my face in her warm flesh, feel the tiny pinpoints of her nipples on my lips.

That's where I always stopped, because to think farther was dangerous, would soil Katerina, would make me blush to look at her, would drive me crazy with impatience for the time to pass, for the years to go, for my face to finally grow a beard, for my body to finally reach adult height, for my hands to grow big and heavy so it would require care to be gentle with her. My mind would whisper 'Katerina' and I would look up at her, bent over her work. Sometimes I would actually speak her name softly, unconsciously, and she would answer. I would have to think of something to say, something inconsequential and commonplace, but the words that were running through my mind were, 'I love you, I love you, my love, my life.'

Those nights I spent with Katerina sitting near me in the kitchen, Grandpa dozing in the other room, Uncle Demetres far away at the taverna, were the happiest moments of my life. Our problems were many, our peace precarious, but there was the hope of a better future, a time when we would be free and she would be mine.

The future had only one possible outcome to me. I

would finish school, become betrothed to Katerina, serve my military duty, get married and work in the bakery. Maybe my uncle would be dead by then. His drinking had to be taking its toll on his health. He looked bloated, too red in the face. He wheezed when he climbed the stairs, and when he played out one of his violent scenes his blood pressure shot up. Any minute he could burst a blood vessel, I thought, and fall on the floor. Then Andreas would be released from the army as a head of household. He would run the bakery and I would grow up, and everything would turn out as I expected.

Once in a while I considered the possibility that Katerina might fall in love with someone else. She was eighteen now, a young woman ripe for marriage. If she had to wait another six years for me she would be an old maid. And she couldn't possibly love me now, not as a man. I still had not entered puberty in earnest. I was a child in appearance and, although my voice was breaking, she could hardly devote herself to so slender a promise of future manliness. But I had every reason to hope. We were the best of friends. She obviously liked spending time around me. More important, there were no likely candidates on the horizon. She was penniless, so although the neighbouring women liked her and praised her, they would be loath to suggest her to their young male relatives as a bride. Besides, she was unlikely to marry for love, since she spent all her time at home, never went anywhere but the market, except with me. Then, too, she was shy, spoke only when and what was necessary, and had none of the sidelong, flirty glances that other poor village girls used so deftly to ensnare the young men of Panorama. She seemed to have no desire to marry, even though that would have released her from her bondage to my uncle. Maybe, considering the treatment she received in both her father's and my uncle's hands, she was afraid of men, I thought. Or, maybe, she was waiting for me after all.

My complacency lasted until that summer. There was a greengrocer in Panorama who sold fruits and vegetables up on Main Street. But the best fruit, the ripest, sweetest pieces at the best prices, were sold out of mule-drawn carts or tractor-pulled bins by the farmers themselves, or farm hands who tried to make a few extra drachmas. They came from the neighbouring villages with hand-held scales and their harvest. They would roam the streets slowly, announcing their presence and what they had to sell in a loud voice, offering free samples to convince the women to come out and buy.

'The best grapes of summer right here!'

'Melon like honey. So good the mother will eat and leave none for her children!'

Most of these itinerant salesmen would only come by once or twice every summer. A few were con artists who kept a few good pieces for samples, and then filled the bag with fruit full of blemishes and bruises. A housewife had to be careful, because they did not depend on return business. Some, however, came by regularly, and could be depended on to sell only the best.

Theophanes was one of the regulars. He was a young man, tall, sunburned and strong as an ox. He wasn't hand-scme, but he had a clear, direct gaze, a ready smile and the look of an honest man about him. He came by about once every week or so, selling whatever he could find. Peaches, plums, sweetest watermelons, and even tomatoes and green peppers. He knew Katerina from last summer.

'Hello, Kalamata,' he would greet her with a smile when she came out with the other women to look over his inventory. He called her Kalamata, he explained to her, because her eyes were as black and shiny as Kalamata olives.

Maybe it was his open, friendly manner. Maybe his direct gaze. Maybe she had just become used to him. Whatever it was, Katerina's eyes began rising from the ground where she usually kept them firmly planted when around strangers. At first she would look at him furtively. Then her eyes lingered a little. By August she looked at him frankly while he spoke to her the few little words that accompanied her shopping. She even answered him, and once she laughed at a small joke that he made for her benefit. Softly and half-heartedly, but she laughed.

I watched, of course. I watched her grow more comfortable with him, and I watched him pick the best fruit to stuff in her bag. I knew from experience what that meant. Hadn't my father kept the best loaves for my mother? Under normal circumstances it was impossible to dislike Theophanes, but these were not normal circumstances. I grew to hate him. Every time I heard his voice down the road my hackles rose and my skin prickled. After he left I would be cool to Katerina, denying her my attention until her punishment grew too hard on me and I went running to find her. I ached with jealousy. I burned with frustration. Most of all, I hurled contempt on myself. Why shouldn't she like Theophanes and laugh with him? He was a man, tall and strong and grown up. If he saw my uncle mistreating her he could shove him aside, punch him in the face, put him in his place. He deserved to win her, because I was nothing but a miserable, weak child who couldn't even play soccer and fell off his bike more often than he stayed on it.

My misery and self-loathing reached their zenith one evening in late August. My uncle was inside doing the books, and Katerina was outside with a few neighbours, listening to Kyra Maria reading the coffee sediment.

'Your heart is heavy, my dear,' she told Katerina. 'You have an enemy, look at him here on the side, see, he's in your house, see the wolf?'

I had looked inside the cups many times to find the shapes Kyra Maria announced and interpreted with so much aplomb, but the sediment always looked like random blots and swirls to me. Still, this was Katerina's coffee cup, so I listened. I also examined her from afar for any signs of anxiety or impatience. Today Theophanes should have come by, but it was eight o'clock and he hadn't.

'I see a package here. You get a small gift, plain as day, nothing big, but nice. And look here, you'll find yourself at a dinner with four people and my, you will have a nice time, but you'll exchange a few angry words, too. I see the small cloud above the table. Nothing to worry about, it will blow over. But, oh my dear, what's this I see, two rings entwined. Katerina, you're getting married. Sure as the sun will rise, you're getting married!'

What! The words shook me to the core. What else could it mean but that she would marry Theophanes. In my panic I forgot my attitude of unbelief towards all this coffee magic. All I could think of were two rings entwined, two bodies entwined, Katerina and Theophanes, Katerina tiny in his strong arms, Katerina lost and swooning in his embrace. Goddamn Kyra Maria, putting ideas in Katerina's head, upsetting my plans, killing them, condemning my love!

The women left and Katerina started picking up the cups and water glasses. I looked on in anger. She showed no signs of being affected by Kyra Maria's words, but in my anger I attributed her impassive demeanour to slyness. Oh, sure, she pretends she doesn't care, but let him come around and she will look at him with her eyes, show him her eyes. She knows how beautiful they are and so she keeps them down only to raise them at the right moment, for the greatest effect. Oh, she's a sly one! Pretending to be my friend and all the time she dreams of Theophanes and wants to marry him!

My rage was at its hottest when I heard Theophanes coming up the road. She went over to him, petted his donkey, waited her turn.

'I'm late today, Kalamata,' he smiled at her. 'Won't you ask me what happened? Didn't you get a tiny bit worried?'

'So what happened to you?' No smile, no look, but she asked!

'My Psares, here, fell in love,' he said, putting his hand on his donkey's neck, no more than ten inches away from hers, resting on the same donkey.

'He did, he fell in love with a lady donkey in Sedes with a bushy tail and ears of velvet, and he wouldn't budge for hours. In vain I talked to him, and tugged at him, and switched his backside. He just brayed at me to leave him alone and refused to move. I had to give up and go have a drink and something to eat, and still he wouldn't leave. I spent half the day waiting for him and now I must sell my peaches this late. So what do you make of that?'

'You're kind to him. Others would have beaten him till he moved,' she said. Eyes shining into his.

'I can't find it in my heart to hurt him. He's like a brother to me and I feel for him. And who am I to stand in the path of love? Maybe some day he can make it possible for me to be with *my* love, who knows?'

Slimy, sweet-talking stranger! What kind of story is that to tell a young girl about a rutting donkey? Doesn't she understand where all this is leading? Can't she see she should never have encouraged him to tell his silly story? Does she think because she's looking down now and blushing, he's not had what he came for? And how much longer will words be enough? Won't he come over soon, as stubborn as his donkey, and demand his own? Ah, but she wants it, that's what it is. She wants it.

'Katerina!' my uncle's voice rang out. 'Come inside this instant, I need you here.'

I followed behind her up the stairs as she hurried to the kitchen, carrying a bag of peaches. He grabbed her by the hair as soon as she was in the door, and yanked hard. She lost her balance and the peaches spilled on the floor. One of them got under her scrambling feet and she landed with a thud.

'You bitch!' was all he said as he dragged her up only to send her back down with a slap. He picked her up again, grabbed her by the front of her dress to hold her steady and rained blows on her, some landing on her face, others on her arms which she had raised to protect herself.

I did nothing to stop him. That will teach you, I thought, savagely.

He let go of her and she fell to the ground, weeping.

'If I see you fooling around with him again I'll kill you,' he said. 'I won't have you making eyes at every two-bit cock that wants to pass his time with you! This is not a brothel, and if you want to be a whore you go somewhere else to do it. You can spread your legs for the whole village if you want to, but not out of this house! You hear me?'

She said nothing.

'Do you hear me?' he repeated, new menace in his voice.

'Yes,' she breathed.

'Well, what will it be? Will you behave and stay here, or will I throw you in the street?'

I stepped outside. My anger and jealousy had left me,

and I was now ashamed that I had allowed him to beat her without trying to stop him. Had she seen me? Did she know I had stood by and allowed this to happen to her without so much as a protest? Did she know that I felt a thrill when the first blow fell, because I wanted her punished, I wanted her to hurt like I was hurting? Could she tell that it wasn't until he let her fall on the floor that the scales were lifted from my eyes and I saw truly? It was too late to help her by then, his anger was spent.

My shame overwhelmed me. I entered the fig tree as I used to do when I was little. I had wanted to hurt Katerina, and because I couldn't I was glad of it when my uncle did. His vulgar mouth spoke to her the words that had been boiling in my own brain. Wave after wave of shame washed over me. What did she have in life to be glad of? All day long she worked and worried over what mood my uncle would be in when he came home. Every night he humiliated her by treating her like a stranger not to be trusted. He hit her, and made her apologise when she was not at fault. And all the time she had to live on charity, accept charity from this man who brutalised her. So she let Theophanes flirt with her. Once a week or so, for three months out of a year. Why should I begrudge her a little joy? Wasn't she mine all the rest of the year? What kind of animal was I to derive satisfaction out of an undeserved beating just to satisfy my jealousy and vindictiveness?

I came out of the leafy branches becalmed. I was wrong but I would make it up to her. Never again would he lift a finger on her as long as I had breath in me. I would bite him, kick him, scratch him, pull a knife on him, but I would protect her, and in protecting her atone for the dark meanness of my spirit.

But he did hit her again and, even though I did try

to stop him, I failed. I didn't die in the attempt, and I didn't pull a knife on him, either. I just got a couple of bruises. And to this day I do not know if I indeed had a better self in me who repented truly in the bower of the fig tree, or if I forgave her Theophanes because I knew that there was no way now that she would ever so much as speak to him again.

13

The Return of the Wayward Son

In September of that year, Andreas finally got his transfer to Thessaloniki. For more than a year I had hardly seen him. Kryoneri, the small village where he had been stationed after basic training, was much too far for him to undertake the trip only to visit what our home had become. Pavlos had visited him and had brought us news that Andreas was well, getting along with his commanding officer and working on his transfer to Thessaloniki.

Kryoneri by all accounts was a miserable place. It was up in the mountains of Epirus, deathly cold in the winter, and not so warm in the summer either, cut off from the world, and hours away from even the smallest and most provincial town. Worst of all, there was nothing to do there. The base was only a few minutes' walk from the village, but taking that walk was an exercise in futility. There was nothing to do there. There was no cinema and no restaurants. There was a tavern with small metal tables under the inevitable buttonwood tree, but sitting there and trying to strike up a conversation with the shepherds was worse than nothing. The natives were inhospitable and considered the soldiers a permanent threat to the virtue of their daughters. They spoke with a thick accent, and most of the time they pretended they hadn't heard when some soldier would try to open a conversation. If they did acknowledge a comment or question directed at them, they either considered the acknowledgement enough of a reply or answered in monosyllables. If any soldier was foolish enough to speak to a village woman, he got in trouble fast. Her father, brother, cousin, whoever, would load a shotgun and escort him away without stopping to listen to explanations. 'We'll have no army bastards here' seemed to be the motto of the village and, the way everyone behaved, you'd think shaking hands was a surefire way to get pregnant.

Andreas told us all this when he came to Panorama a few days after his transfer, over Sunday lunch, eaten in the yard under the acacia trees. Katerina had roasted a leg of lamb with potatoes, and she served it with green salad, homemade fish roe dip and the best seven-grain bread from the bakery. Andreas smacked his lips at every bite.

'Were you always this good a cook,' he asked, 'or is it that army cooking is even worse than I thought?' He was in a great mood, and he looked great, too. He had grown taller and his shoulders had widened some more. He looked in excellent shape. I remarked that the army cooking had obviously done him a world of good, since he looked as strong as an ox.

'That's Corporal Viatsos for you. He had us marching up and down the damn Epirus rocks with our packs on our backs at the crack of dawn every day, and wouldn't let up until we were spitting blood. That man is a maniac. He even loaded our packs with stones so it wouldn't go too easy on us as we started to get used to it. I think I've walked enough to circle the globe a hundred times over, and still he was not satisfied until we dropped on the ground and gave him a hundred press-ups just for the hell of it.'

His voice had grown thicker, too, I noticed. It came to me that grown up though he seemed to me when he had left to go to the army, he actually hadn't reached full growth. Now he really was a man, however, seasoned by experience and by the tough discipline of this Corporal Viatsos.

'So how did you manage this cushy transfer?' my uncle asked.

'Viatsos may be a training freak, but he was bored, too. I just found something for him and the others to do, and I got to be his pal.'

'And what was that?'

'I got a regular poker game going. Viatsos didn't know how to play so I taught him. I took it easy on him at first. Encouraged him by making it so he'd win often. Then I stopped holding back.'

'You mean you started cheating,' my uncle interrupted.

'I started winning all his money,' Andreas continued over the interruption, 'and soon he wanted to get rid of me, because he didn't have enough money left over for cigarettes. He kept saying he wouldn't play any more, but what else is there to do on that Godforsaken mountain except watch the eagles circling their nests.'

'With that kind of trick I would have thought he'd send you to Evros,' I chimed in. Evros is the river marking the boundary between Greece and Turkey. It's considered the worst post possible. The soldiers spend much of their time stationed on the border guard houses nervously watching their Turkish counterparts across the river. It's dangerous duty, too, because the Turks are belligerent and shifty. Sometimes they shoot at Greek soldiers and pretend it was the Greeks who started it, just for sport. And if that is not enough, there is even less to do in Evros than in Kryoneri.

'You're right, but I also took care to get on his good side. I invented the other favourite pastime of the Kryoneri station,' Andreas said with a triumphant grin.

It seems the Kryoneri women wash clothes in a stream by the village. A few old men usually accompany them at a distance, to keep strangers away. Safe and away from prying eyes, the women bare their legs and dangle them in the stream after they work up a sweat beating and wringing the clothes. Some even take their dresses off and wade in, naked but for their soaked and cling-ing shifts, in broad daylight. Andreas tried to find a way to circle the guards and come up from behind, but you had to be a goat to do that.

'I was hiding as close as I could get without running into trouble, and I kept thinking to myself that they were just too far to be able to tell they were women, let alone whether they were pretty or not. And then I got the idea. I went back to the barracks and filled out a requisition form for a telescope, and I wired it to my buddy Haritoglou, who got this cushy job in requisitions because his father pimps for this general by the name of Paparas.

'Haritoglou and I had a good time in Kavalla together, and he owed me a big one. You see, I introduced him to this girl he was crazy about only she wouldn't give him the time of day. He used to pine and get this hangdog look on his face until I asked him one day, "What the hell is the matter with you?" So he says it's that girl Jenny. I follow her around, he says, and try to talk to her, and nothing happens, she won't even look my way, it's like I'm not ever there. So *I* follow Jenny, and of course I'm not a sap like Haritoglou, to beg for her attention and get her to think she's too high and mighty for me, oh no, I just bump into her, hard, by accident, and I flatten her on the ground, and then of course I have to make sure she is okay. So I buy her a lemonade to steady her on her feet, and I apologise, and I insist I must escort her home, the honour of the army demands it. So she asks who I am and I tell her my name and she says, "Vasilikos, you mean like the candy?" and she's talking of course about that big fat cat the chocolate manufacturer and her face lights up, so now I've got her number. No, I tell her, I wish, but no. I'm not rich. I don't even know any rich people except for this buddy of mine. Now those are riches, I tell her, you must have seen him around town, he's like this and like so. Now I see on her face that she knows who I'm talking about, but she won't let on. She just asks his name. Haritoglou, I tell her. So is his family rich, she asks. Well, his father is General Paparas, I tell her. So why is his name different, she asks, she's not as dim as she looks. He's the adopted son, I tell her. His mother lost her husband and got married to the general, and the general can't have children, it's a great tragedy, so he adopted Haritoglou, but Haritoglou was the dearly departed's only son, and the dearly departed was an only son, too, so the in-laws insisted that the kid keep his name. That's okay with the general, he's just happy to have someone he can call a son. So she swallows this whole! We get to her house and her mother opens the door and she's not too happy to see me with her, but I'm on my best behaviour and explain everything, and ask permission to visit later and see how my victim is doing and can I bring my friend Haritoglou with me? The mother wants to say no, but Jenny is no fool, she sticks her elbow gently in her mother's ribs, she shushes her, of course we can come, she'll be expecting us. And as the door closes she is already explaining to her mother that this is a chance of a lifetime.

'So that same evening we show up, showered and shaved and carrying candy and flowers. Jenny and her mom keep talking about the general, and I've briefed Haritoglou but he's too nervous to play along, so I do it for him, I talk about the general and assure them there is no way he will ever have children of his own, old war wound, got him his promotions but took something out of the man. By the time we left Kavalla, Haritoglou had had some fun times with Jenny, and all thanks to me. So when he gets my wire in Athens he's only too happy to send the telescope, state of the art, to Kryoneri, never mind that Kryoneri doesn't rate such fine equipment. I don't know what he wrote to justify the requisition, maybe he pretended he was sending it somewhere else and it got lost on the way.

'Whatever he did we had that telescope in just a few weeks, and we hid behind the bushes and watched the women come in and out of the stream. They were dogs, even the young ones, that Godforsaken rock breeds nothing but the misshapen and the ugly, but it beats chasing the goats, and that's the only other female mammals up there.'

Andreas spoke right through the meal, punctuating his words with greasy fingers, chuckling at his own inventiveness. We all listened to him, rapt. I was in awe. He could leave this village that was all he knew and make his way in the world, get Jenny to pay attention to Haritoglou, spin a fancy story out of bare bones of truth, become the pet of his fierce commanding officer, cheat all his money away from him, and still land in the cushy post of military chauffeur to the top brass in Thessaloniki, by finding a way around the watchful eyes of shotgun-toting guardians of the women near his base. He may have no morals, I thought, but he gets the best in life anyway. I had to remind myself not to let my admiration overshadow the sense of disapproving morality that surely was the only fitting response to this tale of con artistry.

My uncle had no such qualms. He laughed and snorted his way through Andreas's story, drank much of the wine and kept refilling my brother's glass. At the end of the meal the two of them stayed in the yard, talking and laughing like in the old days. It seemed they had forgotten both the scene over my uncle's money and the compulsory labour at the bakery that had robbed my brother of his last carefree summer before entering the world of adults.

We didn't see Andreas much at first. He would only come up once every week or two, always on a Sunday, stay till eight or so and then make his way back to the city again. He and Pavlos were spending all their free time alone, and even though Pavlos was in university they must still have found much in common, because they were inseparable.

I turned fifteen that year, and finally there was a peach fuzz on my face. I kept running my hand over my cheeks so Katerina would notice. She had been very quiet since the episode with Theophanes. She seemed to shrink into herself again, become withdrawn and somehow absent. She went through all her chores same as always, but much of the time she looked like a sleepwalker. I had no explanation for this, because even my uncle seemed to have let up on her a little, and caused big scenes less often than usual, and only when his drinking happened to exceed what had become his norm. More and more he seemed to have come to care for her a little, and now he praised her more often, and many times had a tender word for her. Still, he took every opportunity to remind her that his gentler behaviour was entirely dependent on her remaining obedient and 'not putting on airs and thinking you know best'.

Andreas lent me his razor for my first shave. With his short stubby brush we whipped up lather in his shaving cup and spread it on my face. Then deftly, proudly, I pulled the razor over the foam. Andreas slapped some stinging lotion on my face when I was done, and I had only one cut to complain of. Andreas stuck a bit of toilet paper on it, and with this badge of manhood, flushed and proud, I stepped into the family room, where Katerina was plumping up the pillows on the sofa. I didn't say anything, it was not fitting, but Andreas did.

'Look, Katerina, this little rooster is finally getting his plumage. Tell the girls to beware.'

'Leave me alone,' I said and blushed, but I was secretly pleased that he had drawn attention to my rite of passage and announced it to the one person who mattered most in the world. Perhaps I got a little insufferable about it all. Twice a week I would stand for a long time in front of the small round mirror hanging in the kitchen and carefully go over every millimetre of my skin, shaving away every little hair I was so proud of. I'd throw the soapy water in the sink and never rinse it, so Katerina could see the hair. I am a man, I was saying. Soon now, be patient.

Near Christmas, Pavlos met Litsa. Andreas said she was short, plump, juicy and a tease. She laughed and talked nonstop, never took anything seriously and always moved quickly, darting about in a dreadful hurry, as though time was never enough. She was a hairdresser. Pavlos fell in love with her on first sight, and courted her with single-minded purpose.

'That minx has made a fool out of him, there's no mistake about it,' Andreas would sigh over his buddy.

Litsa led Pavlos a merry dance. One day she was nice to him, the next day she had no time. One day she would agree to meet him in the park, and the next she would cancel and tell him she was just too busy. She smiled and flirted with him, but she was careful never to be alone with him, telling him that her three brothers would be furious and might do him harm if they ever learned that Pavlos was after her. Pavlos was at his wits' end. After two months of this bait and switch, he finally told her he was serious and wanted to marry her. In vain Andreas told him he was falling victim to the oldest trick in the book.

'Women don't want to see you losing your head over them. Give them too much and they will sit on your back and ride you like a mule. You've got to stay aloof, you've got to keep your head.'

Pavlos listened, but kept right on standing outside the beauty shop waiting for a glimpse of Litsa. He wrote her poetry, he sent her gifts. His parents were furious. Who was this two-bit hairdresser that ruled their son? How dare she interfere with his studies? Pavlos had another five years to go before he would become a lawyer, and then he had to go in the army. He was too young. They used to complain about the way Pavlos and Andreas would run around with different women every week, using army cars and jeeps, running the risk of getting into trouble for using military vehicles to escort their whores around Thessaloniki and its environs, but this was worse. This was serious. In Greece all parents want their daughters wed and their sons single. Only when the bride has money, a house of her own or a business to take in the groom, do parents relent and accept a daughter-in-law without too much grumbling. They forbade Pavlos to go to Litsa's house and announce his intentions.

Pavlos lay down on his bed in his parents' home and wouldn't get up. He cried and refused food and wouldn't talk to them. Finally they relented. Better a married son than a dead bachelor. But only an engagement. No marriage until Pavlos finished school. Litsa's parents were not ecstatic at the idea, but they had not as much to complain about. Five years is a long time. But then again, Pavlos would be a lawyer and his parents had money and a shop, and connections that could land him into the safety of a government job. A solid middle-class position with potential. Who were they after all? Litsa's father was a construction worker. Her mother a fat housewife who never finished sixth grade. Their tiny house in one of the humblest neighbourhoods of Thessaloniki was jammed full with their six kids. Litsa slept with her two sisters, and her brothers slept in the tiny living-room, stinking up the place with the sweat of their own labour, working for a pittance with the crews that built the boxy apartment buildings going up all over the city. They gave their blessing. But the engagement would be formal, announced in the papers. And Pavlos could visit Litsa all he wanted to in her own house, but no sleeping together with the tacit family approval Greek couples who were formally pledged to each other often enjoyed. Her parents figured that this way, if Pavlos changed his mind, their daughter would be intact and they could still sue for breach of promise to marry, a charge which, if proven, could result in a judgement forcing the inconstant fiancé to provide a dowry for the girl, giving her worldly goods with which to ensnare someone else, now that her reputation was compromised.

Andreas lost Pavlos to Litsa and love. He had no liking for Litsa's family, least of all the three dull and slow-witted brothers who had none of Litsa's brightness.

'I don't know where she gets it,' he would say ruefully. 'You can't believe what that house is like. Except for her, they're the dimmest people you ever saw, plodding like cattle through their day, always in a bad mood, always complaining. It's like Litsa got all the personality, too much if you ask me, and left none for the rest of them. If her mother wasn't such a gorgon I'd say it was someone other than the father who sowed that seed.'

Abandoned by his friend, who was either with Litsa or talking about her, Andreas started spending more time in Panorama. His chauffering duties were light. His commanding officer was not a demanding man. Andreas once again managed to insinuate himself into the good graces of his superior.

'You've got to figure out what people want and give it to them, George,' he would tell me. 'Now Besios is not a bad sort. But he's short and ugly, and he's shy. He wants women but he doesn't know how to go about it. He figures he's too ugly, so what would they want with him. So he approaches them, when he does, with this look on his face like he's apologising for taking their time. The man needs confidence. Women don't care about looks. They want to see if a man has a backbone. Act like you're God's gift and they believe you. So I'm building his self-esteem. Would you believe it, when I first came here he had never had a woman yet, except for flea-bitten whores from the wharf? He'd go down there once a week or so, and wait for one to approach him, he wouldn't even choose for himself, and pay his two bits so they would lift their skirts in an alley somewhere and let him fuck them standing up, and he would thank them afterwards, for I don't know what. But I took care of him. I know some girls, some regular girls, not whores, but the next best thing, really. They work in the factories. They want nice things. A pair of stockings, some perfume. They figure if it's done discreetly, who's to know. Pavlos is hardly ever in his room any more before eleven. I threw a little party there. Got some wine, some

173

barbecued chicken, a few little gifts, and got two of the girls to come over. I told the one of them what to do. So when she sees Besios she acts like she's in love. She pours his wine, she rubs against him, she puts her hand on his thigh. We run out of wine and I take the other with me. We go to get more wine. So we leave Besios alone with Areti and Areti shows him Paradise. And when I make it back he's a changed man. He's finally fucked on the horizontal and now he thinks I walk on water, because I know women who will bed him down without money. You just have to figure out what they want and then give it to them, and what most men want is either one woman or many. And the ones who want many are the lucky ones.'

I listened raptly to these lectures. They were educational. But I knew Andreas was not giving away his secret. Sure, figure out what they want and give it to them. But to give it, you had to first get it, and that's where the whole thing fell apart. The magic of Andreas wasn't the giving, it was the getting.

He never asked about Artemis, never mentioned her, but then he didn't have to. She was right down the road. Still dragging her foot behind her. Never turning his way. At an age when other girls were looking to get married, Artemis was looking nowhere but straight down in front of her, to avoid rocks that might upset her balance. I noticed that in all of Andreas's stories about women and sex, decent girls were absent. Andreas had learned his lesson, I figured. He was sowing his wild oats in the unfenced fields. Or maybe he just knew better than to boast to me of more seductions of poor defenceless girls.

14

Rite of Passage

The return of my brother to Thessaloniki lightened the atmosphere around the house. He didn't live with us of course, but thanks to the patronage of Besios, he was able to come and go pretty much as he pleased. Whenever he could get away from the barracks, he slept in his old room with me. Grandpa had been installed long ago in my parents' old bedroom. His failing wits made him the only member of the household who could stand to sleep in there. There was no question of Katerina moving upstairs, of course, because it was hardly seemly for an unrelated young female to share a house with three lone males. The fact that the downstairs did not communicate with the upstairs, so that you had to leave the house, go down the steps and turn the corner to reach her door, made her room a separate house almost, where she could have our protection, but none of the gossip that would have accompanied any other arrangement.

My uncle was on his best behaviour when Andreas was around. He did not raise his voice or swear at Katerina, and he didn't make scenes. Part of this was surely the fact that Andreas jollied him and made him laugh with his stories of women conquered and army highjinks. Another part may have been that he was afraid to play the bully in front of Andreas. Whatever the reason, Katerina's life was easier and I was glad to have Andreas back, even though he adopted a flirtatious air with Katerina, and smiled and winked at her as he strolled in and out of our lives in his usual high spirits. Of course, Andreas was never home when my uncle sat down to do the accounts and interrogate Katerina about what she did and how much she spent. At those times his voice alternated between thinly-concealed menace and the wheedling, sly tone he used when he wanted to seem her friend, who had her best interests at heart. This hurts me more than it hurts you, he seemed to be saying, but I'm doing it for your own good.

I continued to grow that winter. My peach fuzz was getting thicker, my voice was sliding lower and my feet seemed to absorb all the food I was eating, because they were growing faster than we could buy shoes for them. I examined them with alarm every night when I sat on my bed to take off my socks.

'It's a sign you'll grow tall,' Andreas assured me one night when he was sleeping over. Actually, he was wrong. It was just a sign that all my life I would be a short man with outsize feet.

'And you know what else they say,' he continued when he saw the look of hope in my face.

'What?'

'You really don't know? Then maybe it's not true and it's just a saying,' he teased me.

'What? Tell me!'

'They say men with big feet have big dicks. So what do you say, is it true?' I was embarrassed at this. I turned off the lights and quickly climbed under the covers.

'So come on, George, how big is it?' he persisted in the dark.

Still no answer.

'Hey, you can tell me. I'm your brother.'

'Goodnight, Andreas.'

'So I take it it's small, huh? Don't worry, little brother. All you have to do is make sure you beat off every single day, at least five times, and it will grow. Just make sure you pull on it real hard.'

'Leave me alone!' I was sick with embarrassment. Masturbation was my secret. I couldn't talk about it. I couldn't even think about it. It always made me feel guilty and soiled. Thoughts and images of Katerina inevitably accompanied my furtive ecstasy, thoughts and images that I tried to chase away, because I didn't want Katerina to be a part of my self-abuse, not even in thought. But then I'd see her every day, going about in her quiet way, and often my erection would threaten to burst my shorts and rear its ugly head in front of her. Every night I fell asleep with thoughts of her running through my mind. Many times I dreamed the pillow I was hugging to my chest was her body. Every wet dream I ever had starred Katerina.

'Okay, so you're embarrassed.' Andreas wouldn't let up. 'You don't have to be embarrassed. I'm your older brother. I've been where you've been. What you need is a woman to set you straight and relieve your mind of all your worries.'

Yeah, Andreas, I need a woman. And where do I find one? Do I get a little girl to fall in love with me and then blackmail her into giving me her body the way you did? I seethed, but I said nothing.

'George, I can get you a woman. You just say the word and I'll get you laid. You just tell me if you're ready and I'll have you between a pair of thighs like you haven't even dreamed of, and you can ride yourself into Paradise, little brother. I know this working girl, this Arletta who specialises in virgins. She will pluck your cherry and you'll love it.'

I threw my pillow at him just as he was finishing his sentence. I heard the plop of its landing, and I heard his muffled laughter.

'Georgie, you're such a prude.'

'And you're such a lech!'

'He speaks, my God he speaks! Listen, shrimp, stop getting so worked up. What the hell is the matter with you? Your friend Nikos would give his nuts to have this kind of offer! What are you, afraid? I'm telling you, Arletta will take care of everything. You don't have to know anything. She knows it all. Oh, how she knows it! Hey, she likes them young! Young and clean and inexperienced. Better than some drunken sailor stinking up the place with his garlic breath and pulling on his lifeless prick to get it to stand up and do the job.'

'I'm not afraid! I just don't want to.'

'What do you mean you don't want to? What are you, a pansy?'

'I'm not a pansy! I just don't want to!'

'So what do you think will happen later on, when you get married or you get a girlfriend that wants to? What will you do? You'll just walk into that room knowing nothing and what will you do? There you'll be on your wedding night, for God's sake, wondering which hole you're supposed to plug.'

'You're disgusting!'

'Georgie, you're acting like a sap! How do you think I started, huh? Uncle Demetres took me by the hand when I was fifteen, and brought me to see Arletta. She took me inside and let me do it, and that was that! He paid for it, too. Said it was his duty since our father was too much the village paragon to do his duty to his firstborn son.

178

Said Grandpa was no better, either, and he had to fend for himself when he was a young man.'

The news didn't shock me. I knew that many fathers took their sons to whores whenever they felt the boy was ready. It was considered a way to keep the boy from homosexuality, which many in Greece considered the outcome of frustrated adolescent sex drive. I had no idea my uncle had done this for Andreas, but the news certainly fit the participants to a tee.

'You sleep on it, Georgie, but I'm telling you,' Andreas's relentless voice continued, 'you need a woman. Beating off is just going to get you callouses. And I don't mean on your hand, either.'

He finally shut up and soon he was breathing deeply. I just lay in the dark, with my eyes closed determinedly, wishing myself asleep. My mind would not co-operate. I kept thinking of my wedding night and Katerina. We would both walk into the bedroom, we would kiss, I would nuzzle her breasts, my prick would stand up straight, just like it was doing now, and then what? The only road map I had was the long-ago scenes between my brother and Artemis. I knew the motion well, I knew how bodies would move, how the woman could be on top or on the bottom, that I could wrap my legs around her waist and drive into her repeatedly, or just grind away in circles. But where exactly did the penis go? When my brother would take his in his hand and guide it inside, what was it he was guiding it in? Frustrated, insecure, unbearably inflamed, I tossed and turned, ground my erection in the mattress and finally fell asleep near dawn. I dreamed of Katerina, naked and waiting on the bed, her thighs open in invitation, but there was nothing between them.

*   *   *

In April, Besios had to travel to Athens, and he pulled whatever strings he had to take Andreas with him.

'He doesn't want to be without me, that man!' Andreas laughed when he came to bid us good-bye. 'He knows that if I'm not around he'll never get a woman to look at him sideways. We'll be gone a month. Can you guys get along without me?'

Andreas was joking, but it wasn't a funny joke. For a month there was no calming influence on my uncle, who got drunker than ever and had Katerina on her knees apologising for breaking a worthless bottle of wine when she was trying to pour him a glass.

It was with immense relief that I saw my brother enter the yard one afternoon, carrying two paper bags.

'I'm back, and boy have I got the goodies for all of you!' he shouted.

Andreas had brought us gifts. A Swiss Army knife for my uncle, a pair of real American Levis for me.

'And for you, Katerina,' he announced dramatically, 'this!' He whipped out the last package with a flourish. Then he opened it in front of her, and took out a length of cloth. The reddest, softest, plushest length of red cloth.

We all gasped at the brilliance of the colour. Katerina was still wearing black, just like she had the first day I saw her. At first she was in mourning for her parents. Then for my mother, and last for my father. A year after my father's death she was still wearing black be- cause it was all my uncle would provide. There was no question of course of her asking for money to buy clothes. Once in a while, however, my uncle would bring her a dress or a skirt, always in black, always loose fitting and drab, perhaps to keep Theophanes and others like him away.

'And these,' Andreas continued, 'are magazines with

the latest styles, so you can have Kyra Toula sew you the best. I'll pay her myself to sew it for you.'

Katerina fingered the cloth silently, but I could tell she was excited. Her eyes shone. I felt a small stab of jealousy. First he provided her protection from my uncle, without even knowing it. Now he was giving her what any young woman might want, a new dress. I was doomed to never give her anything, except my best intentions.

'This was the best one in the lot, I think' said Andreas, wrapping the red length around her. 'You're such a pretty little thing, but enough black, forget the black! No wonder you always look so pale and lost in these rags you wear. This will make a new woman out of you.'

My uncle had sat quietly throughout the whole little scene.

'More like a new whore,' he grumbled now. 'This colour is cheap! She'll have every randy goat in town following her home.'

Andreas ignored him. He was too happy with himself.

'You'll be the prettiest girl in the village with this on. And I'll bet you'll smile more, too. Won't you?'

'Thank you, Andreas. It's wonderful! But it's so expensive. You must take it back,' Katerina said with a fearful glance at my uncle.

'Nonsense!' he replied. 'It has already been cut, and anyway I can't go back to Athens to return it. The thing is, I got it at a great price. There was this cousin of Besios who had just returned from America with all kinds of things, and he was selling them and giving them away to friends and acquaintances. Besios took me to him and explained what a friend I've been to him, and he gave me the stuff for a song.'

'More likely for a lay with one of your whores,' my uncle interjected and, with one of his moods creasing his forehead, he got up from his chair. 'Katerina, get me a clean shirt, I've got to go,' he added and he went inside the house, Katerina following him.

'Is that how you got the stuff?' I asked Andreas.

'Why do you listen to that old drunk?'

'Well, is it?' I insisted.

'Look, George, how I got it and how I paid for it has nothing to do with anything. Katerina needs new clothes. She can't keep going around the village in those old things she wears, it makes us look bad not to dress her properly once in a while.'

'And since when did you become so concerned with what people think? If it's not right for Katerina to dress in her old clothes, then it's also not right for her to wear whore clothes!'

I spoke these words in a querulous tone, but Andreas refused to start a fight.

'Georgie,' he joked, 'I think the lack of a woman is making the cum back up in your system and cloud your head. This is not whore clothing, it's good American polyester. Katerina will be pretty as a picture in it, and if Besios's cousin got laid for them, who's to know? Come on now, did you think about my offer? Do you want me to take you to Arletta? The offer still stands!'

Yes, of course I had thought about it. Obsessively. For months. To penetrate the mystery. To solve the riddle. To prepare myself for Katerina. The idea both excited me and disgusted me, and I kept returning to it. Wouldn't this finally make me a man? Wouldn't this get me closer to my goal? With Arletta under my belt, I would finally know everything a man could know. The experience was bound to change me in some indefinable way, give me confidence, make Katerina notice me as the man I was becoming instead of the powerless little brother I seemed to be. The clothes Andreas got for Katerina by pimping would look beautiful on Katerina anyway. Going to Arletta was the same thing. It was mean and debasing, but the end result would be good. Wouldn't it?

It took me two weeks to steel myself to bring up the subject, but finally I did. In the impenetrable dark that followed the dousing of the light in our room, I finally, haltingly, told Andreas that, if he was still willing, I wanted to go to see Arletta. Casually, softly, without a fuss, Andreas's voice agreed in the darkness to set it up.

He picked a Sunday for my initiation. He told me to wear my America jeans and he instructed me to meet him at the bus station in Thessaloniki. Nervous and sweating, I boarded the bus that would take me to my assignation. The half-hour trip took no time at all. I told the bus driver to let me know when we reached the station Andreas had named, and he did. It was five in the afternoon when the driver nodded in my direction. I got off the bus, into the quiet deserted streets of the city. At this hour in the middle of the summer, everyone would be asleep.

There was a bench under an awning meant to shield bus passengers from the sun or rain while they waited. Since there was no sign of Andreas, I settled on that bench to wait. I was melting in the heat, but I waited patiently. After the first few minutes I wondered if I had the right stop. Did the bus driver nod to indicate this was my stop, or did he mean something else? No, he would have stopped me from getting off the bus if that were so. Well, then, did he hear wrong when I told him what stop I wanted? Anxiously I got up and peered down the street trying to see if I could make out the next stop. Maybe Andreas was there now, wondering how I had managed to get lost. By now worry, nervousness and the afternoon heat were staining my shirt. The American jeans felt hot and heavy. I had never in my life felt less like having a woman.

When another bus traveller joined me at the stop, I was relieved. Now I can ask him if this is the right stop, I thought.

'Why, you're George Vasilikos,' he said, before I had a chance to speak. 'Yiannis's son. What are you doing here?'

Now I recognised him. Kyr Ilias, from Panorama.

'I was going to the stop across the street to wait for the bus,' he continued. 'I'm going back up. I was here to see my daughter and her new baby, and then I saw you and I thought to myself, I know that boy. He's one of us. So what are you doing down here in the middle of the afternoon?'

'Meeting my brother,' I said.

First he assured me that I had the right stop. Then he told me everything about his daughter, her no-good husband who had taken her away from the village and brought her to this evil city so that he had to spend twenty drachmas to see his own granddaughter; her monstrous mother-in-law who lived with them and resented his visits as though this wasn't his own flesh and blood ironing her son's shirts and scrubbing at his dirty collars; his son-in-law had the dirtiest neck in the land, his poor daughter's fingers were red and raw doing the laundry, and she had to wash the monster's clothes, too, and God only knows how dirty *her* neck was. He went on and on, and I just let his words wash over me, limp with heat, exhausted from worry. Finally the bus to Panorama stopped across the street and Kyr Ilias crossed the steaming pavement to get on.

It was six o'clock now. A few people were beginning

to appear on the street. Most were out of town, near the sea or on the mountain, seeking water or a breeze to relieve them of the heat. How much longer should I wait? Should I take the next bus up? I thought of the cool acacia shade in our yard with longing. Not to have to be tested today, not to have to take off my sweaty clothes in front of a strange woman with all-knowing eyes, not to have to worry that the sun had melted my privates.

Finally, Andreas appeared.

'Sorry, George, I overslept. But not to worry. Everything is set up and you'll thank me for the rest of your life! What a lucky son of a bitch you are. Here, hop in! Boy, you look like a drowned rat! Did you bring everything? Hah! Just joking. Nothing to bring!'

I sat next to him in the jeep as he barrelled down the empty streets. Soon we were heading for the waterfront. He finally stopped in front of a small taverna.

'Is this it?' I asked.

'Can't wait, can you? No, this isn't it. We're meeting Besios here. Can't let you have your first woman without proper fortification first, now can we?'

He saw the dubious look in my eyes.

'Trust me,' he said.

We joined Besios, who was sitting outside in the shade sipping his coffee, his short, skinny legs stretched out in front of him. We ordered coffee, too. I sat stewing with impatience to get the task over with. Andreas and Besios were talking about people they knew, and they seemed in no hurry. When they finished their coffee, they ordered ouzo, some cucumber and anchovies, a few meatballs. Andreas poured me a glass, too.

'This will do you a world of good, little brother.'

'Your brother doesn't talk much, does he?' Besios said.

'Sure he does, he's a regular chatterbox. But today is

a very special day for him, and he's lost his voice. He's putting all his energy elsewhere.'

Don't tell him, oh God, don't tell him!

'Oh, yeah? What's so special?'

Just don't tell him. Just this one thing. Don't tell him!

'I'm taking him to Arletta for his first taste of Paradise. My little brother is becoming a man today.'

'Now that is special! So, little brother, how old are you?'

'Sixteen,' I muttered.

'Fifteen, actually,' Andreas corrected.

Now I really felt like a fool. Only little boys lied about their age.

'Fifteen and seven months,' I blurted before I could stop myself. A big fool!

'You must have some pair of balls, little guy, to want a woman at your age.'

'George is a regular fucking machine. I couldn't hold him back. You take me to a woman now, he told me. Or else I'll fuck every girl in the village, and the bitches, too, and the cows, and you'll never hear the end of it! There's no holding back my little brother!'

'I am impressed,' Besios laughed. 'Here, George, have another one. It's too early for whores, they haven't warmed up yet. Give them some time to loosen up so they don't scream when you do them, because that might bring the cops running and you won't have time to finish!'

The heat was still heavy. My embarrassment was even heavier. I downed my second ouzo under a barrage of dull, worn jokes delivered by my brother and Besios. Andreas kept feeding me morsels of food.

'If you don't eat with all this ouzo you'll get too drunk,' he told me.

'Nonsense!' Besios said. 'It's only old goats like you and

me who lose their starch if they drink too much. A young goat like him can fuck even if he is unconscious! Here George, have another one. To young pricks! Bottoms up!'

Drinking was having its effect on me. I got bolder. I forgot my embarrassment. What was there to be embarrassed about? This was the man who, until he met my brother, had never had a woman except standing up in an alley. Of course he couldn't let the subject of my mission drop. He was jealous. I started laughing with them. I told a few jokes, too. The three of us sat at that table for hours, until the sky began to darken, and the waterfront was filled with people walking up and down its length in groups, breathing in the sea breeze that had come to cool the city.

Finally Andreas indicated it was time to go. I got up eagerly. Give me the whore. Give me a thousand whores. I'll split them like logs, I'll nail them to the bed.

It was only when I got to the jeep that the world started spinning. My hand grasped the hood of the jeep. My legs buckled. Andreas and Besios were laughing hysterically over some joke. They didn't realise what I was about until I bent over and retched miserably.

'Oh, God, I think he's sick,' I heard my brother say.

'Ah, he'll get over it. It's just his stomach, nothing wrong with his balls!'

Andreas put his arm around me.

'I want to lie down,' I whispered.

Andreas got me in the jeep. Besios fetched a glass of water from the taverna.

'Snap out of it, Georgie,' he said. 'This is your night, and you've got to get over this. What you need is some coffee and some food.'

He brought some coffee from the taverna. Then he

bought some gyros from a waterfront vendor. The smell nauseated me, but I ate it. I drank the coffee. I felt better.

'What do you think, little brother, should we go?'

I was still drunk.

'Sure,' I answered.

The whore house was in the seamier side of the waterfront. The streets were narrow here, the buildings old boarded-up warehouses or tavernas with sailors at the rickety tables, paper patching the windows where the glass had been broken. A flabby woman with too much lipstick and eye make-up was sitting on a chair placed against a wall, one ankle crossed over the knee, dark hair plainly visible in the cleft between her legs. One of Besios's stand-up whores, I thought. She snapped her gum as we passed.

Andreas finally parked the jeep. He led me and Besios up a narrow staircase. The place looked deserted. When we got to a door, he knocked. Once, stop, then two more times. The door opened with a chain in place. An eye peered at us. The door closed and then immediately swung wide open.

'Hello, Andreas. Come on in.'

The voice was husky, as low as a man's. It belonged to a tall, bloated woman in her forties. She had an enormous mass of dry blonde hair, eyes lined in kohl, the reddest mouth I ever saw. She was wearing a sheer yellow shift that must have seen better days. Her nipples were clearly visible through the thin material, and they were pointing to the floor. The bush between her legs cast a shadow, and her stomach was in two rolls, one resting comfortably on top of the other.

She ushered us into a plain room with dim lighting. There was an ancient horsehair sofa, a table with a ripped lace tablecloth, a radio, two pictures of women in the nude, one bathing, the other fingering herself.

'You're awfully early. You're the first tonight.'

'No sense getting sloppy seconds,' Andreas said with a smile. She didn't seem to mind the crack.

'There's only me and Arletta here. Who wants whom?' she asked as she led us to the sofa and offered cigarettes all around.

So this isn't Arletta, I thought with relief.

'Just my brother, here. I brought him for Arletta.'

The woman bent over me. Her breasts flapped in my direction and a sour smell enveloped me. The gyros ground uneasily in my stomach.

'He's a young one,' she said, and I could see now that several of her teeth were missing at the back. 'I'll tell Arletta.'

She disappeared behind a curtain. Andreas winked at me.

'You okay?' he asked.

'Yes, I'm fine,' I answered, wondering if it were true.

The woman came back and proffered her hand. Her nails were long and painted red. They curled at the tips, like the claws of a bird or a cat. She led me through the curtain.

'Give 'em hell, little brother,' I heard Besios say after me.

We came to a door beyond the curtain.

'Just go in,' the woman said and stood there looking at me.

My hand went to reach for my hair, to pat it down. I willed it to reach for the door knob instead.

The room inside was small and windowless. It had a bed, a wash stand and basin and a chair. A woman was sitting on the side of the bed. She turned and got up as I walked in. She was a small woman, skinny as a rail and bleached blonde like the other one. The skin on her face was coarse, and I couldn't guess at her age. She had a wide mouth, a big nose and small eyes placed close together. Arletta is ugly, I thought, and I tried not to let my disappointment show. How to get out of here. Then she smiled in my direction. It was a beautiful smile, a smile full of kindness and understanding.

'Oh, my, but you're handsome,' she said in a voice as sweet and melting as honey. 'Aren't I the lucky one!'

She took me by the hand, helped me out of my clothes. My prick was small and shrivelled. I was still feeling unsteady from the ouzo. With deft, sure movements she began to wash me. In the warm suds and her hands, my cock swelled and I swayed in her direction.

'Easy, my man,' she said.

She led me to the bed, she lay me down. Then she took off her dress, her bra, her black panties. She leaned over me and offered a small pear-shaped breast to my mouth. Then she settled herself over me and rubbed her body down the whole length of mine. She stroked my leg. She straddled me. She put my hand between her legs and rubbed it there. She was taking me on a guided tour of the female body. She separated one of my fingers and pushed it inside. The wet warmth parted, and I groaned. Then she took my hand away and slid down on top of me. She moved once, twice, three times, and I felt myself coming apart at the seams. Just as a cry escaped from me, she cried, too. Rode me fast and desperate. Then she fell on me.

When she washed me again, she smiled once more.

'You are the best I ever had, honey. You are really

something. Whatever woman gets you, she ought to get on her knees and thank the good Lord.'

When I walked out of that room my stomach was cramped as though it were filled with rocks, a headache had lodged in my skull and my throat was scratched raw from the cigarettes I had smoked with Andreas and Besios. Still, I walked out of that room feeling ten feet tall, knowing for a fact that I was the best there ever was. I joined my brother on the horsehair sofa.

'Everything okay?' he asked.

'Yeah,' I grinned. 'Where's Besios?'

'Well, he's never one to waste an opportunity. Here, have a cigarette.'

By the time Andreas and I had finished our smoke, Besios and the fat whore joined us. She saw us to the door.

'Come back again, any time,' she said.

'Thanks, Katerina. Bye!'

Katerina! The name exploded in my mind. That fat, vulgar woman, the one who had done God knows what with Besios of the stand-up whores, had the same name as my wife-to-be, my gentle, pure Katerina. I felt nausea crowding my throat again.

'That wasn't bad at all,' said Besios, rubbing his hands together as we walked back to the jeep.

'Katerina is a fat beast,' my brother said. 'I don't know how you could go with her after the sweet things I have introduced you to.'

'Turn out the lights, and they're all the same, my friend,' Besios laughed. 'Anyway, those cute young things expect me to be grateful. But take a woman like Katerina and give her a good one and her eyes roll back and she tells you, 'You're the best, honey!'

'They say that to everybody, Besios. Wake up. Not even George here would take that kind of talk seriously!'

In the jeep, I had a hard time keeping the gyros in my stomach, where it belonged. My head hurt and I wanted to be alone. Andreas and Besios wanted to go drinking with me and talk about my experience. I just wanted to go home. I had to see Katerina and remind myself that none of this sordidness had anything to do with her. Arletta's smile was not enough to hide the shame any more. They left me at the bus stop after I refused steadily for half an hour to go with them. On the bus I waited anxiously for the trip to end. At home, I rushed to Katerina. She was in the kitchen washing dishes. Her lips were pale, her face shiny and clear, her body slender but supple. She smiled when she saw me, and her smile was beautiful not because it transformed ugliness, but because it was as pure as she was.

15

An Immigrant Visits

How did he do it? With all the rules and strictures laid down by her father, with her three brothers and two sisters always under foot, with her mountain of a mother always sitting on the run-down tasselled sofa of their family-room sighing and rubbing her fat ankles and complaining of pain in her feet, how did Pavlos manage to get Litsa pregnant?

'How did you do it?' Andreas asked Pavlos who was sitting in our yard. The trees had begun to bloom, the air had the fragrance of spring and the sky was the brilliant crystal blue that only Greece offers. Andreas was sprawled between two chairs. Ever since he finished his military service, moved back to the house and started working at the bakery, he made a great show of how tired he'd get. After work he would install himself in as comfortable a chair as he could find, pull up another one to put up his tired feet, and smoke and drink his coffee with repeated sighs and the look of a man who had spent a week digging ditches and hauling rocks, rather than shovelling bread in the oven and counting change.

'They can't watch us all the time, my friend. I can stay up late, because I don't have to get up in the morning like they do. And I can be very quiet. Anyway, her father snores so loud you could do it with Chrysa, and still nobody could hear!'

At this they both started laughing. I didn't understand. 'What do you mean?' I asked.

They paid no attention. They kept on laughing and Andreas started making this high, screeching sound that got them both laughing even harder.

'Chrysa is this woman we both know,' Andreas said when he could finally speak again, 'who, how can I explain this, lets you know how much she appreciates what you're doing to her by letting out this screech when she gets to the last lap. Heeeeehoow! She is louder than a siren, and if you don't know it ahead of time you're in for a surprise. Pavlos here got so scared he'd hurt her that he dropped everything, including his boner, and hightailed it out of the room with his trousers around his ankles.'

'And at the door I got all tangled up and fell down.'

'And there was Chrysa inside, going, "Pavlos, come back, come back!"'

They started laughing again and I laughed with them.

'Except this isn't funny,' Pavlos finally said when we had all sobered up.

Pavlos's parents were livid. They were afraid of something like that. Pavlos had another four years to go for his degree and then two and a half years in the military. This was no time for a wedding. Besides, they had hoped that in the years it took Pavlos to finish, he would forget about his little hairdresser and find a better girl to marry, someone with a bit of money and maybe a house to her name.

Litsa may have been afraid of the same thing. She may have decided that there was not much time, and she had to go for the big play while Pavlos was still head over heals with her. He had been begging her to let him make love to her, and she had steadfastly refused. But once her mind was made up, she finally let him, and this was the predictable outcome.

When Pavlos told his family, you would have thought he had announced he had brain cancer. His mother fainted straight away, and when they revived her with smelling salts and cold compresses she started pulling her hair, banging her forehead with her fists and crying endless tears. She fell to her knees and begged God to make Litsa lose the baby. His father paced up and down looking apoplectic, and muttered about a future lost and a young man's life wasted, as though he had to bury Pavlos six feet under the ground instead of getting him married to the woman he loved. At first he refused to agree to a wedding. Pavlos stopped eating again and stopped going to his classes. His parents were scared, but his mother wanted to wait to see if maybe Litsa was lying. She counselled patience.

Tired and weak from not eating, frustrated by their wait-and-see attitude, Pavlos decided to change tactics. He announced he was quitting school and moving out to live with his in-laws. He would marry Litsa and renounce his parents, he said in a ringing voice over the Sunday meal. He then grabbed the family table complete with platters of roast lamb for Sunday dinner and tipped it over, sending everything crashing to the ground.

Reluctantly, grudgingly, his parents gave in and agreed to set the wedding date. They consented to take in the couple in their own home while Pavlos was still attending school. They demanded, however, that Litsa's family contribute to the support of their daughter and the baby. This was impossible. It was Litsa who provided money to her household instead of the other way around. Her leaving the house would actually cut her family's income instead of lightening its load. Pavlos's parents knew that, and in the mean-spirited mood that their dashed hopes for their son had placed them, had tried to force the old construction worker into a corner, by insisting on a financial contribution. They wanted to make him lose face, because they saw Litsa's condition as a family ploy to take advantage of the richer family their daughter had managed to hook into.

The old construction worker refused to be cowed. Far from being humbled and admitting his limited means, he took the high moral road. He answered that it was their son who seduced his daughter, so they had to provide everything. He had already sacrificed his honour. He would not countenance immorality, nor would he reward shameless behaviour in his own house, by providing support for the two sinners. It was Pavlos's parents who had neglected to teach their son restraint, and it was they who should pay to set matters straight. Fotini, Pavlos's mother, countered that it was up to the girl to keep her knees together. This was the more popular view on who had to put the brakes on sexual activity, but Kyr Stathis refused to acknowledge it. Instead, he insisted that since Pavlos had taken advantage of his hospitality and seduced his daughter in his own home, the fault was all his. He flatly refused to pay for the wedding.

Pavlos's parents complained to everyone they saw about their in-laws' stinginess and poverty, their rough manners and crude talk, their shameless, scheming daughter, but they had no alternative other than to pay for everything to be done first class. It was that or get their son married on a shoestring, as though he were no better than the son of a shepherd, instead of the only child of a prosperous merchant.

'Just wait till she comes to my house,' Pavlos's mother, Kyra Fotini, told Katerina when she stopped at our house for coffee one day. 'She'll curse the day she trapped my boy with her cheap tricks. If she thinks she's found easy street and she can come to my house with her belly out to here and have me wait on her, she has another think coming. She's ruined my boy's chances, and I'll make her pay. He's a man, what control can he have? If she lets him, of course he'll take it! It's up to the woman to control the man, and not let him till she's married. If that worthless peasant her father had raised her properly, she wouldn't be pregnant now! God only knows what kind of slut I'm putting in my house, but I will show her.'

There was no doubt in my mind that Litsa would curse her fate many times in the next few years. Pavlos would still be living in his room in Thessaloniki while school was in session. It was agreed, at his parents' insistence, that he come up only on weekends and holidays, so his school work would not suffer. Litsa would be living alone with the in-laws who hated her and considered her the ruination of their son, and if she had indeed schemed to get Pavlos to marry her, she would soon regret her scheming and pay for it a hundredfold.

All this was a problem only in theory that afternoon, however. Pavlos had come to ask Andreas to be his best man, and he seemed to have no inkling of his mother's vow to make Litsa's life a misery.

'I'll have the best of everything. The life of a student and my wife at home with my parents, waiting for me to come up and see her. So what do you say, will you be my best man?'

Andreas accepted and the rest of Pavlos's visit was spent exchanging toasts over a bottle of ouzo, and jokes about the best man keeping an eye on the bride to keep other men away from her.

I didn't drink with them. Ever since my visit to Arletta, ouzo had lost its pull for me. In Greece alcohol is not forbidden to children. I had on many occasions been given a glass of this or that, never more than one. When I was a baby, my mother had probably rubbed ouzo on my gums to ease my teething, like every Greek mother did. That evening with Besios and my brother was the first time I had ever had enough to get drunk, however, and the taste of ouzo was forever linked in my mind with the sour smell of the fat whore and the revulsion I felt later for what I had done. To this day I don't drink ouzo.

The wedding was set for June, right after the close of the academic year at the university. It was a month away, but the village was buzzing with gossip, and Kyra Fotini fuelled most of it, with horrific descriptions of the squalor in Litsa's home, the poverty that surely was the result of Kyr Stathis's bad habits, because after all he had three sons and one daughter all working and bringing in money, so it couldn't be that they were so poor after all, not without good reason.

'Who knows what kind of a gambler and drinker he is, or maybe he does drugs, who knows in that miserable neighbourhood they live in! And her mother, she never heard of sweeping or mopping the floor,' Kyra Fotini would say in a torrent of ill will to anyone within hearing distance. 'I wash the soles of my shoes after I visit them to get them clean enough to go into my house again.'

So much venom was unprecedented even for the mother of an only son who had to marry a penniless girl, and speculation on the subject, and reports on further developments, would have kept the village entertained for a long time, if bigger, better news had not descended on the small community to overshadow the upcoming wedding.

The news came in a telegram, delivered to the doorstep of Kyra Parthenopi. Kyra Parthenopi was the old, gnarled mother of Manos, who more than ten years ago had left for the shores of America to escape poverty. He had tried farming as a young man, tilling the soil of the small family plot and trying to grow whatever he could think of. His pumpkins were destroyed by rainfall that broke all records for duration and intensity, his watermelons were eaten by worms, his potatoes rotted by disease. One crop of zucchini survived, but so did everybody else's. The price he got was not enough to keep him and his mother for the year, let alone pay off the debts accumulated over years of bad luck.

Manos was not afraid of hard work. He was just afraid of work in vain. He got his few coins from the zucchini, stuffed them in his mother's hands and told her he was leaving for New York, to make money and build a better future. He was her only son. Her only living family member. She didn't want him to go. But what could she tell him when it was as plain to her as it was to him that there was no living to be made in Panorama? Others had gone away and come back rich. Others had never come back. She kissed him, gave him her blessing and let him board the ship that would take him to the Promised Land, the land of plenty.

Like every Greek son who ever lived, Manos adored his mother. It wasn't easy for him to leave her. He took care to send her letters regularly, and he always put money inside, green dollar bills that Kyra Parthenopi had the postman take to the bank to change into drachmas for her. I learned later that Manos often went hungry himself to send the money to his mother. He had to support her and he had to pay off his debts, to keep the family house out of the bank's clutches so that his mother could have a roof over her head while he was not there to protect her.

The first few years were hard. But Manos worked hard from sunup to sundown. He spent nothing on himself, often sleeping in shops or warehouses owned by other Greeks he met, saving every penny he didn't send home to his mother. The amount he sent home kept increasing. Soon there were packages, too, of good American cloth for his mother to sew a dress or a coat. When she wrote that she was having trouble walking, he sent her a gold-handled cane. And when she complained of arthritis, he sent money to build a bathroom attached to the house, so his mother would not have to walk so far.

By the time I could read, Kyra Parthenopi could no longer see clearly, and I became her secretary, reading Manos's letters to her and writing the letters she dictated to me to send to America. She lived in comfort now, but she missed her son, and she was alone. When Antigone's father died and she was left an orphaned old maid, without a protector and without enough money to make ends meet, Kyra Parthenopi invited her to live with her. Antigone moved in and rented out her own house to supplement her income. The two of them became almost like mother and daughter. Antigone tenderly took care of the old lady and listened patiently while Kyra Parthenopi sighed over her son and lit the candle placed in front of the picture Manos had sent at his mother's request.

I remember that picture, because I have one myself that looks very similar. It shows Manos standing with his hands on his hips in front of his brand new restaurant, a slightly seedy eatery with red letters proclaiming this to be 'Manos Diner'. Kyra Parthenopi kept looking at that picture long after her eyesight allowed her to make out Manos's face.

'It's printed in my heart,' she'd say.

Manos stayed away too long, but finally, in the year of Pavlos's wedding, he announced he was arriving. And upon learning the news, Kyra Parthenopi had a heart attack that sent Antigone twittering her distress and hovering over the old woman's bed with tears streaming down her eyes.

'Don't you dare die, Kyra Parthenopi, you hang on now, because Manos is coming and he wants to see you,' she repeated a hundred times a day, and Kyra Parthenopi would nod her head and smile. She was the happiest patient there ever was, grasping at life eagerly to await the return of her boy.

And the day finally arrived. Manos had landed in Athens where his car, a huge gleaming Chevy, had arrived before him and awaited him like a chariot to lead him triumphant to his birthplace. Kyr Ilias, the man from the bus stop and third cousin to Manos, had taken the bus to meet Manos in Athens and act as his navigator. Together they drove from the capital to Panorama.

The two of them arrived in that Chevy, honking and waving to everyone. People stared as though at an apparition, and then dropped whatever they were doing to follow the chariot in its slow progress through the streets of Panorama. By the time the huge car pulled in front of the house, the whole village was behind it, the kids whooping and whistling, the adults laughing and slapping each other on the back, those with relatives in the *xenitia* misting over with the thought that their loved ones, too, could come back one day like Manos, crowned with success and carried in its most obvious emblem.

Manos had difficulty pushing the crowd away to open the door of his car. Then he had to part the masses shouting welcoming words to him to reach his doorstep. His mother had refused to let her son see her in her sick bed. She had had Antigone dress her in her finest American clothes and set her in a chair in front of the house, her gold-handled cane in her hand, her gold American ring, sent to her a few years ago on Manos's birthday to thank her for giving birth to him, shining on the second knuckle of the arthritic finger that it couldn't fit over. Even if her eyesight had been good, she still would not have had that first glimpse of her boy, because she was crying in earnest by the time Manos reached her.

He knelt in front of her, kissed her hand and hugged her.

'What are you crying for now, Mother?' he asked her. 'I am here.'

She had forbidden everyone to mention her heart attack to Manos. She didn't want to mar his happiness. Time enough later to tell him. He was going to stay two months. In that time, after he had settled down, after the excitement had given way to normality, she would tell him. Meanwhile, she pretended to be recovering from a very bad cold.

That evening there was a celebration in Panorama the likes of which nobody had witnessed before. One of our own had achieved the dream and was back to let us share in it. Out of the cavernous trunk of the Chevy came suitcases full of gifts. Manos had forgotten nobody. There were dresses and trousers and shirts made the American way so they never needed ironing, fitted sheets that a housewife didn't have to keep tucking in, kitchen gadgets and transistor radios, pantyhose, Timex watches, a camera, baby-sized dolls, wallets, belts, aprons, bracelets and brooches, socks, pocket knives, bottles of Scotch, American cigarettes, Zippo lighters, toy cars, a metal erector set, shoes, ties, cuff-links, desk sets, perfumes, lotions, creams, miracle drugs from America, spot removers, icecube moulds in the shape of women's breasts, shawls, bags and yard upon yard of polyester in every print imaginable. Most of the gifts had been purchased with someone specific in mind, but there was a large quantity of small items – rubber balls that glowed in the dark and jumped higher than the trees, small stuffed toys and tiny dolls, plastic earrings and necklaces – that Manos had bought to give to children born too late for him to know of, so nobody would go away from his homecoming empty handed.

All the rest of that day Manos sat next to his mother holding her hand in his and received the line of villagers come to wish him well. They arrived with food and drink, some bringing their own chair to sit on and join the revelry. The gifts were set out all over Kyra Parthenopi's dining-room for everyone to admire. People were awed by the sheer quantity of items. There was more in that dark, high-ceilinged room than in most shops. And it was all American, so it was the very best, the very latest. Men drank their ouzo and puffed away at their American cigarettes, exclaiming over the smoothness of the smoke and the lettering on the packages. In the evening someone put a lamb on the spit and started turning it slowly over a fire built in the front yard. Soon the delicious smell wafted over, proclaiming the celebration to the world. Till late into the night, kids crawled all over that Chevy parked out front. Manos had left it unlocked, and kids quarrelled over who would slide behind the steering wheel to pretend he was driving that magnificent car, bigger than most people's bedrooms.

I got a Cross pen and pencil set from Manos. He gave it to me the next day.

'You were my mother's eyes and ears all these years, and I wanted to get you something special. I brought more of these for other people, but yours is better. It's real silver. Take good care of it.'

Manos fascinated me. Like the majority of Greek men, he was short, dark and narrow-shouldered, but he had an air about him of confidence, of worlds explored and conquered, of obstacles overcome with valour. He wasn't stooped over with hard work and misery. He stood tall and he seemed to shine among the other men. His voice had a slight accent, a curious turn to some words, particularly ones involving the letters P and R, that invested everything he said with special significance. This was the voice of America, with all the shiny patina of that Mecca of technology and wealth. You have to remember the glory of America in the sixties to understand the impact of its imprint on Manos. To Greece in the sixties, America was the Garden of Eden, a heaven of wealth and plenty, a land where factory workers drove Mustangs and bought colour TVs, which didn't even exist in Greece. But it was also an immoral country, where people got divorced and women were unchaste. And it was vast, endless, infinite. A Greek could get lost in it, swallowed up by its giant maw, never to emerge again. That's why most Greeks who emigrated there landed in New York and never moved farther inland. They hugged the shore and hung on for dear life, afraid to let go of the body of water that, if followed through thousands of miles of ocean, traversing the Mediterranean and then tracked to the north, would lead to the Aegean and the tiny coves and bays that make up the shoreline of Greece. That Manos had gone to America and come back a conqueror, marked him as a winner.

He looked a bit funny for someone so venerable. His clothes were outlandish. Maroon trousers, worn with white shoes and a white belt. Shirts with bold stripes and patterns. Loud, wide ties and lapels bigger than anything seen in these parts. His clothes would have made him the object of scorn, if he hadn't been Manos the returning immigrant. But he was. So his peculiar clothes were fingered and exclaimed over, and his undignified ties were much admired for the boldness of the pattern. He had escaped so far from the village, outdistanced everyone so much, that the rules of good taste and dignity did not apply to him, and he could not only break them with impunity, but set new standards.

I attached myself to him. He was a hero. I, too, would have liked to arrive in a shiny car and dispense gifts to everyone. I, too, would have liked to be asked my opinion of everything, and be begged for my advice on every topic from a possible marriage to the sale of a few acres of land. Manos laughed at the villagers' requests for his opinion.

'I've been away too long. What do I know of what you should do?' he said again and again as he sipped his coffee from a green mug with the name of his restaurant on it. He had brought his own coffee maker, which the local electrician converted to European current, so he could drink American coffee. He generously offered it to everybody, but the consensus was that this was a pitiful concoction, with no body and no aroma, more like brown water. After the first day, he drank it alone.

The villagers ignored his protests. They insisted that he give them advice anyway. He had been out in the world, and he would know better.

Like poor people everywhere, the villagers assumed that great wealth equalled great wisdom. And Manos appeared to possess great wealth. He bought rounds every night at the taverna, he took a group of twenty of his closest friends and relatives to a local restaurant and paid the entire bill by himself on at least two occasions that first week, alone. And he made arrangements to buy the house next to his, to some day expand his own house. It was known that he had wanted to build a new house in his lot for his mother to live in two years ago, and the only reason he didn't is that his mother insisted that she wanted to go on living in her old house because she liked the memories in there.

After the first week, the enthusiasm died down a little. People would still come by to have coffee, shoot the breeze and hear about America, and the kids still fought over who would pretend he was driving the Chevy, but life had returned to its natural rhythm. The summer people were arriving and everyone was busy making money out of them. Manos seemed to enjoy his diminished social duties. He sat in his yard with his mother and Antigone, the radio playing in the background, and he relaxed. Often I would join him. I would ask a million questions about his business, how he lived, what New York was like, what Americans were like.

'You ask more questions than anyone, George,' he said one day. 'Are you thinking of going yourself?'

The thought had occurred to me. But no, I didn't plan to go. Maybe some time in the future, after I was married, if Katerina wanted to go. But I wouldn't leave her like Manos left his mother. I wouldn't leave her like Petros left Antigone. What if I got lost in that big country and never came back? Would some street punk tease Katerina by shouting my name in the street to make her wince? Oh, no. I knew first hand what the *xenitia* cost those who were left behind, and I wouldn't do that to Katerina.

'Do people ever emigrate with their family?' I asked.

'You mean, take the wife and kids and go?'

'I mean get married and the two people go together.'

'Well, I suppose it happens, but I've never seen it. It takes a long time to make good, George, and until you do, life is harder than you can imagine. You sleep wherever you find a dry place, and you save all your money. You struggle every day and work sixteen, eighteen hours, as many as you can manage, because the harder you work, the faster your money grows and the faster you can go back. And you struggle to learn the language and get used to the bad weather, and the ways of the foreigners. The worst thing is how you feel. You feel so alone, George, I can't tell you how alone you feel. My second year there, I remember standing on the corner of Madison and 57th selling hot dogs. It had rained for a whole month. The sky was grey and heavy, nobody seemed hungry for hot dogs and I was standing shivering in the rain, and all of a sudden I heard Greek. Two guys were walking fast arguing with each other, and as they went by me I heard their words clearly. They hit me like a ton of bricks. This was my language, right there on this cold, lonely street, and I just left my cart unattended and started after them, yelling for them to stop. They didn't hear me in the noise of downtown traffic until I was almost on them. They turned to see who was this madman coming after them. Passers-by were giving me a wide berth, but pretending not to notice me, like they do in America. The guys were from Athens, I didn't know them and they didn't know me, but I took them back to my cart. By some miracle it was still there. I treated them to a hot dog and I begged them, just begged them to stay and talk to me for a while because I was so heartsick with missing my home. So would I take a woman out there and make her leave her mother and father and live in poverty and sell hot dogs in the rain? Not if I loved her, I wouldn't.'

This speech shook me inside. So far people had been asking Manos to describe the glories of America. The large stores, the opulence, the magnificent cars, the banks that extend credit, the marvels of technology, the availability of work for anybody who wants it. Nobody had asked about the other side of life, missing your home and your family, standing alone in the rain selling hot dogs, chasing strangers down the street to hear Greek.

'New York is a bad city to be poor in, George, and it's an even worse city to be alone. I don't know what it is about Americans, and maybe it's just New Yorkers, but they just don't seem human sometimes. They are all wrapped up in themselves. They come to buy a hot dog and it's like they are buying it from a machine instead of a person. They never look you in the eye. They never want to know how you are.

'Oh, they ask, if they know you they ask. They say, "How are you?" but they don't want to hear. Let's say you're not well. You are ill, someone broke into your house and stole your money, or your wife is cheating on you with your best friend, or you're just feeling mean. If you tell a Greek, any Greek, even one you've never seen before, he'll listen to you, he'll tell you his own problems, he'll put his arm around you, he'll buy you a drink. He will discuss your problem from all angles and give you more advice than you want or need. But Americans, just don't tell them. Say you're fine. They don't want to know. If you're dumb enough to think they want to know how you really are, just start telling them and you will see their eyes glaze over and their feet back up away from you. They think telling them what ails you is bad manners. They think heartache is a sign of weak character. You've never seen people more bent on ignoring their feelings. Every morning they stick a vacant smile on their face and that's that. Have a nice day! They think you have to smile even when you feel like crying. They're not smiling *at* you. They are just deflecting any bit of human feeling that might come their way, even if it's just a bad mood.

'I'd stand in that corner all day, and unless some Latino or Indian or Pakistani stopped to buy, by the end of the day I would be wondering if I had somehow become invisible. I hurt my leg one day, I fell down the stairs on my way up to my room in this hostel where I was staying. It bothered me, and standing all day was not helping. Soon I had pain shooting up and a cramp clamped down on my calf. I sat down to relieve the pain, and nobody, George, not a single person asked me if I was okay, or if they could get me anything. At first I thought it was because I was a foreigner. But no. They're like that with their own, too.

'One night I came upon an old lady wrapped in furs standing in the street crying because some punk had snatched her handbag. Out of all the people passing her by I was the only one who stopped to offer help. And you know what? She slapped at me with her little hands and made to run, and she fell down. I tried to help her get up, but she got hysterical and kept shrinking from me, so I figured I'd better leave her alone. New Yorkers are so unused to giving help that they cannot fathom it when it's offered to them. She probably thought I wanted to take her coat.'

'But it was worth it, wasn't it? Now you're a rich man!'

Manos laughed at that. 'I'm not rich, George. I'm a business man. I owe the banks a lot of money. I'm comfortable, that's all. I have a house and a car and a good business.'

'But all these gifts! All the money you spend buying drinks and food!' I protested.

'Oh, I'm rich enough for Panorama, for a while. The dollar buys a lot of drachmas. But I still háve a way to go before I retire.'

Manos had a plan. He had returned to convince his mother to come with him to America for the years he still had to spend there. She would live in his house, and the two would be together again, the way they used to. Kyra Parthenopi refused.

'I'm gonna die soon, Manos. I want to die in my own land. Go back if you must. And don't go back alone. Pick a good girl and marry her and take her with you. But I can't go with you, my son. There is no time.'

Manos insisted, so Antigone finally took him aside and told him his mother was sick, even though Kyra Partenopi had still not given permission to tell him. Manos listened to Antigone and then turned around and left the house in silence. I saw him walking away, his shoulders hunched for once, and I followed him. He came to the edge of the village and sat down on a boulder. I waited for a while, but then I remembered his stories of loneliness from New York and I went up to him and put my hand on his shoulder.

His eyes were brimming with tears when he turned to me.

'Hi, George,' he said.

'What is it?' I asked him, although I knew.

'It seems I stayed away too long, my friend. I stayed too long and now the person I did it for can't enjoy it. Antigone says my mother has a bad heart. She says the doctor thinks the next attack will be the last. It won't be just New York any more. I'll be alone everywhere.'

I sat next to him. I told him about my mother and how she died. We talked a long time, as though we were contemporaries, even though he was twenty years my senior. We talked and we cried, and when the evening fell around us our hearts had lightened and we were friends. Together we went back to the house, and Manos put on a convincing show of good cheer and ignorance.

Kyra Parthenopi never lifted her eyes from him if she could help it.

'Antigone, fetch a pillow for my boy. He's not comfortable. Manos, do you want some more coffee, do you have enough cigarettes? Is it cool enough over there, do you need the fan?'

She was cramming ten years of care into a few weeks. She couldn't do things for him herself, but in Antigone she had a person willing to be her hands and feet. Tirelessly and without complaint, Antigone hovered around Manos, doing his mother's bidding.

'Don't you ever get tired, Antigone, of waiting on me? Should I speak to Mother to let you rest a little?' he asked her after his mother had retired to her bed.

'I don't mind, Manos. She's like a mother to me. Whatever brings her pleasure, and brings you pleasure, I am glad to do.'

It was always curious to me to see Antigone with Kyra Parthenopi. Antigone was a bitter old maid with everyone else. Humourless, unforgiving, mean. She complained about kids making too much noise, about shopkeepers charging too much, about young girls dressing like loose women and baring their all to see. She had a bitter criticism for everybody in the village. That woman doesn't keep her house clean, this one was pregnant when she married never mind pretending to be virtuous now, that one wore too much make-up in church. This man was a lazy oaf, that one watered down the milk he fed his children, the other beat his wife. Her face wore the expression of her sour character. Her lips were pinched together tight and her eyes and mouth had mean, crimped corners. And yet this miserable, unhappy woman was an angel of mercy to Kyra Parthenopi, catering to her every whim and looking after her with love that you could never have imagined to find in her small and barren heart. I knew this side of Antigone from hanging around the house reading and writing letters from and to America, so I was not surprised to see that it carried over to Manos.

'Thank God for Antigone,' Manos said to me when she went inside to get him a cup of tea. 'She's been a ministering angel to my mother, and I owe her a debt for life. It's too bad her life had to turn out the way it did with that miserable Petros who left her on the shelf, but thank God she was there for my mother.'

'Did you know her before you left?' I asked.

'Yes, I did. She was always a quiet girl. She'd sit in her yard and sew or embroider. She must have made hundreds of handiworks to show off in her house when she'd marry. She used to make the finest stuff, all brilliant colours and fancy stitchwork, flowers and ships and any number of designs. She used to monogram sheets and towels, too. She was the very best in the village, and all the young girls would ask for her help when they couldn't manage a hard part in their own embroidery. Some days there'd be a whole crowd of them around her, watching her explain a new stitch or execute a difficult combination. That stuff she made must still be in her hope chest. God knows there's hardly a woman of her generation in this village who doesn't have some of Antigone's handiwork in her own dowry linens. She was shy and never had much to say. I guess she felt she was not as pretty as the other girls and that made her close in on herself. But she did have a very pretty voice. She still must. When she was sweeping the yard or doing the wash, sometimes she'd sing. Her voice didn't have much power, you had to be close to hear, but it was a sweet voice, like a caress.'

'But what about Petros?' I prompted.

'Well, he didn't get interested in her until after she had started despairing that anyone would take an interest. He lived two streets down, where the Papademas live now. He had to pass by Antigone's yard to go to his house, and once in a while he would look in. Antigone's mother was alive back then. She knew the score. Knew her daughter was too shy and needed some help. So she began inviting Petros in. He loved food, Petros did, and they never had much in their house. Her mother, Kyra Vaso was her name, was on a mission. They didn't have much either, but she spent all of it on stuff for Petros to eat. Her family might eat bread and olives for dinner, but there were sesame cookies made with real butter to serve Petros. And she got Antigone to bake the stuff, too. Petros would stuff his face and smack his lips, and Kyra Vaso would say that Antigone made whatever it was with her own two hands.'

'So did Petros fall in love with Antigone?'

'In his own way, he must have. He wasn't very bright nor very strong in character. He could be bent to someone's will quite easily. And Kyra Vaso had a will. He didn't even know how he found himself engaged. One day he was eating sesame cookies, and the next he was walking up and down Main Street with Antigone on his arm, her face beaming with a smile from ear to ear. Having a young man changed her. She became more sociable, came out of her shell. But there was no money to get married. No money to set up house or raise children. So Petros decided to go to Germany and make some money. He had heard of factory jobs out there, and since the weather was not co-operating with farmers, as though it ever does, he took his cardboard suitcase, kissed Antigone and left. Some time later, I left, too. I came back, and he didn't.'

'Do you know what happened to him?'

'He probably found another yard with food in it and never looked back. Who knows? Maybe he just never made good and was too ashamed to come back. It's a big burden, you know, George, to make it when you are out there. People expect it of you. You see immigrants returning and they all seem to be success stories, lugging TVs and washing machines back with them, cars, record players, all the good things and even money to fix up the old home and make an indoor bathroom with a toilet and live like human beings, and you think it's automatic. You stay in the *xenitia* for some years, you eat its bitter bread, and then you come back rich. But the ones who don't come back, they are the ones who lost. It's not a sure thing. The world is big. You play your cards. If you win, you come back covered in glory. If you don't, you just stay out there and blend in with the foreigners, and no one is to know you failed.'

His words made me sad. I kept thinking of this Petros, whom I didn't know, lost in a foreign land full of the noise, dirt and speeding cars that Manos had described to me, surrounded by people who spoke no Greek and didn't want to know how you are. And I thought of Antigone too, who was a quiet girl and embroidered, and smiled ear to ear when she finally got herself a young man. Manos had no idea what a bitter, self-righteous woman she had become. Was it her disappointment that had soured her inside? If she had got married, would she be another person now, one who smiled and sang and

taught embroidery to young girls? I had always disliked
her before, had even been pleased Petros had left her and
shamed her publicly like that when she complained to the
priest that the boys made too much noise in the afternoon
playing ball, and they should be allowed to play only away
from the village streets. But Manos gave me a new view
of her. When she came back with tea for Manos and a
snack of bread, watermelon and feta cheese, I could see
the slender stem her body must have been before it grew
arid and gaunt. I wished all of a sudden that she would
sing, but I was ashamed to ask.

Manos and I became the best of friends. He had lost the
habit of sleeping in the afternoon, and I was too young
to enjoy it, so the two of us got together after the midday
meal when everyone slept. We would walk to the outskirts
of town where I had found him crying. We would settle
ourselves under the shade of a tree and we would talk
about everything, but mostly America.

'How come you spend so much time with grown-ups,
George?' he asked me one day. 'How come you're always
home?'

I explained to him how bad I was at games. I felt
comfortable with him. I could tell him things I would
never dream of telling other people. So I told him of my
incompetence in soccer, my disgust at my lack of height,
my puny build, my lack of looks and manly stature.

'I'm sixteen, Manos,' I told him, 'and I still look fourteen. I stand next to Andreas and I look like his son
instead of his brother.'

'Some boys grow up slower than others. You're just one
of the slow ones,' he told me.

'But I've got to grow up now, don't you see? I've
already waited too long!'

Manos was smart. He heard more in my words than I had put in them.

'Is there a reason you have to hurry up, George?' he asked me.

So I told him. I told him of my dream of marrying Katerina, of how much I loved her, of how my uncle treated her and of how I couldn't protect her. I told him things got better once Andreas moved back into the house, but that he wasn't around enough. And I told him that I was worried because I was taking so long to become a man that Katerina would be married and her kids in school before she or anyone else would think of me as a man. Manos heard all this seriously, with no protestations that I was too young to know who I would marry or know that I was in love.

'Well, now, there's a way to help nature along,' he said.

For a moment I thought he would suggest I visit a whore. I had never told him about that, and I wasn't about to.

'You just need to challenge your body to make it develop.'

That evening he fashioned an exercise programme for me. It involved running, doing press-ups and sit-ups, chopping wood and carrying a stack of bricks put in his yard for further improvements to the house from one end of the yard to the other.

'You see Thanases?' he would say. 'He works construction. His shoulders are huge and his chest is as big as a barrel. That's because he challenges himself all day. It builds strength and it builds muscles. Now see Kyr Demos. He sits behind the counter every day in his shop. No wonder his arms are sticks. They never have to carry anything heavier than drachmas. And your brother.

Why do you think he got to be so big? Because he played soccer all day, rode his bike, climbed trees, threw rocks. It's a pity, really. The boys who need it most, the small ones, are the ones who are worst at it, so they drop out and they never develop. We're gonna put you on a crash course, and then we'll see who's a man around here.'

And so I started huffing and puffing in the middle of the summer heat, wearing a hat to protect my head from the sun, but otherwise making no allowances. At night I went to sleep with my muscles dazed by all the physical labour. In the morning I'd wake up sore and in pain, my muscles screaming against the idea of moving. But I persisted.

'George, you're crazy! You keep moving the same pile of bricks around in Manos's yard. Is this some kind of punishment from Hades, what are you, Tantalus, to have to keep doing the same thing over and over and never be done?'

'He's bought the farm, Andreas, that's what it is. Little George just lost his marbles, and that crazy American is to blame,' my uncle chimed in.

Laugh all you want, I thought to myself. Laugh now, because you won't be laughing later. And I crossed over to Manos's house to move the bricks again.

16

June Brides

The Saturday of Pavlos and Litsa's wedding dawned clear and sunny. The wedding would take place in the church of Saint George, right next to our house. Tradition was for a wedding to take place in the bride's church, but Kyra Fotini and Kyr Lambros insisted that if they had to pay for everything, then they would hold the wedding where they pleased and to hell with tradition.

The nuptials would take place at six-thirty. Then everyone would go to Pavlos's home, where there would be a band and food for everyone. Andreas didn't go to the bakery that day. Instead he took Pavlos with a few other friends to a restaurant for Pavlos's last meal as a free man. They sang and drank and toasted each other until three, when each returned to his house for some rest before the big event.

We all took our baths early that Saturday, to be clean for the wedding. Katerina steam-pressed my uncle's summer suit and hung it in the family room. She then put out a clean shirt and a pair of trousers for me, together with a tie. She polished everybody's shoes and then she spent at least an hour preparing and laying out Andreas's clothes, but that's because he was the best man, and every eye would be on him.

She had no time at all to prepare her own clothes. The dress she would wear, the bright red polyester bought with Andreas's pimping, had been hanging on a peg on the wall of her room, covered by an old sheet, uncreased and unstained ever since Kyra Toula sewed it for her. There was not much call in Katerina's life for dressing up.

Katerina was the last one in the wash shed. She came out wrapped in a bathrobe, with plastic slippers on her feet. She sat under the sun in the yard and combed her long, dark hair. She had already fed me and my uncle, and he was inside sleeping, so she could just sit and rest and enjoy her time of quiet. In just a matter of minutes the sun started to dry and curl the thick mantle tossed on Katerina's back. I sat away from her waiting for Manos's meal to be over so we could go for our walk, and I admired the curling strands. Her hair seemed alive to me, calling me to run my fingers through it and breathe its scent. Manos whistled for me, motioned me over from across the street and I took off.

'Don't be late, George,' Katerina called after me.

By the time I made it back, Andreas was dressed and ready to leave. He would go to Pavlos's house first, to escort the groom to the church. My uncle would go, too, to help set up the tables for the party and, I suspected, to start drinking early. My uncle found the handkerchief that had been delaying their departure and, sticking it in his pocket and muttering that people were crazy to be marrying in the middle of the afternoon in June, ran after Andreas who was already striding out of the house.

In a while, Katerina went downstairs to dress. I was proud as a peacock that I would be escorting her the few steps to the church. I changed clothes, wet my hair down, parted it carefully on the side and combed it in place. Then I sat to wait for Katerina. She didn't take long.

I still remember what she looked like that day when she walked in dressed in her finery for Pavlos's wedding, the prettiest of the best red poppies of May. Her soft, sun-warmed skin was a perfect foil to the fiery colour of her dress. It caught a glow from the shiny material and seemed as smooth and inviting as the ripest August peach. She usually tied her hair in a pony-tail or a braid, but today it was loose on her shoulders, and kept off her forehead with a ribbon from the same material as the dress. One long black strand was curling over the square neckline of her dress. Kyra Toula must have cut the dress a little small, because her breasts were squeezed up and in by it. Their smooth white tops peeked out a little, and the dress was helping them to form a delicious crease that hinted at warm, perfumed depths. The dress was fitted in the bodice, almost painfully tight, but flared out around the hips after squeezing her waist into a tiny ring that a man could encircle completely with his hands. Underneath the full skirt, her legs were long and slender in high heels courtesy of Andreas, the legs of a prize colt, with calves that curved gently into slender, aristocratic ankles. I had been accustomed to seeing her in her shapeless black clothes and flat slippers, and even then I had thought her beautiful. That day, standing before me in that cascade of bright colour, with her hair and eyes looking like liquid velvet in perfect contrast, Katerina was the most beautiful creature on earth.

'You should wear red on your wedding day, Katerina,' I told her. The smile left her face and she turned a bright crimson. Oh, no, you idiot, I thought, brides wear white to signify their virginity. What are you saying to her?

'Katerina, I didn't mean that you are not . . . I mean, of course you are . . . I just meant . . .'

I stammered and searched in vain for the right words.

'I just meant you look beautiful in red,' I finally managed to say.

Americans, who love elaborate weddings, cannot understand the simplicity of Greek nuptials, but Greece is a poor country, and its customs reflect its poverty. Two wreaths of silk flowers for the groom and bride, a family girl or two to hold the huge decorated white candles that burn through the ceremony, sugar-coated almonds wrapped in tulle as wedding favours, are about all the preparations there are. No festooning the church with every blossom available, no bridesmaids with matching dresses, no wedding march.

Katerina and I arrived to find Kyra Fotini in charge. She was arranging the wedding favours in a beribboned basket and shooing the neighbourhood children who had come to beg the tulle-wrapped candied almonds.

'Later, later,' she told them. 'If there's enough for the guests, we'll give you the ones that are left over. Ten drachmas a piece, I paid for them,' she said to us as we walked up to her, 'and these urchins want to eat them all before we have the wedding! I should have got the cheaper ones, God knows she doesn't deserve the best the way she brought this wedding about, but he's my only son, and I've got a name to uphold. Never let it be said that I didn't start them off with the very best.'

She left us in charge of the favours after giving Katerina the once-over, and moved on to complain to the priest that the church floor was not clean enough. Katerina and I sneaked some favours to the most persistent children. In time, the second cousin arrived who would later take charge of handing out the favours to the guests. We passed our task over to her and joined the rest of the crowd. Katerina's appearance created a mild stir of surprise. I think it made her a little umcomfortable to suddenly have so much attention, but there was too much going on for her to remain the focus. Pavlos was pacing nervously in front of the church and Andreas was running after him, trying to fix the gardenia in his lapel. Kyra Fotini and Kyr Lambros were complaining that the bride and her guests were late, and this would throw everything off schedule. People were kissing Antigone on both cheeks and wishing her her own wedding soon. This is a traditional wish to all unmarried women, and even men, but by now Antigone had heard it enough times to know that nobody believed it would come to pass for her. She received each wish with a crimping of her eyes and a pursing of her mouth, and did not thank the well-wisher as she ought to have, for the sake of good manners. Manos was surrounded by those who wanted to know about weddings in America. His mother was not there because she wasn't feeling well.

The bus from Thessaloniki must have finally arrived, because a whole group of people was suddenly seen rounding the bend and walking the steep incline to the church, lugging plastic bags loaded with Tupperware. Huffing and puffing in the heat, loaded with food for the feast to come later, Litsa's relatives had made it to Saint George. And a motley crew they were. There was poverty in Panorama, too, and Pavlos's family was well-off only in comparison with the rest of the village, but Litsa's family looked badly dressed even to us. The men's suits and jackets were shiny and old, and some had visible patches at the elbow. The women were dressed in an assortment of cheap cotton dresses that strained and puckered over protruding bellies and pendulous breasts, receiving little help from stretched-out bras and girdles. Plastic sandals in uniform white, to go with everything in the summer, were on every woman's feet. The children the women were dragging behind them were an ill-looking bunch, loud, dishevelled, and in at least one case with snot running freely down the face, to be wiped on a shirt tail in full view of everyone. The look on Kyra Fotini's face was priceless.

Litsa's family greeted Kyra Fotini and Kyr Lambros, but when no introductions to the rest of the guests followed, they picked a corner of the churchyard to call their own and talked among themselves while we all waited.

Finally we saw it. It was a cab with white ribbons on it, honking wildly and sending gravel spinning as it came up to the church, followed by another cab.

'Doesn't anybody in their family own a car, for God's sake,' muttered Kyra Fotini, who obviously considered it undignified for the bride to arrive in a hired conveyance.

Stathis, the construction worker, came out first, in what must have been the shiniest suit in attendance. Then he turned to help his daughter out. Her mother-in-law may have been livid, her family snubbed, her chariot nothing more then a common cab, but Litsa shone with happiness when she emerged. Her wedding dress was rented and made no secret of her condition. Still, she looked beautiful in it, dark and quick and delicious. Her huge mother, wearing what appeared to be a once-white lace tablecloth, had to be helped out next. I think the cab driver helped by pushing from the back, while Kyr Stathis pulled from the front. Kyra Agne stumbled out, almost fell on her ample backside and finally steadied herself on her aching feet which bulged dangerously out of her pumps. The rest of her brood, the sullen brothers and the two sisters, with none of Litsa's charm and verve, got out of the second cab with the inevitable plastic bags in hand.

Greek wedding ceremonies are long and tedious. The priest chants in biblical Greek, waving his incense burner every so often. The best man holds the flower wreaths over the heads of the bride and groom while the priest leads the trio in what is called the 'dance of Isaiah' around the small table where the ceremony is enacted. The candle girls hold the lit tapers and hope the tulle adorning them does not catch fire. More biblical Greek, more incense.

The flower girls at Pavlos's wedding were Litsa's third cousins, because her sisters were too old for the part. The cousins were two brats dressed in matching, pouffy white nylon dresses, with their hair fixed in bouffant hair-dos, and supercilious expressions on their faces. One managed to break her candle so that, throughout the ceremony, the tip listed to one side, dripping melted wax on the white tulle and silk flowers tied around it. I watched the dripping with much interest, wondering when the whole thing would topple over and burn the giggling little girl up like kindling.

There is a spot in the ceremony, where the priest says the only words in his entire litany that are spoken in something resembling modern Greek. He says that the wife must stand in fear of the husband. It is customary as the words are spoken for the bride to step on her groom's foot, to counteract the admonition. Litsa was wearing heels, and instead of stepping on Pavlos's foot with her toe, she sank her heel in him. Hard. Pavlos yelped, the candle girls guffawed and elbowed each other viciously, and the broken candle leaned over completely, touching the tulle and setting it on fire. The priest grabbed the wine the bride and groom are supposed to drink and threw it on the flames. Most of it splashed on the little girl who started crying. Her mother rushed over, red and sweating in irritation, and screamed at the priest he must be crazy. That is a rented dress, and how is she going to clean the red wine from it so she can return it and get her deposit back. Kyra Fotini looked made of stone at this point, refusing to give in to the humiliation she felt at the goings-on.

Katerina and I were laughing hysterically along with the rest of the congregation. I was wiping the tears from my eyes when I felt a chill emanating from the side. I looked in that direction and I saw Uncle Demetres by the aisle next to the wall, his eyes pure venom, staring at Katerina. The dress, I thought, he hates her in the dress.

The congregation finally composed itself once more, and the priest rushed through the rest of the ceremony to avoid further mishap. The bride and groom stood to receive the line of guests waiting to kiss them and wish them happiness. Then each guest headed for the door, where he would receive a wedding favour and exit the church to wait in the yard for the departure of the newly-weds. Kyra Agne, as the mother of the bride, was one of the first to kiss the couple. Afterwards, she walked over to Pavlos's second cousin in charge of the wedding favours and, tucking her own in her handbag, asked for extras to take to the relatives who could not attend. The second cousin smiled uncomfortably at the request, spread a protective arm over the basket and cast desperate glances at Kyra Fotini who was talking to some relatives. Kyra Fotini immediately rushed over, just as Kyra Agne was reaching two chubby hands to grab a bunch of favours from the clutches of the second cousin.

'What do you think you're doing?' Kyra Fotini's voice boomed out as she yanked both cousin and basket out of Kyra Agne's grasp. 'There's barely enough here to give to the people who came! I asked you to tell me how many to expect, but you didn't give me the right number, now did you, Agne? I'd be mad at you now, if it wasn't that I know you can't count.'

Kyra Agne did not take kindly to this insult. She rummaged in her handbag, fished out her favour and threw it dramatically back in the basket.

'You can put on as many airs as you like,' she replied tucking her chin up in the air, 'but I know you're not as high and mighty as you like to pretend. Your father used to work in the sewers and everybody knows it. I don't want these candied almonds. They smell too much like shit to me, pardon the expression,' she announced in a voice that carried in the cavernous church.

Kyra Fotini was thunderstruck. It was true, her father, God rest his soul, had worked for the sewer department, and he had in his first few years with the agency worked underground in plastic boots and gloves, fixing leaks and blockages. But Kyra Agne couldn't have known this unless Pavlos had told her. Her own son had betrayed her to this grossly obese woman who was standing like an immovable mountain in front of her, with her tiny fish mouth trembling in fury and her abominable dress hanging about her like a tent. She glanced over at Pavlos, who was kissing relatives, oblivious to his mother's humiliation. There were any number of retorts she was capable of. She chose dignity and moral outrage.

'It doesn't surprise me,' she intoned, drawing herself up to her full height, 'that such as you would use profanity in the house of the Lord.' With that, she brushed her hand across her immaculate summer dress with its cropped, short-sleeved jacket, to emphasise the contrast between her in-law's abominable taste and her own smart get-up, and turned away.

Kyra Agne was not fazed. As far as she was concerned, Kyra Fotini had simply failed to dress with the splendour befitting the occasion. And moral outrage was her forte, too.

'I think the Lord is more upset that you are sitting here in his blessed house like the moneylenders he chased out of the temple in Jerusalem, counting candied almonds like they were gold coins,' she said, grabbing Kyra Fotini by the arm and turning her around. 'It's your only son you just married today, and you ought to be ashamed for your stinginess. If you're as rich as you pretend to be, why didn't you buy some extra favours so you wouldn't have to stand guard over them like you were guarding the royal jewels!'

By now Kyr Lambos and Kyr Stathis had got wind of the argument and had drawn near.

'You dare speak of stinginess when you didn't contribute a single drachma to this wedding!' Kyr Lambros said in outrage.

'You'll probably give us a bill for the cabs you used to get here,' Kyr Fotini added.

'And what price my daughter's honour, I ask you?' Kyr Stathis sputtered.

'Your daughter could do a lot worse than marry my son the lawyer,' Kyra Fotini countered.

'Lawyer! He's a student who's never done a day's honest work in his life. He can't support her, but he knows the rest of his business, it seems to me. How to live off his parents and in-laws and how to get the goods before he gets the Church's blessing.'

Ordinarily a parent would not allude to his daughter's embarrassing condition so publicly, but Kyr Stathis was seeing red, and Litsa's pregnancy was plainly visible anyway.

'Live off his in-laws!' Kyr Lambros exclaimed, arms outstretched and face turned heavenward, as if asking for divine agreement with his outrage at Kyr Stathis's words. 'If Pavlos didn't show up every Sunday in your house with chops and chicken to feed your spawn, you wouldn't know what meat tastes like!'

The fight might have turned uglier, but the priest stepped in. He was a young priest, tall, vigorous, and with the voice of thunder.

'You stop this immediately!' he told the four parents, waving his finger at them. 'This is the house of the Lord, and this is a special day. Do you want God to strike you mute, or worse, right where you stand?'

Then he took aside the two fathers and counselled them to rein in their wives and to shake hands in friendship, so as not to poison the day for their children.

The priest's intervention calmed things down, but it was plain that the bad feelings were still just barely under the surface.

The bride and groom, throwing worried glances at their parents, emerged from the church and were pelted with rice and candied almonds. They got into Kyr Lambros's battered but clean Fiat, with flowers and ribbons tied on its radio antenna, to be driven to Pavlos's house for the party. The rest of the guests followed on foot, whispering and laughing about the in-law fight, which promised to liven up their lives for years to come.

The yard of Pavlos's house was big and full of trees and bushes. There were five spits set up in one corner to roast the five lambs that would be served to the crowd. Four barrels of retsina were set sideways on a cart, a tap in each one, to provide drink. On the other side of the yard, the band was tuning its instruments.

Most villagers would have chosen a folk band to play traditional tunes for a wedding, but Kyr Lambos was a fan of the popular *bouzouki* music, so it was that kind of band he had hired. The band numbered five people. There was a drummer with the look of a dumb animal; a guitar player who seemed already too drunk to stand up; a cadaverous *bouzouki* player with a cigarette stuck to his lips that his hands touched only when he had to discard it and replace it with another; a second *bouzouki* player who was also the lead singer and obviously headed for a brighter future, as was made obvious by his slick hairstyle, flashy tie, and gold pinky ring; and a plump, juicy woman with her hair piled high on her head, dressed in a tight, shiny dress that left one shoulder bare. Her job was to provide harmony for the lead singer and something for the men to gawk at.

Litsa's dowry was spread out inside the house. There were sheets with hand-made decorative borders, pillow-cases, towels, a tablecloth, blankets and the ubiquitous embroidered *semedakia*, made to be spread on every available furniture surface in Litsa's future home, if she survived the initial cohabitation with her in-laws. In the sixties in Greece, there was never a table or a sideboard that wasn't covered by a square, oval or rectangular *semedaki* of point-stitched needlework depicting flowers or abstract patterns in bright colours. Litsa's dowry was neither of good quality, nor abundant. Even I could see that. Kyra Fotini had decided to keep the shutters closed in an effort to disguise this, but after the events in the church she came home and threw the windows wide open, telling Katerina and me: 'Everyone might as well see that her parents are marrying her naked and barefoot.'

The party was soon under way. Chairs and tables had been borrowed from every household in attendance; there was plenty of room to sit. The retsina wine was flowing freely and food was coming in a steady stream from

Kyra Fotini's kitchen. There was a mountain of spicy
meatballs dusted with flour and then deep fried, soft oily
rice wrapped in vine leaves picked from Kyr Lambros's
own vines, cheese and spinach wrapped in filo pastry and
baked to delicious crispiness, small sausages, aubergine
salad, yoghurt salad with garlic and bits of cucumber,
pink fish roe paste to spread on crusty bread, cubes of
feta cheese with a dash of oil, anchovies, french fries,
kasseri cheese deep fried and served flaming in brandy,
clams baked in a lemon sauce with crumbled feta cheese
on top, giant baked beans cracked from the heat of the
oven and resting in a tomato base, tangy fried green and
red peppers in vinegar, pickled green tomatoes, fresh
shredded carrot dressed with oil and lemon juice, vine-
ripened tomatoes cut open like flowers and sprinkled with
oregano, breaded and fried sardines to be eaten whole
with the bones, marinated octopus. Kyra Fotini's kitchen
was crowded with every female from both clans, some
unwrapping stuff they cooked at home, others making it
right there, or waiting for the oven to reheat what they
had brought. They were flushed and laughing, and
they would stride out of the kitchen carrying platters
full of goodies, to be set down in front of the men who
were busy putting a dent in the retsina as they sat around
borrowed tables toasting each other.

The band was finally ready. They sat on chairs in a
row, with the drummer at the back. The woman sat
with her plump knees together and her hands clasped
loosely, every so often opening her mouth just a tad, to
squeeze through grudgingly her few notes complementing
the lead singer. In typical *bouzouki* fashion, she kept her
face devoid of all expression. The lead singer had one
ankle crossed over his knee and the *bouzouki* resting on
his lap as he picked out intricate melodies. He had a

gold tooth that flashed every so often. The songs he sang were all about love gone wrong, but this was not an omen. Just about every *bouzouki* song ever written bemoans the faithlessness of women.

I had a go at turning one of the spits over the coal to cook the lambs. Kids came up every so often to ask that they be allowed to rip off a bit of crispy skin. If you've never smelled lamb roasting over an open fire, then you have never been tempted with food and your mouth has never watered.

Lamb takes a long time to roast over an open fire, so by the time it was ready to cut and serve everyone was in great high spirits from the retsina. People were taking turns on the impromptu dance floor, kids were chasing each other around the trees and bushes, the men were toasting war heroes from the Greek revolution of 1821, and Pavlos was kissing Litsa as though he had decided to give her another kid right there in front of everyone. Kyr Stathis and Kyr Lambos had grown friendly in their befuddlement, and had actually draped an arm around each other as they leaned back in their chairs and sang along with the band the words to 'Mother, why did you give birth to me?' Litsa's three brothers showed no signs of slowing down on their eating. Ever since the first appetisers had appeared, they had fallen on them like starving children from the time of the Nazi occupation of Greece, and they had not let up for a minute. One bite disappeared into their mouths before they had time to swallow the one before it. One of them, the hulking man they called Kostas, was stuffing what he had no time to eat in a bag, to be taken with him when he had to go home. All three chewed and gnawed with relish, their thick moustaches moving frantically up and down and sideways as they tore into loaves of bread and used whole slices to sop up every bit of sauce and gravy, wiping clean each plate that stopped at their table. The two sisters were talking to every young man in sight, simpering and smiling in a futile attempt to imitate Litsa's charm.

The only signs of discontent were in the kitchen, where Kyra Fotini was arguing that Kyra Agne's sardines were not fresh and should not be served.

'No way will you fry those fish in my kitchen! They stink and their eyes are filmed over. They aren't fit for eating. They are only fit for a decent burial.'

'These fish are fresh. They were swimming in the sea just yesterday.'

'They were in the sea, all right, belly up! If you serve these the guests will be poisoned!'

Kyra Agne had had about all she could take. For hours now she had put up with Kyra Fotini's disapproval of every dish provided by Litsa's relatives. Time and again Kyra Fotini had remarked at the inferior quality of every contribution of the bride's family, sometimes with a cutting remark, other times by just wrinkling her nose and asking the girls who were helping to serve a particularly despised dish to Litsa's brothers or her uncles.

'Make sure to take this one to my son's brothers-in-law,' she would say in a voice dripping with false solicitude for the well-being of those three dumb brutes, when what she meant was make sure nobody in our family eats this.

The insult to the sardines was the last straw. With a blood-curdling battle cry, Kyra Agne dropped the sardines on the floor and grabbed at Kyra Fotini.

'You lousy bitch! How dare you insult me on the day of my daughter's wedding. Nothing is good enough for you. You've forgotten the smell of shit on your father and now you put on airs and play the grand lady with me!'

Kyra Agne was fat and slow, but if she found her target, there was no way to shake her off. Kyra Fotini was jammed between the hot oven and her opponent. With no room to run, she clasped a handful of Kyra Agne's hair and pulled with all her might. Kyra Agne turned her head sideways and bit down on Kyra Fotini's arm. The fight was on. I was in the kitchen to bring some lamb in to the women who were cooking and serving, but I was not about to tackle either of the two women to stop the fight. As the others dropped whatever they were doing to try and separate them, I ran out to the men to alert them to the trouble.

'Come quick,' I cried. 'They're gonna kill each other.'

Kyr Lambros and Kyr Stathis stopped in mid-verse. They looked at me dumbly.

'Kyra Agne is biting Kyra Fotini, and Kyra Fotini has her by the hair!' I explained, pointing to the house.

The two fathers jumped to their feet, followed by other relatives. Only the three brothers continued to eat as though nothing had happened.

By the time I could squeeze back into the kitchen, the two women had been separated. Kyra Agne was sitting on the floor surrounded by sardines and raining curses on Kyra Fotini who was a miserable woman bent on ruining the day for her. Kyra Fotini was crying and inviting everyone to smell the sardines and tell her if she was in the wrong. Pavlos and Litsa were standing in the corner shaking their hands, but they were the only people in attendance who were neither talking nor shouting. The din was unimaginable. Everyone was taking sides, registering complaints, trading insults, picking up sardines to examine them for signs of freshness.

The two fathers-in-law at first tried to calm down their wives. When this had no effect, they tried to get them to see reason. They were both the worse for wear, slurring their words and weaving about as they tried to get to the bottom of the trouble and diffuse it. The music from outside was getting louder, and it was plain to see that both of them would rather return to their retsina and their duet.

'Listen here, Agne,' Kyr Stathis finally said in exasperation, 'come out of this kitchen right now. It's not your kitchen. It's her house and she can serve whatever she likes.'

'And you, Fotini,' Kyr Lambros added, 'you stop this nonsense right now or I will beat you myself. Enough is enough! This has to end right here and now.'

'You keep talking to me like that, Lambros, and we'll see what enough is,' threatened Kyra Fotini, who did not take kindly to her husband bullying her. But the fight was over, because Kyra Agne, aided by at least three people straining with all their might, was up once more, and following her husband out the door. Bits and pieces of sardine had threaded themselves into the lace of her dress, particularly around her impressive rump, and I must say that when she swept past me, the fishy smell was unbearable.

Outside, the party was still in full swing. Warmed by food and fuelled by retsina, the guests were laughing, mingling and dancing up a storm. The musicians had abandoned the dirge-like 'Mother, why did you give birth to me?' and had switched to *tsifteteli*, quick, lively belly-dancing tunes. Greek men are macho, but they love the *tsifteteli*. They sway their hips sinuously, shake their shoulders sensuously and snake their arms around their heads and bodies like Turkish harem girls, bending their waist this way and that, and twirling around their partners or on their own. Women dance it more modestly, for the sake of their reputation, so it's the men who give full expression to this dance of seduction. Andreas was in the middle of the circle of dancers, swaying and dipping with the best of them. I watched in fascination, and then I saw Katerina, who had spent all her time in the kitchen, absorbed by the dance, too, as she leaned against a tree in the dark recesses of the yard. She seemed to have a half-smile on her face, and I wished I could dance with her in the crowd, wished I could see her slender waist bending from side to side, her breasts shaking with the Asian rhythm. Instead, I got us two glasses and parted the crowd to join her.

'Here, Katerina,' I said, offering her one. I had been drinking steadily all evening while I was turning the spit and helping with the guests. My mind was feeling light and easy, and the gathering nightfall was making me feel free.

She accepted the glass and drank it down fast, after her hot work in the kitchen.

'Will you dance with me?' I asked.

'I don't think so, George. But it's nice to sit here and have a drink.'

I left, got her another glass and returned to stand beside her, breathing in her scent. The crowd was going wild, the music gathering force. Kyr Lambros and Kyr Stathis were dancing together, Kyr Stathis kneeling on the ground and clapping his hands, Kyr Lambros shaking his shoulders and his rounded belly as though he were a courtesan. The sounds of the celebration seemed to come from far off, from another world. I felt invisible.

'You are so beautiful, Katerina,' I whispered to her, putting my hand on her shoulder and bringing my face close to hers. 'You are so beautiful, and I love you so.'

'I love you, too, George,' she said, leaning away from me. Those were the right words, but they were not said in the right spirit. She was talking to a brother.

'But I don't love you like a sister, Katerina,' I said. 'I love you like a woman. Listen to me. I'm not your brother. And soon I'm going to be a man. Don't you understand?'

My arm went around her waist, and I drew her to me. Her glass splashed retsina. Her breasts bumped against my chest. With my head bent over her small frame and her face drawing away from me, I could see down that cleft. I was inches away from the rising and falling of the downy soft smoothness. I dropped my glass and put my other arm around her, crushing her to me, moving one hand up to the curved base of one breast. Never before, and never since, had I wanted anyone so much. She pushed against me to get me to release her.

'Please, George, you're drunk.'

I resisted her small hands.

'I love you, don't you see? I'm gonna marry you Katerina. As soon as I can, in a few years, I'm gonna marry you.'

She started crying. My arms went slack.

'Katerina, why are you crying? What's wrong? Did I say something wrong?'

She shook her head, but kept on crying.

'Stay here,' I told her, and leaped to the retsina barrel. I brought her another glass, filled to the brim.

'Here, Katerina, drink some of this. Are you feeling sick?'

'I'm sorry, George,' she said between gulps. 'I'm sorry. But I can never get married.'

'Why, sure you can, Katerina. I know you're poor, but other poor girls marry. A girl as pretty as you are doesn't have to stay on the shelf unless she wants to. Look here, I love you. What do you mean you can't get married? You can marry *me*. Maybe I'm not much to look at now, but I will be soon. Manos says if I keep carrying the bricks and doing everything else I will grow big and strong. I'll look like Andreas, truly I will. And I can take care of you, Katerina. You'll see. Will you marry me, Katerina, will you?'

She just shook her head and smiled bitterly.

'You just don't understand, George.'

'What don't I understand? Explain it to me. Just tell me.'

But she wouldn't say. She walked away and I went to follow her; she motioned me not to. My good mood had evaporated. It seemed there were obstacles to my heart's desire that I had not considered. I sank down on the ground and kept on drinking. If she thinks she can't get married to anyone else why doesn't she want me, I thought. It must be that she thinks it's humiliating to marry someone who looks like a little kid like I do. She's twenty years old, twenty-one. It would look terrible to marry a short, skinny sixteen-year-old. She would look desperate and tongues would wag. That Kyra Fotini was sure to find something poisonous to spew her way. Katerina just doesn't realise that I am going to develop into a man and she'll have nothing to be ashamed of being seen next to me. She thinks I'm asking her to get married to a child. In a year to two nobody will be able to tell she's older than me. She just can't visualise the progress I'm going to make. I made a pact right then to move the pile of bricks twice every day, to hasten the process along.

More than a little drunk, but pleased with my conclusion, I moved once again into the middle of the party. Andreas grabbed me by the arm.

'Come on, little brother, it's time for you to dance.'

I protested, tried to get away, but soon I was shaking and swaying with everybody else.

The stars were out now and the party was still in full swing. Kyra Agne was soothing her nerves with food. Kyra Fotini remained in the kitchen. The dancers were wiping their sweaty faces but showed no signs of stopping. In my mad whirling and swaying I saw Katerina in the ring of onlookers. Her face was flushed from drinking and she seemed to have got over her tears. She was singing along with the words of the song and tapping one of her small feet. Andreas saw her, too. He grabbed her by the hand, the way he had grabbed me, and dragged her into the dancing throng, near the band.

'Dance with me, Katerina,' he shouted above the din. Then he reached in his pocket, pulled out a hundred drachma note, spat on it and stuck it on the forehead of the singer, shouting out a request. The singer smiled, put the bill in his pocket and led the band in the wildest *tsifteteli* yet, about a man whose woman is making his life miserable with jealousy.

Katerina looked uncomfortable for a few bars, but encouraged by Andreas, she soon started to move a little, cautiously, modestly. Pavlos was dancing next to them with Litsa. Then Andreas was dancing with Litsa and Pavlos with Katerina, and then the four were dancing together. And just as the song was in full swing, with everybody singing the chorus at the top of their lungs, Pavlos swept a table clean with his arm, and Andreas grabbed Katerina by the waist, and hoisted her up there, to dance for the whole party. Pavlos went to do the same thing with Litsa, but she motioned to her belly and he let go. On top of the table, Katerina was blushing, but the throng was around her, clapping and shouting encouragements to bend her waist and shake her hips. She tried to get down, but Andreas pushed her up again. She gave in, took a few steps, swished her skirt around, then the song was over. Andreas put his hands around her waist again and lifted her off the table and to the ground in a smooth easy motion, as though she weighed nothing. Beside him, she was as small as a doll. He was smiling down at her, and when she smiled back he winked. They looked good together, the huge man and the toy-like girl, and there seemed to be a spark between them. My jealous eyes blinked as a new thought came to me unbidden. Was she in love with him? Is that why she said she could never marry. Because she harboured some secret passion for my brother? She would dance for him. She gave him smiles, but she gave me only tears and enigmas. I hung my head.

The band moved on to the next song, a slow and moody *hasapiko*, the 'butcher's dance'. Only men dance these songs, so the women sat down and watched their husbands and sons, with arms on each other's shoulders, execute the slow deliberate steps and difficult combinations.

The party slowed down along with the music. Litsa's family had to leave or they would miss the last bus. Amidst kisses and traditional wishes for a flower-strewn life, the cotton-clad women picked up their brood and husbands and started the walk to the bus station. The three brothers were still stuffing food in their mouths and they carried with them bags full of provisions for the trip down. Kyr Stathis kissed Kyr Lambros on both cheeks, shook hands firmly to cement their retsina-inspired friendship and took off, followed by Kyra Agne, who complained she couldn't walk fast enough to keep up with him because her feet were killing her.

'Of course they're killing her. Look at the fat cow. Feet were meant to carry people, not refrigerators,' Kyra Fotini, who had emerged from the kitchen now that her rival was leaving, said venomously.

The Beloved Land

I was drunk and I knew it. My shirt was soaked in sweat and I was staggering a bit. The world was spinning a little too fast for comfort, so I sat at one of the tables and waited for the feeling to subside. The band played on, with the woman in the shiny dress looking as bored as ever, and hardly moving a muscle. What was left of the party was the hard core of midnight revellers, who had no plans to clear out in the foreseeable future. Since these were Greeks, the group was large. Pavlos, Litsa, Andreas and Katerina were sitting together at one of the tables, laughing over some of the jokes Andreas and Pavlos were exchanging. I watched them with desperate attention. If Katerina was in love with Andreas, how did he feel about her? Did he know? Did he care? He would know better than to try something with her, wouldn't he? In vain I tried to find further clues in their behaviour. But she had danced with him. There was no denying that.

I don't know how long my bleary eyes stayed riveted to the merry foursome. When I finally tore my gaze away the retsina still flowed, but now there were no outsiders – they had all left to catch the bus – and Kyra Fotini chose her moment to straighten things out with her husband. She drew him aside, and started whispering fiercely to him. For a while he listened, but then he must have turned bored or tired, because he waved her away. This enraged her.

'Don't you wave me away, don't you dare! That you would sit and drink with that man and make a fool of yourself dancing with him after what his wife did to me! Have you forgotten what they are? Have you forgotten what they've done? It's all right to drink and sing tonight, but what happens tomorrow? The sun will come up tomorrow and we will have to provide for their grandchild and their daughter. And are they grateful?

No! Instead they come to my house with their rancid fish and cheap dishes and they try to poison the guests. And when I try to stop her you tell me to shut up instead of sticking up for me!'

'Fotini, you're crazy.'

'Crazy? *I'm* crazy? You kiss that man on both cheeks and *I'm* the crazy one? But that's how it is with you! So long as you drink and eat and have a good time nothing else matters, like loyalty to your wife and protecting your wife. She bit me, goddamn it. I should be tested for rabies!'

She was crying now and shaking with anger and everyone had stopped and was listening to her tirade, except for the band, which played on more determinedly than ever. Pavlos walked up to her, Litsa behind him.

'Here, Mother, calm down.'

'You! You snake that I raised in my bosom only to have you bite me when I least expected it. How dare you tell that woman about my father! What gave you the right to discuss my father with her!'

'Mother, what are you talking about?'

'How did Agne know my father worked in the sewers if it wasn't you that told her?'

'Okay, so I happened to mention it. So what? It's not like he was a thief and we have to keep it a secret! He did an honest day's work for an honest day's pay.'

'She threw it in my face, that's what! She threw the smell of shit in my face!'

'Oh, Mother, so you both got angry and you said a few words. No need to carry on about it so.'

'I have no family!' She was wailing now. 'They've taken you both from me with their wiles and schemes. My own son and husband betray me and take her side.'

Litsa tried to reach out for her.

'You stay away from me, you bitch,' Kyra Fotini snapped at her.

'Mother, I forbid you to talk to my wife like that!'

'Forbid me! My own child whose nappies I changed forbids me to talk to his wife! What else will my ears hear today? You got what you came for, didn't you, you little whore. He's yours now, body and soul, and I am nothing, nothing at all. Not even to my own husband who tells me to shut up as though I don't have a right to talk in my own house.'

Pavlos stormed into the house with Litsa in tow. Andreas went after them. The guests were tiptoeing out of the yard silently. Someone told the band to stop. Kyr Lambros stood over his wife weaving back and forth on his feet, uncertain what to do. My eyes met Katerina's and I nodded to her to leave. As we were walking out, Manos and Antigone joined us.

'I had forgotten what a joy family life in Greece can be,' he said, taking Antigone's arm in his. 'This is one wedding that will go down in history.'

Halfway to the house we came upon the stooped figure of my uncle.

'Demetres, wait up,' Manos cried.

My uncle turned and waited. For the rest of the walk home Manos tried to joke with him, but he was silent. We parted in front of our yard. At the stairs, Katerina bid us good night and turned to her own door.

Upstairs, my uncle sat down at the kitchen table, heavy-lidded and morose. I murmured good night, and went to my room. When I closed my eyes in bed I felt like I was going to throw up with dizziness. I put my foot down on the floor to steady the world, and tried to concentrate on Andreas and Katerina and the monstrous new possibility that I had not before considered. Could there be a rival in my own house? Had I lost Katerina before I could truly compete for her? Obsessed with my newfound worry, I fell into a fitful sleep.

A muffled scream awoke me with a start. It was still pitch dark. The sound had come from downstairs. Our house was built of thick stone and noises didn't carry. For me to have heard it through thick walls in my sleep, it must have been quite loud. Katerina, I thought, and jumped out of bed. I still felt a little unsteady, but I struggled into my trousers and shoes and stumbled out of the room and down the stairs.

Katerina's door was locked. Inside I could hear my uncle's voice and Katerina's whimpers.

'You bitch, you whore! Shaking your tits for the world to see and swinging your skirt to show your cunt!'

A crash, a slap, a muffled sob.

'You won't rest until you've had every man in the village, will you?'

Bang, crash.

'Please, Kyr Demetres. I didn't do anything.'

I pounded on the door. I shook it in its frame. I cursed in frustration. There was nothing I could do to get inside and stop the slaughter.

'Uncle,' I yelled. 'Uncle, stop it this minute or I'll call the police!'

The noises stopped. The door swung open and a heavy fist reached out and grabbed me, pulling me inside.

'You'll call the police? I'll show you to threaten me!'

His fist connected with my stomach, then his foot with my balls. I doubled over in pain and saw stars. When my eyes cleared I saw he had started on Katerina again. Her lovely red dress was torn to shreds all over her little room. The nightgown she wore was ripped down the side. Her left breast was plainly visible, shocking in its whiteness. The rest of her was an angry red from blows that had fallen on her and were still falling on her. He was beating her about the shoulders while pelting her with an unending string of curses and accusing her of every vile act possible between man and woman. I was dragging myself across the floor in an agony of pain trying to reach them when the door burst open on its hinges and my brother Andreas strode in.

In two long steps he was behind my uncle and had him by the scruff of the neck.

'What the hell do you think you're doing, old man,' he said, and threw him aside.

He bent to help Katerina, but my uncle was already picking himself up and preparing to attack.

'Look out,' I yelled at my brother, but he hardly needed my warning. My uncle had had too much to drink and was tired from all the blows he had dealt to Katerina and to me. Once, twice, Andreas punched him. One in the face, one in the squishy gut. My uncle fell down like a sack of potatoes, unconscious.

Andreas bent over Katerina again. Her face was swollen and bore the imprints of my uncle's hands. Her legs and arms were full of marks, and she was doubled up in pain.

'Is it bad?' Andreas asked.

She nodded yes.

'George, we've got to take her to the hospital.'

'Should I get an ambulance?'

'No, we don't want the neighbourhood to know. Get a blanket. We'll wrap her in that and I will carry her to the taxi stand.'

'What about Uncle?' I asked.

'Let the bastard drown in his own swill.'

Thank God it was summer. Thank God it was the weekend. Panorama had a spot dedicated to taxis, but there's never any taxis there in winter. And there's never any taxis there this late except on summer nights, when the summer people or their guests may need one.

With Katerina securely held in his arms, my brother, dressed in his best suit, walked the quiet streets of Panorama. He walked slowly and evenly, so as not to jar her. I followed behind him, consumed with worry. At the taxi stand we put Katerina in the back seat, her head resting on Andreas's knees. I got in the front.

'To the Saint Loukas hospital,' my brother commanded, 'as fast as you can.'

The cab driver threw the cigarette he had been smoking out of the window and drove off like a bat out of hell.

'What's wrong with her?' he asked.

'Bad fall,' Andreas answered.

By the time we pulled in front of the hospital I had muttered every prayer I could remember. I had a kink in my neck from throwing glances to the back seat. Andreas was caressing Katerina's forehead.

At the hospital two attendants put Katerina on a stretcher and wheeled her down a corridor and out of our sight. Andreas sat down to wait.

'So what happened?' he asked as he lit a cigarette.

'I was asleep. Katerina's scream woke me up. He was beating her because she danced and wore the dress.'

'So what if she danced?'

I couldn't hold my tears any more.

'He hates it if she looks pretty or if she talks to men,' I said, water leaking from my eyes. 'He beat her badly a year ago because she spoke to the fruit pedlar. And he slaps her when she spends too much on things for the house.'

'How long has this been going on?'

'Ever since you left for the army. Two years.'

'How come I've never seen it now that I'm back?'

'He doesn't do it when you're around. Ever since you came back from the army I thought he'd stopped altogether.'

'So why didn't you tell me, George?' His voice had a hard accusing tone. 'If you had said something I could have talked to him, threatened him a little, we wouldn't be here now.'

Because I didn't want you to rescue her. Because I hate it that he is afraid to hit her in front of you, but he makes a punching bag out of her when I'm around and he knows he has nothing to fear because he can beat me, too. Because I hate your big strong arms, and your confidence, and your strength. Because all I want is to be like you.

'Because I thought he'd stopped,' I whined miserably, my voice high in pitch as though I had never entered puberty.

'Well, that's just great,' Andreas said, flicking his ash to the floor. 'You think he's stopped and he sends her to the hospital. Fine handiwork, George.'

'I love Katerina,' I yelled back at him. 'Don't you dare make this my fault. I'd give anything for this not to have happened. I was going to call the police. I was going to kill him.'

Andreas just shook his head with contempt. He didn't even bother to look at me or reply. The two of us sat in the stiflingly hot waiting room with the bare floor full of cigarette butts and dust, and waited for the verdict.

I was staring at the floor, fighting back tears of rage and remorse, when I heard another person enter the area.

'Antigone!' I cried.

'Why are you here?' Andreas said simultaneously.

She was crying and seemed very upset.

'Kyra Parthenopi had another heart attack. My God, I think this might be it. We might lose her.' Her tears were hot and earnest. She threw herself in one of the chairs and sobbed.

'It's like losing my mother all over again. I can't stand it. What will become of me if she dies? How will I live alone again!'

Pity swept over me in a rushing tide. Her nastiness and bitter personality were erased from my mind. The image in my head was of a young Antigone plying her needle, singing songs, smiling up at her fiancé. I sat down next to her, unsure of how to give comfort. A young man in a white coat appeared and motioned Andreas to go with him.

'Stay here,' he told me and disappeared with the young man.

I felt awkward alone with the grieving Antigone. I was sad, too, that Kyra Parthenopi might be dead. I thought of Manos somewhere up there in the hospital anxiously questioning doctors. But I had no idea what to say to Antigone or if I should talk at all.

Finally Manos appeared.

'She's alive. They have her hooked up to every machine known to man. I have a specialist coming in from Thessaloniki to look at her,' he said.

Then he looked up at me.

'What are you doing here? How did you know?'

I stammered. And then Andreas was there.

'Katerina complained of a pain in her belly,' he said easily. 'We thought it might be appendicitis. She's in now and they're running some tests. How is Kyra Parthenopi?'

By the time Manos and Antigone went in search of a doctor for an update on Kyra Parthenopi's condition, I was bursting to know how Katerina was doing.

'She's okay, they think. No big harm done, although she got a pretty bad beating. The damn doctor thinks I did it. They will keep her overnight for observation. Now we'd better think of a way for appendicitis to have caused the bruises!'

We waited a while longer to make sure Kyra Parthenopi was in a stable condition. She was still alive, but the doctors were not hopeful. She was old and weak. Her heart might give out at any minute. Manos told us he and Antigone would stay at the hospital.

'Why don't you take the car?' he told Andreas. 'There are no cabs out here at this hour.'

I wanted to see Katerina before I left, but Andreas said she was sleeping and I shouldn't disturb her. We got in Manos's car and swung out of the parking lot and on to the deserted, dark road to Panorama. We drove in silence, weary and heartsick. The sky had begun to change colour and there were birds starting to sing. Andreas had the window rolled down and a cigarette dangling out. His profile was carved in stone.

I woke up very late the next day with a monster of a headache making my skull throb. The house was deserted. My grandpa was sitting in the kitchen, oblivious to everything. When I went in to check on him he complained that Niki had not fed him. Three years after her death, he was still saying her name every day. I fried him a couple of eggs, but felt nauseated at the thought of eating one myself. Neither my uncle nor Andreas was around. Manos's house was empty, too. I sat in the yard and waited. My uncle showed up first. He brought some bread and watermelon in the yard and ate, spitting the black seeds to the ground, never glancing my way. My hatred for him was a dark cloud around me, obscuring everything. I searched his face for a sign of Andreas's punch, but I could see nothing. He finally got up with a belch and went inside to sleep.

In a while, Andreas pulled up in Manos's car.

'She's okay,' he answered my wordless question. 'I got them to keep her in today, too. She's got a bruise on her face. Maybe with another day it won't look so obvious.'

'Kyra Parthenopi?'

'The specialist is here. He keeps shaking his head. I'm just here to pick up a few things from Manos's house and go back to the hospital. Manos says you're to come, too.'

In Manos's house, Andreas opened a small jewellery box and took out Kyra Parthenopi's American ring.

A few hours later, next to Kyra Parthenopi's bed with the intravenous equipment and the heart monitor, Manos married Antigone at the express wish of his dying mother. The old woman's lips were blue and her skin ashen, but she was smiling as she gave them her blessing. The *xenitia* gave Antigone a husband after all.

17

The Betrayal

After the short wedding ceremony, I went to see Katerina.
She was sitting up in bed, in a ward filled with nine
other beds, seven of them empty. There was a wheezy
old woman next to her who was talking in a sing-song
voice about her son the policeman, and a mound in
another bed across the aisle which emitted piteous,
ominous groans at regular intervals. Katerina was wearing
a hospital-issue nightgown, and there was a water glass
with some wildflowers on the stand next to her. There was
only one bruise on her face, a big bump in the middle
of her forehead. I greeted her and pulled the curtain
between the two beds shut, to give us some privacy.
Then I sat on the edge of her bed, my eyes roaming
over her in search of scars and bruises.

'It's all on my legs and arms,' she said. 'Except for
the mountain on my forehead.'

I glanced in the direction of the old woman behind the
curtain, who was still talking a mile a minute.

'Don't worry,' Katerina said. 'She can't hear anything.
She's deaf as a post.'

'Where did you get the flowers?' I asked.

'Andreas brought them this morning.'

This small bit of information hit me hard. My suspicions,

which events had caused me to set aside for a while, choked my brain once more. I could offer no more than a few token words of sympathy, while Katerina played listlessly with the fringe on the bed sheets. I left the ward feeling dissatisfied with myself. I had let her down, I had nothing to offer her, and she seemed a million miles away from me. Still, I told myself, she didn't have the look of a woman rescued from danger by the man she loves, did she? Maybe I was being crazy.

Andreas was downstairs.

'They don't think Kyra Parthenopi will make it through the day,' he said to me.

Kyra Parthenopi made it through that day, but she didn't live through the next. Katerina came home in time for the lying in. I spent most of that second day after Pavlos's wedding near Manos, who seemed to have aged ten years in two days. Antigone was crushed by Kyra Parthenopi's death, too, but there was a sleek look of satisfaction about her. The mourners who filed through the house were more interested in the news of the wedding than in paying their respects. Many parents had cast a hopeful eye to Manos as a possible groom for their daughters. That the old maid Antigone, with her dried-up looks and pent-up frustration, had snagged such a prize seemed unfair to the mothers of nubile young girls.

'She will live in luxury now,' I heard the butcher's wife whispering fiercely to Kyra Fotini. 'The car, the jewellery, everything she wants, and all because she was smart enough to cosy up to Parthenopi. Manos could have had anyone he wanted, but who can compete with a mother's dying wish?'

'Beware of unmarried women,' Kyra Fotini whispered back, with a bitter smirk.

I thought the remarks ill-deserved. Antigone could hardly have anticipated, let alone planned, the events that led to her surprise wedding. She still seemed unable to believe her good luck in the middle of her misfortune. All day long her expression veered from grief to exultation and disbelief. Manos and she did not seem like a married couple. They still acted like no more than friends. She went out of her way to make him comfortable, but this was no different from before. But every time she plumped up a pillow to put behind his back or reached for a glass to fill with water for him, the ring would flash on her bony hand and her eyes would fix on it with happiness. She would have gloated, perhaps, in other circumstances. As it was, the coffin made her almost unassuming in her great triumph.

The funeral was simple. Katerina did not attend. She was at home recuperating from her supposed appendectomy.

The next few days were quiet and subdued. Manos sat in his yard, with Antigone next to him. He told me he would be leaving soon with Antigone, to go back to New York.

'Without my mother,' he sighed, 'this place doesn't feel like home any more.'

At home, Katerina stayed in her room all day, lying in her bed with the curtains drawn. The neighbourhood women stopped by to see her, bringing food for the men in the house who could not be expected to fend for themselves. Those who asked about the shiner on Katerina's forehead, were told that Andreas had carelessly bumped her head against the door when he was carrying her out of the room and to the hospital, after her collapse from the awful pain of an appendix about to rupture.

My uncle went about as though nothing had happened.

I don't know if Andreas spoke to him, or if he threatened him. All I know is that the two acted as though they had had a fight. They ignored each other almost completely, except for looks of pure hatred directed from Andreas to our uncle who seemed not to notice them at all. Instead of cowering and apologising, Uncle Demetres was wearing a look of injured pride and bravado, as if to say he had done no more to Katerina than she deserved, and what was the fuss about anyway.

And that is the end of the golden years of my life. A week after Pavlos's wedding my childhood ended, normal life ended, and I had lost Katerina. I lost my life.

That Saturday Katerina was finally up from her supposed sickbed and Andreas had invited Manos and Antigone over to eat, in a quiet celebration of their wedding. It was just the six of us: the new couple, my brother, Katerina, Grandpa, and me. The table was laid in the yard, the roast chicken was placed in the middle of the table, the wine was poured and Andreas stood up to make a toast.

'May you live a long and happy life,' he said, 'and may you have many children.'

Antigone smiled fondly at Manos, Manos squeezed her hand, the glasses chinked.

'And while you are all here, I have an announcement to make,' Andreas continued. 'Why should you be the only ones to enjoy married life? This may come as a surprise to you, but Katerina and I are getting married!'

I still remember the way my stomach dropped to the ground. The way my heart stopped in mid-beat and left me hanging on the threshold of apoplexy. The way my brain stopped functioning because there was no way to handle the overload short of exploding. I sat like a pillar of salt, paralysed with disbelief. I was no longer a part of the scene in front of me. The seconds ticked by. I swallowed hard. With a great roar in my ears, my heart started pumping again. Feeling returned to my extremities. Had I heard wrong? No. Antigone was up on her feet, hugging and kissing Katerina. Manos was standing, too, and he was hugging Andreas, wishing him the best. Grandpa was cackling without knowing why. What? What? What was this? Where did this come from? How did this happen?

'No!' I yelled and sprang to my feet.

Everything stopped, the company turned in my direction, surprise and puzzlement on their faces.

'What do you mean you're getting married?'

'Why, little brother, I mean we're getting married. What do you mean, what do I mean?' Andreas was looking at me like I was the village idiot. The words I was forming scattered in my brain. They came too fast, and they came in the wrong order.

'Married . . . Katerina . . . You can't . . . I mean . . . how . . .'

I was blushing with the effort. I was stammering. I sounded deranged. I looked at my brother, a smile still on his face. I looked at Manos, understanding dawning in his eyes. I looked at Antigone, a look of disapproval souring her expression. And I looked at Katerina, most of all Katerina, my love, my heart, the centre of my being, and she looked blank, a stranger. I ran. I pushed the table away violently, I heard something fall and crash and then I ran as fast as if the hounds of hell were at my heels.

It was two in the afternoon. The sun was high and the heat strong. I ran up to the villas and then kept going, past the big houses, out where there were no people, nothing but trees and weeds and stones. The sweat poured down my body. My breath came in fast, labouring gusts and my chest and legs were on fire. I stopped out of sheer exhaustion in the middle of nowhere. I crumpled in a heap, lay my cheek on the dry earth and cried enough to flood it. I cried the way I had never cried for anything. I cried like the last man on earth. I cried for the loss of my mother, the loss of my father, the loss of everything that I had loved and held dear. I cried for hours, and when I ran out of tears I lay on my back and closed my eyes and waited for death to take me, because there was no place else to go. And when night-time came and death had still not come to claim me, I got up and started walking back to the village out of habit. My soul was dead.

Manos had been looking for me for hours. He caught up with me in front of the villas. Without a word he put his arm around me and then he led me to our spot, where we had spent the afternoons of another life talking together. When he settled me under the tree and sat next to me, he finally spoke.

'You love her.'

'More than life.'

He put his arm around me again. He drew me to him as though I was a child. He sheltered my head on his chest, and then he told me they were getting married in a week. So soon. So soon. The tears came again. He let me cry and he rocked me back and forth and cradled me like a baby.

'We must go home,' he said after I had stopped for a while.

'Never,' I said. 'I can't go home.'

'You have to, George. It's your home, and he's your brother and you can't just leave and never go back. Katerina has a right to marry whom she wants. You have to be a man about his. You can't act like a child that can't admit defeat. You loved and you lost and now you have to put a good face on it and go back and congratulate them both. You lift and carry the bricks to look like a man. Start acting like one.'

So that's what I did. I squared my shoulders and my chin and walked back with Manos. I entered the yard alone. I wished Katerina and Andreas a happy life. My lips were stiff and dry, my words short and forced, my eyes elsewhere but on those two, but I did it. And then I went to bed to await the morning. It was a very long night, but I was glad of its length, because with the new day I would have to face them again, and I had not carried enough bricks to live through a whole day with this weight on my shoulders.

Without any sleep I rose the next morning. My head felt heavy, my eyes scratchy from all the tears. My brain and my heart were numb. I sleepwalked through the whole day, as the news made the round of the village and women stopped by to check out the situation and give their wishes and congratulations to the engaged couple. As I watched woman after woman smile and nod, kiss Katerina, shake Andreas's hand, say how pleased my parents would have been, my mind started working again. How had this happened right under my nose, without me knowing? Even if she loved him, as I had so recently suspected, why would he marry her? Did he want to protect her from my uncle's abuse? But surely his presence and his knowledge were enough. Did he love her? He who had had so many cheap and easy women in the full flower of plump, vibrant femininity, could he have any appreciation for the delicate, pale Katerina? And when had this happened? How come I hadn't noticed anything until I saw them dancing? Scenes flashed through my mind. Katerina with the red polyester cloth wrapped around her. Andreas complimenting her cooking and casting an appreciative glance at her. Andreas peeking in the washing shed to see her taking her bath. Katerina dancing. Katerina on the table. Andreas with his hands around her waist, helping her down. Katerina smiling up to him. Had I been blind? I watched them avidly as their wedding day drew near. She was a tiny little slip of a girl next to the great height and breadth that was my brother. She seemed happy. She smiled more. She blushed at the talk of the women around her.

Day in and day out, all day long, my mind examined the situation and tried to adjust to the shattering reality of losing Katerina to my brother. While I was waiting to grow up, he who had everything, he who was a man in every sense of the word, had stepped right in with all his accustomed ease and plucked the prize right out from in front of me. I had to go through hell to prove myself worthy of Katerina and earn her love little by little through years of struggle and frustrated waiting. He could just reach out and have her effortlessly, without trying, without deserving her. I hated him with all my heart. His voice grated on me. His big, strong body was an affront to me, seemed monstrously outsized and bulky. Thoughts of his making love to Katerina came to me unbidden and unwanted, and I shuddered, burned with envy, misery, disgust. I had told her I loved her, and she had gone ahead and said yes to my brother anyway. So what was all the talk of never marrying, and all the tears? Lies, lies and more lies. Lies to get rid of me, to get me to take my burdensome, unappreciated feelings and be gone. Lies to get me to clear out the path for my brother to stride through, tall and strong like a young tree, and claim her. Had she known then that he would marry her? Surely she must have known. Surely their plans had been laid even then. Was she meeting him in a corner somewhere? Had they been kissing and speaking of love, and making their plans while I knew nothing, while I laid my plans and sweated in my exercise routine to become strong and manly for Katerina?

I felt like such a fool. They must despise me, I thought, for being so stupid and for not seeing the truth in my own house, right in front of my eyes. Shame, pain, more shame, despair, despondency. Every day was the same. Every hope was gone.

My uncle received the news with total indifference. He shrugged, shuffled off, spent more time than ever at the tavern. He stopped talking to Katerina. She continued to do his washing, feed him and make his coffee, but the two had no other contact. In the evening, it was Andreas who did the accounts. Uncle Demetres and my brother had a little run-in over this one. The first day Katerina returned from the hospital, Uncle Demetres sat down alone to do the books, but Andreas walked in and said he would do the books from here on. My uncle ignored him and went right on counting the money. Andreas banged his fist on the table, making the coins dance.

'I said this is my job now!'

My uncle stopped arranging his neat piles and fixed Andreas with a steely glance.

'Follow me,' Andreas said, and his voice held menace.

My uncle followed him. The two went into Uncle Demetres's room, and Andreas shut the door. They stayed in there several minutes. When they came out, Andreas took my uncle's seat at the table, and Uncle slammed out of the house. That was the only talk the two had, and I had no idea what they had said. But the money was under Andreas's control now.

*   *   *

I don't know why it had not occurred to me before. The shock was too great, perhaps. My pain and jealousy too all-pervasive to allow my mind to see the obvious. It took Kyra Marika's prying eyes, her glance full of calculation at Katerina's waist, to jolt my mind out of its daze. She was pregnant! My God, that's what it was. He was marrying her because he had gotten her pregnant!

My eyes now followed her everywhere with renewed zeal. I compared her figure to Litsa's, who was a frequent visitor. Litsa's breasts were bigger. So were Katerina's. It was hard to tell in her shapeless shifts, but I remembered the way they peaked out of the red dress. Kyra Toula hadn't cut it too small. Katerina was just not pregnant when Kyra Toula made the dress. Katerina's waist was slender in the dress, but I remembered that it was made to constrict the waist, and keep it from spreading in its natural contours. In effect, Katerina had been wearing a corset.

It all made sense all of a sudden. Of course there would be no signs. Andreas was a master at dissembling, perfectly capable of carrying on a love affair in his own home without anyone knowing. He was the king of liars. His casual indifference, his air of hardly noticing her most of the time, were nothing but a smoke screen. It was too much, wasn't it, to expect my brother to live in the same house with a beautiful young girl and not try to have her. He seduced her, just like Artemis, and she let him because she was infatuated with him, just like Artemis, and now she was pregnant, too. But this time he was cornered. He couldn't walk away from this one. Katerina was part of the family. And she would have refused an abortion. Or maybe she was too far along for that. So he had to do the right thing. And rob me of my only chance for happiness.

Rage filled me to the brim. I stalked the yard all day long, and when Andreas came in from the bakery, I confronted him. I asked him to come to our room. I closed the door. And then I lit into him.

'She's pregnant, isn't she? That's why you're marrying her!'

'This is none of your business, George.'

'The hell it isn't. Just tell me, you son of a bitch!'

'Butt out.'

I attacked him. I knotted my whole body into a ball of rage and I fell on him, taking him by surprise, knocking him to the floor. We grappled. I pounded at him, swinging my fists all over his body, biting, scratching, pulling his hair. So what? He humoured me for a while, just avoiding my blows as much as he could. But when I showed no signs of let up, he stopped toying with me. He slapped me, imprisoned me with his powerful thighs, flipped me over, got his arm around my neck, held me in a painful and humiliating vice.

'Artemis,' I sobbed. 'You lousy son of a bitch, you got her pregnant just like Artemis!'

'I'm marrying her, aren't I? You should be happy!'

'Artemis wasn't enough for you. Your whores were not enough for you. You had to have her, too.'

His arm and legs were hurting me. I was panting with the effort and the pain. He relaxed his grip a little. My head sprang up against his own, hitting him hard on the chin.

'Damn!' he spat out, and tightened his grip again. 'What the hell business is it of yours?'

With that he let go of me, shoved me down against the floor, and walked out. I love her, you piece of shit, I thought. That's what business of mine this is. I love her and she was mine until you got her to fall in love with you, and give you everything. And now you're taking her forever, and there's nothing for me. You could have had anyone you wanted, but you took my love.

I tried to adjust to my loss. I tried to make it through the day. I thought of the future. Of endless days and nights. Nights especially, when we would all get ready for bed, and my brother would take Katerina into the bedroom and close the door, and I would have to lie on my own bed and think of the two of them together. I thought of the child Katerina would have, and of the other children Andreas would have on her. Images of his making love to Artemis crowded my brain and then Katerina replaced Artemis in my vision. Katerina in his arms, Katerina with her legs wrapped around him, Katerina taking him in, night after night, with me next door, listening to the slightest noise, trying to catch a breath, a whisper, a sigh. A lifetime in purgatory.

The wedding was small and quick. Pavlos, whose parents had not coughed up for a honeymoon, was the best man. Katerina wore the same rented dress Litsa did. The wedding favours were not wrapped in tulle, they were just candied almonds handed over into the hands of the few guests. People noticed my stricken expression. Time and again I was asked if I was feeling all right, if I was sick, if I had had too much sun. The questions were torture to me. I didn't want to speak, I didn't want to hear. At night Katerina and Andreas retired to my parents' bedroom. My grandpa had been moved into uncle's bedroom, and Uncle Demetres had taken over Katerina's room downstairs, without so much as a single complaint. I lay in my bedroom and made myself ache with visions of Katerina's luminous skin bare in the moonlight, exposed to Andreas's jaded eyes.

I went to see Manos the next day. He and Antigone were getting ready to leave. There were suitcases everywhere.

'Take me with you to America,' I said.

'George, it's a mistake. This is your home. Stay here.'

'Manos, take me with you or I will kill myself.'

My voice must have convinced him. The black circles under my eyes, the despair in my face, must have communicated the truth to him. I couldn't go on. I couldn't live like this. America sounded perfect. A place where nobody would know me. A place where people leave you alone in your pain and nobody asks what's wrong with you. I would live the rest of my life in mourning, and I wanted no sympathy. I wanted only to lose myself in the crowds of New York. Most of all, I wanted to never see Andreas again, never face him again with the full knowledge that he had Katerina's love, and that I never would.

Who was there to protest? My uncle didn't care, my grandpa hardly recognised me. Andreas shook his head in bewilderment, but he had no wish to police my life. Katerina tried to talk to me.

'I wish you wouldn't go, George,' she said. 'I'll miss you.'

But I didn't even look at her. There was nothing to tell her. If she had picked Andreas over me, who could blame her?

The Chevy left Panorama a short while after the wedding. Everyone in the village gathered to wave us goodbye. Antigone waved back serenely, as though she were a queen or a princess accustomed to fanfare. Manos's eyes misted over as he glanced at his house one last time. It was to be torn down and built into a duplex, to be rented out. I sat in the back seat with a heart of stone, impatient for the site of my childhood to grow distant in the mirror. I left Panorama dry-eyed and anxious to be gone. Katerina waved at me, but I didn't wave back. Soon, now, I thought, as soon as we leave Panorama behind, as soon as we leave Thessaloniki behind, my pain will lighten, will become bearable, will feel less like death. Unlike most immigrants, I left Greece willingly, eagerly, and entered the *xenitia*.

Part Three

The *Xenitia*

18

The Edge of the Wilderness

Before I left Panorama, I asked Andreas to give me money. I told him this would be my share of our father's inheritance, and I would never ask for more. I don't know if he believed me, and I don't know where he found the money, but he did give me enough to pay for my plane ticket and have some left over to support myself for a while. Manos assured me that he would give me a job in his restaurant. When the car finally left Thessaloniki behind, I had no money worries and I had none of the anxiety that other immigrants feel, who head for a new land with little more than the address of acquaintances who may or may not receive the new arrival with real pleasure. I was flying off with my good friend Manos, and nothing, but nothing, I might find in New York could be worse than what I was leaving behind me.

Our trip to Athens was uneventful and I, who had never been farther from the place that I was born than Thessaloniki, might have enjoyed seeing Greece if the circumstances had been different. As it was, I simply felt more and more relieved with each kilometre that rolled behind the Chevrolet. Cocooned in its plush back seat, I watched the scenery unfold as if it were a movie.

We got to Athens late and checked into a hotel. At dinner, which the three of us ate together, Antigone tried to question me about my decision to abandon my family and travel halfway around the world, but I avoided her probing questions. Manos got her to stop by indicating that he wanted to talk of different subjects. He entertained her with descriptions of places and people we would see once we arrived in our distant destination. I watched Antigone with some interest. She deferred to Manos on everything, and did not react or comment until she checked his face to see what his reaction would be. It struck me that far from feeling smug or safe, Antigone was trying her damndest to make sure that Manos would not regret giving in to his mother's wishes. When Antigone was sharp with the waiter for splashing some water on her, one look at the disapproving expression on Manos's face was enough to cut her tirade short, and even make her, uncharacteristically, accept the waiter's apology gracefully and with a smile from her thin lips. Antigone was on her best behaviour. I wondered how long she could control her habit of being sharp and unforgiving with everyone around her.

The next morning we took the car down to the port and supervised its loading on to the ship that would, a month later, unload it in New York.

'But don't you need your car?' I asked.

'No, I don't. I didn't even have a car until I decided to visit Greece. The subway goes everywhere. But I wanted to bring a car to Greece. I guess I wanted to show off,' he replied with candour.

Later that day we boarded the plane to New York. I sat next to Manos and Antigone and listened to the prayers Antigone whispered fervently through clenched lips as we took off. The Aegean Sea, blue and gold and studded with sails, receded below us. I was on my way.

It was night-time when we arrived in New York. Kostis, Manos's friend and his general manager, greeted us and led us through doors that receded magically as we approached them. A uniformed black man, standing at least six feet tall, was following behind us with a cart full of our baggage. Only one small bag was mine. When it had been time for me to pack, I had discovered there was very little I wanted to take with me.

Kostis had brought a car, another massive American model, with an interior draped in plush velour. We took off into the night.

My first impression was of immense space. Everything was bigger. The roads were huge multi-lane affairs. The cars were barges floating on smooth wide lanes. Even the people were big. And everywhere there were electric lights turning the night into day. Kostis talked on with Manos about business in the front seat. Antigone and I in the back stared out of the windows fascinated. Kostis pulled into a restaurant after a few minutes. Instead of the bare floors, wooden chairs, naked lightbulbs and oil sheet for a tablecloth that I was used to, this restaurant had a dimly lit, carpeted hallway through which we were led to a table draped in cloth, where a young girl in a red and black outfit brought water as soon as we were sat down, without us having to ask. The water had ice in it! Just like that! But why would anybody need iced water anyway? The restaurant was pleasantly cool despite the heat outside. Air conditioning, I thought. This is what air conditioning does.

I ordered a hamburger even though I wasn't hungry. It came with french fries and coleslaw and a big glass of

Coca-Cola. The Coke tasted different from the Coke sold in Greece. Coke had just arrived there a couple of years ago, and it was sweeter than the Coke the pretty, bright-eyed waitress brought to me. The hamburger looked big and juicy, but it was bland, without oregano or any spices. Just a bunch of meat. The bun was tasteless, too, and had no substance. My uncle made better bread when he was too drunk to see straight. The french fries were all uniform in size and looked delicious, but had no potato taste. The coleslaw was sweet enough to be dessert instead of salad. This was the taste of America.

Manos's house was in Astoria. It had a small garden in the front, but it was squeezed on both sides by its neighbours. There was a family living on the bottom floor, Manos's tenants. He had kept the top apartment for his own use. I felt a little in the way when Manos showed me and Antigone in. He was bringing his wife home. This should have been their moment. He led me to the living-room, switched the TV on and left with Antigone to show her the rest of the house.

Colour TV. I had heard of this marvel, but I had never experienced it. TV in Greece was black and white. There were only two channels, and they were on the air only for a few hours a day, mostly showing news or droning, boring shows on farming, fishing and the army. Even so, people gathered in the houses of those rich enough to afford the new contraption, and stayed glued to the set for hours. Whoever bought a TV in Greece was assured of never spending an evening alone at home. Greeks love company, they don't even have a word for privacy, so this was generally considered an advantage.

I watched for a while. I had expected the colours to be as bright and clear as the movies. They weren't. I could hear Antigone and Manos in the back. His explanations.

Her exclamations of wonder. I let my eyes roam over the living-room. I know now that what I saw was a middle-class home with plain but comfortable furniture and clever arrangement of space. But to my eyes that first night, it was luxurious beyond measure. The carpeting was soft and deep and covered every surface of the floor. The furniture was in excellent condition and all new. No tears, no worn patches. It was a set, with the sofa matching the two armchairs, and the end tables matching the coffee table. No odds and ends accumulated over generations and matched together only in their provenance. No homemade throws and blankets laid one on top of another to make a few wooden boards resting on suitcases into a couch. Money, I thought.

Manos's house had a second bedroom with its own bathroom that was given to me to use. Manos led me to it and brought my bag in. The room was as fine as the rest of the house. A bed with a flowery cover over everything, including the pillow. An armchair. Instead of an armoire with a rickety door and a stained mirror, a closet running the length of the room on one side, with a door that operated smoothly on a rail. The same deep carpet here, too, caressing my bare feet once I took my socks and shoes off. I stepped into the bathroom. The toilet bowl flushed noiselessly and efficiently. Hot water ran in the spotless gleaming sink at the turn of a tap. No waiting for the pot to boil. A bathtub and shower hid behind a plastic curtain. Soft towels with deep pile and a border of embossed seashells hung neatly on chrome rods. I thought of the flat, hard towels, faded from years of use, that Katerina washed and ironed. I thought of the copper basin in the family room. I thought of the boiling of water and the buckets that had to be carried. I washed quickly and used some toilet paper to wipe the sink clean.

The toilet paper was as soft as cloth and dissolved when wet. Back in the room, I sank into my soft clean bed, tugged at the string that operated my night lamp and let my tears roll silently on my pillow. Greece is seven hours ahead, I thought. Andreas is already at the bakery. And Katerina is already halfway through her chores. My pillow was soaked and uncomfortable by the time I finally fell asleep. I dreamed that I was going back, but even in my dream I knew that I had nothing to go back to.

It took a few days for the three of us to get used to the time change. We all woke up early and got sleepy in the afternoon. Manos would leave us every morning to go to the restaurant, but he would return early to take a nap. He telephoned at regular intervals to see if we were okay. Every time the phone rang Antigone would look at me, and I would look at her, each of us wishing that the other would pick it up. We were both afraid to hear English on the other end and be unable to communicate.

Antigone and I stayed inside at first. She spent the day taking an inventory of what there was in the cupboards and closets, and I stared out of the window at the neighbourhood, trying to find the strength to pull myself out of my profound depression. It was no use. At every moment of the day or night, Katerina's face could appear unbidden in front of my eyes, sometimes happy, sometimes sad, always reminding me of what I had lost. On the third day, while we were all sipping coffee in the early morning, Manos insisted that Antigone and I should go shopping in the neighbourhood.

Astoria is almost like a piece of transplanted Greece. It has many Greek shops, so lack of English was no big impediment. Manos assured us that we would find many people who spoke Greek, and we had nothing to fear. Antigone was afraid we would get lost, but my sense of direction was good and it helped that most of the streets were not named but numbered, so that you knew at every moment exactly how many blocks away from home you were. She and I walked all over Astoria. Manos had left a stack of green dollars with permission to buy anything the house or we needed. Antigone declared that Manos had nothing to cook with, and so she and I went on a mission to outfit the kitchen properly. We went into one store after another buying pots and pans, dishes, glasses, plastic containers, strainers, collanders, bowls, ladles, frying pans. Over the course of two days we lugged the purchases home with us.

On the second day of our shopping spree, Manos brought home a stack of records and books guaranteed to teach me and Antigone English. We played the records on Manos's stereo and repeated the phrases to each other. Armed with our knowledge and a dictionary that came with the books, Antigone and I entered the American supermarket and began shopping for meat and vegetables. With a stop at a small grocery shop run by a Greek, we gathered everything Antigone needed, and that evening, when Manos walked in with food from the restaurant, we told him to put it away. Her face flushed with pleasure, Antigone served her first meal in her new home to me and her husband, zucchini cored and then stuffed with rice and hamburger, dressed in a thick egg and lemon sauce. Manos ate it with relish, asked for seconds and thirds, and then sopped the sauce with his bread.

'Antigone, you have hands of gold,' he told her.

Antigone accepted the compliment with a small nod of her head, as if to say this is no more than my duty. But her satisfaction at pleasing Manos was all around her like a fine, gauzy veil. Through it she seemed younger by far than at any time I could remember. Her eyes had a gleam to them, her cheeks were flushed with colour and even her tight mouth seemed to have plumped up and become red, so that all of a sudden Antigone looked almost pretty.

Since we spent so much time together, Antigone soon put it to good use, trying to probe again for information on what had happened to make me leave Greece so suddenly. Her questions were like a scalpel that cut me open without the benefit of anaesthesia. When I outright told her that I did not wish to discuss my family or my home, she stopped her questions, but mentioned Andreas, Katerina, my uncle and Panorama often. Several times I had to bite my lip and squeeze my hands into fists to keep my tears from rolling down my face in front of her. I missed Katerina, oh God how I missed her! And I missed my home.

By the time Manos mentioned that I seemed ready to start working, I would have done anything to get away from the hours alone with Antigone, despite her much improved personality.

Manos hired me as a dishwasher, to learn the work.

'I won't keep you there long,' he promised. 'But it's the only job where you don't need to talk. Study hard, learn the language and I'll have you out front in no time.'

My days became full. I left for work early in the morning with Manos. At the restaurant I swept and mopped, washed dishes and cleaned the grills for ten hours. In the evening, Manos would take me home where, after dinner, I would sit with the books and records to study. Then I would watch a couple of uncomprehending hours of TV, in the hope that hearing the language would speed my learning. Antigone and I would compare our progress. Then I would go to bed and silently cry myself to sleep, praying that I would not dream of Katerina, but actually wishing that I would, so I could spend at least my dreams in her presence.

My eyes would mist over countless times every day. I had no complaints from my life in New York, but I felt dead inside. I missed not only Katerina, but my home, too. Even though America was the land of plenty, it was missing some vital things. Its sky was never as blue as the sky in Greece, its sun never as friendly. Its breezes stank with exhaust fumes, its roads roared with infernal noise. And except for Manos and Antigone, everyone around me was a stranger, with no history and no common ground. I found myself getting sentimental over my village on the mountain. I found myself missing the most surprising things. The cows coming back from pasture in the evening, Kyr Mitsos's singsong voice and his donkey, the women sitting in each other's yard, drinking coffee and gossiping for hours. A hundred times over I would have turned back, I would have swum back if I had to, if only my need to get away from my pain had not been so great.

Above all there was the loneliness. Nobody ever dropped in at home. Night after night Manos and Antigone and I sat alone, with just the TV to connect us to the rest of the world. I didn't mind this at all; it was what I wanted. But I could tell that it was beginning to take its toll on Antigone. She would wait for us behind the door each night, pathetically happy to see us. Finally Manos noticed it, and he asked Antigone if she would like to work.

'Now you don't have to, Antigone, you know that. But I think you're a little lonely around the house, and maybe a few hours of work will help the time pass.'

She accepted eagerly, and from then on it was all three of us who left every morning. Antigone helped in every way she could, dusting the booths, polishing the windows, stocking the pantry with the help of the dictionary, and keeping an eye on the staff to make sure nobody was slacking off more than was normal. In between each chore, she struck up conversations with the waitresses who clustered around a small table taking five-minute cigarette breaks whenever they could. I had noticed that most Americans are impatient and harsh with people who don't have a good command of English. Unlike Greeks, who consider it a major accomplishment for a foreigner to utter even one badly mangled word in Greek and compliment everyone who tries extravagantly, Americans refuse to understand unless each word is pronounced just so. Greeks find accents charming. Americans consider them a disease, to be eradicated and avoided. Unless, of course, you are the boss's wife. Cured of her embarrassment by the gaggle of fawning waitresses, Antigone was stringing words together with abandon. Much of each conversation was conducted through gestures, and most of the rest was incomprehensible on both sides, but Antigone had human contact, so she was happier. I watched her from my post in the back, as I directed the burning stream of water on the racks of dishes to rinse them before shoving them into the dishwasher, and I got my own theory of why Greeks, who don't like to work hard in Greece, become so industrious once they emigrate. Used to being surrounded by family and friends who either live with us or drop in unannounced in a steady stream in our own country, we dread going home when we live abroad, because home there means being alone. We work from sunup to sundown because in America it is the only way to be surrounded by people.

My work did not provide the same opportunities for social contact, but then I went out of my way to take my breaks alone, in the alley behind the restaurant. I worked surrounded by the steam and hot water, and drove myself to wash and rinse faster and with more precision. I kept my hands busy with the dishes, and my mind occupied with my English lessons. Above all, I avoided thinking about home and about my loneliness. I built a shell around myself. But time and again Katerina invaded my thoughts, big dark eyes just out of my reach, and time and again her name came unbidden to my lips.

The weeks and months passed. Autumn came, and the sky became grey and cloudy.

'It will stay that way for months,' Manos informed me.

I didn't care. I slogged through my days and did my lessons, and I was beginning to understand some of what went on on TV. Manos brought some children's books home for me to read. The simple sentences were about all I could handle in the new language.

In October, a letter arrived from Andreas and Katerina. I carried it with me for several days before I opened it. I didn't want to know about their married life. Come home, it said. What are you doing over there? It also announced Katerina's pregnancy. I tore it into shreds that I flushed down the toilet. They disappeared in the soft whoosh of the water.

My seventeenth birthday came and went unnoticed. I floated in a sea of misery. The letter from Greece had renewed Antigone's curiosity about my reasons for leaving home. Her constant chatter about Greece and the people of Panorama, driven as it was by her intense homesickness, was a thorn in my side. How could I forget with her going on about Greece all the time? Besides, it was time for me to move out. I couldn't live on indefinitely in Manos's house.

I broached the subject, and he protested that he wanted me to stay and I should put the idea of moving out of my mind. But I noticed that Antigone did not insist that I stay along with him. I started planning where I would go and what I would do.

The snow came in December. A bitter wind drove it into my mouth and nose and ears every time I stepped outside. It numbed my ears and hands and feet, and the cold made walking painful. On Christmas Day, the phone rang. It was from Greece, it was for me. Manos dragged me to it and handed me the receiver. It was Andreas.

'Merry Christmas, little brother, can you hear me?' His voice was distant but clear.

'What?' I said.

'George, can you hear me?'

'Hello,' I shouted into the phone, as though I hadn't heard a word.

'Merry Christmas' Andreas bellowed. 'Katerina sends her love!'

'I can't hear anything,' I said, and put the phone down.

I had avoided the phone, but there was no avoiding the post. In January another letter arrived with a picture enclosed of the proud parents with the new infant. The baby was rosy and fat, obviously no newborn. The few lines penned by Andreas did not include a birthdate. Rage flooded me again. Did he take me for a fool? Was I not supposed to figure out that this was a baby conceived out of wedlock? I couldn't take any more. I had to leave. I had to go where they couldn't find me. I had to burrow deeper into America, the land of forgetting. I had to get lost in the crowd because as long as I stayed perched on this little corner of New York where Greeks had built their colony, I would forever be haunted by letters and phone calls and Antigone's relentless questions and not so subtle attempts to make me react and gauge my reactions.

Manos was violently opposed to my leaving.

'No! You will stay here and you will live with me. Listen, George, this is madness. You are underage and you have not finished school. My plan is to keep you at the restaurant this year while you study the language and then to enroll you in school so you can get your diploma. Later on maybe you can go to college.'

'College!' I exclaimed. 'Manos, what are you talking about? I'm not going to college. And since I'm not going to college, why do I need to finish school? I'm not going back to school. I want to work!'

'Losing a woman is no reason to ruin your life,' he retorted. 'It's tough to lose the one you love to your brother, but aren't you over-reacting?'

Over-reacting! What did he know, he had never fallen in love: What did he know, who was a man in every sense of the word, of humiliating defeat? I could not be a student any more.

Manos carried on for days, trying to change my mind. I was unmoved. I had to leave. New York was not far enough to cure my heart. Maybe no place was, but I had to try. I felt trapped, forever dreading that the phone would ring, that a new letter or a picture would arrive, that Antigone would unpurse her lips and reminisce again about Panorama.

'Think of the future, George,' Manos insisted. 'Without at least your high school diploma, what will you do? Are you going to wash dishes all your life?'

Future? What future? My life was already over. Manos just didn't see that. I wanted nothing but to work hard and at night go to a small room somewhere, where I could sit with my broken heart and forget.

Manos wouldn't give up. He raised my salary. He spent more time with me. He helped me with my lessons. In every way he could think of, he showed me that he cared.

279

What he didn't understand was his increased attention made me feel more trapped than ever. I had to escape. So I made my plan. I counted my money. I bided my time. I studied a map of America and tried to pick a place that would suit me. The bitter cold winter of New York taught me that I preferred a warmer climate. I looked to the south. And then my eye wandered to the west, and I saw the curve that is California. A big state, with plenty of room to get lost in. As far away from Greece as I could get on the globe without drowning in the Pacific Ocean. My destination was set.

I waited until March. By that time the worst of the winter was over. There was even a day or two of sunshine. But the wind was still heart-stoppingly cold, and icy rain fell regularly. I secretly withdrew my money from the bank where I was keeping it. I still had an amount left over from what Andreas had given me. Plus I had most of my wages from Manos, who paid me well, because he wouldn't let me pay for rent or food. The day I picked for my departure, I pretended to be too sick to go to work. I had a cold anyway, so it wasn't too difficult to exaggerate my symptoms and rub the thermometer to get it to show a temperature. Manos was worried.

'Maybe you should stay home, Antigone, and take care of George,'

Antigone, who was looking forward to another day at the restaurant chatting with the waitresses, looked in my direction with disgust.

'No, Manos, there is no reason for both of us to miss work. I'll be okay,' I said. 'I'll stay in bed, and I hope I can sleep this off.'

'I'll call to check up on you,' he insisted.

'Don't call too soon,' I tried to put him off. 'I feel very tired, so I might sleep for a while.'

Manos and Antigone finally went through the door. I rushed into my room as soon as I saw them from the window getting into the car and driving off. Then I changed my clothes, packed my bag and propped up the note I had written the night before on the kitchen table.

'Thank you for everything,' it said, 'but I have to go. I'll call you some time to let you know I'm okay. Please don't worry about me, and please don't think I'm not grateful for everything you've done for me. I just need to do this.'

Silently, like a thief, so that the family downstairs wouldn't hear and come out to investigate, I closed the door and walked down the steps. All the way down the block I worried that Manos and Antigone might have forgotten something and come back for it. But I made it to the subway undetected. I had studied the subway maps in preparation. I boarded my train and reached the bus depot without incident. At the station I bought my ticket on the Greyhound. It would take three days to reach California.

The trip was everything I could have wished for. Safe and alone in the bus, I rode through the foreign land with my face glued to the window. Finally, after so many months, I had time alone and unobserved, to let my mind dwell on my sorrow. Other passengers saw America through those windows, but I only saw my past. Katerina's face was painted indelibly on the glass for me, and I stared into her eyes for days, trying to find an answer. Lovingly, desperately, I framed her picture in my mind in all the loveliness of springtime Greece, I decorated it with poppies and almond blossoms, I lit it with the golden sun of Greece, I surrounded it with the deep clear blue of my hometown sky. I made a perfect picture, a Garden of Eden, where

I would keep my Katerina and everything I ever loved, and somewhere in that long trip to California, Greece and Katerina became one in my mind, forever melded as the Paradise I lost, forever guarded against me by the snake that inhabits every Paradise, my brother Andreas, the man who tempted my love and cast out only me.

None of the people who sat next to me tried to strike up a conversation. They left me alone, the way I had wanted to be left alone ever since Andreas had announced his big news. I was going into the unknown, but I wasn't scared. What scared me was the familiar. My home, my brother married to the woman I still worshipped. The darkness had no demons other than the ones I carried with me. I was finally where I wanted to be. Nowhere.

19

The Entrepreneur

When I finally got off the bus, it was morning, and I was twisted into the shape of a pretzel. I asked the driver where I might find a cheap hotel and he suggested Hollywood. He might have thought I was one of the scores of young people who come to Los Angeles to become stars.

I had no plans past finding a place to stay. After I checked into a dingy, four-storey establishment where I had to pay in advance, I started walking around the giant city, wondering what my next step should be. I got myself a paper and started looking through the classifieds.

For weeks I stopped at one restaurant after another, asking for work. I was not successful. My heavy accent, my thin experience, the desperation in my eyes, my lack of references, maybe even my sadness, caused every door to close in my face. I began to wonder what I would do if the situation continued to be hopeless.

I was down to my last few dollars when I finally applied for the job of dishwasher at a place that wasn't even looking yet. I had stopped reading the paper for several days. Now I was just applying at every restaurant I found on my way.

Jerry's Place was on the west edge of Hancock Park. It was a mid-priced restaurant, catering to a young and less well-off crowd. It had a simple decor of white walls and dark brown wooden tables and it served standard American fare with a Californian twist, mostly expressed in an abundance of julienned vegetables that accompanied every dish. I walked in at five, just before the dinner hour. I told the tall, muscular man at the door that I wanted to see the boss.

'He's in the back,' the man told me, with a bored expression on his chiselled face. 'What do you want?'

'I'm looking for a job,' I answered.

His face lit up like Christmas.

'Wait right here,' he told me and disappeared.

A moment later, another tall man, older and with a bit of a paunch, hurried over to where I was standing, wiping his hands on a towel.

'Providence must have sent you,' he announced. 'I don't care who are, I don't care if you are an escaped felon. Can you start right away?'

It seems that Phil, the young man scheduled to clear the tables that night, had aspirations for a career in showbusiness, and he had just flown to Las Vegas for his big break in a show. There was a party of forty expected to celebrate an anniversary, and Jerry, the owner, had nobody to help. He tied an apron around me before he even asked my name, and had me setting tables in less than a minute.

I did a good job. I carried all the trays without breaking anything, I fetched water and wine when the waitresses were too busy with other things, I helped with the dishes and I stayed late to clean up.

'Can you come back tomorrow?' Jerry asked at the end of the night, as he was counting the day's take.

'Yes, I can,' I said, 'but can you pay me for today? I need to pay my hotel.'

Jerry counted out my pay and complimented me extravagantly for being a hard worker. I think he was afraid I might not come back. But I did. I worked well and hard that second day, and all the days that followed. I did everything I was asked to do without complaint, showed up on time and never asked for a day off to go to an audition. Twice Jerry called my hotel because he needed someone to fill in, and both times I was there to take his call and available to work whatever shift he needed. People who don't have a life make very good employees. By the time Phil made it back from Vegas, a few dollars richer but still no star, the job was mine. Jerry told Phil, with some genuine regret, that he had had to fill the position.

'This town is too full of actors,' he told me as he watched Phil walking out in a huff. 'You don't plan to be in the movies, do you?'

The entertainment industry was the bane of Jerry's existence. Waiters, dishwashers and cooks are all would-be actors, singers, screenwriters and directors in LA. Jerry could never count on any of his staff to show up when scheduled. But he could count on me.

Once I was sure of my job, I looked for a place to rent. I asked Jerry if he knew of a cheap place I could rent. By this time, Jerry knew I was a fresh Greek immigrant. He had asked me about my immigration status with some anxiety. He didn't want to lose me if the Immigration Department came calling. I had come over as a visitor with no work permit, but Manos knew people in New York and had managed to pass me off as his relative, so I could qualify for an invitation as a permanent resident and attain the precious Green Card. Once Jerry was satisfied that I was not an illegal alien, he asked no more questions. Like any regular American, he didn't want to know more about me than was necessary to do his business. If I seemed a little sad, it didn't matter. I worked like a horse and showed up like clockwork. That's what counted.

Since he felt I was a good sort, Jerry told me of some friends of his who had just bought a house in Hancock Park, with a small guest room. They were looking for a tenant to help with the mortgage payments.

The house was small but beautiful, built in the Spanish style. It had a tiny, lush garden bursting with roses, and a magnolia tree with huge white blossoms. The room for rent was attached to the house, but had its own entrance to the side and its own bathroom. When I went to see it, Jerry's friends were apologetic about the fact that the bathroom did not have a bathtub, just a shower. I thought of the copper basin and the outhouse with the hole in it, and assured them that the lack of a bathtub was something I could live with. The rent was higher than I would have liked, but the house was so close to the restaurant that I didn't need a car or any bus fare. I could afford it.

'And there are English classes for foreigners held twice a week in the high school around the block,' they informed me.

That clinched it. We shook hands, they agreed to wait a month or so for their security deposit, and I had a home.

For five years I worked for Jerry. I was the only employee who ever stayed this long and I was his hardest worker. In time he came to trust me. After the first few months I had to clear tables only when the bus boy didn't show up. I served at the bar, manned the door and filled in for Jerry when he preferred to be somewhere else. He knew that if he left me in charge I wouldn't steal money from the till, I wouldn't feed my friends, of whom I had none, for free and I wouldn't close early to go out. I was as steady and dependable as a rock. In two years, I was Jerry's manager and his right-hand man.

My devotion to my work came easy to me. There was nothing else I wanted to do. I had no friends other than Jerry, and no other interests except learning English. I attended classes a couple of evenings a week at the high school, until I mastered a good vocabulary and basic grammar. Then I became a regular at the public library a few blocks down from my room, and spent all my free time reading one by one almost the entire collection of non-fiction books, and even some novels. What little time I wasn't reading or working, I spent watching my tiny, used black-and-white TV with the crooked antenna. My English became literate and grammatical, but my accent remained heavy and characteristic of my Greek background. Jerry came to me one day with the phone number of two linguistics specialists who specialised in working with foreigners to teach them proper English pronunciation. I thanked him for his suggestion, but I didn't take down the number. Holding on to my Greek accent was a matter of ethnic pride and a sentimental nod to my country. I might speak English all day long, I might spend hours learning it and polishing my skill, but I didn't want to sound anything but Greek when I spoke. There is a limit to everything, and sounding like an American was mine.

My accent and a few clothes were the only things I had from Greece for a long time. I waited a whole year before I contacted Manos, and another year before I would give him an address. He promised not to come and find me and he promised not to let anyone know where I was, including Antigone. But he did send me a package. It contained two pictures, the picture of my dad and the picture of my family in the yard.

'Before we left Panorama,' he wrote, 'Katerina gave me these to give to you. She said you didn't want them then, but you might want them in the future.'

I remember my curiosity when the package arrived, and the shock I felt when I opened the package. There we all were. My sweet mother, my dear father, Andreas, me, and in the corner, a small reminder of Katerina. Had she noticed, I wondered, when she picked that picture, that there was a bit of her in it, and had she chosen it for that purpose? If I had thought that I had put her behind me in my new life, and that after so many years I was finally over her, the hot rush of my blood when I looked at the picture told me that forgetting was impossible for me and that my past could reach out and find me even on the other side of the world. I put the pictures back in their envelope and hid them in my dresser drawer. For several nights, as I lay in my bed, I was aware of them and my impulse to open them up and drink in the memories, but I resisted.

In five years, receiving the pictures in the post was my most intense moment. Every other part of my life was flat and dry. My maniacal devotion to my work alienated my co-workers. They didn't know what drove me, so they assumed it was ambition. They resented the standard I set and thought I might turn them in to Jerry if I saw them eating something they hadn't paid for or giving a friend a free drink. They treated me like a boss long before I became one.

Given these circumstances, Jerry was the only person who could become my friend, and he did. I liked Jerry. He was always fair with me, appreciated everything I did and trusted me. Most of all, he never asked me why I came to America, or what I left behind me. I told him my parents were dead, and he never came close to the subject again.

He did use to wonder why I didn't have a girlfriend.

'You're a handsome guy, George,' he would say. 'That little waitress Mona has an eye for you. Why don't you take her for a spin? You can borrow my car and take a drive.'

Mona indeed seemed to like me. It might have been because I was in charge of scheduling the shifts for waitresses, and she thought she might get special treatment. Or maybe she had a liking for short, dark, serious men. But even though she was attractive in a pert, bouncy kind of way, I never responded to her sidelong glances, and eventually she moved on.

I wasn't a complete hermit. When I was twenty-one, Jerry hired an older woman as a waitress. Her name was Theresa, and she was probably thirty-five or so. She had a matter-of-fact manner, a lanky body and a heavy smoking habit. She also liked to stay after hours and drink a few. Then she would get in her car and drive drunkenly to her apartment in Hollywood. Like many others, she was a screenwriter, or at least she hoped that some day she would be one.

From the first day she came into the restaurant her eye lighted on me and never wavered. She watched me with curiosity, as though I held a secret that she was determined to figure out. She often took her breaks when I was in the back smoking a cigarette, and she would join me back there, smoking silently beside me. At night she'd help me close up, making small talk while I counted the money.

'Do you like women?' she asked me one night.

Her question caught me by surprise. I lost count.

'Do you have to think about it?' she said when I gave no answer.

'No.'

'No you don't like women, or no you don't have to think about it?'

'No, I don't have to think about it.'

'So do you like women?'

Her words were spoken dryly, without the lilt of a come-on, but I could feel an excitement stirring inside of me.

'I like them. A lot.'

'Do you like me?' she asked now, a curl of smoke escaping from her mouth and getting sucked straight up her nostrils, in a neat trick I had watched her perform many times before. My heart beat a little faster. I considered her shoulder-length honey-blonde hair, her clear green eyes, the laugh lines around her mouth. It was not a happy mouth. It curved downwards, and it had a trace of bitterness in the corners.

'You're very attractive, Theresa,' I replied, looking away.

'In a sort of lived-in way,' she laughed.

I went back to my counting and she to her drinking. But she wasn't finished.

'It's my birthday today,' she said after a while. Her voice was cool and did not carry any sentiment.

'Happy birthday, Theresa,' I smiled at her.

'Hey, you're good. You don't ask how old I am. I like that about you, George. You don't ask questions. It's my experience that people who don't ask questions don't like to answer them either. Am I right?'

'Is there something you want to know?'

'As a matter of fact there is.'

'What?'

'If I ask you to leave with me tonight, will you?'

I never would have asked her myself. Or anyone else for that matter. My loneliness was vast, but I was not prepared to do anything about it. Except that here was a human being, speaking to me out of a loneliness that seemed to rival mine, only there was something she could do about it, and she was asking me to help.

We left together, taking a bottle of Scotch with us, that I was careful to pay for. We didn't touch as we locked the door behind us, set the alarm and got in her car. Theresa got behind the wheel and drove us uncertainly to Hollywood, where she parked underneath her building. She was concentrating so hard on keeping to the road despite having had several drinks, that conversation, any conversation, would have been perilous. I wished I knew how to drive.

Her apartment was almost empty of furniture, and extremely small. She went into the kitchen, leaving me standing by the door. She returned with two glasses and poured the Scotch. Then she led me to a small balcony with a view of the neighbouring apartment buildings. We sat on some pillows under the starless, never dark, sky of LA. We drank and we talked about the restaurant, the city, her screenplays, her agent who couldn't get her a job, the newest sitcoms and how she could write better stories in her sleep if only someone gave her a chance. Little by little she leaned on me, and when I kissed her I didn't even have to reach for her.

I had lived for years without being touched. After life in the Siberia of my own making, the warmth of her body was like a brand new experience. I glued my lips on hers and wouldn't let go. I knew very little about kissing, but she knew everything. During that long kiss, I learned everything there was to know. I let her tongue fill my mouth, and then I returned the gift. I fed on her, like a newborn at its mother's breast. For however long we sat under that sky, and it was a long time, the world became this wet dark living place that made me moan with pleasure.

At some point she stood up and took me by the hand. She led me to her bedroom, as empty as the rest of the apartment, except for her futon on the floor. She undressed me and left me standing while she took off her clothes. Then she lay down and made room for me. I lay down next to her. I kissed her long and hard and clutched her to me feverishly, this living flesh next to mine, and my body sang at the feel of another human being. I revelled in the luxury. Her bony frame was the softest, smoothest velvet, her tongue and mouth ambrosia. There was no room for my senses to think of greater pleasure. But after a while she reached down and took my penis in her hand and led me inside her. She was narrow and tight, but thoroughly wet. I felt her parting to receive me and then closing in on me, as first the edge and then the depth of her got a grip on me. Before I could build up to pleasure, before I could taste the moment, I came in torrents, and as I came I started to cry, so that my gasps of pent-up anguish could pass for cries of passion. My prick throbbed its last drops inside her, but my brain was experiencing only the relief of my tears.

She held me without a word. Her flesh tightened and relaxed, and tightened and relaxed, a pump sucking away at me, telling me there was more, I had more to give. I cried and shuddered, and my penis began to swell inside her again. I rose on my arms to get more leverage, but I couldn't bear to be so little in touch with her body. I fell on her, rubbed my chest against her, bucked and swivelled, ground myself in her, drove into her fiercely and roughly. She came. Her legs gripped my waist, her body melded with mine, her heated, revolving vagina became a vortex. On the outer edge of her orgasm, I came again.

The next morning we made love again before she drove me home. At the restaurant we had no trouble acting as though nothing had happened. She had the early shift, so she left many hours before I was free to go, but when I showed up on her doorstep at midnight she was waiting for me. She knew I would be there.

My affair with Theresa lasted nine months. Almost every night for those months, we made love. In the dark I didn't know who she was. She was just this warm, accepting body to me, who sheltered me and contained me, and admitted me again among the living. Several times I cried.

Theresa stopped seeing me for the same reason she became interested in me. As she explained it to me, I seemed to her a man of mystery. She saw sadness and loneliness in my face, but I gave no clues, so she had to keep guessing at their source. My aloofness was a red flag waved in her face. At first she liked the mystery and didn't try to penetrate it. But eventually she became obsessed with getting me to talk about myself.

'You say that what attracted you to me was this wall I've built around me. Why do you try to tear it down?' I asked her near the end, when once again she asked about my past life.

'Because relationships must move forward! Because I want you to trust me! I want to understand you, and help you.'

'There's nothing to help with,' I answered, getting exasperated.

But Theresa would not be pacified. She pushed and pulled and prodded, and when I wouldn't give in, she finally told me it was over. She quit the restaurant and left my life.

I missed the human touch. I missed her warm body, her boozy talk at night, her way of gripping me with her vagina until I had given up every ounce of juice in my body. But I could go on without her. I wasn't shattered and I wasn't sad. I was relieved that I didn't have to deflect her questions any more and get into circular arguments going nowhere with her.

I wanted very much to find another Theresa, but it was difficult. The only women I met were the waitresses at Jerry's Place. I had been lucky with Theresa, our affair had gone undetected at the restaurant, but I knew this was a fluke and I could hardly expect to get tangled up with another waitress and once more escape detection. The customers were out of bounds. They were there too briefly, and I would have had to take aggressive initiative to get something going. This was something I was unwilling to do. So I remained alone.

Jerry had a daughter. She was three years younger than me. She was still in high school when I first met her, a shy, awkward girl, flat as a board and all legs, who would come over after school sometimes to see her dad. Jerry adored his shy teenager and she worshipped him. His wife had left him when the girl was only six, and since then the two of them had been alone. Jerry would occasionally take up with one woman or another, but he never took any home with him and he never seriously considered marrying any of them.

'Diane is the only woman I want in my life,' he told me once, when his current girlfriend was giving him the ultimatum of marrying her or else.

Diane's adolescence and young womanhood took place in front of my eyes. I think her mother's desertion and her failure to ever get in contact again or even remember her daughter with a card or a letter, must have scarred the little girl Diane was. At fourteen, she was painfully shy and uncertain of herself, and she had not an ounce of self-confidence. She didn't date and she had few friends. The only time her warmth and wit came to the surface was when her father was near her. Jerry hired her when she turned sixteen to work at the restaurant part-time, but talking to the customers was too difficult for her. She whispered her greeting to them, felt that she was intruding when she had to go and refill their water glasses. Her second day on the job she spilled a Coke on one customer and shook for the rest of her shift, even though her victim was nice about it and only made a fuss when Jerry wouldn't waive payment of the dinner bill for compensation. Diane quit after a few days.

By the time Diane entered college, she was over enough of her shyness to try working at the restaurant again. This time she did better. She was still shy and introverted, but not paralysingly so. She had known me for three years now, and it was plain to her that her father both loved and trusted me. Since he was my friend, she would be my friend, too. When I mentioned to Jerry that I wanted to learn how to drive, she volunteered to be my teacher. The lessons started in the alley behind the restaurant and progressed to freeway sessions that led us to the beach. Diane instructed me with patience and precision. It was plain that any lingering shyness she may still have felt towards me was melting away quickly from seeing me uncertain and nervous behind the wheel of her dad's Toyota. At the beach she rolled up her jeans to the knees and splashed at the water's edge like a puppy.

The driving lessons became the highlight of Diane's week. When I had become proficient, she came with me to take the test, and in delight at my passing she gave me a quick hug that made her blush and become self-conscious.

'I'm so glad you made it,' she said later, 'but I'm sorry we won't be going to the beach any more.'

Her regret was plain to see.

'Who says we won't?' I replied.

I bought a clean used car, and it was in that that Diane and I continued our outings to the beach. These were not dates. Diane and I were friends. We talked about her school, her plans for the future, her life with her dad. She wanted to become an elementary school teacher, because she liked kids so much. I think she just wanted to give to as many kids as possible the female warmth and care, the lack of which had marred her own life.

She was becoming a woman, and if she was not pretty, she was certainly attractive. She was rail thin, but she had long, beautifully formed legs and a neat face with thin, regular features that were somewhat harsh in their purity. Her mouth was small and tight, and she hardly moved her lips when she talked. It was easy to assume she was cold, but I knew she was just masking her vulnerability.

In my eyes she was a lost little kid who needed someone to tell her everything would be all right. Many times in our hours together I thought of touching her and melting her reserve. At times I thought she wanted me to. When she had revealed some small secret, like her long-ago crush on her biology teacher in high school, or when she proudly told me of a school assignment she had completed particularly well, she had a look of tenderness and yearning in her eyes that seemed an invitation to take her in my arms. But she was Jerry's daughter, and I thought any move I might make on her would be a betrayal of Jerry's trust in me.

I was being hopelessly old-fashioned and Greek, of course. I just assumed Jerry saw me as his daughter's guardian instead of a possible boyfriend, because that's what a Greek in his position would have wanted. Besides, because I worked with Jerry and was not going to school, I considered myself part of his generation, even though I was almost the same age as Diane. Kissing her seemed like the act of a dirty old man. Much later I realised that Jerry was throwing us together, thinking that his daughter could do worse than getting a hardworking, honest, trustworthy immigrant for a husband. Jerry knew that LA was overrun by flaky entertainment types who might bring his daughter to grief, and he trusted me. But back then I kept my hands to myself.

It wasn't hard on me. I liked her and enjoyed her company, but I felt no overwhelming passion for her. It was nice to be friends with her and enjoy her company, and if occasionally I had the urge to put my arms around her and bruise her prim little mouth with a kiss, I could have the satisfaction of holding back and congratulating myself on my honourable behaviour. And so we went on, Diane occasionally dating one classmate or another, but never more than a couple of times and never with any real interest.

After five years, I was practically running Jerry's Place single-handedly. I still lived in the same small room in Hancock Park, because even though I could afford something better I relished the proximity to the restaurant. More and more I had to spend time there, because Jerry was absent for hours on end. During that last year, he was changing rapidly. He seemed preoccupied and stressed. He had grown fat with the years, so that his once-slight paunch now hung pendulously over his belt. Diane tried to get him to eat right and exercise, but he didn't seem to hear her. He had always been a drinker, but now his drinking was almost out of control. The danger signals were there, but I didn't take them seriously enough. Diane confided her own fears about her father to me, but I was too private a person to feel comfortable questioning Jerry.

I assumed Jerry's problem was the declining popularity of Jerry's Place. Our clientele was deserting us for newer and more exciting places that were sprouting up all over the area. We needed an uplift, a new image, new decor, some fanfare. I approached Jerry with some ideas, but he didn't want to listen. When I persisted, he did what he had never done before. He got mad at me and shouted for me to leave him alone. So I did.

One night I was awakened out of a deep sleep by the ringing telephone on my bedside. It was four a.m. and the hysterical voice on the other end was Diane's. She had just been awakened, too, by a call from the police, informing her her father was involved in a car accident and had been taken to the hospital.

I hurried over to Jerry's house, to find Diane still in pyjamas and furry slippers, crying and wringing her hands. I told her to go and change and then drove with her to the hospital. There we were told that Jerry had been dead on arrival. While driving under the influence, he had veered off the road and smashed his car into a post. He was wearing no seat belt and he was travelling very fast. Diane collapsed in my arms.

The next few days were harrowing. Diane was on the edge of a nervous breakdown. Losing her one remaining parent was more than she could cope with. I made arrangements for the funeral, ran the restaurant and sat for hours cradling Diane, who was inconsolable.

There was more bad news. It seems Jerry had been playing the commodities market, and he was not winning when he died. His life insurance could erase some of his debts, but left most of them intact. His house was still not paid off, and the restaurant was heavily mortgaged, with the loan money going to pay off Jerry's losses in the cotton and timber futures markets. No wonder Jerry did not want to consider renovations. There was no money for them.

Diane and I visited the bank together. We were ushered into a small office and shown to two chairs facing a desk cluttered with pictures and souvenirs. A small wooden plaque announced the loan officer's name as Ms Sanchez. Small-time, I thought to myself. The loan officer was sitting behind the desk. She was a middle-aged woman, with neat grey hair in a short hair-do, and a smart jacket with a pocket handkerchief. She shuffled the papers in front of her and then gave Diane and me a rueful look. She summed up the situation with something approaching regret colouring her voice.

'I'm afraid the news is bad, Ms Warren. Your father had already missed three payments at the time of his death. You probably know that the restaurant has not been doing well. The bank wants to call the loan.'

Diane swallowed hard and looked at me. I reached out and took her hand.

'The restaurant just needs some care. It was profitable once, it can be profitable again.'

'And who are you?' the loan officer asked, not unkindly.

'My name is George Vasilikos. I am the restaurant manager and a family friend.'

'Mr Vasilikos, Mr Warren's landlord wants to terminate the lease. I've gone over the lease and he has the right to do so.'

I had gone over the lease, too.

'The landlord has the right to terminate the lease only because the loan is in default. If we can work out something he will back down.'

'The lease. gives him the right to terminate the lease regardless of the default, in view of Mr Warren's death,' the loan officer replied, casting a glance at Diane at the mention of Jerry.

'I know the landlord, Ms Sanchez, and I can assure you that if your bank doesn't carry through with its foreclosure then he will go away.'

'He'll use the change in management to ask for more rent, Mr Vasilikos,' Ms Sanchez said ruefully. 'At any rate, supposing the bank doesn't call the loan, what do you propose to do? It is unlikely that Ms Warren will find a buyer for the business in view of the circumstances, and I don't believe she has the expertise to run it herself.'

'I will run it.'

'I thought you were merely an employee.'

'And a family friend,' I said, squeezing Diane's limp hand.

Ms Sanchez shuffled her papers some more.

'So what is it you want?' she finally asked.

'A chance to turn things around. If you foreclose you will only get part of your money. If you let me turn the restaurant around you'll get all of it.'

'You need cash to stop the foreclosure, Mr Vasilikos. Mr Warren's death gives us the right to call the loan, just like the lease, regardless of the default, which cannot be ignored anyway. I'm sorry to do this to you and Ms Warren, but there are guidelines I must follow in these situations.'

'There is Ms Warren's house,' I said reluctantly.

'Any equity?'

'I'm not sure how much,' I answered.

Diane left the bank with instructions to bring the house loan documents over.

The house had some equity in it, but it was Diane's only asset. If she sold it to pay off the debts, she would be left with only a few thousand dollars, not enough to live on, let alone pay for school until she could get her degree and start working. I knew this, but I dangled the equity in front of the loan officer to gain some time.

We returned to Diane's house from the bank, Diane silent beside me. At the house she made some coffee and we drank it side by side on the living-room couch.

'I'm nineteen years old,' Diane said. 'So I don't have someone to pay for everything any more! Lots of people my age don't. I'll just work. I'll quit school and I'll work.'

I had been thinking hard for days. What we heard at the bank had not been complete news to me. It just confirmed my suspicions. I had a plan, but now I had to see if Diane would welcome the chance I had to offer her.

'I have some money,' I said. It was true. I had spent only a fraction of my wages over the years, and Jerry paid me well. The money was not enough to make a difference, but it was something.

'Diane,' I continued, 'if we offer that money to the bank, tell them I will stay on to run the restaurant and present my ideas for some changes to attract new customers, we may be able to buy some time. The landlord will back down if the bank does, and we can keep the restaurant going to pay the mortgage on this place and keep you in school.'

'I can't let you do that. That's your money. I can't take it from you.'

She started crying as though her heart was broken. I put my arms around her and pulled her head to my shoulder. Her thin body was racked with sobs that had all the heartbreak of a child left alone in the world, without protection and comfort.

'Let me do this, Diane. I want to. We'll draw a contract. We'll split the profits. It will be our restaurant. You can work there too, if you want. We will turn things around. I have a few ideas that I think will probably bring the people back. If the restaurant becomes profitable again, we'll both benefit. And you'll be contributing, too. It's your restaurant. The goodwill, the lease, it's all your father's and now yours.'

She lifted her tear-stained face to mine. Her clear blue eyes were red-rimmed and her nose was swollen. Her mouth was trembling and she looked about ten.

'I love you, George,' she said, and I don't think she meant as a brother. I hugged her, kissed her on the forehead and beat a hasty retreat.

We went back to the bank. This time we were ushered into a bigger office, with a couch and low coffee table in one corner. At my request, Ms Sanchez had brought her boss in on the meeting. His name was Biaggi, and he was a tall man, with close-cropped curly hair and a thick New York accent. He sat in a chair across from me and asked me to explain why the bank should not call the loan.

This was my chance. I knew I had to make it good. I started off by offering him my life's savings. I explained that this was all I had in the world, and it represented five years of saving. Then I spoke about my plans to change Jerry's Place.

'It's a great location, close to theatres and Hollywood with all its clubs and discos. The problem is that it hasn't changed with the times. I plan to change it. I'll keep serving lunch and dinner, but I will expand the hours of operation. At eleven, instead of closing down the kitchen, I will have a jazz band playing. I will serve coffee, hundreds of varieties of coffee, French, Italian, Turkish, Irish, with chocolate, with mint, you name it. And I'll serve dessert. I'll keep the prices low and I will cater to the younger crowd. At night they come down from Hollywood on their way home. Jerry's Place will be the last stop. A place where they can sober up while listening to something other than disco and rock and roll. And I'll change the menu. I'll serve more sandwiches and health-conscious meals. I'll drop the prices and I'll target the young people.'

My voice had been rising in volume and speed. I was up halfway through my speech, waving my arms and pacing up and down. My accent was thicker than ever. Biaggi looked on with his hands steepled under his chin. At the end of my speech he uncrossed his impossibly long legs.

'You're from Greece, George, may I call you George?'

He could call me anything he wanted. Just don't call the loan.

Biaggi asked questions. He asked my age, where I was from, how long I had worked for Jerry, what I did, what my relationship was to the Warrens. He listened to everything I said with one eyebrow cocked halfway up his forehead. At the end of the questions, he shook my hand and told me he would let me know.

A few days later, he called me in. He had sent someone to scout out the restaurant and see me running it. He had asked questions and investigated the market. When he told me this, I took heart. This was an ambitious and hardworking man. He did his homework and then some. That was exactly what I needed. Someone who, if convinced he could score a success, would not hesitate to bend the rules or even break them.

'I have confidence in you,' were the first words out of his mouth. 'I believe we can work something out.'

The bank would take my money. And it would not call in the loan at this time. I had to take over the payments and agree to run the restaurant for a minimum of five years. The payments would be restructured, so they would be lower for the first year, but would rise steeply after that.

'I agree with you that the restaurant needs to change,' Biaggi told me. 'But I don't agree with the direction you've chosen. Youth-orientated businesses don't turn enough profit to dig you out of this hole. You would need an enormous volume, and the place is too small for that. Now, I'm from New York, and ethnic restaurants are all the rage there. Here we have a lot of oriental food, and the usual Italian and French, but nowhere near the variety we have in New York. I believe what you need to do is switch the restaurant into the ethnic food market.'

I was a little taken aback, but I listened. What choice did I have? Whoever pays the piper calls the tune. Biaggi's brainstorm was to open a Greek restaurant. Not a gyros joint serving greasy mystery meat, but a clean, classy place with authentic cuisine at reasonable prices. He thought I could do it.

'There are not many Greeks in LA,' he added, 'but there are enough to give you a good start. They will all come at least once to check out the place. It will be up to you to keep them coming. Give them a spot they can call home.'

Biaggi probably thought I had ties to the Greek community and could fill the place with just my friends. He was wrong, but I wasn't about to tell him.

'This means a radical change in decor,' I said. 'I'll need money.'

'Of course. The bank is willing to loan you personally what you need to change the look.'

And one more thing. They wanted a second mortgage on Diane's house.

There was no choice. If we didn't do this, Diane would have to sell the house, quit school and get a job. If we accepted the terms, Diane would have a running business to finance her studies and keep up the payments on the house. And I would have a restaurant to run.

It bothered me that the restaurant had to be Greek. I had stayed away from the small Greek community of Los Angeles because I wanted no ties to Greece. If I now opened a Greek restaurant they would be sure to find me. They would speak Greek, reminisce about the old country, maybe even ask me if I knew so-and-so, comparing names of people they know, in that obsessive way expatriates use to establish commonality with new acquaintances.

I didn't like it, but I had to do it. Without this alternative, I would have to look for another job and start again from zero. My money was not enough to start a business of my own, and anyway, I had a responsibility to Diane that I was not taking lightly. I accepted, signed on the dotted line and became a restaurateur.

Diane and I worked together to transform the restaurant on a shoestring. We had it painted blue and white and hung huge pictures of famous Greeks on the wall. Photographs of Melina Mercouri, Maria Callas, Onassis and Agnew mixed with drawings of Alexander the Great, Socrates and Plato. In between the pictures, we arranged copper pots and pans that Manos located for me in New York. We covered the tables with pristine white tablecloths and placed a small basil plant on each. We sold the old chairs and found some with seats made of interlaced straw, almost identical to the ones that proliferate in Greece.

The big challenge was finding the right cook. For this I had to visit the Cathedral of Saint Sofia on Pico Street.

The priest told me that yes, there was a newsletter that the church put out and that counted every Greek in the area as a subscriber. I placed my ad and waited.

Leandros was the first applicant who answered the ad. He strolled into the restaurant as though he measured nine feet instead of five four. He shook my hand vigorously, told me his home was Volos, but he'd not been back for four years.

'I'm your man,' he announced in his quick, loud Greek. I had forgotten how rapidly Greeks speak. Not because they are pressed for time – there is always time for talking – but because they are carried away by their need to communicate whatever they happen to be talking about. Greeks talk fast out of passion and conviction.

Leandros was not one to rely on talk alone. He pulled me to his car, drove to Farmers' Market and bought a basketful of meat, produce and oregano. Then he took me back to the restaurant, and in front of my astonished eyes cooked up spicy meatballs in tomato sauce, and a delicious vegetable stew made with olive oil. He tasted everything, pronounced it satisfactory and presented me a plate with a bow and a flourish. I took a bite, took another, and hired him on the spot.

Leandros and I worked out a menu and interviewed waiters. Leandros thought the waiters should all be Greek, but I thought this was too hard. There weren't enough Greeks answering the ads if we were going to be choosy. We compromised by hiring men who at least could pass for Greek if God had been a little more generous with inches to the Greek people, and if successive wars and poverty had not worn the race down.

As the last touch, we piped in instrumental versions of popular Greek songs sent in by Manos. I remember popping the tape into the sound system for the first time and having the sound pour out of the speakers. What is it about music that speaks so directly to the heart? As the melancholy melody about the sea that stole the life of a beloved man reached my ears, I felt the sharp sting of memory inside me. I bit my lip, busied myself with the silverware, staunched my tears. I am too nervous and unsettled about this new venture, I told myself. I am in a vulnerable state.

Artemis is Greek for Diane. The restaurant, renamed Artemis Garden, was a success from the first. I expected that Greeks would come, and I had advertised heavily in the newsletter that brought me Leandros, but Americans flocked over, too, to try something new. And Armenians and Arabs came, too, because their food resembles Greek cooking. After the first two weeks it was impossible to get a table at the weekend without making a reservation in advance. Biaggi came for a meal on the house, and I was careful to thank him for his excellent idea.

It was one of the happiest times of my life. I was there all day long. During the day I consulted with Leandros while he fine-tuned the menu, ran all over town looking for fresh ingredients and interviewed applicants for the various positions that were always coming open. At night I greeted my guests and hovered over everybody, making sure things were getting done right. Later, I did the books and dropped the cash off at the night deposit. I was flushed with success, consumed by my thriving business, kept flying high by the buzz of activity around me. Each night I went to sleep grudgingly, eager to get sleep over with so I could return to my restaurant. Here I was at the age of twenty-three, an immigrant with a thick unwieldy accent and no high school diploma, a boss to more than twenty employees, making it in LA.

Diane was in the restaurant often. She was excited about how well we were doing, but the success was not hers and so it did not fill her with excitement and accomplishment. She was more alone than ever. I was the only family she had now, but I was too busy to go to the beach with her or talk the way we used to. She would come in and sit in a corner until I could spend some time with her. When I did approach her it was to explain the books to her. In my utter lack of sensitivity, I was treating her as the part owner that she was, instead of a lonely young woman who had just gone through the painful experience of losing her only parent.

'George, can't we put the books away and go for a drive?' she asked me one night, as I was trying to explain to her a sudden rise in the cost of supplies.

'I don't have time, Diane,' I replied.

'But you would spend at least an hour explaining all this to me. Why not put it away and go for a drive instead?'

'Because you need to know this. It's your restaurant too.'

I looked at her as I said this, and it was my first real look at her in months. Her face looked pinched. Her small features were all bunched up and crimped. She seemed to have lost weight and grown shorter somehow. She wore no make-up and her black shirt was draining the colour from her face, making her look pale and wan.

'Diane, are you sick?' I asked, suddenly worried.

'No, I'm fine. I just miss Dad sometimes,' she whispered, averting her eyes.

With my finger I raised her chin so that her blue eyes were level with mine.

'You spend too much time alone,' I told her, sounding like an uncle. 'You need to get out more. Tell you what.

This Monday I'll come and pick you up, and the two of us will go to the beach. Just like old times.'

'I have classes in the daytime,' she said, an unmistakable spark in her eyes. 'Can we do it in the afternoon?'

I really wanted to work in the afternoon, but she seemed so eager for me to spend some time with her that I couldn't say no.

That Monday I picked her up and we headed for our favourite spot in Malibu. We had dinner at Gladstone's, a restaurant right next to the ocean. We sat on the patio outside and fed the gulls that visited the tables regularly for the peanuts Gladstone's provides to its patrons in large barrels. We ate seafood, had a few drinks, watched the sunset and talked like old times. When we got up to go it was already dark.

'Let's walk on the beach,' Diane suggested.

She took off her shoes and we strolled for a while, listening to the sound of the waves and the fading noise from Gladstone's. We threw rocks at the water, made footprints on the wet sand where the waves crashed and receded.

'Do you ever think of what happens to the dead?' she asked me as we stood shoulder to shoulder in front of the ocean.

'Yes, I do. At least I did when my own parents died.'

'Do you think we'll ever see them again?' she asked turning to me. There was urgency in her question and her eyes were searching mine for reassurance. Without shoes on she was only a little taller than me.

'Yes, I do,' I answered. 'I think that when we die we join them in heaven or the hereafter, or whatever, and then we never have to leave them again.'

Her eyes were filling rapidly.

'Do you really think so, George? Because I can't bear the thought of never seeing Dad again. I miss him so.'

I reached out and took her hand in mine. I caressed her long slender fingers.

'You'll see him again,' I whispered, and I leaned over and kissed Diane's sweet lips. It was to be a light kiss, a feather touch, a simple gesture of sympathy and caring. But Diane's lips opened to meet mine, and they anchored my lower lip between them, gently sucking at it. My body was ready to pull back, but her action caught me by surprise. I kissed her back, and my arms went around her slender waist. She tasted of wine, and I hadn't been with anybody since Theresa, almost two years ago. I continued the kiss, never going deep, just playing at the surface of her mouth, nuzzling at her and pressing my tongue lightly to hers. She moved closer, clung to me. I pulled my hips back so she would not feel my erection, but I gripped her tightly around the shoulders and went on kissing her until I heard a soft moan in her throat.

'I love you, George, I love and I need you. Please don't ever leave me,' she whispered against my lips, and I fell to kissing her again, delighting in the small sounds she was making. As we made our way back to the car, my mind was racing. Why not? Why not?

Mondays became our days. We would have dinner, hold hands, kiss for increasingly longer periods of time and finally part, Diane with a glow of happiness about her, me in a confused state of mind, wondering where I was going with this. I cared about her, there was no doubt. I wanted to take care of her, and she was so alone. I was alone, too, and it was good to have her beside me, the look of love in her eyes, the smile on her lips that always met me when I turned to her. At times I felt I had no business spending time with her. I didn't love her. I had known love in my

life, and the comfortable feeling I had with Diane bore
no resemblance to the storm Katerina had stirred in me.
Since I didn't love her, shouldn't I leave her alone? But
she loved me! There was no doubt that she had loved me
for some time. If I stopped going out with her she would
grow sad and lonely again. And I couldn't just put her out
of my life and hope she'd forget and get over me, because
the restaurant was our joint endeavour, binding us tightly
together. It was her future and mine.

The only thing to do was to marry Diane. I knew it,
had even decided it subconsciously, I think, but I didn't
tell her until events put a stop to my endless dithering
and second thoughts. Diane got sick. She had a cold and
she was running a temperature. I went to visit her in the
house. She was lying in bed with a box of Kleenex in her
hand, dressed in a pretty white nightgown with lace.

'You look awfully good for a sick woman,' I told
her.

'I don't feel so bad. I really shouldn't be in bed at all,
but it's been raining all day, and this seemed better than
roaming campus jumping over puddles and getting my
feet wet.'

I sat on the edge of the bed. She really didn't look
sick except for her flushed face. Her hair was clean and
combed back neatly, and she smelled of perfume. I noticed
a few wet blonde strands.

'You took a shower!' I said. 'Don't you know patients
with a temperature are not supposed to take a shower?'

She looked a little embarrassed.

'Well, when you called to say you were coming over
. . . I was such a mess . . .' her sentence trailed.

'So this folly was done for my benefit,' I laughed and
leaned over to give her a kiss.

'I couldn't let you see me a mess,' she giggled.

'You're never a mess,' I said, hovering over her, my nose taking in her delightful scent.

'Oh yes, I am,' she said, and grabbed my head to bring it down to her lips again. Her breath was minty. She had obviously overlooked no detail in her grooming despite her stuffy head and raised temperature. Her kiss was strong and ardent.

At first it was playful. We mock-wrestled on the bed, crushed the box of Kleenex, kissed for a long time. The light coming from outside waned and we found ourselves in the dark, in her bed, her breath coming faster, my penis strangling in my trousers. What else was there to do? With awkward hands I unbuttoned her nightgown and took her breast in my mouth. The fever was making her flesh burn. Her body arched as I circled her nipple with my tongue. Her hips under the covers stuck to mine, pressing my erection and sending shivers down my spine. I had never allowed this to happen between us before. The die was cast. I joined her under the covers. I ran my hands over the length of her and she kissed my neck. When my hand separated her legs and covered her mound, her kiss turned into a bite. With infinite care I slipped a finger inside her. My thumb made circles over her clitoris. Her hips rose by their own volition, and she gasped. I stroked her while she clung to me, whispering her love with heated breath into my ear. I ground myself against her thigh, that was now flung wide and reckless. Her muscles inside clenched at my finger. When she reached a hand to fumble at my zipper, I almost lost control. I took a few deep breaths, helped her pull my trousers down. Under the covers, with her nightgown bunched at her waist, I held myself above her and gently eased my penis inside her. There was some resistance. A soft moan of pain. I kept myself very still, half inside her, half out, and applied my hand to her clitoris again. She forgot the pain. She only felt the pleasure now. With each rising wave she would impale herself a little more, as her hips moved this way and that in excitement. Finally, with a mighty shove, I buried myself to the hilt, exploding as soon as I hit against the soft mouth of her womb. She had been a virgin, but if there was any pain, the pleasure was greater.

We remained in each other's arms. The clock was ticking. The rain was falling.

'Diane, will you marry me?' I said, before my penis had time to slip out of her. Her kiss was her answer.

20

The American Dream

Childhood and adolescence take forever to pass. The years are endless, a month is forever. But once you finish your preparation for life and arrive at the state where you plan to spend adulthood, life speeds up and the years collapse together. With Diane as my wife and Artemis Garden humming along, time gathered up speed and carried me along.

I was happy. The popularity of my restaurant – and thanks to marrying Diane it was now all mine – did not wane. People came flocking to taste Leandros's tangy rice wrapped in vine leaves and his one-of-a-kind *pastitsio*. The *Los Angeles Times* food critic came to try the place and wrote a glowing article praising everything to the skies. He even mentioned me by name. 'The portions are huge,' he wrote, 'the atmosphere lighthearted, and the whole place hums with the quick, nervous energy of its young, diminutive owner, George Vasilikos, who I am told is present all day and all night, to preside over everything.' It was true. I was at the restaurant all the time. When I wasn't there, I thought about it.

I had always worked hard before, but as a way to escape my problems, and not with pleasure. Owning Artemis Garden changed all that. This was my baby, and I cared about everything. Its success was my success, and every satisfied customer was a feather in my cap. Diane took a picture of me standing in front of the sign. That picture says it all. There I stand, drawn up to my full height, a short man who obviously feels tall and proud and brim-full with the happiness of accomplishment.

Artemis Garden became a gold mine. By the time the bank loan kicked into higher payments I could easily afford them, despite the higher rent and the expense of changing the restaurant around. Soon I was making the payments with ease. Biaggi had spoken to me already about opening a second restaurant. At first I had not wanted to. There are many restaurants that splash into the scene triumphantly, only to reign for a year or so and then lose their popularity. I was a little scared. But once the years passed and Artemis Garden entered its fourth successful season, I revisited the idea. Part of my motivation may have been that Artemis Garden now practically ran itself. I was beginning to feel a little unnecessary and unchallenged. Biaggi wrote the cheque before I even had time to finish asking for it, and I began the new venture.

I found a location in Santa Monica, bargained hard over the rent and went to work. My idea was to open Artemis Garden 2, but Biaggi disagreed. He thought I should open a totally different Greek restaurant, something that wouldn't compete in the same league as my first. His advice had been good the first time, so I listened to him again.

Artemis Garden was a mid-priced place, but Poseidon was a diner. Here the tablecloths were white oil sheets, just like in Greece, and the fare was simpler. There were no menus. In the time-honoured Greek tradition, the customer had to come back to the kitchen to make his selection and look into the pots and pans to see what the cook had prepared for that day. The waiters were instructed to bring whatever appetiser was freshest and most plentiful out to the table as soon as the people sat down, without asking. The lighting was bare and bright and the decor nonexistent, except for a gaudy picture of a mermaid, taking up the entire east wall. Poseidon was more Greek than any Greek restaurant outside of Greece.

Poseidon took a while to take off. The neighbourhood had too many plush restaurants, and we had to wait for our clientele to find us. But they did. And once they did, they kept coming back for more. Biaggi was right to steer me away from the idea of an Artemis clone. Many times people would come into both my restaurants in the space of a week, something that would not have happened if they were identical.

A big part of Poseidon's success was owed to the cook. Kyra Euterpi was hard of hearing and already in her fifties, but she could cook up a storm. More important, she had a decidedly eccentric personality. She scolded the customers and refused to serve them what they wanted but insisted they finish every bite of what she chose for them. She wandered around the dining-room looking over everybody's shoulder, sitting down to have a glass of retsina with her favourites, and on several occasions tried to arrange matches between her endless array of nieces and nephews and the customers. She served Greek coffee in tiny demi-tasse cups, and if she liked you she would read your fortune in the coffee sediment for free. She was the only cook–fortune-teller in existence, and the clientele loved it.

I was worried at first by her peremptory ways and her insistence on reading even bad news in my customers' coffee cups. I told her to tone it down and stay in the kitchen. She would not listen to me, or maybe she didn't hear me. She continued to boss everybody around and pronounce impending doom when she felt justified, and I soon realised that far from scaring my customers, she was actually the evening's entertainment. Sure, some of my more Anglo-Saxon diners grew a little impatient and a few left in a huff. Most, however, laughed and joked along with my imperious cook, listened raptly to her pronouncements and then brought their friends to see this new phenomenon. Poseidon took a little getting used to, but it was soon filled to capacity almost every night and did brisk trade for lunch, too.

I spent my days in a whirlwind of activity. I shuttled back and forth between my two restaurants, supervised the buying of provisions, the hiring of help, the greeting of customers and the bookings for large parties. I pored over the books, refereed fights among the staff, averted catastrophes and visited the bank to make deposits. Late at night I would drive home humming, to have a quiet drink in the living-room, retire to make love to my wife and then sleep the sleep of the just. When the alarm shrieked in my ear, I would bounce out of bed, eager for the new day.

There was very little to my life besides the work I loved. After Diane and I married, I moved into her house. She continued attending college, but she also made a home for me. She learned to cook my favourites and cooked them often, even though I hardly ever came home for dinner. She bought my clothes, laid them out for me every morning, and made a mean cup of Greek coffee. She even went through trade magazines and cut out articles she thought I might be interested in. When she realised I had no time to read them, she started taping them on cassettes for me, so I could play them in my car on the way to work. She stayed up to wait for me at night, and had a drink and a smile ready for me at whatever hour I happened to make it home. She dropped in to the restaurants occasionally, but kept away from me so as not to disturb me, and simply helped out when there was need. I guess I was ignoring her, but she seemed to understand. At night, in bed, I made love to her often, sometimes out of guilt rather than desire. She didn't seem to notice the difference. She took what little I had to give and never asked for more.

After we had been married for more than a year, she gave birth to our son. I rushed over to the hospital when Leandros finally caught up with me with the big news, and found Diane happy and resting, our small baby boy in her arms. She quit school after that and devoted herself to full-time motherhood. A year later my daughter Niki made her appearance. Diane had her hands full now. The house was full, too. It was never meant to house an entire family. Still, we put up with the close quarters because I didn't want to buy a bigger house yet. But once Poseidon opened and demonstrated its money-making abilities, I finally decided to take the big step.

Diane located the house in Brentwood. I inspected it briefly, pronounced it satisfactory and signed on the dotted line. I had already checked with Biaggi, who believed the area was bound to appreciate and was more than happy to make the loan. So there I was, not even thirty yet, with two restaurants, two children, a wife and a four-bedroom house in the suburbs. I had arrived.

Considering that I lived with her, I saw little of Diane during these years. Our lives were on parallel orbits. She was at home with the kids all day long and I was out making our fortune. She still waited up for me and we still made love often, but we hardly ever talked. Because of the hours I worked, our social life was slim. Once in a while I would take a night off, the babysitter would come and we would go to a film or, more often, attend a dance at the Greek church.

Yes, I had finally done it. I had joined the Greek community. It was hard not to. My restaurants attracted the Los Angeles Greeks. They came in to eat and made great efforts to get to know me. There were even some who had ties to Thessaloniki, but none from Panorama. I was scared at first that one of them might know my family, might say something I didn't want to hear. After a year or so of worrying about it without it ever happening, I relaxed. It was okay. I was safe from detection. The danger lay elsewhere. There were among my customers Greek immigrants who often travelled back and returned with stories of Greece, their voices dripping with the thick, sweet honey of their love for their home, their tales full of the welcome they received. One of them had actually visited Panorama for the filo pastry served at Stamos's. My heart writhed in my breast. A strong longing to see again my beloved village coursed swiftly through my blood. Katerina, Katerina. But I was too unsure of what I had achieved. In a few years, I told myself. Maybe in a few years. If Katerina doesn't hurt me any more.

I found that I liked being part of the Greek community. I liked the occasional pain of remembrance. It had the sweetness of a razor cut, and the irresistible pull of a sore tooth that the tongue cannot leave alone.

It was nice to speak Greek again and to be among people who thought and acted the way I did. I had come to America very early in life, before I had had the chance to get fixed in my ways and to cement my beliefs. Comparing myself with the foreigners around me, I was convinced that I was too loud, too emotional. I seemed to over-react to everything, to be too aggressive, too obvious, too moody. In embarrassment I had toned myself down, accepting the foreign way as a standard. Now that I found myself with my own people, however, I noticed that they were all the way I used to be. I watched them in my restaurants next to my American customers, and at times it was the Americans who seemed to me in need of overhaul. They were too quiet, too reserved, too deadpan, too unemotional. The Greeks roared with laughter, interrupted each other in their eagerness to be heard, argued with murder in their eyes and then kissed and made up in the space of five minutes, lived life fully every minute. Smoothly, easily, like a key fitting into its well-oiled lock, I slipped into my place in Greek society. I made friends with my repeat customers and joined them at their table. We waved our arms back and forth, raised our voices, argued about inconsequential matters and threw our passion into everything. I felt fully alive again. But America had left its mark on me. After a while I would get tired of the fever-pitch of emotions and the relentless involvement in each other's lives. Then I would drive home to Diane and her calm serenity. I had the best of both worlds.

When I turned thirty, I took my first vacation. Diane had to talk me into it, and it took her three years, but finally we packed up the kids and our bags and flew to Hawaii for ten days. We rented a bungalow on the beach. I didn't understand then, and I still don't understand, why Angelinos go to Hawaii. It's no different to our own beaches, and it's five hours away by plane, and more expensive than going to Malibu. But this was what Diane wanted, and since it took her weeks to arrange and she was obviously eager to please me, pleased I was, and I told her so.

The kids played on the sand all day and Diane ran

after them so they wouldn't come to harm. I sat uncomfortably under an umbrella, shocked at the whiteness of my skin. I had always considered myself dark-skinned, but I guess staying indoors and never seeing the sun has the effect of a bleach, because I was the fairest person there, my family excepted.

I had meant to read while on vacation, and had brought books with me, but I found it more interesting to watch my family from afar. Those are my kids, I repeated to myself as they made sand castles and carried pails of water from the ocean to wet the sand where they were working. They were both fair haired until their hair darkened a little in adolescence, and they resembled their mother. I scanned over to where Diane was standing, telling my son John – American for Yiannis, his grandpa's name – not to demolish his sister's handiwork. Diane was wearing a one-piece yellow bathing suit. Her legs were just as long and lovely as they ever were. Her two pregnancies had filled her out a little, added some weight to her hips and breasts and a small swell to her belly. Some might have found the changes unappealing, but to me they were welcome. Diane looked more like a woman. And the tender way she handled our kids, her infinite patience and her enjoyment in spending time with them, completed the impression of soft, warm womanhood. My wife is a fine-looking woman, I thought, and made a note to tell her so at the first opportunity.

At dinner that night, I gazed at my children, scanning their faces for any resemblance to me. They both had dark eyes, but that was it. Everything else, from their thin lips to their long limbs, belonged to the other half of their ancestry. There was something familiar about my son. When he pushed his hair out of his face, when he screwed up his mouth to refuse food, that reminded me of someone. Yeah, Jerry. He was the spitting image of Jerry. And Niki, my mother's namesake, did she hold anything of my past? No. She was Diane all over again. Diane as she must have been when she was four and still had her mother and her father. They are strangers to me, I thought, my children are strangers, and that's why I'm searching their faces to find something I recognise.

In bed that night with Diane, I made love to her as though it were the first time. Afterwards she turned to me with heavy lids and buried her face in my chest to whisper how wonderful it was.

'You were the most beautiful woman on the beach today,' I said in her hair. Before I let sleep claim me I resolved to get to know my children.

I put my plan into effect the next day. When they ran to the surf I followed after them. When they threw sand at each other and Niki chased her brother around, I tried to join in. But something was wrong. They didn't include me in their game, the way they included their mother. If anything, my presence puzzled them and they thought they should stop their horseplay and sit quietly on the towel. I tried to engage them in conversation, to play games with them, but although they didn't flinch or turn away, they were not altogether at ease.

Diane saw what I was doing.

'Don't give up,' she counselled when I gave up in frustration. 'They are not used to being with you. If you keep trying they will come around. They do love you, you know, but they don't know you very well.'

What she said seemed reasonable. I gave up on sharing their games, but I made an effort to engage them in conversation. In little more than a day they were chatting about everything to me. When John confided in me that he wanted to run restaurants when he grew up, just like me, my chest swelled with pride. This was my boy. I resolved to take him with me now and again, so he could see the business close up. My own plans were to make him a doctor, of course. This was the normal progression of things. Most American Greeks follow the unspoken rule. The father opens a restaurant, but the son becomes a doctor. Still, there was no harm in indulging John for the moment.

After a week or so of rest and relaxation, I was convinced that Diane's idea for a vacation was excellent, but ten days was too much. I had been on the phone to LA every day, my calls were getting longer and my anxiety to go back was growing unbearable. I began to complain that the weather was too hot, the bed too hard, the sand too fine and impossible to keep out of my shorts, the crowds too intrusive, the topography too boring. Diane suffered through my tirades, and replied to each one by suggesting that maybe I should call Leandros to check up on everything.

'What's the matter with you?' Leandros said when I called him for the third time on the eve of our departure. 'Can't you relax? I told you already that everything is fine. What do you think, that the minute you turn your back we will sell the furniture and set fire to the place? Go back to your wife, go back to your children, have some fun.' And he hung up on me.

We arrived in Los Angeles the next afternoon, and I left for Poseidon the minute we were in the door. I was back to my old ways in no time at all. My good intentions of getting more involved with my children and taking John with me to visit his dad's restaurants remained just that. Good intentions.

21

Grecian Cave

Despite my success, I remained afraid that my luck wouldn't last, that something would happen and my thriving restaurants would stumble, or that nothing would happen and people would just get tired of them and stop coming. The fear kept me working hard even when the love of my work would have finally let up enough for me to kick back and take it easy.

Finally it happened, and when it did I was not surprised by it, but instead relieved that it was finally here. Out of the blue, with no warning whatsoever, Kyra Euterpi, my star cook and entertainment at Poseidon, announced that she was leaving to open her own restaurant. I tried to dissuade her. I was already paying her well, but now I offered to give her a percentage of the profits. I had already been doing that with Leandros for some years. Her eyes glinted at the offer, but she refused. When more money didn't do the trick, I tried to appeal to her sentiments. She was like a mother to me, I told her. The place could not go on without her. I couldn't go on without her. I didn't feel guilty lying to her like that. I didn't much like her. She had been a humble, energetic woman when she first came to me, but as soon as she realised she had become a star, she grew too proud, and impossible to please. On the job, she still remained eccentric but lovable, but in my dealings with her she had grown arrogant and full of self-importance. I thought her ungrateful and insufferable, but it was true that the place couldn't go on without her. I was humbling myself in front of this miserable woman, but I was doing it out of love for what Poseidon had become.

I should have saved myself the trouble. She was leaving to help her daughter, and nothing comes before family to a Greek. She packed her special cooking implements when her two weeks' notice was up and went over to Venice Beach, where her son-in-law was already open for business with his own Greek restaurant. She never even thanked me or said goodbye.

I hired another cook, but braced myself for a slide in business. And it came. Euterpi was the soul of the place. Without her the oil sheets and the tacky mermaid didn't seem to work. Her fans came in, looked around and didn't return. Her own hole-in-the-wall in Venice was filled to capacity every night.

In desperation I searched for another cook. I found several who could handle the simple menu, but none with a personality to hold the place together and a knack for telling fortunes. What could I do? Instruct my new cook to go out to the floor and intrude on the customers' dinner? Either you have a gift for prophecy and bossing people around or you don't. Euterpi was one of a kind, and there was no replacement.

Poseidon slipped into the red, even though I spent all day running the figures obsessively over and over again and cutting corners. I was in despair. All my worst fears were coming back to me. The fact that Artemis Garden was doing just fine didn't matter. My confidence was gone. When you've created a place like Poseidon, nurtured it from its first day, seen it struggling to stand on its own two feet, watched it grow healthy and strong, it becomes a living thing. It was like watching a beloved child fight some dread disease and standing helplessly by, unable to help. I advertised everywhere, I tried to drum up business, but nothing could turn things around.

I brought frustration home with me every night. I slammed doors, muttered curses when my slippers or car keys were not where I wanted them to be and yelled at the children at every opportunity. At night in bed, I would turn my back to Diane, determined to make my misery as complete as possible.

Diane waited patiently for me to come to my senses, but each passing day made me worse. One Sunday morning, as I sat at the kitchen table adding up the numbers one more time before we left for church, Niki, who must have been seven at the time, came over to see what I was doing.

'Can I have a dollar for the donation tray, Daddy?' she asked.

'Speak Greek,' I barked at her, annoyed at the interruption, but more annoyed at the figures in front of me.

When my kids were babies I had resolved to teach them Greek, but I was never around to do so. Diane knew how much I wanted them to speak my native language, so she enrolled them as early as possible to the language school run by the Greek church, where she attended classes with them every Saturday morning. I found Diane's accented Greek charming, but it was a sore spot with me that my own children sounded like foreigners and seemed to have no special aptitude for my language. Most of the time I let them talk to me in English, because it bothered me to hear these two Greek children wrestle with what should have been their mother tongue. That day, however, my daughter's flawless American was a thorn in my side.

Niki tried to think of the words in Greek, but couldn't. She decided to get a glass of water instead. She got a tumbler from the dishwasher and then took the water bottle from the refrigerator to fill the glass with. Her hands were small, and the bottle full. The tumbler overflowed and then tipped over, drenching my papers. I exploded. I grabbed my daughter by her tiny shoulders, shook her and yelled at her that she was a careless, thoughtless, bad girl. I yelled at her in Greek.

Niki may not have had an easy time with the language, but she knew rage when she saw it. Tears started flowing as soon as my hands laid hold of her, and she was wailing as I shouted that she was grounded for the rest of her life. Diane heard the commotion and rushed in to save her. She took Niki away from me, settled her in the other room and came back to help me arrange my papers back in order.

'If I put these in the oven for a while, I bet they will dry just fine,' she said. I resented a solution to my problem. I wanted the papers to be ruined, and I wanted to be mad about it.

'Why don't you add some potatoes along with them and we can have a roast,' I said, my voice dripping with sarcasm.

'Listen to me, George. For weeks now you've been going around like a rabid dog. We are afraid to approach you and we don't even dare breathe in your presence. I know Poseidon is in bad shape, but darling, stop acting like your best friend is about to die. It's just a restaurant. Even if you have to close it down, you can always open another one.'

My anger, which had receded only slightly, returned full blown.

'Another one! And I suppose if one of the children died you wouldn't mourn because you could always have another one!' My words were meant to shock and hurt, and they did.

'How can you say something like that to me? And how can you compare your own children to a lousy restaurant?' Diane did not often get angry, she had too much of that American restraint, but she was angry now. There were two bright red spots on her cheeks, and her hands, bunched up in fists around sheafs of wet paper, were trembling.

'Poseidon *is* like a child to me, and if you don't understand that, then you understand nothing. Leave me alone! Give me those papers!' I grabbed the papers she was holding from her hands. 'Why don't you all just leave me the hell alone!'

I slammed out of the house and drove to Poseidon. I stayed there all day long, and then all evening, as my few customers walked in. My mood got worse and I finally drove over to Artemis Garden. I got myself a drink and sat at one of the tables in the back, speaking to no one. After the kitchen closed, Leandros came and joined me.

'Things got you down, boss?' he asked.

'Don't even ask. Get me another Scotch.'

Leandros did.

'I think I know what you need,' he told me as he set the drink down in front of me. 'You need some *bouzouki*, to forget your troubles.'

Leandros was not married, and he had no family in the area. Like me, he never talked about what brought him to America. He did his work well, stayed till closing time and then drove over to a Greek nightclub called Grecian Cave, where I believe he stayed till four or five in the morning, drinking and listening to Greek music.

I had been to the Grecian Cave a couple of times with Diane, but it wasn't really a family place. It was tucked

away into the worst part of Hollywood, and kept late
hours. It had live Greek music that started every night
at eleven, and a belly-dancer who did a couple of dances
in between sets. It served food to those who wanted it,
but made money mostly on its watered-down drinks and
the high-flying types who took their pleasure by breaking
plates and overturning tables after they had had a few, for
all of which they were charged a pretty penny. The bar
was always filled with mysterious men who had probably
left Greece because they got in trouble with the law and
would stay in America until their drug habit or shady
deals got the American law enforcement agencies after
them. When one of them disappeared from one day
to the next, nobody would say a word about it. It
was taken for granted that the missing person was on
his way to Argentina, Brazil, or some other such place.

I had never gone to the Grecian Cave without Diane,
but now the thought of going home to her was unbearable.
She didn't understand my pain, she didn't understand me,
and I would punish her by withholding my presence from
her. I nodded my agreement to Leandros's proposition
and the two of us left Artemis Garden.

At the Grecian Cave things were just getting started.
Most of the tables were empty, and several of the night's
singers were at the bar, drinking the evening's first drink.
The minute we came through the door, everyone greeted
Leandros like an old friend. We took two stools and
ordered our drinks. Leandros talked to his buddies and I
sat nursing my drink and feeling out of place. When
the spotlight hit the stage and the band began to play,
Leandros and I moved to a table at the edge of the seating
area.

The place was beginning to fill up. There were no
Americans here. The place was hard-core Greek, with

some Armenians thrown in because the owner always had one Armenian singer on the entertainment roster, and with several Arabs who came in because their own music at times resembles what Greeks listen to.

The first singer was a man, dressed in a tight-fitting white suit and much put out by the band's unsynchronised performance. He turned to them often, waving his hand in the beat he thought they should follow. The *bouzouki* player kept shaking his head. The music sounded too loud. I complained to Leandros that this was too much like random noise.

'Drink some more,' he shouted over the din. 'It will get better.'

Through the performance of the irate singer in the white suit, and the follow-up act of a bleached blonde with a big mole on her cheek, I drank determinedly. By the time the two performers joined each other in a duet, my head was feeling light and the band seemed to have improved. The volume was about right.

The lights went out, a drum roll sounded. When the spotlight hit the stage again, a new performer was on centre stage. She was a slight girl with long black hair, worn loose down her back. She had the waist of a wasp and she wore a bright red dress. Dazzled by the quick switch from darkness to brilliant light display, I sucked in my breath in shock. Katerina.

The girl was cradling the mike as she waited for the musical intro to lead into her song. No, it wasn't Katerina. But to my bleary eyes, it was close. Fascinated, I watched her wait with a thoughtful expression on her face, and finally begin singing a slow ballad about heartbreak. I motioned the waiter to bring me another drink and riveted my eyes on the stage. Her dress had sequins on it that caught the light and reflected it back. She seemed surrounded by a shiny cloud, a brilliance. Leandros said something to me, but I shushed him. I was enthralled. She stood on centre stage, with her hands around the mike as she sang. She sang modestly and wistfully, with none of the lascivious moves so common to performers in nightclubs like the Grecian Cave. Her voice was soft and sweet, perhaps a little weak, but she had the face and body of an angel, and this was not just any angel, but my own personal angel, the angel of all my dreams. I watched her leave the stage at the end of her set with a pang. I turned to Leandros.

'Who is she?'

'That's Angela. She's been here a few weeks. She'll come out soon. She likes to mix with the customers.'

I drank impatiently while I waited for Angela to come out of the dressing-room. She seemed to take an awfully long time. I drank some more.

She finally came out, still in her red dress, and made straight for the bar. With a drink in her hand, she joined a couple of men who were sitting there. She seemed to know them. She talked easily and laughed at something. She was more animated than she had been on stage.

'Can you ask her to come over?' I asked Leandros.

'Oh, she will. She knows me. She always stops by to say hello.'

I waited some more. Drank some more. And Angela finally sauntered over.

'Leandros, you old sinner, here you are again. Why don't you ask Theo to put you on the payroll?' she said as she kissed Leandros on the forehead, her long slender arm around his neck.

Leandros invited her to sit, ordered her a drink, introduced me. The two of them talked about the show and the first singer's tiff. I sat silently contemplating her.

Her face, which looked so delicate from a distance, was not as pretty close up. Her skin was coarse and lined and she had fillings in several of her teeth, which showed black when the threw her head back and laughed a full-throated high-pitched laugh. Unlike her presence on stage, her movements at the table had a coarseness about them that stamped her as a singer in shady nightclubs. She cussed freely and she made risqué jokes, flirting openly with Leandros. She was definitely not Katerina. But with several drinks blurring my vision and with the dim lights of the floor, when she wasn't talking, when her head was turned just so, so that her hair hid most of her face, I could pretend that this was Katerina, come to me at my lowest hour to redeem me.

I stayed at the Grecian Cave with Leandros until Angela did her second and last set of the night. Then Leandros and I stumbled out and we went back to Artemis Garden so I could pick up my car. I tiptoed into my house and found nobody waiting up for me. When I slipped into bed, Diane gave no sign that she was aware of me.

The next night, after I closed down Artemis Garden, I went to the Grecian Cave again, drank quickly and efficiently, and managed to be quite drunk enough when Angela came on stage to dream without reality intruding.

It got to be a habit. For two weeks I went to the Grecian Cave every night. Diane and I hardly spoke, and indeed hardly saw each other. During the day I was depressed and miserable as I watched Poseidon slipping farther down the road to disaster, but at night I was back in Panorama, safely and without risk to myself, because with a few drinks and clever lighting Katerina visited me and sang to me of love.

Angela noticed how I stared at her. She asked questions about me. Leandros noticed it, too.

'She likes you, boss,' he told me. 'I bet she wouldn't say no if you wanted to spend some time with her.'

Normally I would have found it offensive for one of my employees, even Leandros, to speak to me in that way, but this was not a normal time in my life and I was already on my fourth drink when he said it. It got me thinking. Would it be so bad to have a go at Angela? Would it be so bad to have a small victory when all around me was failure?

I started buying Angela drinks and giving her flowers sold by a Korean woman who was allowed, for a fee, to peddle half-wilted roses to the patrons of the Grecian Cave. She accepted them with a smile and she began to dedicate songs to me from the stage, never mentioning my name but glancing at me with meaning every time she announced that the next song went out to a very special man. Finally, I followed her home and into her bed.

In the back of my mind, I guess I was wondering if in the darkness of her bedroom the magic that happened every night on stage would repeat itself. I was wrong. It wasn't my fantasy. It was something else entirely. My fantasy was possible only when Angela sang in her modest, unassuming way centre stage, bathed by a lone spotlight, in her red dress with the sequins. In her bed, she was a grown woman who had been around and seen a lot, and liked to talk dirty and fuck violently.

She shrieked and moaned her pleasure, but I never knew if it was real. I left her bed each time a little disgusted with myself, but then the next night she would work her transformaton again on stage and I would follow her home once more in an alcoholic haze, to look for what wasn't there.

After the first couple of times, Angela started hinting broadly that I might show some generosity. She interspersed her hints with all manner of declarations of love

and shameless flattery, not even bothering to conceal very
well that she just wanted to use me. I didn't leave. Instead,
I bought her jewellery, a set of diamond earrings and a
bracelet. Her eyes flashed greedily when she opened each
of the small velvet boxes, and she outdid herself with
sexual tricks to thank me. I felt cheaper than ever as I
drove home, but the way this relationship debased me
seemed fitting to me in a way. I kept going back.

Diane and I were still not talking except for the
bare necessities, spoken in a dry and sullen manner. I
tried talking to Angela. Until I figured out that Angela
was taking the measure of my wealth, I was surprised
to find her interested and even eager to hear about my
business.

'So if you close down Poseidon, will you be broke?' she
asked me.

'No, but that's not the point,' I explained. 'Poseidon
is my baby, and I want it to do well.'

'So why don't you put some music in there? I bet
that would get things going. Maybe I could sing there.
Wouldn't that be nice? And in between songs I could take
you in the cooler and blow your socks off.'

My sordid little affair came to an abrupt end. One
night, as I tiptoed home once more, I found Diane waiting
up for me. She was sitting at the bottom of the staircase, determined to intercept me.

'Would you follow me into the kitchen?' she asked,
her voice calm and collected.

With a sheepish look on my face, I followed her as she
asked. In the kitchen she handed me a cup of coffee and
sat across the table.

'You're seeing someone,' she said.

I tried to part the drink fumes and decide whether to
confirm or deny her accusation. She didn't wait.

'You have to stop immediately. Or this cannot be your home any more.'

Her face was set and hard. I fiddled with my keys, still in my hand, took a gulp of my coffee, swirled it around in my mouth. She waited. I was tired of hating myself. I was tired of living in the gutter.

'Okay,' I answered.

She got up and washed out her own cup.

'We need a vacation,' she said with her back turned to me. Her voice sounded normal. As though we hadn't just had the most important conversation of our married life together.

'Okay,' I said again.

I didn't hire Angela to sing at Poseidon. Indeed, I never saw her again. I didn't even speak with her. I just told Leandros to mention that I wouldn't be going to the Grecian Cave any more. Angela had received the bracelet only a few days before my confrontation with Diane. She must have felt that this was the most she could hope for, because she made no effort to contact me.

I did hire musicians for Poseidon. I set them up in one corner, and had them playing at a volume that allowed conversation without shouting. And I hired waiters who could dance. Right in the middle of the dinner rush, they would put down their trays and dance around the tables, as though the music had tempted them away from their duties. And they would grab the customers, too, and make them dance in a long snaky line that ran the length of the restaurant. The gimmick worked like a charm, and Poseidon was in the black once more. The wages of adultery are not always grief.

Diane and I left for Mexico after Poseidon seemed well on its way to recovery. This time we left the kids behind, so that when I would get on the phone to check up on my restaurants, Diane would be talking to John and Niki. The rest of the time we strolled and swam and sunned. We were careful with one another, but we were trying. At night we made love. The act had lost some of its innocence, had been tainted by my foray into the underbelly of the Grecian Cave, but we persisted, and near the end of our two weeks it was the same as ever.

In the aeroplane on the way back, I drank my Scotch thinking that if this second honeymoon was meant to restore our relationship, it worked. Unfortunately, restoration did not mean a return to passion, because passion had never been a part of the bargain for me. My marriage was simply this calm and steady presence in my life. It would never bring me wild happiness, but it would not bring me utter desolation, either. This is what I had wanted, and this is what I had got. And as a marriage it had its own value, if it could survive my affair with Angela and my depression over Poseidon with so little damage.

A month or so after our return, Diane told me she was pregnant again. I received the news with mild pleasure, and was little aware of Diane's pregnancy until I arrived home the day of the birth to find my children locked out and their mother missing, driven to the hospital by Christos the inscrutable. Little did I know during those months when Diane knitted booties and got the basinette out of storage, that my third child, the light of my life, the joy of my heart, the one person who would restore to me my capacity for feeling love, was on her way to me.

Part Four

The Return

22

The Arrival

It's six in the morning of the day of my return to Greece.
I'm still here, in the living-room where my family's
pictures, the ones Katerina sent to America with me,
hang on the wall. I've been sitting here with my Scotch
and my memories all night, but I don't feel tired and I
don't feel sleepy. If anything, my mind is sharper and
more alert than it has been in twenty-five years and I seem
to see everything with a new clarity of vision. Daylight
is beginning to stream through the windows, and it's
taking away the brightness of the small lamp that has
accompanied my vigil. It's funny, but as I'm looking
around the room in the new light, this house in which
I've lived for five years seems unfamiliar to me. Every
piece of furniture, every little knick-knack, is brand new
to my eyes. I'm going home. But if I'm going home, then
I'm not home now. No wonder I recognise nothing.

I've already made the call to the airlines to book my
flight. The clerk has informed that my best flight path
is to take a plane to London and then hook up with
Olympic Airlines, which flies straight from London to
Thessaloniki. No need to waste time flying into Athens.
United has taken my reservation to London already,
but Olympic Airlines is Greek, so they don't have a

round-the-clock reservations desk to book my connecting flight. Everything can wait until tomorrow for Greeks. Well, almost everything. *I* cannot wait till tomorrow, even though it is tomorrow already.

There are six hours to go before my flight, and one hour to go before my household awakens. Diane will wake up first, and then wake John and Niki and help them prepare for school. It's June, and this is exam week. John will get As again, and Niki's teachers will remark that she is smart, but doesn't try. No, she doesn't try. The only thing she tries to do is frustrate me at every turn. If I express a preference for something, whatever it is, she will oppose me. If I tell her to be home by ten, she will waltz in at midnight, with some fabricated story about cars breaking down, or her watch having stopped. If I tell her to go and study, she will lock herself in her room and crank up the music, swearing that it is the only way she can concentrate. When I told her her friend Linda was a mindless shopping robot and she should drop her and get better friends, she went shopping with the clothes horse and ran up a shopping bill that was over $500. When I took away her charge card, she screamed that I was a tyrant and wouldn't talk to me for weeks. I have been cursed in my eldest daughter.

I've been much luckier with my son, but there is something missing there, too. John is a good student, plans to go to medical school just like I want him to, never screams or yells or throws tantrums, but sometimes I forget he exists for days at a time. He never says anything. He is a silent presence in the house, spending most of his time in his room with his books and his computer. I've never had a conversation with him. He is polite and respectful enough when I talk to him, but he answers in monosyllables, and speaks only when spoken to. I would have worried that he might be stupid, if his report card was not always perfect in every way. John does everything that is expected of him, but he gives me no affection and he gives me no pleasure.

Is it any wonder Katie is the light of my life? Between John's silences and Niki's cursedness, what parent wouldn't have a preference for that bright warm little girl who lights up like a Christmas tree whenever she sees me? She even lisps Greek words to me, as many as she knows. Her brother and sister attended Greek school every Saturday for six years each, but they never use the language. John knows quite a bit of it, because he did as well in that class as he does in every other class, but Niki knows nothing. She probably plugged her ears every Saturday morning to stop herself learning any Greek by accident while she sat in class, just to spite me.

I pace around downstairs waiting for the time to pass. I like this new game where every object is revealed to me in this new clarity. I know that I should feel familiar in the house, but I don't. Look, here is the piano where Diane has learned to pluck out Greek tunes at parties. Her sheet music is neatly stacked to the side. But I never before noticed the whiteness of the Steinway baby grand, and I never before was struck like this with the grace of its form, or the purity of the gold letters spelling out 'Steinway' above the keys.

And here is the dining-room, where Diane insists that we have dinner every night, shunning the kitchen. Katie always sits on my right and asks for this and that morsel out of my plate. John always sits next to his mother and he eats slowly and deliberately, without pleasure, the way he does everything. He always measures his food just right, so that he gets done with the meat and potatoes and vegetables simultaneously, loading each perfectly balanced bite on his fork with precision. He butters his bread so every single bit of surface is covered by butter in even thickness, and he folds his used napkin neatly before getting up from the table. Sometimes as I've watched him go through his routine, I've wondered if maybe we ought to get him to have a physical, to see whether it's flesh and blood he's made of.

Niki usually eats in a hurry because she has to go somewhere, or because she can't wait to get on the phone with her friends. She demanded her own phone when she turned thirteen, and I refused her. But you refuse Niki at your own peril. She kept the family phone busy for hours at a time, hanging up when she was asked to do so repeatedly, but then sneaking to another extension only minutes later, to continue her interminable conversations. I finally had to give in and install her own line in her room, because I was worried that if anything happened, I would be unable to get through to my family.

I walk into the kitchen through the study door that marks the passage. This used to be a swinging door, but I had it replaced. Somehow, little Katie was always getting hit by it every time John and Niki were in the kitchen, until I finally got suspicious and decided to remove this instrument of torture from my house. John and Niki would not admit to anything deliberate, of course. John gave me his inscrutable look when I accused him, and denied any evil purpose. Niki looked at me with contempt.

'If she wasn't always trying to spy on us, she wouldn't get hit. But she sneaks up and stands close so she can hear, and of course the door lands on her when we try to leave the kitchen,' she told me. As if a little girl would know enough to spy on her brother and sister! She just wanted to be included. She's like a puppy dog with her brother and sister. No matter how many times they hurt her, she always brightens up when she sees them and runs after them to get their attention.

'Why can't you be careful when you open the door?' I asked Niki reasonably enough.

'Am I to live my life on guard because I have a sneak for a sister?' Niki retorted.

I didn't take this lying down. I told her that yes, she had to live her life so as not to hurt her sister. Then I made a rule that if Katie ever got hit again, both John and Niki would be grounded for a week. I never got a chance to impose this punishment, however, because the next time the door hurt my darling it was Cora, the cook who later died of a heart attack, who had done the swinging. So I had the door replaced.

I also told Katie not to stand behind doors. Closed doors can often let out enough sound to hurt whoever listens behind them, and this particular kitchen door, the new one which never hurt my Katie, did hurt me. I was standing behind it when I overheard Niki talking to Diane one night. Niki has many times tried to hurt me deliberately, but she inflicted her most significant wound unwittingly.

It was almost time for her fifteenth birthday and Diane had suggested that we let Niki throw a party for her friends. I agreed, and that night Diane told Niki the news at the dinner table. Niki looked pained for a moment and then said that she didn't want a party. I thought it strange at the time, but did not pursue it. Later on, as I made my way to the kitchen for another bite of dessert, I heard Niki and Diane talking in there.

'I would be embarrassed to have a party here,' I heard my daughter tell her mother.

'But Niki, we have a beautiful home, and a nice pool, and I'm sure your friends would like it!'

'It's not the house. It's him. He'll be all over the place talking in his loud voice and mispronouncing everything! I can't take it, Mother. He's been in America all his life, and he still can't talk like a human being!'

'Niki, you're way out of line on this,' Diane chided her.

'I don't care if I'm out of line. It's embarrassing to have him talk like that, and it makes me wince. People make fun of him!'

I gave up on dessert. I just tiptoed back to the small living-room. I am a successful man, a pillar of the community. I have a home with a pool in Beverly Hills and our old home in Brentwood that I'm renting out, two thriving businesses and a position on the Board of Directors in our church. The bank rolls out the red carpet for me whenever I go by, and Biaggi made his career off of me. People are always asking my advice and pointing to me as a man who has everything. I have the respect of every man I meet. And my daughter's friends make fun of my accent. But my accent is who I am. My accent is my link with my past. I always knew that Niki didn't love me, but I just assumed I had her respect. I hurt for a long time after her cruel words, and my only consolation to this day is that she has never dared to say anything to my face. She may not respect me, but she sure does fear me.

I sit in the kitchen and think about my wife and children and my life here. Except for Katie, it seems unreal, too, just like the objects around me this morning. What's real to me at this hour is the life I ran out on twenty-five years ago. Panorama! I will be there in twenty-four hours! And I will see Katerina. How will she be now that she's grown up? She must be forty-six now, a middle-aged woman. Maybe she won't bear any resemblance to the girl I loved. Maybe she has grown old and grey, the way so many Greek women do before their time. They live a hard life out there, which lines their faces and makes them old in their thirties even. So how has time treated my Katerina? Has her life been happy? Did my brother make her happy? Suddenly these questions are the most important thing in my life, and I cannot wait to see for myself the very people I have done my best to forget.

Diane walks into the kitchen. I tell her I am flying to Greece. She shows no surprise. She only asks my plans. I have no plans other than that I'm going there. I don't know what is happening with Andreas, I tell her. I will call when I get in. Meanwhile, I call Manos and ask him to let everyone know I'm on my way. Manos is relieved at my decision. I can tell because his voice is suddenly happy.

I say good-bye to the children. John and Niki don't care. After they leave, and Diane is upstairs preparing my suitcase, I sit down with Katie and we have a long talk.

'Why can't I go with you?' she asks.

'Let me get there first. And if I'm going to stay longer than a few days, I'll arrange for you to come over.'

Her little face lights up with glee. She wants to go to Greece, my little darling.

Finally it's time, and I drive over to LAX, with Katie beside me and Diane in the back seat. Diane is unnaturally silent. I have a good view of her face in the rear-view mirror, and I know that she is thinking. At the airport Katie reminds me of my promise to send for her. Diane kisses me solemnly.

'I hope you find your brother all right. And call me if you want me to come. The kids will be out of school by the end of the week. We could all come.'

The thought is strange to me. My family in Panorama! It's only Katie that I can think of in that setting. She is the only one who fits the context. Diane kisses me again.

'I love you,' she says, and I know that this is where our conversation stopped last night.

'I'll call as soon as I get in,' I tell her, and go through the metal detector.

As I follow the stream of travellers to the gate, my step is firm and sure. I'm walking fast, as though this will help me get to Greece faster.

In the plane I drink as much as the stewardess will allow, and then I sleep. Scrunched up in my seat, I actually dream. It's Katerina I see as I'm dreaming, walking towards me in a field of red poppies. She is just as young as she was when I left, and even in my dream I think this is impossible. She's dressed in black, but she is smiling. 'He's dead, George,' she tells me. 'Now I am yours.' Happiness floods me in my dream, but it's a guilty happiness.

I wake up only when we reach London. I have a six hour layover, and I spend it walking around the shops and having coffee, determinedly pushing my dream out of my mind. My nerves are getting tight, and time crawls by agonisingly slowly. In the airport coffee shop I sit next to four Greeks who seem to know each other. The young two are students, studying in London. The others are parents who were visiting their son, who is also a London college student. They talk about the housing situation. The two young people found this great apartment at a low price, and the parents can barely conceal their envy at the savings that could have been theirs, if only their offspring had shown similar scouting abilities. I give no sign that I understand them, or that I am listening to them. I don't want to be social, and I don't want to talk.

When I show up at the counter of Olympic Airlines, all is confusion. The plane is late, the attendants are rude, the people refuse to wait in line. There is much pushing and shoving, and everywhere there is a stream of Greek flying from mouth to mouth rapidly. At the Greek church in Los Angeles, many people speak English with only a few Greek words thrown in, sometimes spoken in an American accent even though the speaker grew up in Greece. This curious phenomenon is one of my regular annoyances with the Greek community. It is nothing but affectation; how can you forget your mother tongue? My own Greek is as Greek as it ever was. I may have some trouble coming up with a word now and then, but I sound like what I am.

Finally I am in the plane and waiting to take off. The announcements are in Greek. The airline magazine is in Greek. My eyes are red with fatigue, my head hurts, I worry that my bag has not been loaded on the plane. I sit up with my jacket on my knees, ready to leave the plane at a moment's notice as soon as we arrive, unwilling to sit back and relax and admit to myself that there is another three hours to go before we land. I worry for no reason that the plane will be hijacked, or that we won't be able to land in Thessaloniki after all. Whenever I stop worrying, I have to keep swallowing hard to hold the tears at bay. My heart is so full! In a few hours I will see my village, I will see Katerina. I will see my brother. I have no idea how I will feel, but for now I am a naked nerve, an open wound, in my vulnerability and sensitivity. Fly, damn you, fly! Take off! Take me there!

We fly over Europe, but I never once look out the window. Instead I just concentrate on the sound of the engines. It is my willpower alone, my concentration, that keeps the plane flying, and I am hurrying it on its way. I part the clouds in front of it and I provide the pressure that keeps the wings afloat. The pilot doesn't tell us when we cross into Greek airspace. I only know we are there because the command comes to fasten our seat belts. Now my face is pressed to the tiny window. Greece! This is Greece below me! Thessaloniki, white and golden and bathed in the light of the Greek sun. The sun takes a long time to go down in Greece in the summer, so even though it's seven o'clock, it's still full daylight. Slivers of light are playing on the water of Thermaikos Bay. Somewhere down there, on the ground we fly over, Katerina may have heard the hum of the aeroplane. Will she be at the airport? Will anybody be at the airport? Is Andreas alive? There is no stopping my tears now. They wet my face and blur my vision. Oh God, I cannot bear the strength of my own feelings. I am home. Thank God, I'm finally back home.

The plane touches the ground with a thud. I've wiped my eyes a hundred times, but it's no use. The tears keep coming. I try thinking of other things, I try doing the multiplication tables, but Greece has its arms around me and it's cradling me to her breast. This is what I have missed most of my life, and what I have found again in large measure with my Katie. A feeling of love so vast and sweet and intense that I feel I cannot possibly contain it, and I will die of it. The man next to me is not put off by my strange behaviour. He's Greek. When I cast a glance at him through my watery mist, he smiles and nods his head.

'Been gone long?' he asks me. His teeth are bad, his hair is shiny with some oil, but his smile is warm.

'Twenty-five years,' I tell him in my strangled voice.

'Welcome home, *patriotis*.'

There is Greek music coming through the sound system of the plane as I line up with the other passengers to get to the door. We are a small distance from the terminal and there are buses waiting to take us there. First we must leave the plane by the large metal staircase that has been wheeled over for that purpose. There is a woman with a five-year-old behind me. The kid is obnoxious and keeps kicking at my legs as I wait my turn. It's okay, I understand. He is impatient to get off, too. I wish I could do some kicking. His mother slaps him hard just as I set foot on the stairs and breathe in the balmy air. It's hot. I descend on wobbly legs. My shoes clank on the metal steps. The kid kicks me again, and with one more step I'm finally here. I'm standing on Greek ground.

There is a crowd gathered at the windows of the terminal, but I'm afraid to look as I go into the door that leads to passport control and customs. The usual pushing and shoving as people try to be first through the line does not concern me.

At the baggage carousel, I hand a dollar to the attendant who lets me have a cart. He gives me some Greek coins as change. They are different from the coins I remember. Smaller and lighter. I find my bag easily. I load it on the cart and go to customs. The man in attendance just waves me through, too engrossed in a political argument with a co-worker to worry about smugglers. There is a crowd gathered at the door, bodies pressed together in a tight crunch, shouting names and waving. A fat lady lets out a scream next to my ear when she sees whoever is waiting for her on the other side. I push the cart in front of me, and I walk slowly. I don't know what to look for, or if I should look for anything.

'Vasilikos! Vasilikos!'

I hear my name. I look around. I see the young man. He's about twenty-five, and he's holding a sign with my name pencilled on it. My face contorts in a grimace but fresh tears break through anyway. The young man lets me hug him, and even hugs me back. He slaps me on the back affectionately.

'You're Uncle George,' he tells me, and I nod. 'I'm Petros. Dad is alive,' he says.

He's talking about his father Andreas, of course. But he's the spitting image of my father.

23

The Invalid

It's two hours past midnight and I'm sitting next to my brother's bed in hospital. This is Saint Loukas Hospital, the same hospital where Manos married Antigone, and Katerina had her bruises tended to the night of Pavlos's wedding. Andreas was a strapping young man back then. Now he is tethered to a heart monitor and an IV. His lips have a bluish cast and even though I've been here for hours, he has slept the whole time through, so he hasn't seen me.

I'm here this late because I cannot sleep. Jet lag has me in its grip. Everyone else has long since gone home. My brother breathes rhythmically. His doctors say he is as well as can be expected. He might have another heart attack and he might not, but the important thing is to rest, give up smoking and drinking, follow his diet and pray.

He has changed. His hair has thinned, and even under the covers I can tell that he has put on some weight. His body probably doesn't have that V shape he was so proud of any more. But he is still tall, his feet reach the end of his bed. And his shoulders are still massive and wide. His face is drawn and haggard, but that's probably the effect of his heart attack. He's seen Hades with his own eyes, and if that's not enough to make a man haggard, I don't know what is.

I haven't gone to the house yet. I've been in the hospital since I arrived. After I collected my wits about me and stopped snivelling like an idiot, my nephew Petros put me in the little Ford that belongs to Andreas, and we left the airport. Twenty-five years is a long time, but you don't know how long until you visit a place you haven't been to all that time. Thessaloniki has changed. It's bigger, brighter, richer. I recognised the road leading to Panorama, but only because the signs jogged my memory. It used to be that there was a long stretch of undeveloped land separating the city from the village. This is not so any more. The city has spilled out of its boundaries and is doing its best to climb all the way up the mountain. There are charming condos and beautiful houses at every turn. And there are hundreds of cars going up and down what used to be a country road.

Petros spoke to me all the way up to the hospital, explaining about Andreas and telling me about the family. Petros has two younger brothers, Yiannis and Nikiforos. My father and mother have certainly been honoured in the naming of the grandchildren they never met.

'Everybody is up at the hospital,' he explained. 'Mom practically lives there.'

Mom is Katerina, I thought. I will see Katerina in just a short while. And this young man with my father's look about him is Katerina's child of shame, the child she conceived by my brother before marrying him. This is the child that triggered my unhappiness and sent me to the other side of the world. He seems a nice young man. His driving is a little reckless in these narrow streets, but that's a sign of machismo, and Petros is the son of Andreas in every way. He has a cockiness about him, a bit of a swagger. But he is Katerina's son, too, so there is more to him.

'I'm running the bakery with the help of Yiannis. Thank God this happened in the summer. Yiannis is going to college, but now the term is over, so he can help. Nikiforos is in the army, stationed in Crete. He flew in to see Dad, but he had to go back today.'

Petros kept up his chatter throughout our hair-raising drive, negotiating the turns expertly but too fast, treating the Escort as though it were a Ferrari. He would turn to me every so often, waving his cigarette to make a point, and I would pray silently that he would keep his eyes on the road so we could reach our destination. I didn't want to die so close to Katerina without seeing her first. When I wasn't praying for dear life, I listened attentively to all he said. I found my curiosity to be enormous after lying dormant for twenty-five years. Besides, the chatter kept me from getting nervous about my meeting with Katerina. I glanced surreptitiously in the side-view mirror as the car approached the hospital. What will Katerina think of me? I wondered. Will I finally look like a man to her? Have I finally grown up?

Katerina was in the waiting-room when we arrived. She was visible from the moment I started down the long corridor leading to her. At first all I saw was a woman sitting in a chair. Then her head snapped into attention. And with only a moment's hesitation, she rose and came to me, the two of us covering the distance in half the time, me walking steadily, trying to delay the moment so I could get my emotions under control, she hurrying to me until she was in my arms, sobbing.

My brother stirs in his sleep and his hand slaps at the air. Some garbled word escapes him, and then he settles down again. He must be dreaming. As for me, I have no more need of dreams. I've seen Katerina. So how is she after all this time? Her eyes are still round and enormous and made of black velvet. Her lashes are just as long as they ever were and still cast shadows on her cheeks when she looks down. Her mouth is still a delicate almond blossom pink, her teeth small and pointed, her shoulders fragile, the curve of her throat slender and long. Her widow's peak still shapes her face into a heart. She's still my Katerina. Time has changed some things, but it's been gentle with her, and generous. It has scored her skin with lines, but it has left the light of sweetness that shines from her face undiminished, so that the lines are blurred and barely visible. It has plumped up her slender figure, but the new plumpness makes her softer, more inviting. It has planted white strands in her coal-black hair, but she wears it short now, to the chin, and this short hair suits her. The new hairstyle makes the white look premature and out of place. Hers always was a beautiful face but time has made it finer. Her cheekbones are more visible, her jaw more chiselled. Now that I know about these things I realise that Katerina has marvellous bone structure. Time can take away a lot of things but it cannot take away that. So, Katerina has aged well. Better than that; Katerina has aged beautifully. Maybe when she walks down the street men don't stop and stare, but I think it must be impossible for any man to sit down and speak to her, to hear her sweet voice and look into her incomparable eyes, and not want to take her in his arms. Some women fade when they lose the freshness of youth. Katerina is blossoming for the second time.

Katerina hugged me for a long time. Then we sat and talked. She updated me on Andreas and then asked about my family and my life. She repeated the names of my wife and children. She didn't seem to notice that Katie bears her name. When I named my baby I never thought there would come a time when I would say that name to Katerina and now I am relieved that Katerina didn't comment on the sign of the extent of my obsession.

'It sounds like you're happy, George. You don't know how many times I've prayed that would be so.'

She was holding my hand when she said that, her fingers caressing mine. Her nails are short and broken, and her skin rough. Katerina has the hands of a woman who has spent a lifetime washing and cleaning. As I provided answers to her many questions, I kept thinking of the years we've spent apart. The lines on her face, the veins on her fingers, even the age spots where once there was only clear young skin, filled my heart with tenderness as I spoke calmly of my kids and business. Katerina, Katerina!

I asked Petros to call Diane in Los Angeles and say I've arrived and am all right. I don't want to leave the hospital, and it's impossible to reverse charges in Greece. Katerina left with Petros and Yiannis around ten. She wanted me to go with them, but I said I wanted to stay in case Andreas woke up. The truth is I want to be alone. In this quiet, half-lit room, I have what I need most right now. Sensory deprivation. I need to get my emotions off this roller coaster. I wish I could sleep, but it's four in the afternoon in Los Angeles. Sleep mocks me.

'Who's there?'

It's Andreas. He has woken up with a start.

'Andreas, it's me, George.'

There is a pause.

'George, you came! Come over here, let me see you.'

I go over to my brother. I look down on him. He smiles.

'So does this mean I'm dying?' he asks, but he asks it lightly, like a joke.

'No. They were afraid when they called me, but that was almost two days ago. You're fine now.' I don't know if I'm telling the truth, but how do you answer a question like that?

'Look at you. You look good. How come you still have all your hair? If it's some fancy American shampoo, I hope you brought me some.'

'You have to rest, Andreas. Don't talk so much. Go to sleep. I'll still be here tomorrow.'

'So why the hell did you leave like that, eh? And why do I have to get a visit from the Grim Reaper to get you to come see me?'

'Sleep, Andreas, or I will call the nurse and have her give you a shot.'

'You wouldn't say that if you'd seen her, little brother. She's got a pair on her that could feed an entire orphanage of starving babies.' He chuckles, but his voice is already drifting. He's falling asleep again.

Sensory deprivation! What a joke! I'm crying again. My brother just spoke to me. His voice is just like it used to be. He called me 'little brother' again, just like he used to when he didn't call me 'little fool'. For someone who didn't love anyone for years, I sure do love a lot of people today. The man next to me in the plane, the horrible five-year-old, Petros, Katerina. Even my brother who stole my happiness. I don't want him to die, oh God, I don't. Even though he's a bad man, and always has been, even though he robbed me of Katerina and broke my heart, spare him, oh God. Even if it means I have to see him with her the way I never wanted to, please let him live.

I lie down in the bed next to my brother. Memories assault me and I wet the hard hospital pillow with more tears. This is my brother, my friend and my enemy.

Take of my strength and live, I tell him in my thoughts.
Don't leave me.

Morning surprises me. I have fallen asleep in the empty
bed next to Andreas without even realising it. What wakes
me up is the nurse, and she wakes me up out of a very
deep sleep. I take my shaving kit to the bathroom and
try to make myself look presentable. I am exhausted. It's
eight o'clock in the morning here, but ten the previous
night in LA, and my sleep patterns are so messed up that
my body is ready to collapse.

When I come out of the bathroom, Katerina is there
with Yiannis, my second nephew. He is tall and dark
and he resembles neither of his two parents overmuch.
Katerina fusses over me and declares they are taking me
to breakfast. We drive into Panorama. There's very little
here of the look I remember. Panorama has become a
slick suburb. All the streets are paved. Luxurious shops
line Main Street. Cars whizz by. The cinema does not
exist any more.

'People go to the city for movies,' Katerina explains.
Now that everyone has a car it seems that Thessaloniki
has moved closer. Nobody thinks twice about making the
trip any more.

We have coffee and toast with butter and marmalade in
a coffee shop shiny with mirrors, and I'm starting to feel
like a human being again. I catch up on what's happened.
Pavlos and Litsa have two children. The first one, the one
that precipitated the wedding, died a few days after it was
born. Birth defect. Kyra Marika the nurse died of heart
failure. Kyra Maria the sediment reader didn't foretell her
own death. She died from cancer. Uncle Demetres is dead,
too. His liver finally succumbed to all his drinking. I'm at
an age where catching up means learning how people died.

Back at the hospital, as we pass the front desk, we hear a sharp voice.

'What room is he in?'

The voice belongs to a buxom woman dressed in a flower-print dress that stretches valiantly over her curves. She has pouffy red hair of a shade that doesn't occur in nature. She's holding a large white bag in her hand and she is punching out a rhythm of impatience with her heel on the floor. I hear the nurse give the number of Andreas's room. The woman is here to see Andreas! I don't know who she is. I turn to ask Katerina. What I see startles me. Katerina's face has gone completely white. She is staring at the woman as though she is her worst enemy instead of a cheap little piece. A cheap little piece! I have a suspicion.

Katerina throws herself in a chair, as the redhead starts making her way down the hall.

'I won't have it,' Katerina says. 'Yiannis, get that woman out of here.'

'What's going on?' I ask, but nobody pays attention to me. Yiannis takes off after the woman and I follow him. He catches up with her just as she's ready to go in the room.

'Stop right there,' he commands.

She must be used to orders. She stops instantly.

'You can't go in there,' Yiannis tells her.

'And why can't I? I can visit a sick man as well as anyone can!'

'You are not anyone. You are nothing but a trouble-maker, and you are leaving right now!' Yiannis has laid hold of her arm, and he must be hurting her because she's wincing.

'Nurse!' she cries out to a nurse who is walking by. 'This man is hurting me!'

'She's trying to disturb my father,' Yiannis explains to the nurse.

'Who are you, miss?' the nurse asks.

The question is giving the young woman trouble.

'A friend,' she answers finally.

'Well, you can't go in there. This is not visiting hours. Only first degree family allowed.'

She must have lied at the front desk, but she can hardly do so now with Yiannis close by to contradict her. She's getting ready to obey when Katerina walks up.

'You stay away from my husband,' Katerina hisses at her, and disappears triumphantly behind the door of Andreas's room.

Yiannis and I walk the young woman to the door. We let go of her there, but she makes no move to get into any of the waiting taxis. She just sits on a ledge and sniffles into her handkerchief.

'Who is she?' I ask Yiannis, although I know the answer already.

'Some whore Dad keeps on the side,' Yiannis says. His bitterness makes him spit the words out. 'You might as well know. He was with her when he had the attack. She's the one who called the ambulance. She was here when we arrived, after the hospital called us. She didn't even have the decency to leave when she saw my mother. Mom threw a fit when she saw her. Dad's been going around with her for two years now. Mom knew about her. Dad's taken her all over town and people have seen him with her, and they couldn't wait to come and give Mom the news. Mom demanded that she be made to leave, and Petros got her out of there pushing and shoving all the way. And now she's back.'

It's plain to see that Yiannis takes his mother's side in this. He is disgusted with his father. So am I. The same old

Andreas. So he hasn't made Katerina happy after all.

Yiannis takes off after his mother and I remain near the entrance. This is the man I prayed for last night. Nothing ever really changes. Still and always Andreas disappoints me and makes me regret whatever love I feel for him. Oh my darling Katerina!

The woman is standing in front of me. Her face is wet with tears and much of her make-up has rubbed off on her handkerchief.

'Mister, how is he?'

She is only in her twenties. She has amber eyes, a heart-shaped face and a soft, tremulous mouth. She looks cheap, but she is very pretty and in the full flush of her youth. Her distress is very real.

'He's doing fine,' I tell her, conscious that I am talking to the enemy.

'Who are you?' she asks me.

'His brother.'

'George? The one from America?' I nod. She is fascinated.

'Oh, but he talks about you all the time. About how you left and never write or call. He wonders what happened to you every time he has a bit to drink. You flew in?'

I nod again. This is probably the friendliest anyone in the family has ever been to her.

'Will you tell him I came by?' she asks me now. 'Will you tell him I'd be there if only they'd let me?'

'I can't do that, miss.'

'Voula, my name is Voula. Please, Kyr George, please tell him. At least give him this note.'

She's pressing a folded piece of paper in my hand. I've been Andreas's message-bearer before, and no good came of it.

'I can't,' I repeat, refusing to take the note.

'Please take it. I love him so.' She's very pathetic in her wrinkled finery and ruined make-up. Her feelings are real, and she is in so much pain. But my loyalties cannot be swayed by any amount of pity.

'I'm sorry,' I repeat.

She stares at me for a while. Then she puts the note on the window ledge.

'I'll leave it right here,' she tell me. 'Think about it, and if you find it in your heart, please pass it on to him.'

She leaves, this time getting into a taxi, with a flash of leg. She looks out of the rear window at me as the car pulls away, mouths her last plea. I pick up the note when she can no longer see me. I open it. It has a crude drawing of a heart on it, and in the heart a few words: 'I love you my darling. I pray for you all the time. Get well soon and come see your Voula again. I'll be waiting.'

I crumple the note and throw it in the bin. How does he do it? He is not a young man any more. He has a pot belly and he's losing his hair, he drives a beat-up car and obviously has no money to speak of, and still a young woman risks everything to come and see him when he is at death's door, and writes him love letters with hearts in them. What is it about Andreas that makes everybody love him? What is it that he has? What is it that I do not have?

Back in my brother's room, Katerina is combing his hair while he fusses. Yiannis is staring out the window. Andreas's eyes light up when he sees me. He waves Katerina away impatiently.

'So I didn't dream you up last night! Come here, sit down. How are you? Tell me everything.'

I sit next to him. I tell him about America, answer his questions. But I'm really watching Katerina. She shows no outward sign of having seen Voula. Is she mindful not to upset Andreas in his condition, or is open and indiscreet infidelity something she's used to?

At noon we all leave. Andreas needs to sleep again, and so do I. But first, I pull a wad of dollars out of my pocket and pass the money around to nurses and other staff. Greece has socialised medicine. Everything is free, in theory. In practice, the care is as good as the tips the patient can pay. Something tells me my brother's family has no money for tips, so I ask to meet the staff, ostensibly to thank them, and as I shake hands, I pass money surreptitiously to each. You have to mind their pride, too. As the grand finale, I meet up with the attending physician. No hand-shaking here. Instead, I put a cheque in a white envelope I've procured from reception, and at the end of the brief interview, I ostentatiously place the envelope on the doctor's desk. He doesn't acknowledge my gesture, but he's been paid.

Yiannis drives us back to the village. This time we veer off Main Street and head home. My heart constricts again. There is the taverna and the buttonwood tree. It's still alive. I can see the dome of Saint George. The car ascends the small rise, then turns into the yard. I'm home.

The yard is more bare than I remembered, and so much smaller. The fig trees are gone, but the almond trees are still there. And there's the house. It looks run down and in need of a coat of paint. The walls are scratched and marred. One of the wooden shutters hangs from its hinges. The outhouse is gone. The wash shed still stands but there's no cauldron next to it to do the wash.

The house is dark inside, shuttered against the heat. There is a bathroom now next to the kitchen, and it contains not only a shower unit but a washing machine as well. Modern conveniences. But the furniture is the same. The same odds and ends pulled together out of necessity. Everything is clean and neat, but shabby and old.

'I prepared your room for you last night,' Katerina tells me. 'Petros sleeps there, but I thought I would move him in with Yiannis for a while, and you could have your old bed back.'

She lets me enter my room alone. It still contains two beds. The cot where my grandpa used to sleep has been removed. He died many years ago, his mind completely eaten away by old age.

Diane has packed for me neatly, forgetting nothing. I go out and ask Katerina if I can take a shower.

'I just turned on the water heater for you. It will take about fifteen minutes for the water to heat up.'

I had forgotten. There is no instantaneously hot water in Greece. Energy is too precious and expensive to be wasted. I go back to my room and unpack my things. Katerina comes to ask if anything needs ironing. I hand her a few shirts and she goes to work immediately.

While she irons I take a shower. I'm too old to go so long without proper rest and comfort. The water is barely lukewarm and comes out in a pathetic trickle, but it's a godsend nonetheless. My face in the bathroom mirror is pale and tired. Black circles ring my eyes.

We eat outside. Petros has closed down the bakery and has brought some roast chicken for our meal. Katerina has cut up tomatoes and cucumbers for a salad, and has added bits of feta cheese and onions. I bite into a tomato, and the taste explodes in my mouth. It's the most delicious thing I've tasted in years. I had forgotten how much more delicious fruits and vegetables are in Greece, where they are allowed to ripen on the vine, and make it to table only a few days at most after they are harvested. Tomatoes are more tomatoey, cucumbers more cucumbery. I eat hungrily off my mother's ancient and cracked china, soak my bread in the oil and vinegar, drink two glasses of retsina. Then I retire to my room. It's time to sleep.

I'm sitting under the acacia trees drinking coffee with Katerina when visitors arrive. A tall portly man and an enormously fat woman. It's Pavlos and Litsa. She's changed so much. She looks a lot like her mother now, but the change is all outward. She flirts outrageously with me when she sits down. She's still quick and bright. She still sparkles.

'We finally got away from the old gorgon,' she says, her voice full of merriment despite the topic of her conversation. 'Ever since she broke her hip she thinks I have no right to leave the house, not even to visit an ailing friend. We tell her a hundred times that Andreas has had a heart attack and still she will not believe us. She thinks we're making it up to leave the house and get away from her.'

She's talking of her old nemesis, Kyra Fotini. It's been Litsa's fate to live all her life with a mother-in-law who hates her and has never recognised Litsa's claims to a husband and a life of her own. Kyr Lambros died five years ago, but Kyra Fotini lives on, demanding care and attention and never showing even a bit of gratitude for all the time and labour Litsa spends on her.

Pavlos agrees with Litsa, but what can he do? This is his mother and he is an only son. He has to live with her. He finished law school, became a lawyer, but found it hard going to get a practice established. Finally he gave up and took over his father's shop. It was a good move. Maybe at one time the shop would not have been enough to keep both his parents and his own growing family prospering, but Panorama has grown and developed, and the shop has bought them everything they could have wished for. Thank the good Lord, he has no complaints on that score. He can even slip a bit of money to his shiftless brothers-in-law every so often, and he was even able to get Litsa's sister married off. All over the protests of his mother, of course, who has never stopped complaining that Litsa and her family have been a millstone around Pavlos's neck.

The phone keeps ringing while we sit in the yard. First Katerina and then Petros and Yiannis answer it, but the caller keeps hanging up. I think it's Voula, and I think she's trying to get hold of me to see if I passed on the message, but I don't say anything, and I don't answer the phone.

We all go to the hospital together. When we come back at night, I call Diane. I tell her I don't know how long I'm staying. No, she shouldn't come over yet. I can't have my family descending on my brother's household at a time like this. Diane says she understands. I speak to Katie. She misses me. Is Uncle Andreas okay? Yes, my darling. Can she come over? Not yet, but maybe soon.

The days fall into a pattern. I spend a lot of time at the hospital. What time I spend at home I spend receiving visitors, curious to see me after all these years. My friend Nikos has moved away, so I don't see him. I spend a lot of time talking with my nephews. They're trying desperately to keep the family business afloat, but things are not good. The bakery has competition, and has had it for several years. Still, I don't understand why they seem so strapped financially. Panorama is big enough to make short work of the output of two bakeries, as well as the prefabricated bread sold by the two supermarkets that have opened for business. Petros finally tells me that Andreas is a spendthrift. He gambles, he drinks and he spends money going to clubs. Until the boys stepped in to help with the bakery, the shop could not be depended on to open every morning, and many people went over to the competition. The boys are turning things around, but habits are hard to break.

Things are beginning to make sense. There are lines of bitterness around Katerina's mouth, and now I know what put them there. While all around her her contemporaries have prospered, her family alone has lagged behind. The only improvement Andreas has made in her life is to get the indoor bathroom built and to buy her the washing machine. The washing machine was bought used. When it runs it makes in infernal noise. Its crashing and banging reach a crescendo when it spins the clothes, and the vibrations make it move, so that it crosses the floor and bangs against the bathroom door. The door has the scars to prove it. To limit the destruction, Katerina drops whatever she's doing when it's time for the spin cycle, and hugs the machine to keep it from running away. If she doesn't get there on time, the door gets banged and the draining hose, which she places into the toilet because it is not linked to the piping, gets dislodged, spilling wash water all over the floor.

Katerina lives in privation in her ancient, crumbling home. She has few clothes and her shoes are worn. At night, when the temperature gets cool, she throws one of Andreas's sweaters over her shoulders. She's very careful about turning off lights to keep the electric bill down, and she puts meat on the table only once a week. She buys the cheapest cooking oil, made of crushed olive pits, she reads the newspaper the neighbours throw out, she recycles left-overs obsessively, and she saves paper, cans, rubber bands and throw-away bottles. Katerina lives in graceless, grinding poverty. And it's all Andreas's fault.

It's hard to feel resentment against a man who just had a close brush with death, but I do. Every time I see Katerina carefully count the money in her wallet, I want to grab that man and shake him. He's shamed her in front of the whole world by parading his mistress for all to see, and he doesn't even have the decency to provide properly for his long-suffering wife. I recall that Voula was wearing a gold bracelet when I met her. I bet it was a gift from Andreas. Katerina has no jewellery. Still, she does her duty by her husband. She hovers over him at the hospital, plumping his pillows, paring his nails, bringing him water, helping him wash and change.

When we finally bring Andreas home, she watches him like a hawk to make sure he doesn't sneak cigarettes or drinks. She sets up an armchair in the yard for him to sit in, and she goes up and down the stairs a million times a day to fetch whatever he wants to be comfortable.

He is a bad patient, querulous and grumbling, demanding this and that and never being satisfied. He complains about the diet he has to follow, and he declares that life is not worth living without a drink and a smoke. Lack of nicotine makes him irritable and he yells at everybody. His blood pressure rises when he does so and everybody cowers and obeys no matter how unreasonable his anger is, because they are afraid of causing another heart attack.

I try whatever I can to lighten Katerina's load. I buy food for the house – steaks, cheese and cold cuts that my brother's family tastes only on holidays. I sneak the telephone bill and the water bill in my pocket and pay them without anyone knowing. I pay a man to fix the shutter. I try to keep Andreas distracted with stories of America. He questions me minutely, and with wonder.

'Two restaurants! And how much do you make a year?'

When I tell him that I paid taxes on $500,000 of personal income last year, he whistles.

'That's a hundred million drachmas!'

He asks the price of everything. My car, my home, my clothes, my shoes, my belt, my wallet. As soon as I give him the figure, he converts it to drachmas. Then he tells everyone who comes to visit. He's very proud of my money. He seems to think it reflects well on him, even though he had nothing to do with earning it. I protest when he starts his recitation of prices and income, but it's all a sham. Deep down I am glad to have my finances bandied around publicly. I've come empty-handed, so how else will the world know that I've done good? What if they all thought I was staying away in shame at not having made it? My brother's boastfulness serves my purpose and feeds my pride. Most of all, it soothes the feathers my brother ruffled all my life. It's particularly sweet to speak of my wealth in this setting, surrounded by my brother's crumbling home. He may have beaten me at everything when we were children, but I have the last laugh! If he didn't ask so many questions, I'd have to find a way to volunteer the information.

Andreas's inquisitiveness pleases me, but my patience with him is running out. Whenever he sends Katerina to bring him yet another thing, I want to scream at him to let her rest, and stop being such a pain, but I am afraid of the consequences of a confrontation. We all treat him with kid gloves. His illness has disarmed us and we have become his slaves. The phone keeps ringing and the caller keeps hanging up.

It's Andreas's sixth day at home and he and I are sitting alone under the acacia trees. I'm sipping coffee, but Andreas is only allowed fruit juice.

'All this clean living will kill me,' he sighs. 'They keep saying how all this stuff is bad for me, but I ask you, can it be good for me to sit here and pine after a glass of wine and a smoke? I think they've got it all wrong. It's not having the stuff that's gonna send me to an early grave!'

'Just do what the doctors tell you and you'll live to be a hundred.'

'What good is a hundred if I have to spend it like this, sitting in this yard eating bland food and counting bird droppings? You've never come close to death so you don't know what you're saying. Even if I don't have another heart attack, who's to say a truck won't mow me down the next time I cross the street? Life is short, George. I've got to live it while I still have some left.

'If you're trying to get me to let you sneak a smoke, you might as well give up,' I tell him. 'You may die tomorrow, but it won't be me who sends you to the grave.'

'Forget the cigarettes. I'm talking about other things. George, there's this girl.' His voice is low now, conspiratorial. 'She's the hat-check girl at this place I go. The sweetest thing you ever saw. Hair as red as fire, lips like honey.'

He's talking about Voula. My brother is confiding in me.

'She's been with me for two years. She loves me. I was with her, you know, when I had the heart attack. I was nailing her to the bed, pounding away like a young bull. Ah, but I can't tell you what she does to me. It's like I'm twenty all over again. She's got the sweetest little box you ever felt. All tight and fat, not stretched out from children coming through.'

He pauses, an ingratiating smile on his face. His words repulse me, but I say nothing.

'So George, I hear she came to the hospital and they didn't let her see me. She must be frantic. I've got to get word to her. I want to see her. I may not wake up tomorrow, and I want to see her. So what do you say, George, can you help?'

'You're joking!'

'Come on, little brother. This is your big brother talking to you from death's door. Do me this little favour. Tell Katerina you're taking me for a drive. It would be easy as pie. Come on!'

'No I won't, Andreas. Don't you have any shame? Don't you have any decency? Here you are surrounded by your family, by the best woman in the world who waits on you hand and foot and puts up with the way you humiliate her for all the world to see, and you want me to lie to her and take you to see your whore? You want to make me a part of your sordid life? No! I won't do it!'

'You always were a prig, George. Don't think I don't know you! I know you inside and out. The only reason you always take the high road is that you can't make it like I can. You've always hated me for getting on with the ladies, but it's just the green-eyed monster. If you could do it, you would be fucking everything that moves. But you can't so you make out you are a saint. I've got your number, little brother! I bet the only women you ever fucked were the ones you paid and the one you offered marriage to. No woman would have you just for the pleasure of your dick! That little girl loves me, and when I put it to her she squeals with glee, and you can't stand it!'

I lose sight of his condition. I see red.

'Oh, yeah, they squeal with glee. And they cry for more. Until they are crippled trying to get rid of your spawn.' I've seen Artemis around, still unmarried, still limping, sewing away in her dark cottage. 'You've brought your women nothing but misery. Even Katerina, our own mother's daughter of the soul, was not safe from your big dick. Even her you had to bring down to the muck with you!'

'Don't you dare talk to me about Katerina. I saved Katerina!'

'Oh, sure. You saved her. First you seduced her through God knows what lies, and then you were kind enough to marry her so you can shame her while you parade your girlfriends where everyone can see them and report back to her!'

'*I* seduced Katerina! You always were a fool, George, where she was concerned. You always had a thing for her, mooning at her with your calf's eyes, muttering her name in your sleep. And what about you? Wasn't it your biggest dream in life to have Katerina, or did you think I didn't notice? How many times would you have snuck into her room downstairs if only you'd thought she'd let you? Well let me tell you something, mister high and mighty—'

'Dad, Uncle, what's going on here?' Petros interrupts his father's tirade. He's casting accusing glances at me. 'Not another word. Are you crazy?'

I walk away. My heart is racing in anger and I cannot see straight. I walk out of the yard and head on down to the square and up towards the villas. Up here there is quiet. The houses don't seem so grand now. Some of them have an old-fashioned, unkempt look to them. Others are better maintained, signalling the owner's continued prosperity. The Karras villa is shut down. I've heard that Anna lives in Athens now and never comes up here. Lila lives in Paris, married to a Sorbonne professor. I turn Andreas's words in my mind. Is it true? Would I have seduced Katerina if I had had the confidence, the courage? If I had thought she might have me? Would I have snuck down to her door and knocked on it softly for her to let me in? Would I have lain down next to her and taken her in my arms? Would I have got her pregnant? Would it have been me, then, who married her? Was the only difference between me and my brother not a difference in morals but a difference in abilities? No! Maybe I would have slept with Katerina if she would have me, but I loved her. If I had married her I would have treasured her all my life. And I had morals. I wouldn't run around with other women. Angela flashes through my mind. What morals? Didn't I rut with Angela even though I was married? And there was no love there, not on either side. I bought Angela's company, just like Andreas bought for me the company of Arletta, the skinny whore with the beautiful voice. So what is the difference between me and Andreas? He doesn't love Katerina, so he sees other women. I don't love Diane, so I got tangled up with Angela. The only difference between us is that I love Katerina and he doesn't. But in my universe, loving Katerina is the litmus test. Whoever loves her is my friend. Whoever causes her pain is my enemy. My brother is my enemy.

24

The Hero Everybody Loves

Andreas never carries a grudge for too long. He doesn't feel anything too deeply, and that includes anger. By the next day he is back to his usual ways, complaining and grumbling, but not looking at me any differently than he did before our fight.

Things last longer with me. I hate him for the things he said and the things he's done. I would leave, if it weren't for Katerina. I stay for her sake. She protests every time I buy something for the house, but I brush away her protests and keep carrying home food and drink, and even new pots and pans for the kitchen and a clock for the mantel. She thanks me repeatedly.

'But you must stop this, George. It's we who owe you. You never got your share of the bakery, and this is your house, too. You own half of it.'

I tell her that as far as I'm concerned this house and the business belong to her and her sons. I have plenty in America. I think of my plenty in America. I think of my beautiful Beverly Hills home with the four bathrooms and the pool. I think of my brand new Mercedes. I think of my wife's fur coat, her jewellery and silk dresses, her pink dressing table with the silver-backed comb and brush and the bottles of expensive perfume. Katerina fixes

375

her hair in front of the small bathroom mirror and she has no perfume. She has but one good dress, and she hardly ever has occasion to wear it. She's beautiful in spite of having none of the things women use to adorn themselves. But then, she always was.

I love the new relationship that's developing between me and Katerina. I am no longer the little kid who was always staring at her. I am a man now, a man with a lot of money, who can buy whatever he wants and who commands a small army of employees bent on doing his bidding. I tell her stories of my life on the other side of the world, but it's not enough. I wish I could show her my home and my restaurants. I wish I could whisk her off on a shopping spree on Rodeo Drive, and then to L'Orangerie for a candlelit dinner. I wish I could watch her exclaim over the elegance of the waiters and the dining-room and then over the contents of the small velvet box that in my imagination I slide towards her after the waiter cleans off the crumbs from the table. I daydream all the time about a different life, a life where there is no Andreas and no Diane. Just me and Katerina and my Katie, in our beautiful home in LA in the winter, in our villa in Panorama in the summer.

My daydreams make calls to Los Angeles difficult. I probably would call even more infrequently, but I miss my pixie. I need to hear her sweet voice. She misses me, she tells me so every time I call.

My conversations with Diane are strained. I have nothing to tell her, and all she can do is ask if I want her to come over or if I'm coming back myself.

'I think that would be too much, Diane. My brother is sick, he needs rest. But, say, Katie sounds really down. Do you think, maybe you could send her over here?'

'Darling, that's a bad idea. She's just a little girl. She can't travel halfway around the world on her own. We could all come. Your brother doesn't have to be put out. We can stay at a hotel.'

'No, don't do that. My sister-in-law would never let you. Anyway, I'll come home soon.'

But how can I leave? How can I leave my Katerina again? Now that she's learning to depend on me, now that she finally seems to see me the way I always wanted her to, how can I go back? She must be reliving the past, too, just like me. Maybe she's telling herself that she picked the wrong brother after all. I am the one who started with nothing and made good and who treats his wife like a queen. Andreas is the shiftless, no-good brother who made a hash of a good bakery and who has not managed to take care of his own family even though he found everything, job and house, ready and waiting for him. She takes good care of him and she never complains, but she doesn't love him. She can't love him after all he's done to her. He ruined her life. She only stands by him because that is her duty, and because there's nothing else she can do. How can I save her? How can I save my Katerina?

We are all sitting in the yard when the bombshell drops. Pavlos and Litsa have come over, and Andreas is showing off for them, telling jokes and behaving like he's perfectly fine. He keeps reaching for Pavlos's cigarette pack and makes faces when Katerina snatches it out of his reach.

'This woman will be the death of me. She never lets me have any fun!'

Andreas's bluff manner disgusts me. He does not deserve a loving family around him, and yet he has it. His sons obey his every wish even though they resent his treatment of their mother. And they are good kids, friendly and open, taking me into their confidence on nothing more than my claim to a blood tie. They've never seen me before, and yet they treat me like family. Their father has squandered the inheritance that is theirs by rights, and has taken money that belongs to them and spent it on cards and loose women, but they don't throw tantrums, they don't fiddle obsessively with their food and they don't demand BMWs. Oh, no! Andreas's sons talk to him with respect, toil at the bakery without complaint, keep their resentment to themselves and never slam doors or give any indication that they are embarrassed by Andreas and his vulgar talk. I would have been proud to call them my own. Petros returned from the army and went straight to work. He wasn't a very good student, so college was out for him, but as a young man, didn't he have some dreams of his own? He told me that he wanted to be an electrician, that he had practised the trade somewhat in the army and he liked it, but the bakery was in a shambles and his family needed a firm hand to take control. It's Petros who started keeping regular hours at the shop again. The truth is that even before Andreas had his heart attack, it was Petros who did most of the work, including getting up at the crack of dawn to bake the bread.

Yiannis is smart. Book smart. He studied hard in school and took the college entrance exam. College is not so easy to get into in Greece. Space is limited and entrance is awarded only to those who score in the stratosphere when they take the entrance exam. Tuition is free, but few pass the exam. Parents with money send their kids for years to private preparatory schools that teach them what they need to know to pass the dreaded entrance test. Rich kids who still fail are sent abroad to college, to England, Italy, Germany, France, even America. It's not uncommon for an adolescent in Greece to spend all day in school and all evening in the preparatory classes. It's time and money well spent. Often the exam topics have not been covered in the public schools. Only the kids who did outside reading can respond to the questions. Why the public schools can't get around to teaching all the information included in those exams I don't know, but it's been this way ever since I can remember. Maybe the guys who run the private preparatory schools know people in high places. The kid who gets into college without taking years of private lessons is as rare in Greece as the kid who gets a scholarship to Harvard is in America. Yiannis knew there was no money to send him to Rome or London to study. He also knew there was no money to send him to preparatory schools, because his father was pissing it all away. Other poor families scrimp and save and go without bread to give their kids the help they need to get into college. Andreas didn't even give up his ouzo. So Yiannis set his butt down and he studied on his own. He didn't pass the first time, but he didn't give up. The second time he made it. He's going to be a teacher, and I bet he'll be a fine one, too. And how does he spend his summer holiday? He works at the bakery. And does he have a bitter word to say against his father? No.

I don't know Nikiforos, so maybe he's the bad seed, but somehow I doubt it. He's probably a great son, too. He certainly calls often enough from Crete to check up on his father, even though he is a soldier and has very little money and the long-distance bill must be big enough to squeeze him pretty hard. Add to this a wife who is still beautiful in her forties, and you have to ask yourself – what kind of a fool behaves the way my brother does? And how does his family put up with it? I could be lying sick in the gutter and Niki wouldn't get off the phone long enough to call the ambulance. And my son, I have no major complaints, but why can't he be a little more like his cousins and laugh and joke and let the world know he's alive?

I'm thinking of all this, so I'm not paying attention to the company. I'm just looking out and thinking, and there she is. She's standing near the entrance to the yard, half concealed by a bush. I've only seen her once, but there's no mistaking the loud colours and the jutting breasts. She's watching us.

I look around me carefully. So far I am the only one who has noticed she is here. I try to catch Petros's eye to alert him to the situation, but I am not successful. Oh, God, what can I do? How to avert disaster? Katerina rises from her seat and my breath stops. But no, she's just going in to get more refreshments for the guests. And as soon as she disappears, Voula comes out from behind the bush and shows herself. Andreas sees her. He stops in mid-sentence. He chokes.

'Ah, look who's here. Voula, come in, come in!'

'Andreas, are you crazy?' I ask him.

Petros and Yiannis rise from their seats. They don't know what to do. They know Voula must not step into the yard, but they don't want to oppose their father, particularly in his condition. Pavlos and Litsa are embarrassed. They are looking around like the place has suddenly got much too hot for them. Voula steps across the yard's threshold shyly, tentatively. She's all decked out again, in a bright orange frock that nips her waist. Her hair is bigger than it was in the hospital, if that is possible, and she has two bright spots of red rouge sitting high on her cheeks. Her eyes are black with mascara and eyeliner. She clutches her handbag in front of her as she advances and there is this disbelieving smile on her face. She never expected to be be invited in. I'm flabbergasted. I've never heard of a man's mistress walking into his home in full view of his family and friends in broad daylight, as though she were a cousin or something.

'Andreas, tell her to leave this instant,' I command under my breath, but he's not listening. He's got a grin of pure bliss on his face. His heart is melting.

'Voula, my girl, you came to me,' he says, and he is standing up and holding her hand in his.

'Andreas, tell that woman to leave my house right now!' It is Katerina. She's standing at the top of the steps leading down from the house to the yard, and she is holding a tray with glasses full of orangeade.

'Now, Katerina, there is no reason to act this way. Voula is just here for a visit, aren't you, Voula?' Andreas has a big smile on his face and his voice is cajoling. He wants Katerina to indulge him in this. After all, didn't he knock on death's door not more than a few weeks ago?

He's asking too much.

'Right now, Andreas!' Katerina's face is made of stone. Litsa and Pavlos are looking at their shoes. Fani, the neighbour next door whose white cotton panties Andreas revealed to the world so many years ago, has stopped watering her flowers and is staring openly at the little drama.

'Katerina, stop acting like a fool. There is no harm in this!' Andreas makes his voice stern. But he still hasn't let go of Voula's hand.

Katerina throws the tray down the stairs and runs into the house.

'You piece of shit!' I tell him, and I run after her, just as Petros and Yiannis exit the yard to escape the impossible task of taking sides. Pavlos and Litsa are left to chaperone.

I get to the bedroom door, which is shut. This is partly my fault, I think. If I had taken him to see her, or even if I had spoken to her on the phone, she wouldn't have shown herself here. But the harm is done. Katerina is thoroughly and publicly humiliated.

I try the handle. The door opens. Katerina is lying on the bed, sobbing into the pillow. I go to her on tiptoe. I sit on this bed where my brother has had the use of her body all these years without the least appreciation for what I would give my life to possess. I sit down on the edge gingerly and put my hand on her shaking shoulder.

'Katerina,' I whisper, and she half sits up, reaches for me. I put my arms around her. I hold her close to me as she cries, big heart-wrenching sobs that are breaking her heart and mine. I hold my darling as she cries and I murmur soothing nonsense to her. I pat her hair and kiss her forehead and I rock her back and forth like a baby. The voices in the yard are faint murmurs. The shutters are closed against the heat, so the bedroom is dark but for thin shafts of light climbing in through the slits in the shutters. I feel hot. My anger, the weather, my dash to the bedroom, Katerina's nearness. I don't know how long I've been sitting with her on the bed. Her sobs are growing rather than diminishing. I take her face in my hands. I wipe her tears with my bare hands. I look into her red, swollen eyes. There's pain in them. I kiss her lightly. I kiss her again. It starts as a brotherly kiss, but her lips are swollen and wet, tasting of salt. Her mouth is slightly parted. And I am lost. I keep my lips on hers. She lets me. and then I push my tongue into her mouth. It scrapes on her teeth and meets hers. And suddenly there's nothing else in the world except my sweet love's mouth, and her body pressed to mine, and her sighs. I kiss her with all my pent-up love, and my mind spins. I lose track of the years, and of who I am, and what she is, and where we are. Nothing exists but this heat and this need, denied for so long. I eat of her, I feed on her mouth. I revel in her taste, her smell. In a thousand ways I kiss her, and when I let go of her mouth it's only to kiss her eyes, her cheeks, her ears, her throat. My body is burning. My hands are holding her face to mine, and it's the only thing holding me tied to the earth. My love, my life, my darling. Right here, right now, oh let me, let me. My hand moves to her shoulder, travels down her arm. I lift my face from hers, undo a button and bury my burning mouth in the coolness of her breast. A chair scrapes in the yard, a soft giggle sounds.

'No!' Katerina whispers and pushes me back. 'No, stop!'

My heart is pounding. There is a roar in my ears.

'She's still out there,' I say.

'Leave me, please leave me.'

I rise on wobbly feet and stumble out of the bedroom. I go to the bathroom and throw cold water on my face. I wait for my erection to subside. Oh, Katerina!

I finally emerge into the yard. My face is still red, my knees are still weak, but I have murder in my soul.

Voula has left. So have Pavlos and Litsa. Fani is still pretending that she is watering her flowers. She's stuck around for act two. Andreas is still under the acacias. He's telling some story to Petros and Yiannis, who have come back and look pained and uncomfortable.

'What you have done,' I tell him when I reach him, 'is the act of a criminal. You have no respect for your own

383

home and your own wife, and you have no respect for
your sons.'

'Don't tell me how to run my own house! I could
be dead tomorrow, and I can do as I please. I didn't
fuck her in the front yard, for Heaven's sake. She just
paid a visit. What is the point of pretending? Katerina
knows about her. The whole world knows about her.
Am I to never see her again, not even to say hello,
just for some silly female pride?'

'The whole world knows because you let it know, you
bastard! You've shamed this house and this family and I
hate the thought that you're my brother!'

'Who the hell are you?' He yells this out and rises from
his seat. 'Who the hell are you to come here after all
these years and tell me how to run my house? Get the
hell out of here. Go back to wherever the hell you've
been all these years!' His face is getting red as his voice
rises. Petros and Yiannis are casting alarmed looks in my
direction. The neighbours are staring at us from all sides,
curious but unwilling to intervene.

'Please, stop this,' Petros pleads. But I am too far gone
to listen.

'*Your* house! It's my house, too, you asshole! Half of
this house is mine and I will stay as long as I please!'

'You gave up this house and this family when you
turned your back on us twenty-five years ago! Don't
you dare come back now and give orders to me! You
gave this up! You gave this up!'

His face is bright red. His vessels are bulging at his
neck. He knows what he did was wrong. Half his rage
is guilt at what he's done.

'Yeah, I gave it all to you and you ruined it! Your
sons have to work to support you, instead of the other
way around. The house is falling apart around your ears!

Katerina has to wear rags because you don't provide for her, and now you've stripped her of those as well and left her naked for all the world to see!'

'She's my wife, goddamn it! I'll parade her naked if I want to, I'll give her to the dogs if that's what pleases me! This is what it's all about with you, isn't it? You'll never get over the fact that she married me! Well, she did, you damned fool! She married *me*! And you couldn't even—'

My brother stops shouting. He clutches his chest frantically. His face has turned from rage to pain. His other hand waves frantically around, looking for support. Petros and Yiannis rush to grab him, but they are too late. By the time they've reached him he's down on the ground, his features a grimace of suffering. Oh my God, I've killed my brother! Die, you bastard! I hope you die!

Petros drives him to the hospital. Yiannis asks Kyr Milios across the street if he can drive the rest of us there. Katerina is saying nothing as we pile into the car, Yiannis in front with the driver, me in the back with her. Tears are streaming down her face. I can't reach out to touch her in front of Milios, but I want to. There is so much I have to tell her. She's mine, now. Whether he dies or not, she's mine! I'll get a divorce, I'll give Diane everything. I'll renounce my life and my home and I will grab Katerina and make her mine. If she wants to leave Greece, I'll take her to America. If she wants to stay by her sons, I'll stay with her here. We'll rent a house in Thessaloniki where people don't know us. Yiannis can stay with us and go to college. Petros can come with us, too. I'll pay to get him training as an electrician. I'll pay for everything. If Andreas pulls through, I'll even give him money to go to hell if he wants. One thing I know for sure. Katerina will never have him back! I will take her away from her nightmare and I will give her everything a woman could want. I will make her happy! For the rest of her life, she will have neither humiliation, nor pain, nor want. She had to wait a long time for me to finally come to her rescue, but I am finally ready. Soon now, my darling. Soon.

At the hospital, the doctors tell us what we already know. Andreas has had another heart attack. They don't know if he will pull through. The doctor comes to talk to our mute little group. What happened, he asks, and Petros and Yiannis cast furtive looks at me.

'My father is an irritable man,' Yiannis says. 'He got upset and—'

His voice drifts off, but I know his meaning. The boys don't blame me for what happened. They love and honour their father, but they love their mother, too. What Andreas did is inexcusable. As his sons, they couldn't stand up to him, but they are glad someone did. I think they respect me for what I did, despite the consequences. They know I had right on my side. Mothers are sacred to their sons in Greece. You don't treat the mother of your sons in the way Andreas treated Katerina today and expect them to back you up, or even to resent your getting your comeuppance. I have no regrets. My conscience is clear.

We come home at dawn. Light is painting the horizon and birds are beginning to sing as Petros drives us back to the village. We are all silent and exhausted. Andreas is alive and his doctors can't hide their amazement at his stamina. He's pretty much back where he was right before I arrived. I feel relieved. I don't want his death on my hands.

I glance at Katerina, riding in the back with Yiannis, who is holding her hand. She looks tired and drained of all feeling. I feel tired, too, tired to the bone, but I'm also elated. I've made up my mind. I'll do it. I'll seize my happiness no matter what the cost. I'll give everything up for her. I'll fight to keep my Katie, but I'll give everything else up. As the car passes through empty streets, I'm thinking that Diane knows well how devoted to me Katie is. Katie will want to follow me and Diane will let her because she'll never make her own daughter miserable. Diane will agree to this. Diane always lets me have my way. Diane will agree. There are no obstacles.

Of course, with Andreas alive, I'll have an uphill battle convincing Katerina to leave him. She's bound to want to stay with him and do her duty by taking care of him, no matter what the cost to her. But I think I can do it. Voula is my secret weapon. Voula will take care of Andreas, leaving Katerina free and in all good conscience, to be mine for ever after. So there is no reservation in my relief that Andreas is alive. His life will not stand in my way. Instead, it alleviates any guilt that might have marred what will be the fulfilment of a life-long desire. Soon now.

At home we stand around silent as shadows. Katerina makes some coffee. The boys drink theirs and leave for the bakery. They are late already. Katerina and I sit at the kitchen table. In a way it's just like old times, with the two of us in the kitchen, the house silent around us, and me in love.

I'm ready to speak to her, and take a deep breath before I start, when she gets up from the table. She goes into the family room and she picks up the phone. I rise, too, and stand by the door to listen. I don't know whom she is calling.

'It's Katerina,' she says in a dry voice. 'Andreas had another heart attack.' She pauses and listens. 'No, he's alive. He's in the hospital. Pavlos, listen to me. I want you to go find Voula. Tell her for me that if she wants to go to him, no one will stop her, I promise.' She stops again. 'Yes, I'm sure. Just tell her as soon as you can.'

She puts down the phone. She looks so small and defenceless. She looks defeated. I'm at a loss to figure out why she just did what she did. It's as if she knows what I was about to tell her and is already passing the care of Andreas on to her rival so she can follow me. I stare at her nonplussed.

She tugs at the doily lining the phone to straighten it and then she bites her lip. Her face spasms. She sits down on the sofa and begins to cry silently. I kneel down in front of her. I take her hands in mine and look up at her bowed head. Her hair gives off a fragrance that hurls me back to the past. She has no inkling of my plan after all. She probably considers allowing Voula access to Andreas part of her duty to her husband.

'Katerina,' I begin, but I find it hard to continue. I swallow and begin again. 'Katerina, it doesn't have to be this way for you. You don't have to hurt this way. What you just did is hard on your pride, but my darling you never have to hurt this way again. You don't have to stand by and watch Andreas humiliate you with Voula. Leave him. Let Voula stand by him and take care of him. You don't need him.'

She bows her head lower and cries harder. She shakes her head no. Her fingers are squeezing mine and her pale, ragged fingernails are digging into my skin. I lift her work-ravaged hands to my mouth and I kiss them. My heart aches for her. My poor injured darling.

'Katerina,' I begin again, and my emotions are thickening my voice, so that I hardly recognise it as it reaches my ears. 'Katerina, I love you. I love you more than life itself. More than anything and anybody. I always have. Even when I was a kid, you were all I ever wanted. I spent years thinking of you, Katerina, and dreaming that some day you would be mine. I thought you were lost to me forever, my love, but now I come back and I find you tied to this man who cares nothing for your feelings, and who can't even provide for you properly.' She's looking at me with her velvet eyes wide open, as if I'm speaking a language she doesn't understand, but I can't let her stop me now. I tighten my grip on her hands, pull closer to her face, force her to listen to me. 'He took you from me once, my love, but now things are different. I couldn't do anything about it then, but I can now. Katerina, if you want me, if you'll have me, leave Andreas and come with me. I'll get a divorce. We'll be together. Anywhere you want. Here, America, just say yes!'

'Are you mad?'

'I mean it. I mean every word. Oh my darling, I've thought it through. I love you. I've loved you all my life. Like a sister, like a daughter, like a woman, like a mother. In every way, with all my heart. Nothing else matters. I've been half a man without you. I've been half alive. Be mine, Katerina. No one will blame you. Your sons will understand. They'll be welcome in our home. They can stay with us. We'll get a place in Thessaloniki—'

'George,' she stops me, her hand free from mine and flying to my mouth to stop the flow of words, 'George, what you're saying is impossible.'

I wave her hand away. Imprison it in mine.

'No, it's not. Andreas had a heart attack. You or I could have a heart attack. Now, before it's too late, while there is still time. Let's do this, Katerina. Let's live! I've loved you so long that you're part of everything I am. I'll cherish you and love you all the rest of your life. I'll dress you in satin and silk and I'll tell you I love you every day, every hour—'

'I don't want to leave Andreas, George!'

'Don't say no! I knew you'd say no. But just think for a minute. What is Andreas to you? He doesn't love you, he doesn't even need you now that he has Voula. He thinks nothing of hurting you. You owe him nothing! He ruined your life. He seduced you and bound you to him when you weren't old enough to know better—'

'George, no! You are upset. You don't know what you are saying. I owe Andreas everything. He saved my life. I love him!'

She says the words a scant two inches from my face. She loves him! How is it possible that she loves him? Even if she had a silly crush on him back then when she let him talk her into sharing her bed, how could she still love him now? I get up off the floor. I pace the small room.

'How can you say you love him when he treats you like he does?' My voice sounds angry. 'How can you offer your love to this bum who showcases his little whore in front of all the world with never a thought to your feelings or your pride? Are you a saint who likes to suffer? Is that it, Katerina? Is that it?' I go to her and lift her by the shoulders so we're looking at each other eye to eye. 'How can you say you love him when he shows you no respect? You can't love him, Katerina. You just can't. If you look into your heart you'll find nothing but contempt for him. Do it, Katerina. Look into your heart! Look into your heart and tell me that you love him and I'll go away and never bother you with my love again. But do it honestly.'

She's passive as I hold her within a few inches of me. Her coal-black eyes are unfathomable. 'You don't understand,' I hear her tell me.

'What is it I don't understand? Tell me so I can understand, because, so help me God, I'm dying!' I have a feeling in the pit of my stomach as I speak these words. A premonition of what's coming. I don't suspect the truth, but I know that something terrible is on its way and I must meet it. That's why I tell her I'm dying. The thing at the end of this tunnel feels like death. A cold, hard, dark thing, the name of which I do not know yet.

She looks at me, and I must look like a madman. I'm breaking into a sweat, I've had no sleep, my nerves are stretched taut. She considers briefly. And then she tells me.

'I was pregnant when Andreas married me, you know that. What you don't know is that it was not his child I was carrying. I had no one to turn to. I was scared and alone and terrified that any day the world would find out and I would be tossed out on the street. I used to pray for death even though I knew it was a sin. I would think about killing myself and then I would fall on my knees and ask God to forgive me. I lived in hell! And then Andreas found out. He stepped into my life when I had no hope and he gave me a name and a ring to shield my pregnancy. He took another man's child as his own and he never again said a word about it. I love him for that, George! I'll love him forever for what he did! And you think I'd leave him now! So he has his Voula, and the world knows. Yes, it's hard on me, but I owe him this! I just paid back a small part of what I owe him. What is a bit of pride to what I owe him?'

I let go of her. There is a roar in my ears, as though I have been standing next to the turbines of a plane preparing for take-off. Small bits of information crowd my brain. Petros was not given my father's name. That was handed over to the second son. I wonder that this didn't seem strange to me before. Why would a Greek man name his *second* son after his father? Because the first son isn't his. But if Petros isn't Andreas's son, then whose son is he? Petros's face flashes in front of my mind. He is the spitting image of my father! I know the truth, I know it somewhere in the back of my mind, but I have to ask.

'And Petros?' I ask, and she knows what I'm asking.

She has a hard time telling me, but it comes out. In fits and starts, with her face red in embarrassment, Katerina tells me the awful story of the years I've treasured in my memory. My uncle's face fastening on the young Katerina. His cruel games with her over the household's shopping, his threats to throw her out on the street. His first soft knock on her door one night. His going into her room on the pretext that the accounting was all wrong. His advances. First a few pats on the arm and leg, then a hand insinuated down her dress. Honeyed words of affection when she resists. Threats when cajoling fails. Hurtful pinches and smacks on parts of her body that are hidden by clothes. At last a heavy body pinning her to the floor, the alcoholic breath fanning her face, the thick hand covering her mouth, as my uncle drives into her and takes from her her self-respect, her privacy, her peace of mind. Night after night, while I slept peacefully dreaming of a time when Katerina would be mine, my uncle was forcing himself inside her violated sanctuary with threats and violence. Night after night while Katerina danced naked in my dreams he raped my love. For more than a year. Until she got pregnant and had nowhere to turn. Until the guilty secret was about to announce itself to the whole world. And then my brother rode in on his white stallion, and with one stroke of his mighty sword he saved Katerina from her nightmare and gave her a life free of fear and shame. Like the best of heroes, my brother saved the damsel in distress. And if he didn't take her to live in a tower or a palace it doesn't matter, because compared to what

Katerina had been living, the life of a married woman *was* a palace.

Katerina speaks for a long time, and her words reveal this place I thought I knew so well to be an alien landscape. Speaking costs her. This is her secret, a secret that still has the power to shame her. I've known her all my life, but I'm just learning about her. Both of us are crying by the time she is done talking. I embrace her. I kiss her on the forehead. I press her to my breast and I repeat in a whisper, 'I'm sorry, I'm sorry, I'm so sorry to have been so blind.'

'How could you know? You were so young.'

Her words tear at me.

We separate to get some rest before we head out to the hospital again. I go into my bedroom, but there is no rest for me. This is where I spent so many years in my stupid ignorance. This is where I slept in comfort while my love was crucified mercilessly on her bed. What kind of fool am I to have been so oblivious to the plainest truth? There were signs! Memories flood my mind. My uncle's leer. His rage, out of all proportion, to the mildest flirtation with Theophanes. His heavy hand landing on Katerina's face and sending her spinning to the floor.

And another memory. The memory of his short stubby penis in his swollen hands the night he saw me with Lila. The smell of his breath, heavy with alcohol and stale cigarettes rushes out of the past and assails my senses. This is what Katerina smelled the night her virginity was stolen from her and every other night that my uncle touched her slender young body with his gross, profane hands. Insufferable images attack my vision. I'm almost driven mad with impotent rage. He got away with it! For years he reigned supreme in this house, his victim taking care of his every need, afraid to renounce him to the world, and afraid to deny him. He lived well and he died in old age, and never did he have to pay for what he did. I sit on my bed and I loathe him. I loathe his big bulbous nose and his big gut that hung over his belt, his thick short legs, the mouth he used to purse to sip his coffee. I loathe his body even though it's long since been eaten by worms. But most of all I loathe myself. Too small, too young, too ignorant, too late. I don't deserve Katerina. I let her down when it counted most. And Andreas, shallow, prodigal, bright Andreas, Andreas the con man, Andreas the lady killer, Andreas who never felt love, he deserves her. He won her fair and square. He won her love. A love so great that still it lives now that Andreas is a faded shell of what he used to be, drooling after a vulgar hat-check girl with the dugs of a cow and the mind of a ten-year-old. Katerina made him a gift of the passion of his dotage today. A supreme gift of love and devotion. Everyone loves Andreas. Why should it be any different with Katerina?

I laugh at myself, with a mean, dry cackle. So I thought I had it all figured out, did I? Katerina doesn't love her husband, and he makes her life a living hell, so I will come over from America with my riches and my solution to everything, and I will pluck her out of her miserable life and ride off with her into the sunset. Still and always the fool. I can't see what's in front of my nose now any better than I could in the old days. Still and always a fool.

I come out of my room humbled. I have a hard time meeting Katerina's eyes. I am ashamed. I am embarrassed. Katerina, God bless her, acts as if nothing has happened. As if I'm not the biggest idiot in existence.

In the afternoon we go to the hospital. Andreas is pale and drawn, and his lips are blue again. Voula is there. She gets up and leaves as soon as she sees us. She doesn't say a word as she gathers her big white purse to make her exit, except to mouth a 'thank you' to Katerina as she goes to the door. Katerina does not acknowledge her. As though nothing out of the ordinary has happened, she takes charge of Andreas. She fusses around him, arranges the water glass and medicine on the night stand. Then she takes out a comb and combs Andreas's thinning hair. She smoothes lotion on it and then sweeps the long side strands from one ear to the other across his bald pate, in the universal style of balding men who refuse to admit their deficiency to the world. They must know it fools no one, but they persist. Andreas complains as usual, but when she is done, he takes her hand and kisses it. He says nothing, but it's plain to see that he is thanking her for letting Voula come to him. And this is the marriage that I thought was dead.

Katerina leaves the room after a while. She knows I want to talk to my brother.

'Forgive me, Andreas,' I tell him.

'Nothing to forgive,' he grunts.

'The things I said—'

'Forget it, I told you!'

'Katerina told me. About Uncle Demetres.'

'She told you?'

I don't want to explain the circumstances of Katerina's confession. 'How did you know back then?' I ask him quickly.

'The night we brought her to the hospital, after Pavlos's wedding. I told the doctors she had been hit. They examined her and told me she was four months gone.' It's hard for him to talk, he gets winded.

'Four months!'

'She carries small in the beginning. And she was wrapping herself up and eating close to nothing. It didn't show much. I talked to her about it the next day, after I spoke to the doctors. It took some time to get the truth from her, but with half the cat out of the bag, what could she do?'

She told him. Andreas always had a way of getting people to talk. I can imagine the scene. Andreas is coaxing Katerina, accusing the most likely suspect, to gauge her reaction or get her so afraid the wrong man will be blamed that she blurts out the truth. Andreas has his ways.

'An abortion was out of the question,' Andreas continues after he catches his breath. 'It was too late. Making the bastard marry her would be punishing the victim. Only one thing left.'

'So it had to be you.'

'I had no plans to marry, but I couldn't just do nothing.' He pauses. Nobody thought of me, I think. Too young.

'Artemis,' he says, and I know what he means. He had one victim of his own. He married Katerina to save her, but he also married her to atone for his own sin against the seamstress's daughter who still drags her foot behind her. Who would have thought he had it in him?

'Artemis,' he says again, and his eyes are fastened on me. I think he's asking me to forgive him, now that I know he did his penance. We sit for a while in silence, me and my brother the hero, my brother the penitent. I think of what might have happened if Andreas had not found out the truth. Katerina might have killed herself. Or she might have run away to hide her shame.

'I wanted to beat him senseless,' Andreas speaks again. He means Uncle Demetres. 'But I was afraid the story might get out. Couldn't have that shame in the family. So I threatened him, and then I left him alone.'

'Does Petros know?'

'No. Nobody does.'

We sit quietly again. I hold my brother's hand. I squeeze it.

'I'm sorry,' I say again, and I don't know for which of all my failings I'm apologising.

'Forget it. I'll be right as rain in no time.' Andreas assumes I'm apologising for bringing on his second heart attack.

'I love you, little brother,' he tells me. His voice is drifting. He's falling asleep again.

'I love you, too, Andreas.'

25

The Fool

Andreas continues to do well. We are all back to the routine where we spend most of our time at the hospital. I spend a lot of time thinking. Many of my thoughts are thoughts of impotent rage at myself and at my dead uncle. If I hadn't been such a fool, I could have rescued Katerina, and now it would be me who'd have her undying gratitude and love. And if it hadn't been for my uncle, perhaps she would have come to love me in time as I grew up, and even if she didn't maybe she'd marry me because there would be no one else for her to marry. Even like that, even without her love, I would have taken her. I would have taken her and taught her to love me. But I am a fool, and my uncle was a monster, and so my life spun off in the direction of isolation and pain.

I think of the years of loneliness and hard work, when I ate the bitter bread of *xenitia* and had no one to tell my troubles to. I used to hate Andreas for robbing me of my home, my love and my country. Now I know there was nothing to hate him for. Andreas didn't take Katerina from me. I lost her myself. Why was I so quick to believe that if Katerina was pregnant he must have been the culprit? Why didn't I ask more questions? Why didn't my mind fasten on the more obvious candidate? Because all my life, where my brother is concerned, I am an even bigger fool than usual. I've never had a middle road in my feelings for him. I made a god out of him and worshipped him when I was a kid, and when that got too hard on me and jealousy threatened to choke me, I tossed him off his pedestal and called him a devil. I was ready to believe the worst of him, and I did. But I know better now. He's not a god, and he's not the devil. He's just my older, bigger, smarter brother, and thank God he had the eyes to see the truth and save Katerina. I think this a hundred times a day, and just as often I feel the old envy gnaw at my heart. It's hard to know myself for a fool, but it's even harder to be a fool when Andreas is my brother.

I daydream about things being different. What if I had been smart enough to realise what was going on? What if I had realised the truth? Then maybe I could have saved Katerina, and married her, and lived out my days in my home in Panorama, tending the bakery and raising my kids and loving my wife. Andreas would marry, too, another woman. I can't picture this stranger, so in my thoughts I give her Artemis's face. My brother and I and our families live happily in our house in my dreams. On Sundays we all have dinner under the acacias, our noisy kids yelling and fighting and chasing each other. Katerina and Artemis bring out the coffee and then sit down to while away the time with gossip and embroidery. Andreas and I talk about the bakery. Evening falls. The kids ask for money to go to the movies. Andreas and I dig into our pockets and send the lot forth. We sit some more, until night-time falls thickly. There is a fragrance of flowers in the air. The smell of Panorama in my childhood. Andreas and I take our wives for a stroll on Main Street. We stop at Stamos's for some ice-cream. Later we come home. We wait up for the kids and put them to bed. Then

I take my wife, my Katerina, by the hand and lead her to our bedroom. We shut our door and get into our bed, and all is well with the world.

That is my fantasy. In reality, I visit the cemetery. There are framed pictures of my mother and father over their grave, but there is no picture of my uncle. I stand above his grave and curse him. I hope he rots in hell. Katerina tends the graves regularly. She weeds them and sweeps them clean. She tends his grave, too, the man she's hated through the years. I've asked her already how she could stand to live with him once Andreas had put a stop to his abuse of her.

'What could I do?' she asks. 'We couldn't ask him to leave. People would wonder. He might talk. We had to think about Petros. It had to be enough that it was over.'

It's hard for me to meet her eyes these days. I feel embarrassed in her presence, both for my ignorance and stupidity in the past, and for my ridiculous misreading of the situation in the present. I shudder to think what she must think of me. If she wasn't so good she would laugh in my face. Then again maybe she forgives me, because after all I'm just George the fool. What can you expect?

I watch her go through her days. Katerina has learned to make do with little. She cooked and ironed for the man who raped her, and even nursed him when his liver rotted away. For twenty years after Andreas pulled her out of his clutches she fetched my uncle's slippers and made his coffee the way he liked it, and even washed his underwear and sheets. She thinks her life is good because somebody saved her from her nightmare, instead of complaining that her nightmare happened in the first place. Katerina was never a complainer. I guess when you're the daughter of a drunk shepherd who beats you and your mother, you learn that happiness is the absence of pain. But then, maybe I'm looking at this all wrong. Katerina has been happy in her marriage. I have no more illusions on that score. Katerina didn't love Andreas before he rescued her, but she did love him the day she married him. She loves him to this day. She's made a sacrifice of her pride for his sake. Let the world say what it will, and it does! The village is abuzz with talk of Voula. Katerina just sails through the gossip. She's paying back her old debt.

Besides, Voula is not a threat to her. Now that Voula is allowed to come and go as she pleases, it's plain to see that Andreas is not making a choice between them. He has no plans to leave his wife and his home to be with his mistress. Oh, no! He means to have them both. Katerina is his wife. Voula is the sop to his aging ego.

Petros and Yiannis mind that Voula is so visible. They do not take kindly to this affront to their mother. But Katerina has silenced them with her dignified tolerance and a few sharp words. It is not their place to raise the issue. Voula visits when they are not around, anyway. That makes it easy for them to joke and laugh when they visit their father. They love him, too. Nikiforos calls every day and he has managed to get permission for another leave from his commanding officer, who is his good buddy. He will arrive next week to see his father. It sounds to me like he has the same knack Andreas has of getting along with people and getting them to give him what he wants.

Yiannis plans to take a year away from school to tend to the bakery.

'It's too much for one person,' he tells me. They cannot afford to take on a helper to help Petros. The year away from school will keep down expenses and keep the bakery working full steam. Andreas's family doesn't have much money, but it sticks together.

*   *   *

It's the fifth day after my brother's second heart attack.
He's still in the hospital and I am sitting in the yard with
my coffee, which I prepared myself, waiting for Katerina
to wake up from her afternoon sleep so we can go up to
the hospital again. I still have a hard time being around
her. I wish I could take back my impassioned confession
of my burning love. She does her best not to remind me,
but I know she hasn't forgotten. How could she? I still
want her, I'll always want her, but now I feel embarrassed
when she's near. She knows what a fool I've been. As soon
as Andreas is home and it's decent for me to leave, I will. I
will go back where no one knows I am the village idiot.

I am alone out here and I feel lonelier than ever. I'll
never have the love I've dreamed of. I'll have to live with
this void all the rest of my days. And I know exactly
what that means, because I've done it before. Katerina
loves someone else. Worse yet, she loves my brother. And
worst of all, I cannot even hate him for taking her any
more. He saved her, and in the same instant redeemed
his own guilt and paid back his own debt. My brother has
depths I never suspected. So how can I begrudge him
Katerina? I have myself only to blame for losing what
I most desired. I could have been the white knight. Instead, I am the fool who tells a woman in love with
her husband that she should leave the white knight to
go and live with the court jester. Oh Andreas! What
a man you are! I haven't won a single battle against
you in all my life, and you've never even known there
was a war. Here I am, rich and prosperous and finally
grown up, and still you are a step ahead of me. Whatever I do, whatever I become, it's not enough, because I
want what you have and I can never have it. Katerina is
yours, and she will never be mine. Katerina, Katerina!

I barely notice the taxi that stops outside the yard. I only hear the voice.

'Daddy!'

It's my girl, my darling girl, and she launches herself towards me, she runs as fast as her slender legs can carry her, and she runs to *me* and falls on my lap.

'Katie, my darling Katie,' I say through her wet kisses. My heart is fit to burst. Where did she come from?

Diane is standing in front of me. Niki and John are behind her. The driver has opened the boot and is taking out suitcases. I rise to greet my wife. I kiss her, and I kiss my son and Niki, too. I'm just so glad to see them!

'Are you surprised, Daddy?' Katie laughs at me.

'We won't be any trouble,' Diane says.

That night I take my family and my brother's family to a restaurant for dinner. We eat outside, near the villas, facing the twinkling lights of Thessaloniki and the bay. Niki wrinkles her nose at everything and complains that she wanted to stay in Beverly Hills with her friends.

'Greece is so far away,' she whines. 'We were in that plane for days! And why do people smell this way? I had to stand next to this disgusting old lady in the bus that took us to the terminal at the airport in Athens, and I swear she hasn't had a bath in years!'

My daughter, the ugly American! I find her words offensive and insensitive. I prepare to scold her, but her cousins are laughing and chiming in with their own stories of the great unwashed of Greece. They know a little English, and they try hard to communicate with her. Yiannis knows more, so he translates when Petros is stumped. Their blonde, sophisticated cousin is a source of delight to them.

My son is playing with his food as usual. He's still in

shock because the waiter's finger was two quarters deep into his french fries when he put the dish down in front of him. He has separated the contaminated fries and he is examining each one before he puts it in the ashtray. He has already polished his silverware to a shine and examined his water for foreign particles. He takes no chances.

Diane is next to me. She seems a little preoccupied. She talks and laughs, but there is something on her mind. We still haven't had a chance to talk, but I know she's rehearsing a speech in her head.

Earlier, we all visited Andreas. He's not supposed to have a crowd exciting him in his room, so after the briefest exchange Diane and the kids left the room. All except Katie, of course. She, too, was told to leave the room, but she would have none of it.

'I want to talk to Uncle Andreas,' she announced, and there was no putting her off.

So Katerina followed my family out, and I stayed with Katie. Katie climbed on the bed and had a long conversation with her uncle mostly in English while I played translator. Andreas laughed with her, tickled her, told her she is the prettiest little girl in the world and won himself another fan. He always was good with women. When he sent her to bring him some magazines, she went willingly.

'Your little girl is a charmer,' Andreas told me. 'Your whole family is great! I tell you, George, I envy you. You've got it all. Who would have thought that it'd be you who made it! Remember how you were? This snotty little kid who couldn't get into the soccer team except when the ball was his. And look at you now! What is that ring on Diane's finger, three carats, four?'

'You have a great life, too,' I told him. 'You have great sons, and a great wife, and you're in Greece.'

'Bah! Greece! There's no getting ahead here. If I knew then what I know now I would have left with you. So I drank and caroused and had a great time. What do I have to show for it? Money is the thing, little brother. And you got it!'

Everyone came in to say goodbye when the time came to leave. Diane and I were the last out. As I turned to leave, he called to me.

'Hey, George,' his voice dropping to a whisper now that he had my attention. 'That Diane, quite a looker!'

She really does look good. She seems taller in this land of the short. Her legs go on for miles. She's wearing pink, which always looks nice on her, making her look blonder and more fair than ever. In Greece, my wife stands out in a crowd.

Katerina is across from us. She is enjoying her night out. She hardly ever eats away from her own yard or kitchen. She's wearing her one good dress, yellow and sleeveless. On her ears she has a pair of gold earrings that Diane brought her. My thoughtful wife brought gifts for my brother's family. Walkman tape players for her nephews, a shaving kit for Andreas. I asked her how she knew there were three boys. She smiled and showed me two more tape players, stashed in her suitcase.

'I was ready for one brother, one wife and up to five kids,' she says with a mischievous grin.

With my wife and kids around me, my embarrassment abates. Their presence fades a little the memory of what happened. They are so much a part of me, so tied to me, Katie hanging around me, Diane on my side, that Katerina must view my words to her as an aberration, a spur of the moment thing that maybe I didn't mean. That's what I tell myself.

I compare my wife to the love of my life. Diane is

handsome, but she's too pastel, too washed out next to Katerina's vivid colouring. Katerina's face hints at passion. Diane's is all restraint. But Diane has a smoother look, the look of a woman who lives in luxury. Has Diane noticed the coincidence of Katie sharing Katerina's name? She didn't flinch when I introduced them. Right now she's busy talking with Katerina in her accented Greek. Katerina speaks to her of my childhood. She speaks slowly and distinctly, so Diane can follow with only occasional help from me. I have the strange feeling that this is a dream.

Katerina insists that we must not stay in the hotel Diane booked from LA, but we will not hear of it. My family's luggage has already been brought there, and Yiannis has put my things in the boot of the car. Abruptly, I have moved out of my family home. It's how I always leave it, with hardly an opportunity to say goodbye. But all in all I'm glad to have my family here. Their presence distracts me from my shame and embarrassment. And my Katie, my darling Katie who is sitting in Petros's lap and feeding him her french fries, takes away my sadness and my sense of defeat. How can I regret my life when it has led me to this love? How can I wish for things to be different if different means no Katie? In that yard in Panorama, with Katerina and Artemis, there would have been no Katie. I guess I wouldn't have missed her if I hadn't known her, but now that I do, can I honestly say that I would choose a life without her?

The restaurant is part of the hotel where Diane has booked us rooms. When it's time to part, Katerina leaves with her family and I am left alone with mine. We have three rooms, one for us, one for Niki and Katie and one for John. The kids follow Diane and me into ours. As Diane unpacks, Niki and John plop on the bed.

'At least the rooms have baths!' Niki, who apparently expected to find Greece living in the Dark Ages, comments. 'But, Dad, that family house is atrocious! Did you really live there?'

'It was a good house when I was a kid.'

'The yard has definite possibilities, but why don't they plant some grass?'

'I like it just the way it is,' says Diane. 'Lawns are too manicured and boring. And your family is very nice, George. They made us very welcome.'

'I like the cousins!' Niki says. She always likes people who give her their undivided attention. 'Yiannis is just so cute! I've got to take a picture of him before we leave to show the girls. They'll just drool! They'll be buying tickets to Greece to come see him up close and personal. Too bad we're related!'

'I'll marry Petros when I grow up!' Katie pipes in. Up until I left America she was going to marry me.

'By that time he'll be an old man!' Niki cuts Katie's enthusiasm. 'He'll look like Uncle Andreas. Fat, bald and coarse. What a gross old man he is! I saw him leering at me and Mom! Dad, is he a pervert or something?'

She's only trying to bait me.

'Uncle Andreas is not gross!' Katie answers her.

'Young lady, you are to speak of your uncle with respect,' Diane admonishes Niki, but there's a smirk on her face. She noticed Andreas leering, too.

'His wife is lovely.' This from my son, who hasn't said a word all day.

'Boy, she sure is! How on earth did she ever end up marrying him?'

'Andreas was quite a catch when he was young,' I say, and I can see him in my mind's eye, tall and straight like a young pine tree, tossing his hair out of his eyes as he runs after the ball on the soccer field. 'He was tall and slender, built like a Greek god. He was an ace football player, and all the girls were after him.'

'I don't believe it!' Niki exclaims. 'Anyway, I don't care what he looked like! The man could not have had any class even back then! Dad, he doesn't even look like he's related to you! He just looks like a country bumpkin! White trash!'

'Niki, that's enough!' Diane scolds. I don't believe it! I think Niki just paid me a compliment!

'Well, okay. I won't say anything more, but it's amazing that Petros and Yiannis turned out so well.'

'Maybe they take after their mother,' John again. So help me God, my son may not be a total wash-out after all.

'I think it's time to go to bed,' Diane says.

'But I'm not sleepy at all!' protests Niki. 'It's the middle of the day in LA.'

'So get in bed and read.' Diane is determined to shoo the kids out to their rooms. I take Katie by the hand, and Niki follows. I settle them in their room. I wait for Katie to brush her teeth, and then I tuck her in.

'I don't think Uncle Andreas will die,' she tells me.

'Then he won't, my heart.'

'Say, Dad,' Niki pipes in from her bed, 'how come everybody bows and scrapes to you at the hospital?'

'They know quality when they see it,' I answer with a smile. She doesn't miss anything, that Niki. By now I've passed around so much money, most of the hospital staff can retire. I may be a fool, but I'm a rich fool.

In our room, Diane is in her nightgown She's sitting on the edge of the bed, putting lotion on her hands. The lotion smells of roses.

'Everything okay?' she asks, and I nod.

'I don't fell sleepy, either,' she continues. 'How about a drink?'

'I don't know if they have room service at this hour.'

'Never fear,' she says, and pulls two tiny aeroplane bottles out of her travel sack. 'No ice, we'll drink it straight.'

We go out on the balcony. Thessaloniki winks at us from its many eyes. We sip the Scotch.

'It's beautiful out here.' Diane sighs. The night is warm and balmy, the sky is full of stars. I murmur in agreement. It's beautiful. But there's something coming.

'You know, if you want to move back to Greece, that would be all right with me. I would come with you. Niki might be a problem, but we could work that out.'

I expected something, but not this. This seems to come out of left field.

'I don't want to move back, Diane. Whatever gave you that idea!'

'Well, there's something. I heard it in your voice on the phone. You sounded so far away. And I don't mean the distance. You were emotionally absent.'

'I was just preoccupied with everything. And it's been difficult to come back after so long.'

It sounds hollow and false even to my own ears. Diane turns to me.

'George, look at me.' I obey. 'Something is going on, I know it. Is it someone else?'

'There's no one.'

'Then why do I feel like I'm losing you? Why did I get this feeling in the pit of my stomach that made me hop a plane and cross two continents to see you?'

I don't know what to say to this, so I say nothing. I turn away.

'How come you named Katie after Katerina?'

So she noticed. I had prepared myself for this, but the words still shock me. I have an answer prepared, something innocuous.

'I always liked the name. And Katerina is someone I always liked, a pretty girl, very nice, like my own sister.'

Again the hollow sound of a lie. Diane takes another sip of Scotch. She ponders my words. Her eyes never leave me, and I feel naked and vulnerable under her unnerving stare.

'George, look at me,' she says again. I turn to her, unwillingly, reluctantly.

'George, are you leaving me for Katerina?'

What did I expect her to say? George, are you fool enough to be in love with your sister-in-law? George, are you stupid enough to think she will leave her husband whom she obviously adores and follow you to the ends of the earth? But no. Diane asks me if I'm leaving her for Katerina. So I put my drink down and put my hands on my wife's shoulders as I turn her squarely to me.

'No. Diane, I'm not leaving you.'

Her body slumps in relief. Only now I realise that she has been holding herself tensely, braced for a shock, for pain. She moves into my arms and she lets her tears flow.

'Oh, God, I was so scared! Every time we talked on the phone you sounded more and more away from me. I could find no peace. Finally I just grabbed the kids and put them on the first plane. I couldn't bear it any more! I had to know. And I was so scared when I was coming over. I thought, what if he tells me to go back, what if he tells me it's over and he wants a divorce.'

I stroke her soft hair. I kiss the top of her head. Her body trembles in my arms. She pulls away from me, just enough to look at me.

'I love you,' she tells me. 'I couldn't live without you! All through dinner I was thinking that if this woman plans to take my husband I will fight her tooth and nail. If you didn't want me I was going to move here by myself and camp on your doorstep and stay until I won you back.'

She says it plainly. Without histrionics, without drama. But she means it anyway. To Diane I am not a fool. To her I am a grown man who might leave her for another woman. To Diane, the idea that Katerina might agree for love of me to leave her ailing husband is not absurd. I hug her to me.

'You don't have to worry, Diane. Katerina chose a long time ago.'

'You did love her then.'

Why not? Why not just tell her?

'Yes, I did, once. She was my first love. She married Andreas, and I left Greece.'

'You named Katie after your first love?'

Is she getting mad? No, she's too relieved not to be losing me.

'Only as a remembrance of a time long ago. It had been almost twenty years since I had last seen Katerina at the time.'

'I would have still loved you, even if twenty years had passed without seeing you.'

I am Diane's big love. I am the Katerina in her life. Warmth floods me at her words. This woman with the guileless blue eyes and the infinite patience loves me as passionately as ever I loved Katerina. Her reserve belies the strength of her feelings. I am moved.

'It was just a childhood love. It doesn't matter.'

This lie doesn't sound hollow. It is a loving lie. It is a lie of caring for my wife.

We make love, tenderly and with infinite care.

Everything about Diane's body is familiar to me, but the depth and strength of her love adds a new dimension. As she grips at me and wraps her body around me possessively, I am flattered and soothed. In Diane's arms I am the man I want to be. Strong, dangerous, powerful. A man who saved her from economic ruin. A man much loved and not to be taken for granted.

Afterwards we lie apart to let our bodies cool down. In the Greek summer the heat does not abate at night the way it does in LA. We hold hands across the damp sheet.

'Right about now Katerina must be regretting choosing your brother over you,' says Diane through the darkness.

'She didn't exactly choose,' I answer, and I tell Diane the story of how and why Katerina married Andreas. Now Diane feels guilty to have had evil thoughts of Katerina. She is appalled at what the woman she considered her rival went through.

Dawn is coming by the time we're cool enough to snuggle together to sleep. Before sleep claims her, Diane nestles in the crook of my arm and kisses my ear.

'I love you,' she whispers.

Why not say it? Will it kill me to say it?

'I love you, too,' I whisper. What is love after all? I don't feel for Diane that earthquake of the soul that Katerina elicited from me. But maybe there are many kinds of love, and I've just been blind to the love there is between Diane and me. For the first time in days, I fall asleep in a happy state of mind. There is much to be said for this other love, this quiet love.

We stay in Panorama two weeks. Andreas is sitting under the acacias by the time we leave, complaining about everything, and getting the kids to catalogue all my possessions in America for him. We meet Nikiforos, who is just as bright and engaging as his brothers. Niki raves about her cousins, but complains bitterly about the lack of air conditioning, the mosquitoes, the dust. John keeps wiping everything clean, but seems to be coming out of his shell under the constant barrage his cousins aim at him. They will not leave him alone. They want to know him and his shyness does not put them off. By the end of the two weeks, he's laughing with them and even initiating conversations.

Before we leave I buy a washing machine for Katerina and I pay a handyman to paint the house. I say good-bye to my brother in the yard.

'Come back again, George,' he tells me. 'You should come every summer!' There are tears in his eyes as he embraces me.

'I will, I will,' I tell him, and I mean it.

Katerina waves us off as we take off in the car with Petros. Diane, Katie and I are riding with him. Yiannis, John and Niki are in a cab behind us.

At the airport Petros and Yiannis help us with the luggage. Niki keeps snapping pictures of her cousins.

'Goodbye, goodbye. Be sure to write!'

My face is glued to the window as the plane ascends. There is Thessaloniki, the bride of Thermaikos, hugging the bay in the early morning, laughing up at me. I cannot see too clearly, for my eyes are blurring. Diane squeezes my hand.

'You know, I meant it when I said it. If you want to move back, we can do it.'

'Niki would kill me!'

'Niki will be going to college soon. What if we send her to school in London? She'd love that. And it would just be a three hour plane ride to see her, closer than if she went to school on the East Coast.'

Niki in London! I know where she can find a reasonably priced flat!

'John could go to medical school in London, too. And there's Anatolia, the American Academy, not a stone's throw away from Panorama for Katie. We could do it!'

Yes, yes we could. In a couple of years I could sell the restaurants and take my family to Europe. I could live in Panorama and sit in the yard with my brother and our families, picking almonds and pomegranates from our own trees, playing backgammon under the buttonwood tree in the village square. I could buy a villa. Maybe even the Villa Karras. I could come in from the *xenitia* and I could live in Greece forever. It's my choice. And I have plenty of time to think about it.

I squeeze my wife's hand. I raise it to my face and kiss it. She would do that for me. She would put herself in the *xenitia* just so I could come back.

THE END